I0746852

FOOL ME Thrice

LIZZIE MORTON

© Lizzie Morton 2022
All rights reserved.

Published: Adeen Print
ISBN: 978-1-7391175-0-4

Cover Design: Covers by Gillian
Edited: Hayley Ramsey Editorial

The right of Lizzie Morton to be identified as author of this work has been asserted by her in accordance with the Copyright, Designs and Patents Act 1988.

No part of this publication may be reproduced, distributed, or transmitted in any form or by any electronic or mechanical means, including photocopying, recording, information storage and retrieval systems, without the prior permission in writing of the author, except for the brief use of quotations embodied in critical reviews and certain other noncommercial use permitted by copyright law.

This is a work of fiction. Names, characters, businesses, places, events, and incidents are either the products of the author's imagination or used in a fictitious manner. Any resemblance to actual persons, living or dead, or actual events is purely coincidental.

Peter – For helping me fly

Prologue

Evan

Eugene Belmer smiles straight at me. Pure evil in his eyes.

Even behind bars, he manages to get under my skin.

I stare. He stares back.

Finally, I blink, allowing my eyes a well-deserved break from the montage of images on the bed. Too many bodies, hand marks around their necks, hair spread out like a halo. If only their deaths had been that peaceful.

And then there are the children ...

"Mommy lost the game."

Dammit. There's something about this case I can't let go of. It's the reason I'm here, despite all the evidence suggesting I should be elsewhere. Alone in a motel room in Jacksonville, responding to one text after another from the eldest of the Becket children, Michael. But he's not a child, not anymore, and my gut is telling me there's something more to this than a 'child' having nightmares, like Hewson, my superior, keeps suggesting.

I stare back down at 'The Cat', as the world knows him. His murders play out like a game of cat and mouse. He stalks his victims. Always female. Always blonde—of a sandy variety—and always widows. He preys on their loss, uses it, manipulates them.

And then he pounces, leaving nothing behind.

Until the Beckets.

"Can I trust you?" Michael Becket asks, glancing over his shoulder.

His teammates are too busy bumping shoulders and leering at the cheer squad further down the pitch, stretching with their cheer pants on display. Small mercies. I doubt FBI agents are regular attendees of high school football practices, and the tirade of females provides a well-needed distraction.

"Can you trust anyone?" I ask. His shoulders sink and he shakes his head. "Tell me what happened."

He glances over his shoulder again. "Not here."

With a tilt of his head, he begins walking further along the pitch, small and dejected, despite the extra layers making his huge frame like that of a small house. No amount of padding can protect him from the emotional wounds he's suffered.

We're almost off the grounds when he stops and turns back, green eyes swirling with too much darkness for someone his age. "Josie saw someone in a black hooded jacket."

"Freya," I remind him. There's no point in any of this if they're not going to use the names witness protection provided them.

Ignoring my comment, he continues, "It was outside her window. When I went down, there was a lily." I wait. "Our borders are full of begonias."

"Could she have made it up?"

We both know it's a stupid question.

"Josie's never been the one with issues," he comments, then stares off into the distance. "I thought I saw something, too."

I school my expression. "Thought?"

Dragging a hand down his face, he lets out a ragged breath. "I don't know. Ever since Jo— Freya told me, it's been messing with my head. I was driving to school last week, and it was there, standing on the sidewalk. I almost crashed the fucking car, and when I looked in the mirror, it was gone."

"Leave it with me," I reply.

He frowns. "That's it?"

"I'm chasing a ghost, because we have a culprit who's behind bars." When he narrows his eyes as if he wishes the ground would bury me six feet under, I add on, "I'm sorry I can't do more right now. If it happens again, call me."

And he does. Too many times.

My phone lights up on the bed, drawing my attention to the image next to it.

A child, sitting, lost beside their mother's body.

I grab the phone and open the message.

Michael: *The figure was at my game.*

My head throbs. Too many late nights finally catching up on me. "Who are you?" I murmur into the empty room.

A pair of eyes glint up from Eugene's mugshot, taunting me. There's not a sign of remorse, because to him, this is all a game.

We're raised to believe monsters don't exist and not to fear the dark. From the first day I set foot in the bureau, I learned what we're taught as children is a lie. Monsters do exist, but they don't always lurk in the shadows or hide under your bed. The worst kind of monsters are the ones who walk beside you in the light.

Fed up with his face, I flip the image over before replying to Michael.

Me: *I'll be at your house within the hour. Make sure you're not alone.*

***

Michael Becket stares at me like I've grown an extra head.

I try to explain what he would need to do, the façade he would need to present to the world. "... they can't dig if they don't know where to find the secrets."

The last word has barely fallen from my lips when the sound of feet stomping up the stairs filters into the room. We all freeze, and I curse. There's only one other person in the house. One who hasn't had any say in this decision to uproot their life, yet again.

A door slams on the second floor so hard the water in the jug in front of me ripples. Feet thunder above our heads and my eyes move across the ceiling, following their path until they stop.

Michael huffs, making it clear he's had enough of the conversation. Angela Becket pulls her hair over one shoulder and her chair screeches along the floor when she slides it back, preparing to go and deal with the younger of her two children.

"I should go speak with her and explain."

I clear my throat. "Maybe I should?" Angela waits for me to explain. "Sometimes it's easier to hear things from outsiders than it is those close to us."

"She might speak with you if we go upstairs?"

Making our way upstairs, I follow her along a hallway, almost to the end. She stops outside a door adorned with a simple sign with the name Freya. I anticipated it looking like a unicorn vomited all over it, decorated with glitter and ribbons and whatever other crap makes girls squeal at a pitch only dogs can hear.

Apparently, Freya isn't the fluffy unicorn type.

Angela knocks and calls through, "Freya." When she gets no answer, she smiles at me politely and tries a second time. Still nothing. Letting out an exasperated sigh, this time she hammers her fist against the door. "Josie Miller, do not ignore me."

"What?" snaps a voice from somewhere on the other side.

"Agent Price is here to speak to you."

"Tell him to bite m—"

"Josie!"

Angela throws an apologetic look my way before opening the door and stepping inside the room. I stand, trying to listen to the muffled voices, but struggle to make anything out. I look across the hallway, finding another sign which says Michael. Again, no personality. It would appear the Beckets left behind any semblance of who they were in New York, along with their real names.

Eventually, everything goes quiet and Angela steps out from the lion's den. This is the first time I've met the youngest of the Beckets.

"Call if you need me," says Angela, before turning her attention to her daughter. "Freya, be kind." She walks out, leaving the door open. Her retreating footsteps stop halfway down the stairs.

The culprit of the snapping is perched on a window seat, surrounded by cushions, eyes trained on the glass. Her room is as colorful as her mood. The rug, bedspread, even the lamps, are a shade of purple so dark it could almost be confused with black.

I remain standing in the doorway. "Freya …"

"Josie."

Feigning a smile, I ignore her reminder. Her past self has no place here. Not if she wants to remain safe. Silence falls around us and I take her in properly. She's so like her mother and brother it's uncanny, the same sandy blonde hair falling around her shoulders. Then there are the eyes, which, as big and startling green as hers, should sparkle. There's no shine, not even a glimmer.

She looks my way with an overly sweet smile plastered on her face. "Yes, Agent Price?"

Huh. I wasn't aware fourteen-year-olds knew how to sass and it throws me. She watches me, unblinking.

"I need to talk to you about what you heard."

"It was pretty self-explanatory," she snaps, then turns her attention back to the window.

"Not entirely."

A rogue tear makes a steady path down her cheek. She crosses her arms over her chest and huffs. "Did anyone consider what I might want in all of this?"

"Of course we did." I lie. The only thing I considered was her safety, not how she might feel about what it would take to get it.

She looks back over and narrows her eyes. "Bullshit."

I wonder how much her mother can hear.

"I'm trying to help you. A little respect would be nice."

"I'll show *you* respect when you do the same for *me*. I'm not eight-years-old anymore. I wish everyone would stop treating me like I am."

"Freya …" I exhale.

"It's Josie."

After straightening my already perfectly positioned tie, I set foot in her room. Walking over to her desk, I rest my hand on the back of the chair, then glance over my shoulder. "Do you mind if I sit?"

"Is this going to take that long?" I don't answer. "Fine," she huffs, "you can sit."

My attention focuses on the wall above her bed. "Nice poster." I take in the huge framed sketch of a feather. I read aloud the quote that accompanies the image. "What if I fall? What if you fly?"

"Erin Hanson." Her tone softens slightly. "My mom got it me."

"It's interesting."

"It's a reminder that I can be whoever I want, even if it doesn't always feel that way." She stares back out the window, signaling the end of our little heart to heart.

"You weren't included in the conversation because I didn't want to scare you."

She throws her head back and laughs bitterly. "You can't scare me anymore than the figure outside my window." She arches a brow. "Or are you a serial killer, too?"

Dull eyes hold my gaze.

"We should have included you."

"I hate this," she mutters.

"I know."

She laughs again, hysterically this time. "What do you know?" she asks when she manages to catch her breath.

"I understand a lot more than you think I do."

"So, are we moving?" Regret takes over my face. "That's a yes."

Leaning forward, I rest my elbows on my knees. "It's the only way ..."

"... to save Michael's football career," she finishes.

I shake my head. "To keep *you* safe."

Her eyes turn to saucers. "Me?"

"I wish I could give you all the answers you need. But I can't, because I don't have them. All I know is I have to trust my gut, which is telling me to get you far away from here."

"This isn't just about my brother getting to play football?"

"It was *never* about Michael playing football. Not as far as I'm concerned. It's a bonus for him, but a perfect setup for *you*."

Her eyes water and she says so quietly I barely hear, "I've only just started to figure out who Freya could be."

Guilt pierces my chest when another tear spills over, then another, making a path down her already blotchy cheek. The urge to protect and keep her safe washes over me like a tsunami, destroying every rule I have about remaining detached from cases. I'd do anything if it meant I didn't have to watch her cry again.

"I wish things could be different, but my job is to keep you safe. You aren't safe here anymore."

She hiccups. "Where are we moving to?"

"Silver Spring, Maryland." Her cheeks pale. "You need to be close to the bureau so we can keep an eye on what's happening."

"Michael?"

I shake my head, and she raises her chin defiantly. "And what about what I want?"

I harden my expression. "What you want is irrelevant if you're dead."

Her bottom lip trembles. "I hate you."

Taking the brunt of her anger, I stand up and walk to the open door. I rest my hand on the frame. Before walking out, I glance back. "I'm not here to be your friend, and I don't care if you hate me. Sometimes in life, to be the hero, you have to be the villain first."

This is the way it has to be. That's what I tell myself as I walk along the hall. But fuck, if I could change things, I would. Rolling my shoulders, I make my way downstairs. Michael is waiting at the bottom, the clanging of pots and pans coming from the kitchen behind him where I catch a brief glance of his mother busying herself.

"Can we talk before you go?" he asks.

"Sure."

I follow him into the living area, and he sits on the couch, setting the TV to a sports channel with the volume louder than necessary. I sit on the opposite end, and he turns to face me.

"Is this going to work? Really?"

I stare at the screen, watching the players smash into each other with such force it seems impossible they don't break every bone in their bodies.

"I don't know. But are you prepared to sit and wait to see what happens?"

His throat bobs when he swallows. "I'm scared."

"Good."

"Good?"

"A little fear isn't always bad."

He arches a brow. "How so?"

I stare at the screen again, watching the players intently. "When you catch the ball, what makes you run so fast?"

He shrugs. "I dunno. Fear of losing, I guess. It's instinct."

"Fear. Fight or flight. It's your body's way of keeping you safe. If you weren't scared, you'd be complacent. When you're complacent, you slip up with the little details, and it's the little details that will make this plan work."

He follows my gaze to the screen. "Will you watch out for them?"

"If I can."

If. It lingers in the air like a rancid smell.

"Why are you the only one who believes us?"

I choose not to answer. Because there's a small part of me, the 0.0001%, that's still not sure I do, because on paper, none of this makes sense. "Don't let your guard down," is all I reply.

"Do you think he'll come after me?"

I shake my head. "Not if we stick with the plan. When you get to college, the media will be following your every move. It'll be too risky."

Michael whistles as he exhales. "Okay."

I stand, ready to leave. "You have my number. Try not to use it, unless of course there's an emergency. I look forward to seeing you in the NFL one day."

"Because it's part of the plan?"

"No," I say honestly. "Because I've been to one of your games and seen how happy playing makes you. Goodbye, Michael."

I leave before exhaustion takes over and I let slip how rattled I really am.

For the plan to work, whoever is following them needs to believe the lie, that Michael is the one who saved their mom. If they believed it, Michael would have been who they appeared to first.

But it was Josie, sitting upstairs, unaware she has another reason added to her already huge pile of hate, with a target on her head.

One

Josie 9 years later

"If you stain the ceiling, you'll be painting over it." I freeze, the batter in the pan sizzling as I get ready to flip the pancakes. She always has to ruin my fun. Smiling, I turn and find my mom beside the grand central island—the type you see in all the fancy lifestyle blogs. I guess there have to be some perks to having an NFL brother you haven't seen in years. Money might not be able to buy happiness, but the occasional luxurious item helps to soften the blow.

Mom tosses her keys down on the counter with a chink, before sliding off her coat and revealing her stained uniform beneath.

"How was work?" I ask, turning my attention back to the pancakes and opting for turning them with a spatula over flipping. The last time she made me cover up my mistakes it took me over a week to get the paint out of my hair.

"Fine," she sighs, then pushes the plate I set out ready for her forward for me to fill.

We've done this routine for years. Each time she works nights at the local diner, where I also work at the weekend, I have breakfast ready for us both when she returns. You'd think she'd already be full when she gets home, you know, because she works with food for hours on end, and whenever I have a shift, they feed me.

When I questioned her about it, she just shrugged and said, "No one makes breakfast like you."

And that was that.

While she sleeps, I study. The local community college I attend is hardly Ivy League, but I've learned to take whatever I can get. It's small, discreet, and somewhere easy to remain insignificant.

The pancakes only take another minute on the other side. When I turn around, I find mom sitting with her chin resting on the base of her palm, eyes shut. Black circles sit beneath her eyes, mirroring my own. We wear them like a badge of honor. Life might not be perfect, but we're still here, fighting, and that's what matters.

"Mom?"

"Hmmm?" she replies, a faint smile plays on her lips.

"You can't eat if you're sleeping."

"I'm just resting my eyes for a second."

With a chuckle, I fill her plate and add a generous amount of syrup and berries, then a dusting of powdered sugar. When I'm happy with how it looks, I move onto my own plate, giving her an extra couple of minutes before I slide hers over. The sweet scent rouses her and her lids flicker before opening.

Inhaling deeply, she grabs her knife and fork, then tucks in. I wait with bated breath, watching as she chews slowly. "Eleven out of ten. Best you've made in a while."

I grin and tuck into my own plate, aware of the time and that I'm far from ready for the long day ahead. Tuesday is the worst, most pointless day of the week.

"Do you have to work again tonight?" She nods and my stomach sinks. I can't remember the last time we spent a significant amount of time together. Keeping my expression neutral, I comment, trying not to grumble, "You've worked ten shifts in a row. Aren't there, like, rules against this kind of thing?"

She sets her fork down and pushes her barely eaten food away. "I'm tired. I'm gonna go to bed."

Disappointment doesn't come like it used to. I stopped expecting another reaction from her a long time ago. This is how things are and probably always will be. Everyone has their own way of dealing with their fears. When the night goes still and most people sleep, Mom works, avoiding the nightmares that creep in with the darkness. But even in the day, things lurk in the shadows and her attempts are futile.

When we first got to Silver Spring years ago, I was angry at her, and the world. At some point, the anger was replaced with acceptance, and as I grew older, I started to learn things weren't always black and white. The life we live is somewhere in the gray, where actions and choices that would normally be frowned upon make sense. Survival goes against every rule and expectation. We do what we can to get by.

I'm hit with a wave of sadness. Not for me, but for my mom. I'm still at the beginning of my life and at some point, in the future, things might change, but for her, there's a chance this could forever be her reality, and it's a tough pill to swallow. Watching your mom lose herself to sadness and fear isn't for the fainthearted.

I grab both of our plates and scrape the pancakes into the trash can, my own appetite gone. When I've sourced my textbooks and laptop and shoved them into my checkerboard black and purple Eastpak backpack, I slip on my Vans and oversized parka.

Outside, the cold sweeps through my layers, settling in my bones. I shiver and dart to my car in search of heat, my breath billowing through the air as I go. I seriously doubt the Arctic's chill factor is much worse than what I'm expected to deal with each winter. Years spent in Jacksonville spoiled me, and I've never acclimatized to Silver Spring.

Forty minutes later, I'm walking through the warm corridors of college. Keeping my head tucked down, I head toward the library. I don't have class for another couple of hours, but I want to make sure I get ahead on one of my papers due in a few weeks. An associate business degree doesn't come without legwork—a lot of legwork. Sometimes, I think I'll never get to the end. No part of it comes naturally, but dreams remain floating in the clouds if they don't have something to tie them to the ground. It might be painful at times, but this is the sensible route to take if I stand a chance at getting anywhere further down the line.

Settled at my favorite table, hidden in one of the far corners of the room, I slide in my AirPods and lose myself, as much as you can, in business communication. An hour or more passes and one of my favorite songs by a new artist called GAYLE comes on. It's the kind of happy, angry song, that when you sing it, feels cathartic. Probably because of all the cursing.

I find myself humming, and the lyrics to the chorus of "abcdefu" are out of my mouth louder than I realize. Cheeks blazing, my eyes dart up when I find a guy standing at one of the stacks just ahead. His head turns to the side a little and I catch the way the side of his eye is crinkled in a way that tells me he heard me loud and clear.

Without a word, he grabs a book and walks away. I'm left reeling at how I can be so socially awkward at times. Then I remember it's probably because the words social and Josie don't tend to find themselves in the same sentence. That's the last time I use my AirPods in the library.

Studying vibe out the window, I close the textbook and grab my things, deciding coffee is in order if I'm going to get through the day. With my usual mocha, I make my way to my first class, sliding into a seat near the front—the ones no one goes near because you end up having to answer questions. I'd happily take all the questions the professor has if it means avoiding my peers. I'm here to get in and out, hopefully with some understanding of how to run a business. I'm not here to make friends.

Being earlier than usual, I find myself checking over my shoulder to see who is around. Like always, the class gives me a wide berth. God knows what they think my story is, but I'd place bets their assumptions are far from the truth. I'm about to take a sip of my drink when someone sits in the seat beside me.

My arm jolts and the searing liquid pours down my front, soaking through my black band shirt and burning the skin beneath. "Shit!" I hiss, jumping to my feet and pulling the material away from my chest quickly before it can cause any serious damage.

The person beside me jumps up at the time and says, "I'm sorry. I didn't mean to scare you."

When the burning lessens, I turn and take in their red checkered shirt. The same shirt the guy in the library was wearing. He even has the same black beanie sitting over his dark blond hair. I'm dazzled by the way his teeth sparkle when he grins. I thought teeth like his only existed in infomercials, and their astonishing shade of white highlights how clear and blue his eyes are.

"You've got quite the potty mouth on you for someone so quiet ..."

He looks like the guy in the library because he *is* the guy in the library. The red on my cheeks matches the shade of his shirt and my heart gives a little flutter when the dimple in his cheek pops. If you were going to mockup my dream guy, the person standing in front of me could potentially be him. It all comes down to the shoes. I glance down, taking in a pair of black and white DCs. My kryptonite. The red on my cheeks moves to my ears.

If he notices, he doesn't show it, for which I'm thankful. Instead, he holds his hand out. I gape at it like he's asked me to grab hold and jump off a cliff with him. I don't talk to my peers. *Touching* is a different stratosphere and here this gorgeous guy is, waving his hand around, enticing me to touch the skin of his palm, which looks oddly soft. Amusement passes over his face when all I do is stare and he drops his hand to the side.

"I'm Duane," he says, and his pearly whites catch my attention once more. There's something about this guy that is mesmerizing.

He watches me. I watch him. A few seconds pass. I really am crap at this. I can't remember the last time I spoke with someone in public where my academic journey wasn't the subject matter.

Library guy, who I now know to be Duane, chuckles. "And you are?"

I clear my throat awkwardly. "Freya."

I omit the surname. Nobody in this room needs to know who my brother is, not that they'd ever believe me if I did stake a claim to his gene pool. The loner at the front of class hardly screams NFL. And then there's the size difference. Little and large is an understatement. My brother is a giant, and I'm ... not.

Duane coughs and I realize we're still standing up in the front, for everyone to witness our awkward introduction. Sheepishly, I drop into my seat at the same time the lecturer comes in, saving me from any more failed attempts at communicating with the opposite sex.

Anyone would think I was a virgin in every sense of the word, but I'm by no means a nun. Not that the awkward event known as my first time, right before we left Jacksonville, with my then best friend, really counts as a whole heap of experience. The texts between us dwindled over the first few months apart, despite his determination to keep the spark he thought was there burning. He wasn't the one. A victim caught in the crossfire during my war against the world would be a better description of the final role he played in my life.

He was my control in an uncontrollable situation.

Do I regret my actions and losing my V-card so young? A bit. But I've learned from my mistakes and come to terms with what I did. Since then, there has been the odd tryst. I mean, come on, I'm a twenty-three-year-old woman. However, the vibrator hidden away in the top drawer of my nightstand has helped me avoid any unnecessary bad decisions over the years.

The professor's voice is somewhere in the distance, but I don't really hear him, too busy recollecting my sexual experiences. It's Duane shoving a note on my small desk which breaks me from my musings. I open it with the subtlety of a steam train, the paper rustling in the virtually silent room. When the professor glances over with a frown, I shrink into my chair. So much for flying under the radar.

A few minutes pass before I allow my eyes to move down and read what he's written.

I owe you a mocha.

Scribbled beneath is his number.

All I can focus on is the word mocha. How does he know my drink? The hairs on the back of my neck prickle until I sniff, greeted with the sweet chocolate now embedded in the fibers of my shirt. That's how he knows, idiot. I have to remind myself multiple times a day that not everyone is out to get me, and if anyone were, that's what the three bottles of pepper spray I have with me each day are for. One in my bag. One in the pocket of my coat. A spare in the car. Always.

I shoot Duane a brief glance, smiling when I catch his eye, and tuck the note in the back of my notepad.

Class goes by unusually quick, the paper in front of me remains blank. I spend the whole time fretting over what I'm going to say to Duane at the end. Things can't get much worse, as I haven't exactly set the bar high. The class suddenly bustles to life, and I freeze, waiting for what disaster is going to come next.

"Where's your next class?"

I look up. Duane towers over me like an Adonis. Why the hell is he talking to me?

"Erm ... I can't remember." I cringe. "I'm sorry. I'm not used to this. The whole talking thing."

"I know."

"You do?"

He smiles. "I'm not new to the class, Freya." My pulse quickens; out of fear or excitement, I'm not quite sure. "I've seen you around and wanted to say hi. Being serenaded in the library sealed the deal." When I don't say anything, he finishes our mainly one-sided conversation. "I'll catch up with you next time in class. Don't forget to save me a seat." He winks, knowing the row on either side and the one behind me are always empty.

His shirt disappears from the room, and I'm left wondering if Tuesdays might become my favorite day of the week.

***

It's late when I finish. Later than I usually allow myself to stay behind, especially in the winter when the light disappears early. The dark plays funny games with my mind, ones that could give the figure in my past a run for its money. It's not until I'm outside with only the dull orange glow of the streetlights for company that I realize how late it is and what a stupid idea it was not to go home earlier when my stomach growled in protest.

Bag bouncing against my back, my Vans slap against the sidewalk, soaking the bottoms of my jeans. My stride increases with the pace of my heart, my breath coming out in quick pants, which cloud in front of my face, distorting my vision. A vibration from my phone draws my attention down. I slide my hand into the pocket of my parka, fumbling when nerves get the better of me.

One lapse in concentration is all it takes. I collide with a hard, human-shaped object and tumble to the ground. Disorientated for a second, when I come around, all I see is a black jacket. A figure looms over

26

me. A hand comes down and I brace myself for some kind of impact. I frown when it never comes.

Taking a deep breath that barely fills my lungs, I look up, finding a young guy in a hoodie. Not the zip up that appears in my nightmares, but a pullover with a dark gray logo in the middle, barely visible in the poor lighting.

"Sorry," grumbles the guy, still holding out his hand, "I was checking my phone and had my headphones in. I didn't see you."

I offer him a tight smile and avoid his hand, choosing to scramble to my feet on my own. "It's fine."

"Are you okay?"

"Apart from a bruised ass, I'll be fine." I laugh lightly, but it falls flat.

The guy looks at me like small talk is the last thing he wants to be doing.

"Great," he grunts, deeper than expected for someone so young. "Bye."

I'm left with just the dark for company, not out of choice. I make the journey to my car in record time, clutching my pepper spray the whole way. My chest heaves when I hit the central locking system and collapse back against the seat, closing my eyes and allowing myself a moment to get my shit together.

When I open them. A figure in a black hooded jacket is there in the rearview mirror. I stifle a scream and blink. The mirror's empty apart from a few bushes. Accepting that calming myself down isn't going to happen until I'm home with all the doors locked, I turn on the engine and hit the gas so hard I wheel spin, screeching into the night.

I've never been so happy to see our home. Even with all the lights out, it welcomes me like an old, trusty friend. Two felines circle around my feet as I struggle to unlock the door. "Stop it," I hiss.

One mewls and continues rubbing its face against my leg. When the door swings open, I scurry inside, turning on the entryway lights and slamming the door behind me. I slide the bolt—which Mom and I agreed was necessary—into place, and lean back against the door, finally relaxing. Two friendly faces watch me expectantly.

"You can't leave me for five minutes?" One meows. "Fine," I huff, making my way into the kitchen and pulling out their food from one of the cabinets.

When their bowls are filled and they're pre-occupied, I go about my usual routine. No room goes untouched and when I'm finished, the house glows brighter than a Christmas tree. A shower has major appeal; I need to thaw out. There's something about the cold here. It doesn't let up. I grab what I need from my room, then go to the bathroom, turning the shower up as hot as my skin can handle.

Steam fills the room and when I step under the streaming water, I let out a small hiss of air when it makes contact with the area where I spilled my coffee this morning. I turn, trying to minimize the contact. It's really not my night, because after washing my hair and preparing to run conditioner through my thick locks, I squeeze the bottle too hard and it goes shooting everywhere, turning the base of the tub into a death trap.

"Gah!" Admitting defeat, I set the bottle down on the side and glance up.

My blood runs cold.

In the extendable mirror is a figure in a black hooded jacket, watching. I blink. This time, it doesn't disappear. Fear trickles down my spine and I take a step forward, preparing to run. My foot slides and I start to fall. Trying to stop myself, I move my other foot, making things worse. I slip and slide, trying to catch my balance when my hand darts out and grabs the curtain. The force I apply as I tug while starting to spin is too much. It pulls away from the rail and I drop down, hard. The left of my face collides with the tub with a thump. A searing pain shoots through my hip and side when I land. My elbow fairs no better.

The hot water of the shower cascades over my skin. Dazed, I take in the ceiling, for a second forgetting how I got down here. My cheek throbs like I've never felt before, the bone feeling like it almost shattered. I struggle to get up thanks to the mess. Naked flesh slaps against the sides of the tub as I scramble. I might as well have coated it with oil. Somchow, I manage to clamber out, snatching a towel and wrapping it around me before standing straight and facing the mirror.

Nothing.

Not prepared to take any chances, I race out of the bathroom to my room and grab my phone. I bring up the only number I have saved besides my mom's. The one she entered for emergencies of this nature.

Shakily, I raise it to my ear, the shrill ringing making my cheek throb. As it goes on and on, I bounce between my feet.

"Come on," I mutter. It goes through to voicemail, and I wait for the beep. "Agent Price, this is Freya Becket. I need your help."

Two

Evan

The day turns into shit the second I set foot inside the main unit and find a petite female sitting at the desk next to mine.

Lights flicker on the dark screen behind her like lightning bugs. They're every live case we have in the country. Hundreds of them. Too many cases, not enough agents. That's what Hewson keeps informing me in our one-to-one's. It's like the scene from *Batman Begins* when everyone is stuck in Arkham City with no backup. Someone lifted a rock and all the crazies decided to crawl out and wreak havoc. One of them being Eugene Belmer, managing to fuck with my head despite sitting behind bars.

My temples pound, stress getting the better of me, and it's not even nine AM.

"Hey, partner," Mara chimes.

Ignoring her always chirpy mood, I switch on my computer, nodding at a couple of other agents when they pass by.

I feel a pair of eyes watching, and irritation floods through me. "What?" I ask, typing in my login code.

"What's on the agenda for the day?"

"*I* have a list of things I need to work through. *You* can work through whatever you need to."

"Price," her voice lowers and when I look over, her brightness dims. I'm the black cloud in our duo, casting a shadow over everything around me.

"Yes?"

"Do you know what partners means?" she quirks a brow and purses her lips, waiting for my response.

"I do," I reply. The muscle in my jaw quivers, and I fight the urge to grind my teeth.

It landed me with a cracked tooth earlier in the year, something I don't wish to repeat. A voice in my head shouts as loud as Mara when she gets overexcited with a case, encouraging me to indulge in my nasty habit. The powers that be could have been a little kinder when they assigned my new partner.

She's been a pain in my ass since the day she took residence on the desk beside me months ago. Five long months, to be exact. Too often she messes with my things, pulling the partner card, claiming my space is her space, and vice versa. Yeah, never happening. I'm a lone wolf, which everyone in the bureau knows. Mara is no exception; she just chooses to ignore my not so underhand comments and somehow flips them into a compliment in a way only she knows how.

Apparently, she's my protégé. She's been through the basic training, now it's my job to make her a field agent. I decided against it the day she asked if Veronica Mars was a reliable role model. The only reason Hewson wants her on the team is because she can hack anything, even Chinese intelligence, without breaking out in a sweat.

Good things come in small packages. That's what he claims.

Our small package has raven hair and a sense of humor as blunt as her bangs. The fact I know what bangs are is living proof we've spent too much time together already.

Black-lined eyes stare. "Good. Then you'll give me something *you're* working on, so that we can work on it *together*."

An idea sparks and I question how I didn't think of this sooner. "The Kraken Case." She groans. It's a fucker, and we all know it, up there with my man, Eugene. All the clues point in one direction, we're just lacking hard evidence, which is sometimes hidden in plain sight, like in the codes of some of the biggest trading sites in world. Something only a hacker knows how to find. "Have at it, *partner*."

Rolling her eyes, she turns back to her screen, muttering under her breath.

And that's pretty much how my day goes. Holed up in the main unit, no sunlight to be found. If I didn't know any better, I could almost believe my lack of vitamin D could have a part to play in my cranky mood. But it's not. It's something more than a vitamin deficiency and a dislike for my desk neighbor.

My gut stirs and I feel unsettled. I just don't know why.

It's late and I'm ready to call it a night when my phone vibrates. I'm surprised I actually have enough signal for something to come through. I ignore it, assuming it will be Mara pestering me, and go back to staring at my screen, trying to finish up the last of my work with bleary eyes.

It's no good. Sleep is needed in copious amounts. Grabbing my phone, I tap the screen, frowning when I find a voicemail from an unknown caller ID.

A soft voice floats down the line. "Agent Price, this is Freya Becket. I need your help."

I snap the phone away from my ear like it's on fire. One tiny bar of signal that keeps appearing and disappearing is all I have. Something in her voice makes urgency take over. I don't want to waste time getting outside if I don't have to.

I type back quickly.

Me: *How did you get my number?*

I watch blue steadily progress across the bar at the top of the message screen.

The last time I saw Freya was when her mother and I agreed to uproot their lives and move them from Jacksonville to Silver Spring, so they were closer to DC. Up until a couple of weeks ago, the case was like stagnant water, sitting untouched, becoming more rotten with each day that passed. Until someone dipped their toe in, causing a ripple effect. Saving her contact into my phone as F, in case it ever gets tampered with, I delete the voicemail.

When I click back into the message thread, I find my reply hovering at the end of the line in virtual no-man's-land, refusing to budge, but then it suddenly shoots to the end and the message appears as sent.

Three small dots appear, disappear, then reappear, letting me know she's typing.

F: *Mom gave it to me in case of emergencies.*
Me: *And is it? An emergency.*
F: *I think I saw someone.*

I frown. The timing is uncanny.

Me: *When?*
F: *Over an hour ago.*

I go to reply when a whoosh fills the room as the doors to the unit slide open and Hewson steps in. I look up briefly, taking in his large frame, highlighted by the light of the surrounding computers, then turn my attention back to my phone.

"What are you doing here so late?" he grunts.

"I could ask you the same thing." I close the message and place my phone face down on my desk before he reaches me.

"Price ..."

"Frank ..."

"It's almost ten."

"I've been finishing jobs."

His brows knit with concern. "You can't keep working these hours. It's not healthy. You need to sleep."

"I'm fine," I reply. I'm not the only one who's tired. The dark circles he's sporting are a dead giveaway. My phone burns in my hand when I pick it back up, the messages from Freya unsettling me. "Actually, I need a favor. Can you bring up footage of Belmer in Sing Sing? Tonight," I add on. This is the second time I've asked to see him in the past few weeks. The other being when Michael Becket called me in the middle of night for the first time in years, claiming to have seen a figure in a black hooded jacket. The accident that followed, landing him in the hospital unconscious, and removing him from future games, has been all over the news. "You're the only one who has the access code."

He shakes his head, defeated and over-worked. I know the feeling. "Don't go down this path. There's nothing to find."

"But what if there is?"

"Are you questioning my judgement on this?" he asks with a scowl.

"No, I'm just asking to see him."

"He's behind bars, Price. He's one of the most heavily guarded inmates." He's about to walk away; if he does, I'll have no hope of figuring out what the hell is going on.

Clutching at my final straw, I call after him, "There have been two sightings."

He stops. His back straightens, and he glances over his shoulder. "Who by?"

"Do you really need to ask that question?"

He turns back round, folding his arms across his chest. "Which Becket?"

I swallow. "Michael and Freya."

A bitter laugh fills the room. He hates this case as much as I do. "Sightings in Jacksonville *and* Silver Spring. Meanwhile, our culprit is in New York? Impossible."

"Nothing about this case is impossible. We both know that."

"It could be a coincidence."

"Or it couldn't, and we'd be offering them over like lambs ready to slaughter."

His jaw ticks. "Price, you *have* to let this go. We spent months chasing nothing the last time. It was a waste of time and resources then, which we don't have available now."

I stare at him, and ignoring my pride, plead. "Please, I just need to see the footage. Then I'll leave it, I promise."

With a resigned sigh, he says, "Fine. Follow me."

I follow him out of the unit. Neither of us say a word. A couple of dimly lit corridors later, we're inside his office. I wrinkle my nose; the smell of stale takeout is as foul as his mood. Peering at the trashcan, I find it overflowing with boxes. So much for the healthy eating plan he was meant to be sticking to.

His phone hits the wooden desk with a clunk when he tosses it down, before sitting and switching on his laptop. We wait a moment for the system to fire up, then he types in his password. He moves his finger over the keypad, opening the main server.

"Here," he says grimly, swiveling on his chair and pushing back from the desk. I step in and look closely at the screen. "What other evidence do you need?"

I frown. Eugene's there, perched on the edge of his bed, book in hand, swinging his legs. I find the date and time in the top right corner of the footage, pull my phone out from the pocket of my suit pants, and double check. It's legit.

"I don't need to see anything else." Hewson doesn't pull me up on my shit or say anything when I go to leave. I pause at the door and look back. "Thank you for showing me."

Hewson's lips form a tight line, as if he's trying to smile but failing. "How many more times will it take before you trust me?"

He already knows the answer. We both know my trust doesn't come easily, if at all.

"An infinite amount." I step out of his office and shut the door before he has a chance to reply.

He's right. I shouldn't be here. It's been another long day, the kind that starts before the birds wake. I don't bother going back to the central unit—I have my phone, keys and gun. All I need is sleep.

The crisp air hits me when I step outside. I take a deep breath, allowing it to awaken my senses enough to drive. I'm almost at my car when my phone vibrates from the right-hand pocket of my suit jacket. Begrudgingly, I slide it out.

F: *Hello?*
Me: *Is your mom home?*
F: *No. She's working the night shift.*

My breath clouds in the night when I let out a long sigh. So much for sleep.

Me: *I'm on my way. Stay out of sight.*

Once in my car, I slam my hand against the wheel. Frustration takes over that we're back doing this dance again. I should tell Hewson what I'm about to do. This isn't protocol. Despite my better judgement, I turn on the engine and drive in the direction of an old case I have no right in revisiting.

Forty minutes later, I pull to a stop outside a large house. It's a mirror image of those around it. White picket fence, white walls, white everything, apart from the goddamn door and its matching colored roof. Nothing untoward. Nothing that could make it stand out to anyone. That's why it was chosen for them. It's exactly what it needs to be.

I don't knock when I reach the door. Freya's probably spooked as it is, so instead, I open the new contact on my phone and hit call, then raise it to my ear.

"It's Agent Price," I say gruffly, when the ringing stops before she has a chance to say anything. "I'm outside the front door." I hang up and shove the phone back in my pocket.

My ears prick, listening to the sound of metal scraping against metal as she unlocks the door. My hand rests on my gun in its holster, hidden beneath my suit jacket. The door slowly opens and my eyes dart from left to right, searching for any sign of movement. If anyone's watching, this will be when they take their chance. A light breeze rustles the trees surrounding the house. The door opens fully, causing light to spill out onto the porch. That's when I hear it. The snap of a branch. I spin around, flicking the safety off my gun as I pull it out and hold it in the air.

"Agent Price?" Freya's soft voice reaches my ears from behind as two cats skit across the path of light on the front lawn.

Scouring the rest of the street, I find nothing. I turn back. Huge emerald eyes, as bright as a summer's day, stare up at me, features as pixie-like as her frame. It's the huge red lump covering the left side of her cheek that throws me.

A long second passes between us. "Can I come inside?"

More amenable than I remember, she smiles and nods, stepping back with her hand still resting on the door. The door clicks shut behind me and silence thickens around us when I turn back to face her.

"Water?" Freya asks, looking uncertain.

I nod, and she walks away. The faucet is already running when I step into the kitchen. I hover by the central island, pulling out my phone, ready to take any notes needed. When the glass is almost full, Freya turns off the faucet and slides it across the counter toward me.

"You can sit," she says quietly.

"I'm good." If I do, there's a chance I'll fall asleep. My eyes focus on the red lump on her cheek again. She looks like someone took a fucking hammer to her face and a feeling I can't quite put my finger on simmers inside me. "What happened?"

She swallows, tucking a piece of damp, sandy blonde hair behind her ear. "I was showering, and I made a mess with the conditioner." I try to figure out if what she's telling me is relevant to what she thinks she might have seen, or if she's explaining why her face is a mess. "I put the bottle down and when I looked back up, I saw a figure in the mirror, watching me."

My eyes don't move from the bruise forming. "And you were injured how?"

She looks down, sheepish. "I panicked and tried to run. I forgot I'd spilled the conditioner and slipped."

When she raises her hand to tuck her hair back again, her shirt rises, revealing the start of a red mark up her side. My eyes dart to her elbow, which looks as bad as her other injuries. She looks like she's fought a few rounds in a cage.

"There was no one in the house? No one did this to you?" My eyes trail over her, searching for any other injuries. I come up with nothing. All the bruising is on one side, suggesting she's telling the truth and she literally hit the deck. Hard, by the looks of it.

She shakes her head. "It was an accident."

I tap a finger against the countertop. "Eugene Belmer is safely behind bars in Sing Sing Correctional Facility. I've seen it with my own eyes."

She bites her lip, refusing to meet my gaze. "Oh." When she finally looks up, all I see is fear. "I saw something. I know I did."

"Why are you here alone at night?" I ask, picking up my glass.

She huffs. "I'm always here alone at night. Mom covers the night shift at the diner where she works."

The thought of her alone night after night doesn't sit right. "It's not safe."

Her expression changes and she glowers. "If Eugene is *safely* behind bars, then I should be fine. Right?"

I pause. She's got me by the balls. Something I didn't predict happening. Apparently, what she's lacked in growth physically, she's made up for in confidence. Bold is a word that springs to mind as she stares at me with narrowed eyes.

I gesture to the ceiling above us. "Why don't I check things out? Just to be sure."

She smiles sweetly, failing to cover her slight wince when her cheek moves. "That sounds like a great idea."

Appeased for now, she walks around the island and directs us upstairs to the bathroom. When she flicks on the light in the bathroom, she stands back so I can go in alone. I'm hit with the sweet smell of wild rose and vanilla. If only she were as flowery and sweet as she smells. Despite the rational part of my brain telling me Freya's imagination is running away with her and she's just scared, I take everything in, even the droplets of water still clinging to the marble tiled walls. Nothing seems out of place.

Freya stands at the door with her hands on her hips. I carefully climb in the tub, remembering what she said about the conditioner. The shower curtain crinkles beneath my shoes. Positioning myself where she would have been standing, my eyes settle on the extendable mirror, taking in the clear image of the trees through the window. A drip of water lands on my head, finding a path under the collar of my shirt. Irritation creeps in. Have they never heard of frosted glass?

When I climb back out of the tub, Freya opens her mouth to speak. I hold up a hand and walk over to the bathroom window. A huge ass tree blocks most of my vision and the windowpanes rattle from a strong gust of wind. Freya shivers behind me even though we're standing in a hot box. I keep my eyes focused outside, struggling to see anything until clouds part, revealing the inky sky. The moon illuminates the lawn, highlighting a large branch.

"Freya, come here." She walks to my side, and when I point through the window at the branch, she pales. "Was that there earlier?"

"No," she croaks.

I open the weather app on my phone and check the day's forecast. Wind reported, but not the kind that would cause any damage to a tree. "Huh."

"Did you hear a loud thud?"

"I-I don't know. After I hit my head, I was a bit disorientated."

Even in the reflection of the window, I can see her cheek is becoming more swollen.

Freya grabs my arm in a vice-like grip. "What's that on the branch?"

There's another stiff breeze and I think I see what she's talking about. Stepping closer to the glass, I cup it, blocking out the glare from behind. Something moves on the branch again. It's small, but it's there.

"Wait here," I say, walking out of the bathroom.

She doesn't listen. "Where are you going?" she asks, rushing down the stairs behind me.

"I'm going to see what it is."

She's hot on my heels. "You can't be serious."

Managing to slide between me and the door, she presses her back against it. She knows I won't touch her. This is the last thing I need right now, and my voice drops low. "Freya. Move."

"You can't go out," she squeaks. "What if he's there?"

I slide my jacket to the side, revealing my gun, and her mouth drops open. "*You* called me. What did you think would happen? If you want me to help you, then you need to move." She keeps her chin raised defiantly. "Now." With a huff, she shuffles to the side. "Do not come out. No matter what."

"Okay."

"Promise me, Freya. If anything happens, you will not leave this house."

Gripping the door handle, I push down.

Her small hand finds my forearm and squeezes over the top of my sleeve. "Be careful."

With a swift nod, I open the door. "Lock it behind me," I mutter, stepping outside.

Chilly air closes in, threatening to swallow me whole. The trees rustle, but there's only one I care about. Moving down the steps of the porch, my eyes take in the other white houses on the street with their obscenely colored doors. There's nothing untoward. But it's not about what I can see, it's what I can't. That's the thing about the darkness, no matter how hard you look, if something doesn't want to be found, it will remain hidden, and there's nothing you can do about it.

I move to the right of the house, finding the tree standing just outside the bathroom. The branch is still there, on the ground. Up close, it's even bigger. And there it is, the small piece of material. Black and the kind a hooded jacket would be made from. I reach inside my suit jacket, the opposite side to where I keep my phone, slide out a pair of rubber gloves, tear open their sealed packet, and put them on, before pulling out an evidence bag. Retrieving the material carefully from the branch, I slip it into the bag, then seal it and put it back in my pocket so Freya can't see.

Back at the door, I wrap my knuckles against it and call through. "It's just me."

When it opens, I step back inside.

"It's him, isn't it?" says Freya.

I keep my voice level. "No." Freya purses her lips, assessing me. I give nothing away, too busy focusing on the now giant lump on her cheek. "Grab your coat."

She blinks. "Why?"

"We're going to the emergency room. You need to get that checked out."

"I'm fine."

"You could have chipped the bone. Shoes."

She holds my gaze. Seconds tick by, neither of us budge. "Fine."

She disappears and a couple of minutes later returns wearing a pair of Vans covered in cats. I stare at them and when I meet her eye, she simply shrugs, grabbing her parka and slipping it on.

"Can we go now? This could take hours, and I have classes early."

"Classes?"

"College," she explains.

"Right."

We leave the house, and she locks the door behind us, leaving every light in the house on.

Three hours and a giant bag of pain killers later, we return.

"I told you I was fine," she grumbles, fighting back a yawn.

"Great," I reply. "At least now we know." Even the doctors were concerned with the swelling, but scans revealed everything was okay. Lots of ice and anti-inflammatories. Freya sways a little on her feet, eyes glazed. "You need to sleep."

"That's what I wanted to do, but soooomeone decided we needed to go on an adventure," she slurs, jabbing a finger into my chest. That will be the pills strong enough to tranquilize a horse kicking in.

"Shut the curtains and turn out the lights," I say, a slight bite in my tone. "You're living in a goldfish bowl."

Freya chuckles. "Yes, mister super-secret agent. Right on it."

When she sways again, it's my cue to leave. "Lock the door."

"Got it, Dad."

I shake my head and step back into the night. When I hear the lock click and the bolt I noticed grind into place, I turn and make my way back to my black SUV, now sitting just out of sight from the house.

My eyes burn each time I blink, feeling like sandpaper is scraping against them. I get myself settled, ready for the stretch of darkness left. Grabbing the coffee I picked up in the hospital when Freya was being discharged, I watch the lights in each room go out.

Only when Angela Becket pulls up after the sun has risen and the shadows are gone do I let the house with the youngest sleeping Becket out of my sight.

Three

Josie

I t feels like an elephant's stamped on my face and crushed my cheekbone as I begin to wake up.

Late afternoon sun spills through the gap in the curtains and I nestle deeper into the cocoon I've created with my blankets.

Late afternoon sun.

I bolt upright. Dammit, I've missed all of my morning classes. Reading the time on my phone, I find it's three-thirty PM, which confirms I've missed my afternoon classes, too. Annoyance passes over me, replaced with pain when my cheek, ribs and elbow throb in unison. Why do I feel like I've been in battle?

A glance at the nightstand, finding a huge bag of painkillers, brings everything back. I shiver and bury myself under the covers. There's no way I'm leaving the house for the next few days, not after what happened, and not looking like I fear I'll find when I look in the mirror. I'll catch up online.

Tuesdays have a whole new meaning to their usual crappiness. It's no longer a nothing day, and will now forever be known as the day two people I never thought I'd see again appeared back in my life. One definitely not welcome, the other I'm not sure about.

Uncertainty has always been the sucky thing that comes with my past. Never being certain from one day to the next whether I'd be Josie, Freya or someone else. Never certain whether I'd see my brother again or if I'd come home one day and find my mom gone. Never certain who I could be or where my life could lead, not wanting to commit to something to have it ripped away again.

Everything has always been one big ball of uncertainty, and the thing I feel most uncertain about at this moment in time is Agent Price.

Opening the door and finding him ready to shoot the only two friends in my life, even if they aren't human, wasn't the best start to our reunion. I considered forgiving him when warm brown eyes like a cup of hot chocolate locked with mine. Then he put on the same bravado he did when he walked out of my life as quick as he walked in, spouting some crap about being a villain in order to save me.

He can keep his alpha crap. It's only appealing in novels of the spicy variety. If you can't follow it through in the bedroom, there's no need for it in the world. It is a shame, though. He could totally pass as an older version of Christian Grey, if Christian had dark eyes and walked around thinking he was *Batman*. Come to think of it, he's more of a Christian Bale—without the brooding appeal. He's just grumpy and bossy.

I give it another ten minutes before I decide to climb out of bed. Mom clattering around the kitchen getting ready to go to work makes the decision for me. She's going to get the medical bill from last night and want to know where it came from. Plus, with the growth I've got sitting beneath my left eye, it's going to be weeks before I look normal, and I can't avoid her for that long. I might as well tell her now and get it over and done with. My stomach feels like a lead weight is sitting in it as I pull on a sweater, slowly, trying to avoid all the bruising. What I find in the mirror is worse than predicted. My face looks like it's been slammed against a wall repeatedly. The lump takes over most of my cheek and is so big and puffy I can see why Agent Price took me to the emergency room. The bruising is going to be exceptional.

Basically, I'm a mess, and Mom is not going to be happy. I can predict her reaction. I've seen it before. She's going to panic, the tailspin kind where all logical reasoning goes out the window and she makes rash decisions. But I don't want to uproot my life again. I don't want either of us to. We just need to be careful.

I'm done living in the shadows, hiding away with my anxiety and all the what ifs and maybes. What if they didn't get the right guy? What if there really is someone still out to get us? Last night made it perfectly clear this wasn't all a figment of my imagination. But what's the point of being alive if neither of us experiences what life has to offer? We might as well have lost whatever messed up game we've unwillingly been drawn into.

Taking a deep breath, I pad downstairs and into the kitchen. Mom is dancing around humming to the radio, unaware I'm in the room until she spins around. She smiles at first. That quickly changes when the mess of my face sinks in and she drops the heavy-bottomed pan she's holding. It lands with such force I'm sure the hardwood floor suffers injuries worse than my own.

Mom rushes around the island and stands in front of me, looking horrified. "What happened?"

When she goes to cup my face and assess the damage further, I pull back, flinching. Just the gentle stirring of the air from the movement of her hands feels like she's dragged a knife across my cheek. I hope it doesn't stay like this for long. The doctors only gave me a few days' worth of the super strong pain meds I'm sure are responsible for my mammoth sleep. It's been years since I've slept so deeply.

"Freya? Answer me. What happened?"

God, I wish she could call me Josie again, just once. I gave up fighting 'the process' when we left Jacksonville. The day we packed our bags and left Michael behind, something changed. I feel like a part of me gave up on fighting for the life I wanted and began to accept that this was the way things needed to be.

For a second, I consider lying to protect her. It's taken too long for us to get to this point, and I hate that we're about to go back to the beginning. I don't want to see the terror in her eyes, but it's the only way to keep us both safe.

Struggling to swallow over the lump in my throat, I say, "I fell in the tub."

Her shoulders sag with temporary relief. "That's it? You had me worried."

I shake my head, stomach twisting as an image of the figure burns the backs of my eyes. "I fell because I saw someone watching me in the mirror while I was showering."

The blood drains from her face and she rests a hand against the stool at her side, steadying herself. It shakes and her legs buckle. I catch her before she falls, ignoring the pain screaming in every part of my battered body when she leans against me for support. The hiss of air I release through my teeth seems to snap her back to reality. Enough strength returns to her legs that she's able to rest her weight against the counter without sliding to the ground.

I hobble closer to one of the stools and climb onto it, expecting her to follow suit. Instead, she walks back around the island and drops down out of sight. I hear a kitchen cabinet open and rustling coming from her direction. She curses when she bangs her head, before standing back up waving a large water bottle in the air.

"You could have just gone for normal water," I comment.

Ignoring me, she grabs two glasses and pours a couple of fingers' worth of liquid into each. One slides dangerously across the counter toward me, while she raises the other to her lips, grimacing when she lowers it back down. Yeah, that's so not water.

The clear liquid lures me in. I'm not a drinker, because I've never really felt the need, but last night was way too eventful and I decide something to settle my nerves won't hurt as a one off, even if it is the afternoon. Taking a large swig, I choke when it hits the back of my throat, burning more than the coffee I spilled down myself yesterday.

"What's that look for?" I ask raggedly when Mom stares at me, amused.

"At least I don't need to worry whether you're secretly drinking while I'm working."

"It's hardly a secret if you're just never here." The words are out of my mouth before I can stop them, and I'm instantly filled with regret. We don't have that kind of relationship; the kind fueled with resentment. The last time I spoke so out of place was when I didn't understand that every sacrifice we've had to make—that my mom has had to make—was in order to keep me safe. "I'm sorry," I stammer. "I didn't mean it."

She takes another sip of her own drink. "I'm sorry, too."

I frown. "For what?"

"Not being here."

"Mom," I sigh. "You don't need to apologize. I get it. It's okay."

"No, it's not." Her eyes water and I'm riddled with guilt. First, I drop a major bombshell on her, and now this. If I could take back the past five minutes, I would. I never should have come down to face her.

"I can quit the diner. I don't need to be there. We have your brother's money ..." she tails off.

The sincerity in her words is there, but there's something in her voice that tells me it's the last thing she wants to do, even if she'd never admit it. Everyone has their escape; their way of coping. We don't need to understand why people make certain choices or act the way they do. Working at the diner provides her with whatever it is she needs to escape the painful memories that, too often, have threatened to tear her apart.

Which is why I say, "You're not quitting. I don't need you to."

"Bu—"

I shake my head. "No buts, Mom. You need the diner. I get it. Conversation done." She bites her lip and takes another sip of her drink, gazing out of the kitchen window thoughtfully. "I called Agent Price."

Her head snaps back. "You did? And?"

I shrug. "He came by and checked things out, said it was nothing." It's a lie. I know what I saw on that branch, and I don't doubt it was hidden inside one of his pockets. Mom doesn't need to know all the extra details yet, though. Well, apart from one. "He took me to the emergency room. Expect a nice bill for nothing."

"That was kind of him and I'm happy he did. But you should have called me. You can always call me, Freya." When I don't say anything, she asks, "What did the doctors say?"

"Bad bruising. Rest and lots of pills." Her eyes widen at the last word, and she snatches my glass away. "Hey, I wasn't finished."

"No way am I having you mixing pain meds and alcohol."

"Fine," I huff. The horse tranquilizers will probably do a better job of numbing the pain anyway.

Mom glances over at the clock on the wall and her face twists. She looks torn. Before I have a chance to ask what she's doing, she fires a text off her phone. "What would you like for dinner?"

"I'm fine. I'll make something later when you're at work."

She picks up the pan she dropped what seems like hours ago off the floor. "You'll eat now. No meds on an empty stomach."

"You have to go soon."

"I texted in sick."

My mood brightens. She's not had a sick day since we arrived here. "Really?"

She smiles. "Really. Now, what will it be?"

I ponder and then an idea strikes. "Eggs Benedict. Like Dad used to make when he wanted to be fancy."

Her face drops, but she quickly saves the moment before I can take my choice back. A risky choice, but if we're doing things out of the norm, then I'm all for talking about him openly. Something we never do. She nods and fills the pan with water, a smile on her face that shows no joy. Turning, she places it on the stove, setting it so the water can get to a simmer. I watch her like a hawk, taking in every detail. It's the one dish I've never dared make, not once in all the time I've been practicing. The desire to want to be just like him never left, even though a lot of the memories of him did.

Pouring just the right amount of white vinegar into the pan to help set the whites, Mom chuckles to herself. "He loved bending the rules. He's who you and your brother get your strong will from. It's definitely not me. When we first got married, his favorite thing was to have meals in reverse. He said it felt like we were living life on the edge."

"Do you miss him still?"

She turns back and all I see is pain, pain I feel deep inside me and would do anything to make disappear for her. "Every day. You never forget your first love."

"Is that why you've never moved on?"

My bold questioning has her brows pulling together. We've never been this open with each other. I can't decide if it's refreshing or terrifying, but I have so many questions I've always wanted to ask and never had the chance.

Her voice comes out darker than I've ever heard before. "I've never moved on because I've never wanted to bring someone into this reality only to risk losing them." An image of Duane with his ridiculously white smile and offer of a replacement coffee pops into my head. The little flutter in my chest feels bittersweet. Mom isn't finished, though. "But there's a risk of that no matter what your circumstances are. Life isn't a given, Freya. If you have the chance, take it by the horns and make every memory, good and bad, worth it. Sometimes, it can seem like love is all around, but true love is a rare find. If you get a shot, don't waste it."

"Is that what you're doing?"

"What?"

"Waiting for another shot."

She smiles again. This time, it could light up the whole room. "Yeah, I suppose it is. Come on, let me show you how to make the sauce."

Hours later, stomach full, a little woozy off my pain meds, but more content than I've felt in years, I make a choice.

Mom's sleeping peacefully next to me; she gave up halfway through our third movie. Being careful not to wake her, I grab my phone from the arm of the couch and stand carefully, walking to where I remember leaving the bag that I took to college yesterday. I pull out my notepad and find the small piece of paper I slid into the back.

I enter Duane's number into my contacts and pause. Before I have a chance to second guess myself, I fire off a text to him.

You owe me a shirt, too.

Something about this feels right, despite what happened last night. I don't want to keep living in the shadows, and I don't want to keep living in fear. I want to make memories. I want to start living and I want to start now.

***

Evan

"I need you to come with me." Mara jumps to her feet, looking far too excited, until she takes in my face. Her eyes move from the overgrown stubble on my jaw, down to yesterday's suit. She wrinkles her nose and I raise my brow. "Yes?"

She purses her lips. "Can I make a comment without you biting my head off?"

"It depends on what it is."

"You look like shit." I roll my eyes. "Is that yesterday's suit?"

"What does it matter if it is?"

Mara wrinkles her nose again. "It's kind of gross, and out of character. You usually smell like the type of guy that would shower three times a day if he got the chance."

I frown. She's not far off the mark. Mostly it's twice. Once at night, to wash away whatever follows me home, and once in the morning to wash away the dreams that sometimes creep in with this line of work. Occasionally, on a really bad day, there might be three. There's something about the warm flow of the water that helps to wash away the darkness. Even if it is only temporarily, it helps. The fact Mara has picked up on my bathing habits has me wondering if there's something behind Hewson's request to train her up in the field.

"We need to go see Hewson," is the only response she gets before I walk off in the direction of his office.

Hewson looks surprised when Mara and I enter the room together. Usually, I do what I can to avoid her at all costs. His eyes move to my suit. He frowns, then leans back in his chair with a harsh exhale.

Nodding at the two chairs on the opposite side of his desk, he says, "Take a seat." Long seconds pass and we all find ourselves surrounded by a tense silence, broken now and then when people pass outside the door, chattering. "What happened?"

I reach into my pocket, pulling out the evidence bag from last night and toss it on his desk, as if it explains my shoddy appearance. His eyes focus on the black material.

"Freya Becket reached out to me late last night."

Hewson's eyes dart up. "That explains the need to see Belmer." Mara remains uncharacteristically quiet beside me. "And the reason for her reaching out was?"

"She saw something." Mara stiffens. "She was showering, and she thought she saw a figure watching her through the mirror. Her face was messed up, she fell and hurt herself."

"And you would know that how?" asks Hewson.

"Because I went to check things out."

Hewson drags a hand down his face, groaning. "Are we really doing this again?"

"You tell me," I smart, hating how quickly he's ready to dismiss the case without knowing all the facts.

It's always been the same. It doesn't matter who I go to, all anyone can see is the fact the main culprit is behind bars. Main being the most important word, because even though Eugene Belmer is locked away for the rest of his days, it doesn't change the fact there is still an obvious threat to the Beckets.

Neither Hewson nor Mara says a word, so I do what I know I have to, given what happened last night. There's a chance I could get in serious shit for what I'm about to admit, but it's clear now, giving my number in case of emergencies was the right choice to make.

"Michael Becket has also reported a sighting."

"When?"

"Two weeks ago."

Hewson scowls. "And why am I only just hearing about this?"

"Because I didn't know if there was anything behind it," I admit.

"And now you think there is?"

I nod in the direction of the evidence bag on his desk, waiting patiently to have its shining moment. "There was a fallen branch on ground, directly outside where Freya reported seeing someone. *That* was left behind."

Hewson leans forward and grabs the bag, raises it in the air and peers at it through the clear plastic. "It looks like ..."

"The material of a black hooded jacket, I know."

Mara sucks in a sharp breath while Hewson shakes his head.

He drops it back on his desk. "Have it run for DNA, not that I think we'll find anything."

Mara clears her throat and raises a hand. "Erm, how is this possible?"

Hewson looks to me expectantly. "Agent Price, care to explain?"

I turn to Mara. "We have a copycat," I deadpan.

She snorts and starts to laugh. When she takes in my expression, she stops. "Wait. Like an actual copycat? You weren't making a joke, because you know, the media calls him 'The Cat'?"

"No," I say, shaking my head. "I think we have an actual copycat. It's the only thing that makes sense. It explains why this was left behind. Whoever it is, is lazy, disorganized."

"Unless it was on purpose," mutters Mara.

"What?" I snap, feeling a little riled that she's challenging me.

Hewson looks between the two of us in amusement, holding up a hand when I go to speak again. "Keep going," he says to Mara.

Mara shrugs. "I'm good."

Something in the recess of my mind stirs. She could be onto something. I clear my throat. "No, go on. I want to hear what you think. Please."

Mara looks at me like I've had a personality transplant overnight but doesn't say anything out loud. Instead, she dumps a ton of shit into the office neither Hewson nor I could ever have predicted would come from her.

"You might have a copycat, but to me, this looks far from disorganized. Even a copycat wouldn't chance being caught and would take whatever precautions they could to cover up any evidence. Maybe this isn't just a simple case of a copycat."

"What are you suggesting?"

"Maybe the unsub has been inspired."

"By?" I bounce back.

"The game," Mara answers. "Only this time we're the mice."

Silence settles between us. Hewson watches intently in the background, but I'm barely aware of my surroundings, my brain going haywire, trying to piece everything together. "He's made a bold move. He wants to prove he can't be caught. He's playing with us. But why would he still be going after the Beckets?" I muse.

"Because they're part of the game that was never finished. He's still a copycat, but he could be more dangerous. The M.O. isn't his own. He wants to prove he's better."

"He's turned it into a competition?"

"It's only a guess," Mara says quietly, biting her lip.

"A good one," I say. Both her and Hewson's eyes widen in surprise. "I want you on the case with me."

"What?" Mara chokes. "You don't work with anyone."

"Now I do." I face Hewson. "I have five other cases. I can't do this alone."

Hewson throws me a shit-eating grin that grates my insides. "And he finally admits he's human. I want all eyes on Freya Becket. If this is about finishing the game, our copycat is going to go after the person who ruined it."

Mara looks confused. "But I thought the brother saved the mom?"

Hewson and I give each other a knowing look. I clear my throat and explain, "That's what we let the media continue to believe. Belmer sustained multiple head injuries from a baseball bat, but when he was finally questioned, he recalled being pushed. Michael Becket admitted to covering up what his sister did."

"Surely the truth would have come out during the trial?"

"It was filed in Belmer's report that his account could have been inaccurate due to his head injuries. It took him five days to regain consciousness." When Mara frowns, as if she's going to challenge what was done, I finish. "The officers at the time did what they had to do to keep everyone involved safe."

I don't acknowledge out loud that it's only been a matter of time until the truth came out.

I also don't have it in me to admit that Freya might have a target on her head, and that whoever it is that's doing this, if Mara is right and it's a competition, won't stop until she's dead.

Four

Evan

Weeks of tailing Freya Becket have led me to believe she's either an enigma, or a really good actress.

She floats through her daily life like she doesn't have a worry on her shoulders.

Her only tell is the lights.

Every room, in quick succession as soon as she sets foot through the front door of her home. Whether it's light or dark, every single one is turned on. Oddly, she sleeps in the dark and I haven't figured out why. I hate not being able to read people, and watching Freya from afar is like trying to make sense of a book written in wingdings. Impossible.

Mara is sitting beside me in the passenger seat of my SUV, lost in her laptop. I glance over, blinking when I see a huge image of Eugene Belmer filling the screen.

"What are you doing?"

"Practicing," she replies without looking up.

A brief look at the exit Freya always uses when leaving college tells me she isn't finished with class. Everything is still. "Practicing what?"

"Trying to get into his head."

"You're trying to profile?" I quip, amused.

"I find him interesting. You're the one who said I can't hide behind my computer forever, so I'm doing my homework."

"What do you want to know?"

She straightens and closes her laptop. "You'll help me?"

I glance at my watch. "I have nothing better to do for the next six minutes."

With a roll of her eyes, she says, "I want to know it all. Well, as much as you can fit into six minutes."

"Can't you just magic up his file?"

For the first time since becoming my desk partner, she looks uncertain, like a lost puppy. "I'm new to this, remember? Some of the technical stuff doesn't make sense."

"Fine," I sigh, getting ready to quote Mara the file. "Eugene Belmer. Organized killer. The media refer to him as 'The Cat.'"

She nods. "Where did the name come from?"

"He's driven by fantasies. He calls it his game. He's the cat, his victims, always widows, are the mice. It always starts innocently. At least, that's what the victims think. He shows them his mask of sanity. He takes his time, meets them in an unsuspecting way, gets to know them, works his way into their life, dates them, and then the switch flips. He becomes more possessive, and eventually aggressive."

"But the victims never report him?"

I shake my head. "Typical narcissistic behavior. He makes them believe they need him. He embeds himself so far into their lives they can't see the truth. In the hours before he kills them, he has lilies delivered, then he strangles them."

Mara swallows. "I don't need to hear the rest."

I frown. "If you're going to do this, you need to do it properly. We can't hide from the truth. We can't change it. This is reality. This is our job."

"Go on ..."

"He carves the names of his other victims into their skin with a knife, tallying up how many games he's won. He leaves a child behind with the body. Each time they tell the officer, 'Mommy lost the game,' and then he moves on to the next."

I give her a moment to digest everything I've just said. I might come across as robotic when it comes to these things, but even I know it's a lot to take in.

"What went wrong with the Beckets?"

"He showed classic traits the more he killed. He got arrogant, missed important details, like the fact there were two children in the Becket household. He also believed he was untouchable, never realizing that one day, one of the children might fight back the way Freya did."

In that moment, Freya steps through the college doors in the distance, walking alone, eyes scanning all around her, sand-colored hair swaying in the icy breeze.

Mara watches her. "She's strong. I don't mean physically."

"She's a survivor."

In that moment, I feel something I never have before with someone related to a case. Respect. Saying out loud what Freya has survived and watching her try to live her life like she is—it's commendable. Also, reckless, considering the situation she's currently in, but that's because she doesn't know the truth about what we suspect. Not yet, at least.

"Does she have a boyfriend?" Mara asks.

I peer through the front window, trying to get a clearer view to see what Mara's talking about. It's hard when she's surrounded by a snowstorm of people, all rushing to wherever their next destination is. Then I see it, Freya laughing as she walks with a guy beside her. Tall with a ridiculous hat. She playfully shoves him in the arm when he rubs the top of her head, messing up her hair. She looks the happiest I've ever seen her.

Until she looks up. She stops dead in her tracks, blinking as she stares directly at me.

"Shit," I hiss under my breath.

Confusion is replaced with anger, and she scowls. The guy beside her looks around, clearly trying to figure out the source of the abrupt change to her mood. He says something and she shakes her head, narrowing her eyes at me before walking off. The guy scurries after her.

Mara lets out a long whistle as she exhales. "Looks like the cat's out of the bag." My jaw ticks. "Too soon?"

I fire up the engine and pull out into the road, feeling agitated. Why do I care that she caught us watching her when we're only trying to keep her safe?

Oh yeah, probably because I told her there was nothing wrong. Basically, I lied to her face. Still, something doesn't sit right seeing her with that guy. My protective instinct kicks in and it has a one-track mind. It does what it needs to in order to achieve the desired outcome, not caring about the chaos it might create in the process.

"I want you to do some searching into Freya's phone records, see if you can find out who that guy is she's with."

Mara's eyes widen out of the corner of my eye. "Are you sure that's a good idea?"

"Why wouldn't it be?" I ask, slowing at the stop sign, blocking out every answer she rattles off.

Like I said, one-track mind. One goal. Protect Freya Becket, no matter what it takes.

***

Three hours later, with the name Duane Jackson on my lips, I hammer my fist on the front door of Freya's home for the fifth time in a row. Mara watches in amusement back in my SUV. The spectacle unfolding is my penance for making her do something she fought tooth and nail against. The problem? I have my blinkers on, unable to see the reason why she didn't want to pry into Freya's private life.

"Freya, it's Agent Price. I need you to open the door." Nothing. I hammer again. "Freya?!"

Panic creeps in out of nowhere, a feeling so alien, at first, I don't recognize what it is. I never fucking panic. What if something happened to her?

This time, when I hammer my fist, it's so hard the front of the house rattles. It does the job, because the door flies open, revealing Freya standing behind it, huge green eyes full of fury.

"What is so important you feel the need to almost break down my door?" I go to answer, but she carries on before I get a chance. "I can't keep out the monsters without a door, *Agent Price*. Oh wait, no, you said there was nothing wrong. If that's the case, there's no need for you to be here, and definitely not to be following me, right?"

The way she says my name has my skin bristling. No one ever speaks to me like she does. No one ever challenges me with the truth. I don't know what the hell to do with it.

"Who's Duane Jackson?"

63

She tilts her head back and lets out a shrill laugh. "Un-fucking-believable."

And with that, the door slams in my face and I hear the bolt slide back into place.

Nostrils flaring, I crack my neck from side to side and go back to the SUV, slamming the door behind me.

"You're doing an excellent impression of someone unhinged right now," Mara comments.

I ignore her and stare out into the street. "Anyone else would be happy to have an FBI agent doing whatever they can to keep them safe from a serial killer."

Mara snorts. "Apart from the little detail you've skipped is that Freya doesn't technically know you're keeping her safe from one, because you haven't involved her in anything."

I turn and face her. "What are you trying to say?"

"That Freya isn't a little girl anymore. In fact, she never was. But you're treating her like one by keeping her in the dark. She deserves more respect than that and she deserves to know, so she can keep herself safe."

"She doesn't trust me."

"And she never will if you constantly work behind her back rather than with her. You need to get past whatever perception you have in your mind that she's easily breakable. The fact she's still here fighting proves she's not. Like you said yourself earlier, she's a survivor. Treat her like one."

I watch the house, every light on, twinkling in the dusky sky.

"Order an Uber."

"Why?"

"Because I'm not going anywhere until she talks to me."

Josie

Agent Price has been sitting outside on our front porch steps in the freezing cold for four hours.

Every now and again, I find myself gravitating toward the window in the living area, surprised each time I check and he's still there.

I've given up on studying. My books, notes and laptop remain scattered across the central island, my favorite place to work. There's something about the kitchen—it's the place I feel most at home. I guess that's where my passion for cooking comes from—at least part of it. I'm pulling things out of the refrigerator when my phone lights up on the counter. The chime of its alert filling the room. Still dancing to The Score, I pick it up, my mood sinking when I see Agent Price's name on the caller ID.

When I open the message, I almost drop the phone when I see two words I never expected from someone like him.

I'm sorry.

I don't know what to do with that. I tiptoe into the entryway, scared he'll hear me approaching if he has supersonic hearing and whatever other mad skills secret agents have. I pause by the door, pulling aside the sheer curtain covering one of the panels of glass. All I can see is the back of his dark head of hair and black pea coat. When he lets out a long huff of air, it clouds in the air and I'm pretty sure I see him shiver.

The words 'I'm sorry' play through my mind. I feel my anger start to thaw, enough that I open the door without realizing. He turns, but I'm already walking away, calling back over my shoulder, "Come in. You can't protect me if you freeze to death."

A smile plays on my lips when I hear him grumble. I might be inviting him in to prevent hypothermia, but it doesn't mean I'm going to make this easy for him. He had no right doing what he did and the fact he's here proves he knows it too.

Back in the kitchen, with my attention on the food, I hear the door shut and the bolt move into place. Ignoring his presence in our home, I set my playlist on Spotify going again before filling a pan with dried penne, covering it with enough water and setting it to boil. Then I begin working on the sauce, chopping the onions and garlic, then sautéing them in oil, before adding fresh tomatoes, pepper and a bit of salt. The best bit comes last, adding in the basil. It transforms the sauce, and the smells that fill the house every time I do are unreal. Lost in my happy place, I get a shock when I spin round and find Agent Price hovering by the central island; his skyscraper form taking in the mess in front of him.

He doesn't say a word, and neither do I. I'm still mad, and I don't know what the hell he is, as a scowl so deep it forms a line between his brows sits on his face. Only the sounds of JXDN singing "Angels and Demons", along with the boiling pasta and simmering sauce, keep me company. I go back to preparing the food. When the sauce is ready, I drain the pasta, saving some of the water to help thicken the sauce. The final touch before mixing it all together.

I hear a grumble that can only be Agent Price's stomach, and despite my better judgement, I pull two bowls out from the cabinet.

"Are you allergic to anything?" I ask over my shoulder.

A gruff "No?" is the answer I get.

I fill the two bowls, piling his full to the brim, then place it in front of him on the counter. I walk around the island and set mine down next to his, then climb onto the stool. Agent Price doesn't move a muscle, staring down at the pasta like it's offending him.

"Don't worry, I haven't poisoned it," I say, digging into my own bowl. He still doesn't move. "You can sit down, you know. I'm sure eating isn't against the rules."

I'm not sure whether he huffs or sighs, but eventually he sits next to me and picks up his fork. He definitely sighs when he takes his first mouthful, and the second and third. I fight back a smile and keep my focus on my own bowl. He strikes me as the type to spook easily.

I could almost convince myself I'm enjoying his company, until I remember the reason why he's been freezing on the porch, and I stiffen. Damn cooking, it always puts me in a good mood and helps me forget— even the things I shouldn't. When I've finished, I go about clearing up, rinsing the pans and my bowl before setting them in the dishwasher.

When Agent Price finishes, he places his fork neatly in the empty bowl and says, "That was amazing."

I shrug and say coolly. "It was just pasta."

"Seriously," he says, sincerity behind his words. "It was really good."

I fold my arms and stare at him, wondering if I can burn him alive with a look alone. Now the food high is passing, the anger is back with full force, and I have to count to ten to stop myself from screaming at him.

"Why were you following me?" He holds my gaze but doesn't answer. "Agent Price, if what happened that night was nothing, *why* were you following me? You owe me the truth."

His jaw ticks and a battle rages in his eyes. I can see him fighting against what he should do. A large hand settles on the black marble counter and taps. "We think there's a copycat."

I laugh bitterly. "Is that a joke?"

He grimaces. The first bit of emotion I've ever seen him give away. "I wish it was."

"A copycat?" He swallows, still battling with what to do. I know he's considering holding things back. "I want the truth, Agent Price. All of it."

"Someone is mimicking Eugene Belmer. We think he's competing."

"What does that mean?"

The brown in his irises turns darker than night. His pupils are barely distinguishable. "It means he's more dangerous than Belmer."

My future and everything around me start to fall away. I had something. I was building something, and now it's slipping through my fingers like sand. This is why I never made a life for myself, because I didn't want to feel the stabbing feeling in my chest like I am at this moment when it all got torn away.

I school my expression. The backs of my eyes burn, but I refuse to cry. I don't want him to know that I'm scared, hurt and everything in between. "You should have told me."

His face softens and he opens his mouth to say something, stopping when my phone lights on the counter with expert timing. We both look down, Duane's name staring back up at us both. Usually, there'd be a small flutter in my chest. Instead, all hope I had of something between us that's been steadily growing over the past few weeks plummets into the ground, leaving me feeling empty.

"Who's Duane Jackson, Freya?"

I narrow my eyes. "Why are you asking? The fact you know his name proves what you've done. I'm guessing you know more about him than I do. You read his record, right?"

His apology text from earlier seems worlds away.

"I did what was needed," he replies through gritted teeth.

"No. You did what was needed to help yourself, not what was right for me."

"You can't trust anyone, Freya."

"Don't worry, I gave up on trust a long time ago. You can see yourself out."

I leave him behind sitting at the island, staring at the bowl that was temporarily our white flag, before I say something I can't take back.

Up in my room, it's not long until I hear the front door open and close when he leaves. Straight away, I go down and slide across the bolt. It's almost midnight when I finally feel sleep taking over. I amble through the house, shutting off the lights. Just before I climb into bed, I glance out of the window through the crack in the curtains, finding Agent Price's black SUV still parked outside.

It's around four AM when I get up to use the bathroom, my bladder protesting against the glass of water I drank before bed. When I look out of my window, the SUV is still there, and I'm just able to make out Agent Price's silhouette.

Five

Josie

Three nights in a row, Agent Price has been sitting outside my house all night long.

It's the fourth night when the temperatures plummet that I decide to let him inside.

Around seven-thirty, I unbolt the door and race to his SUV. He watches in shock and dives out of the car, gun raised.

"What's wrong?!" he shouts, eyes wild, darting from left to right, taking in everything behind me, his whole-body tense.

A small whimper escapes at the sight of his gun pointing at me and my pulse skyrockets. Involuntarily, my hands find their way in the air, palms facing out. I'm a walking, talking cliché. Well, no walking. I'm frozen to the spot and at serious risk of peeing my pants if he keeps the gun pointing at me for much longer.

"C-can you put that thing down?" I stammer.

He asks again, "What's wrong, Freya? You ran out like someone was chasing you." Thankfully, he drops the gun while he's speaking, and my life stops flashing before my eyes.

"I ran because it's freezing. I was coming to get you." He looks at me blankly, clearly not understanding what I'm getting at. "You can't stay out here every night like you are doing." A cold breeze hits me, and I shiver. Fearing my nipples are going to pierce through the material of my shirt, I turn and walk toward the house. When I don't hear him following, I look back. "Why aren't you coming?"

"I can't." He frowns. "It's against procedure."

I fight an eye roll. I should have known. Agent Price is a sucker for the rules. Of course he is. Perfectly pressed dark gray suit, perfectly straight tie, perfectly cut and styled dark brown hair, never too much stubble. Even his brows are perfect.

I smile. "Fine. It's your choice. You can either freeze, or there's a couch with your name on it." He still doesn't follow. "I'm sure protecting me from inside the house will be classed as legit to your boss."

I'm almost at the front door when I hear his fancy shoes tapping against the path leading up to the porch. I don't hang around. He's probably second guessing himself as it is. Instead, I make my way into the kitchen and pull out some leftovers, setting them down on the counter at the same time Agent Price walks in, thankfully with the gun out of sight.

I'm about to mention the food when one of my feline friends hops up on the island. Agent Price jumps slightly, hand resting on his gun, now tucked beneath his suit jacket. My eyes widen. I've never seen a gun up close in real life and I've been faced with his twice in the space of a few minutes. When he realizes there's no threat, he drops his hand away and my heart settles. I reach up and grab hold of the cat, nuzzling my face into his black fur for comfort. They don't usually come in until right before bed, but the cold has them both being needy.

Agent Price stares at me in disbelief when a second jumps up onto the counter. "Cats, really?"

I smirk. "I figured if you can't beat them, join them."

My joke falls on deaf ears. Agent Price doesn't do jokes either. Of course.

He watches them prowling up and down the island. "What are their names?"

"Cat One and Cat Two."

His brows shoot up into his hairline. "Cat One and Cat Two?"

I grab a couple of pouches of food and fill their bowls, placing them on the floor so they'll hopefully stop jumping around. "Do you have something against my choice of names?"

"They're just ... different."

"They're replaceable."

I wouldn't have said it was possible for his brows to get any higher up his head, but somehow, he manages it. "Replaceable?"

"Do you always ask so many questions?"

He does the last thing I expect. He smirks. A hint of a dimple appears in his cheek, softening every judgy assumption I've made about him so far. "Questions are my job, Freya."

"Funny, Evan. Not." Are we really doing this, bantering in the kitchen? I wonder if I stepped into a parallel universe when I came back through the front door. That's the only explanation for whatever this is, and the dimply smirk.

He scowls, sucking all the humor out of the room. "Don't call me Evan."

"Why?"

"It's too personal."

"Right ... well, on that note, I think I'm going to call it an early night. I don't want to get you in trouble by being in the same room as you. By the way, that's for you," I say, nodding at the plate of leftovers which, thankfully, the cats didn't walk all over.

I'm almost out of the room when he asks after me, "What did you mean by replaceable?"

"Sorry," I call over my shoulder. "I can't give you the answer. It's too personal."

***

Evan

Knuckles hit the driver's window of my SUV and I startle awake. Disorientated, it takes me a second to come round and figure out whcrc I am. I take in the community college Freya attends to my left and try to shake away the sleep. My eyes blink slowly when it presses back in. Damn, I can't remember the last time I had more than a couple of hours sleep and it's beginning to wear me down. I never fall asleep on the job, ever.

Knuckles hit the glass again.

I look to my right, straightening when I find Hewson peering through the steamy window. I roll it down slowly, taking in his stern expression.

"Sir?"

"Don't sir me, Price. You only call me that shit when you know you've messed up."

"Have I? Messed up?"

His lips form a flat line, and he looks over at the college, taking in a few of the students milling around on the steps. "No. But you will if you keep this up. A little bird told me you've been covering every shift you can, watching Freya Becket."

"Would that little bird be Mara, by any chance?"

"Don't go taking this out on her. She's looking out for you. You need to sleep, Price."

"There isn't time," I grit out.

"Then I'm making time. You can't protect anyone if you burn out. Home, now, and sleep. That's a direct order."

"What about Freya?"

He waves his keys in the air. "I'll make sure Freya is okay. You make sure you're okay."

I look between him and the college a couple of times, torn over what to do.

"You're sure?"

"Yes. We have the brief for the Kraken bust at five. Don't be late."

Fuck. I forgot all about it. I really do need to sleep. I'm dropping plates left, right, and center.

"Okay," I sigh, exhaustion consuming every part of my body. "Thanks."

"Don't thank me," he replies, brows furrowing. "The unit is a team, don't forget that. Heroes don't work alone. Even Batman has someone helping him from time to time." He winks and reminds me as he starts to walk to his own SUV parked directly in front of mine. "Don't forget. Five PM. If you're late, *then* there will be trouble."

Not needing to be told twice, I roll up my window and make the journey home, only just remembering to set my alarm before passing out on my bed.

***

Josie

"I'm never going to get this," I groan to myself, staring at one of the many textbooks sprawled across my usual table in the library.

The sweet, sweet smell of coffee mingled with chocolate reaches my nose as a paper cup swoops in front of me. "Need some help?"

I tilt my head back to find Duane smiling. "If by help you mean someone to take this quiz for me and ace it, sure."

He chuckles. "Sorry, I can't do that." My shoulders slump with disappointment. "But I can help you study?"

I bite my lip, feigning pondering my answer. Since the day we met, Duane has continued texting me. Thankfully, he's the kind of person who doesn't pry, and accepted my 'I slipped in the tub' explanation for my face, without any extra questions.

I'd be lying if I said it didn't feel nice, acting like a normal girl with a normal guy. Doing the normal dance that people do when they first start getting to know each other. It all feels alien, though. The way my tummy flutters when my phone lights up with a text. The way I can't stop grinning for hours after he makes a joke or blushing when he gives me a subtle compliment. I want to bottle it all up in a jar to keep it safe so nothing can ruin it, because it all feels too good to be true. I just hope this bubble doesn't pop.

Crystal blue eyes twinkle, and Duane clears his throat. "Freya?"

I hadn't even realized I'd drifted off into my own little world. Awkward.

Releasing my lip and praying my nerves will settle, I grin. "Sure."

He beams back, sliding his backpack off his shoulder and sitting in the seat next to mine. "What is it that you're struggling with?"

My face twists into a grimace. "Business Law."

He pulls over the textbook I've been staring mindlessly at for the past hour and scans the page. "Easy."

My eyes widen in surprise, and he chuckles. "I have a fascination with the law. I want to study it ... eventually."

"How convenient for me," I muse.

"Very." His eyes drop to my lips for a brief moment, and every butterfly flying in my stomach picks up their pace, wings flapping rapidly.

I hold my breath, wondering if he might kiss me. I mean, it would be a little bit weird considering we've only met twice, but I've been speaking with him by text more than anyone before and I feel like I already know him. He's a nice guy. Normal. He's the obvious choice if I want to branch out and start living like normal women my age. It doesn't have to be anything serious. Dating can be fun—it doesn't have to be anxiety inducing, at least, that's what I've read on Google. Maybe that's why I don't pull away when he starts to lean in.

His lips never get the chance to meet with mine though, because my phone vibrates on the table, startling me and breaking the moment for both of us. Duane blinks rapidly before turning his attention back to the textbook.

And the source of our disruption ... Agent Goddamn Price.

Frowning, I open his message.

I have to work late on something. Two agents will be outside your home when you get back. Don't be alarmed.

My irritation waivers. He's just trying to keep you safe, Freya. You can't keep being mad at the guy every time he does his job.

I text back:

I'll be studying later than normal at the library with a friend. If you can, let them know not to expect me at my usual time.

I want to get back to studying and Duane, but three dots appear, then disappear. The next thing I know, Agent Price's name is flashing on the screen with an incoming call.

I mouth 'sorry' to Duane as I slide my chair back and walk over to the stacks for some privacy.

"Hello?" I answer reluctantly.

Agent Price's voice sounds groggy, like he's just woken up. "What friend?"

I roll my eyes because he can't see me. At least, I think he can't. I stop rolling them, just in case. "You know who."

No way am I saying his name out loud and making this super awkward.

"Duane Jackson?"

"Yes," I answer curtly. Silence. "Are you still there?"

"Be careful."

"What, that's it? You're not going to go all Batman on me?"

"No need. I already ran a background check on him."

More silence. When I look at my screen, I find he's hung up on me. My nostrils flare as I walk back over to the table. Duane is still focused on the textbook when I sit back down.

"Everything okay?" he asks after a couple of awkward minutes.

"Fine," I say, trying to sound it, even though irritation is still crawling beneath my skin in a way I only ever associate with Agent Price. No one has ever been able to draw such a reaction from me with so few words. Probably because there technically haven't been many people in my life to try. Minor details.

Hours pass without me realizing and when I finally acknowledge the time, I realize it's dark outside.

"Damn," I murmur, quickly starting to pack away my things. I told myself after freaking out last time that I wouldn't stay late, yet here I am, letting a guy distract me. At least I have my pepper spray.

"What's wrong?" asks Duane, seeming surprised by my sudden change in mood.

I don't really blame him; it's not even seven PM. After how much he's helped me, I feel like I owe him an explanation.

"I hate being out in the dark alone," I admit.

His eyes twinkle. "I'll walk you to your car. Problem solved." He jumps up, towering over me and flexing his muscles in one of those weird poses body builders do on stage. "I'm stronger than I look."

He looks ridiculous with his black beanie and blue checkered shirt. I don't like to stereotype, but the wraps around his wrists and the peek of a tattoo on his arm where his sleeves are rolled up make him look like he'd be better suited at a gig than in a weight-lifting environment.

I throw my head back and laugh. It feels good, really good. I could almost convince myself I'm a normal person walking a normal path in life. Unfortunately, my unkind brain thinks this is the perfect time to remind me of what happened the last time I was here late. An image of the figure in the black hooded jacket watching me through the mirror flashes through my mind. The blood drains from my face and Duane frowns but doesn't comment.

Outside, we walk quickly in the direction of my car. It only takes a few minutes and I feel much calmer having someone by my side. I pull out my keys when we're close, getting ready to unlock it. I never do until the very last second getting in. I read an article in a magazine once about a guy jumping in the backseat of a woman's car and kidnapping her. My routine was changed forevermore, and I haven't bought a magazine since.

Duane shoves his hands in his pockets, looking nervous for the first time since I met him. He stubs his toe against the sidewalk awkwardly and says, "So."

"So," I reply.

He chuckles and rubs the back of his neck. "We should do this again. The studying thing."

I smile. "We should."

We hold each other's gaze and my heart thuds. I think back to that night with my mom when I made the decision to start living. I think this would be considered a moment to seize. I take a couple of steps closer, removing most of the space between us. Duane doesn't seem surprised, and the nervousness disappears from his face when he brings both hands up to my face. He strokes my cheeks with his thumbs before reaching round and tangling his hands in my hair. He holds my head in place, leaning down. He pauses. There's a millimeter of space between our lips. And then he kisses me.

It's like a candle wick being lit. That's how I'd describe our first kiss. He's tentative, but firm, and with each press of his lips the flame grows a little bit stronger from the first spark. Something aches inside me. It's not hormone-driven passion, it's something much more, much deeper. It feels like hope.

After a few seconds, Duane pulls away. My smile drops when I catch his troubled expression.

"What made you afraid, Freya?"

The glimmer of hope diminishes as quickly as it appeared. I'm not sure if it's the question, his use of my fake name, or both.

I want him to call me by my real name. I want to be able to tell him the truth. But I can't.

Stepping back, I unlock the car without a word. I slide into the driver's seat and close the door, activating the central locking system before rolling down the window.

"Thank you for walking me to my car," I say with a sad smile, trying to hold it together.

"No problem," Duane replies. He doesn't say anything else and I'm grateful.

After rolling the window back up, I pull away into the night, watching his figure disappear in the rearview mirror.

I remind myself, over and over, that this is the way things have to be.

***

Evan

Hidden in the dark behind a tower of crates, the only potential giveaway of my location is my short, sharp breaths, clouding in the dank air. It's eerily quiet bar the murmur of voices in the distance and the steady slosh of water occasionally breaking against the sides of the dock.

Staring straight ahead, I lower my chin to the lapel of my black pea coat and breathe into the small mic for the rest of the unit to hear, "Target in sight. They're about to exchange. Dispatch on my count." My eyes narrow in the dim light, fighting to see through the slight mist rolling off the water. They burn and I fight the urge to blink. I can't afford to miss anything. "Three." A masked figure approaches a group of suits. "Two." Words are exchanged. "One." With a subtle nod, something is handed over. "All unit's dispatch, now!"

Swarms of agents swoop in from every angle, guns raised, surrounding the group. One of the taller suits lets out an audible groan and tilts his head to the sky as if he's praying to God. With the shit he's knee deep in, I doubt God will answer any of his prayers.

I keep my gun trained on Andres Moreno, the leader of the group. He grins like the bastard he is, then winks. Shit. I dart forward at the same time he lobs our whole case, in the form of a black box, into the dark water. Our bodies collide and tumble to the ground. My gun is knocked from my hand and skirts across the concrete as we go.

Nobody moves or tries to intervene in our hustle. I have him pinned to the ground, but right at the last second, Andres gets in a swing. His fist collides with my jaw. My flesh ripples and jaw cracks from the force he puts behind it. Fucker. Frustration-fueled anger charges through my veins. I raise my fist to return the favor, knowing everyone around me will turn a blind eye, when I remember the box. Grabbing his coat, I shove him back against the ground. Hard. Enjoying the thud his head makes, hard enough for it to remind him not to fuck with me again, but not hard enough to cause a problem.

Before anyone can stop me, I rip off my coat and rush to the edge of the dock, steadily lowering myself into the water. My balls retreat inside my body as the ice-cold water swallows me in, trying to pull me down. I tread lightly. Shit, it's cold. I can't stay in here much longer.

"Torch!" I bark at one of the other agents who's followed me to the side. They pull one out from their coat pocket, leaning carefully over the edge to hand it over. I switch it on and right before I hold my breath, I hear the screech of tires. Hewson and the rest of the team, coming into the docks like planned.

I dive under the water. The torch is useless. The water's too murky and it's too dark to make anything out clearly. I need to get to the bottom where I pray the box will be. That's if it hasn't moved with the water already.

My lungs grow tight the deeper I go. Finally, my hand collides with the bottom. It's colder than freezing and I'm dicing with death, but I've always believed in chance. It's chance when the tip of my finger touches something hard that could be plastic. I squeeze my eyes shut as they burn from the icy water, then open my hand gently, trying not to disturb the water. I close my grip around something that feels like a box.

I don't have time to second guess myself, I just hope chance is on my side. Pushing off from the bottom, hard with my feet, I kick against every ache and protest my muscles make, trying to get to the surface. When my head breaks through, I gulp in air like it's my first breath.

I turn back to the dock, finding Hewson frowning down at me. "Swimming wasn't on the agenda."

"Plans changed," I mutter.

He holds his hand out and I pass him whatever is in mine, before grabbing onto the arms of two other agents who help heave me out of the water.

My teeth chatter as I watch Hewson intently, needing to know what I found. "You're a fucking idiot, but you got it."

Mara rushes over with a towel. "What the hell, Price? Are you trying to die from hypothermia?"

"Thanks," I say, taking the towel from her.

Luckily, I have a spare set of clothing in my trunk. I inform Hewson what I'm doing and trek to my SUV. Inside, I turn the heat on full blast, staying hidden in the back thanks to the tinted windows. Teeth still bouncing against each other, I head back over, finding the unit has made quick work of cuffing the group. They remain silent apart from Moreno, who bitches and moans any chance he gets.

Hewson and I both stare at the months of hard work that's sitting in his hand. The USB from inside the box holds the details of each past and future transaction of the Kraken Cartel, known worldwide for their dealings in child trafficking. When I look up, the group is secured in the back of a transport van, ready to be taken to the main unit for questioning. The van pulls away as quickly as it arrived. There should be a sense of accomplishment that we've finally got them, but all I feel is regret for those we let down in the past.

"Good work today," says Hewson. He follows my gaze, staring into the distance at the disappearing vehicle. He knows what I'm thinking—he always does. "You should be proud. You and the unit saved a lot of lives today and a lot of families the heartache of being torn apart."

"It's not enough."

We both know I'm talking about more than the Kraken case. I've been unsettled since the night Michael Becket called, even worse since his sister joined the picture. It's starting again, I can feel it in my bones, but damn, I don't know if I can deal with it. This case does something to me. It has since the first day I opened one of the files, years ago, and saw an image of a terrified child next to its mother's mutilated body. Not that I'd ever tell anyone that. We're taught to desensitize ourselves to these things. The fact I feel anything toward this case proves I'm far from desensitized.

"Evan ..." Hewson murmurs, reading my mind. "We all have a case; one we can't let go. One that gets under our skin to the point we forget where it ends, and we begin. It's one of the many downsides of the job. But if you let it take over, it will be the end of you. Don't let it win."

"There's been nothing since that night." I don't need to expand; he knows which night I'm referring to.

"The DNA report came back with no match for the material."

"Like we expected anything else," I reply bitterly.

"What's your gut telling you?"

His question throws me. I think about it a moment, then answer honestly. "That the game hasn't even started yet."

He nods, the lines in his forehead deepening. "Then we better get ready to play. It's late, you should get home. Take the day off tomorrow, you need the rest. Freya Becket's home is already covered for the night."

I'm about to argue that I don't need rest, but he walks away before I get a chance, getting into one of the waiting black vehicles and speeding off.

Accepting he's right, I plan a date with my tub, wondering when the hell I'm going to warm up.

85

Six

Josie

I haven't seen Agent Price in almost two days. I was surprised when I stepped out the day after my study date with Duane and found another agent watching the house.

I'm getting ready to go to college and glance out the window, finding the same figure as yesterday sitting in an SUV similar to Agent Price's. My curiosity piques, and when I'm almost finished getting ready, I step outside and walk toward the vehicle, making sure not to run and risk having another gun pointed in my direction.

When the Agent catches sight of me, he jumps out with a look of concern. "Is everything okay, Ms. Becket?"

"I was just wondering where Agent Price is," I say sweetly.

He pauses, contemplating whether he should tell me what's going on. The same small ball of worry that came with seeing Agent Price's gun grows, sitting heavy in my chest. It's the realization that his job isn't like in the movies. He doesn't have a stunt double for all the fancy tricks—what he does is real and dangerous. Every day, he sets his life on the line. I'm just not sure why I suddenly care so much.

Whatever internal battle the Agent is dealing with passes, and he answers, "He has the flu."

I arch a brow. "The flu?" It seems ironic that a giant like himself could be knocked down by something so simple. It's another reminder that he isn't invincible like he makes it seem.

"Okay," I reply, turning and heading back into the house with the agent shooting me a confused look as I go.

I don't have much time, but I make it work, bustling around the kitchen and ignoring the growls of my stomach, protesting against its lack of breakfast. There's a chance I'm going to be late for class, but my mind is on one track, and I bat the concerns away. When I'm finished, I loop my backpack over my shoulders, then pick up the small box, balancing it carefully when I lock the front door behind me.

Before going to my car, I walk back over to the agent's SUV. He's already standing on the sidewalk when I get to him, watching me quizzically.

"Your shift's over soon, right?" He nods and I offer over the box. "I was wondering if you could take this to Agent Price."

Amusement flashes in his eyes. "Can do." That's all I get. Maybe lack of conversational skills is a universal trait in the FBI, who knows. He takes the box from me, setting it carefully in one of the footwells in the back of the car.

"Thanks," I say, before walking to my own.

I'm about to turn on the engine when my phone vibrates.

Duane: *How about another study session?*

I smile to myself, remembering the kiss from a couple of nights ago.

Me: *Sounds fun. Tomorrow?*
Duane: *Great. It's a date.*

I beam all the way to college. Being normal feels better than I ever could have imagined.

***

Evan

Taking a swim in freezing water wasn't the smartest idea I've ever had, even if I did get what we needed. I've been on my back, struggling to open my eyes since I collapsed into bed after closing the Kraken case. I've never taken a sick day, and now I've taken two. It's pissing me off, but no matter how hard I try, I can't get warm, and exhaustion keeps taking over. I ignore the little voice in my head trying to tell me this is where things were heading anyway. Burnout really is a thing.

A knock at the door of my apartment has me stirring from a restless, fever-fueled sleep. Nobody ever comes here. I'm not even sure anyone knows where I live. When there's another knock, I resign myself to getting up and pulling on some clothes, swaying as I go. I grab my gun en route, just in case. Through the peephole, I find Sanchez from my team, and open the door with a frown. I'm sure Hewson said he was covering my shift watching Freya.

The hairs on the back of my neck stir with unease as I open the door, my brain jumping to conclusions.

"What's wrong?" I ask before he has a chance to say anything.

He looks at me, confused. "Wrong?"

"You're supposed to be watching Freya Becket. Has something happened? Why didn't anyone call me?"

Sanchez chuckles, watching me as if he knows something I don't. "Freya is fine. I clocked off my shift. She asked me to bring you this."

He raises a box in the air.

"What is it?" I ask, taking it from him.

He chuckles again. "A care package. Looks like she's the one watching out for you for a change." He backs away, yawning. "I need sleep. Call if you need anything." Realizing what he's said, he corrects himself. "Please don't though, I really do need to sleep. I don't know how you've done this for weeks. No wonder you're sick."

"Yeah, thanks, bye," I mutter, unable to take my eyes off the package.

I close the door and walk over to the kitchen, setting it down on the counter. My stomach growls at the sight of two pots of chicken noodle soup. She's even made sandwiches. I open the wrapping of one and lift the top slice of bread tentatively, finding it filled with Swiss cheese and a combination of other things I wouldn't normally go for. I'm a plain chicken, rice and veg kind of guy. Simple. Predictable.

I place one of the containers of soup in the microwave oven before diving into the sandwich I've already opened, almost devouring it in one go when the nutty taste of the cheese combined with rocket, mayo and something I can't put my finger on coats my tastebuds. Damn it's good. I could eat the others without them touching the sides. The microwave pings and I grab the soup. It's even better than the sandwich.

Satiated, I place the rest of the food in the fridge for later and climb back into bed. Sleep threatens to take over, but this time it's the calm and restful kind. The kind you have when you've been cared for. The problem being that the person doing the caring is the one person who shouldn't. The same person who's been playing on my mind, because of one word in particular that fell from her lips.

I blame my lingering fever for the fact I pick up my phone and do something I promised myself I never would with a case. Something personal.

Me: *Thanks for the soup. Why 'replaceable'?*

It doesn't take long for her to reply.

F: *Because it will hurt less when they're gone.*

I set my phone down, wishing I'd never asked the question, because her answer resonates with me more than it should.

***

Josie

"I think it's starting to make sense. You're a good teacher."

Duane gives me a lopsided smile and some of his dark blond hair falls across his forehead into his eyes. For once, he isn't wearing a beanie and his glossy hair is on show. I've concluded he conditions.

"Does that mean we get to move on to the date part of our study date?" he asks.

I set my pen down on the coffee table where all my textbooks are spread out, along with hours' worth of notes. Duane really is a good teacher and there's a possibility I'm going to ace the upcoming quiz thanks to his help.

"What did you have in mind?" I ask playfully, a faint blush covering my cheeks.

"Well," he leans in closer, eyes focused on my lips. "I was thinking we could pick up where we left off the other night."

My heart starts to race when I feel his breath tickle my skin. I close my eyes ready, and his lips skim across mine at the same moment a throat clears behind us. Duane slowly pulls back. Meanwhile, I dart back across the couch like I've been electrocuted.

The source of the throat clearing is, of course, Agent Price, in his perfectly pressed, dark gray suit with his perfectly styled hair, staring at the two of us with an unreadable expression. What are readable: his eyes. When his mood is light, so is their color. The fact they're almost black is a dead giveaway that he's pissed. I'm hit with a dilemma when I realize I don't even know who I should introduce him to Duane as. He's older, not like super old, but maybe old enough I could get away with saying he's a friend of my mom's if needed? It sinks in what a bad idea it was to have Duane come over. The FBI agent standing in my house is a prime example of how far apart our worlds are.

Duane jumps to his feet and rushes around the couch, holding out his hand, grinning. "Duane Jackson."

Agent Price gives his hand a look of disdain. I follow Duane into the entryway, my cheeks turning a deep shade of red, which is now for entirely different reasons.

A few long and torturous seconds pass.

Duane might be oblivious to the role Agent Price plays in my life, but it's clear he isn't oblivious to the tension passing between us all when he gestures at the front door.

"Maybe I should go?" he asks, facing me.

"That's probably a good idea," Agent Price answers before I get a chance.

"I was asking *Freya*," snaps Duane, anger flaring in his eyes.

Agent Price tucks his hands in the pockets of his pants. As he does, his suit jacket pulls back revealing not one, but two guns sitting in their holster.

Duane blinks in shock and scurries to the door, grabbing his things from the floor. I barely hear him say, "I'll see you around," as he darts outside.

My brain struggles to catch up with what's just happened and the door shuts, leaving just me and the overbearing FBI agent together. I keep my eyes focused on where Duane was standing seconds ago, scared I'll lose my shit if I look at Agent Price.

"What was that?" I ask, removing 'the fuck' from the sentence, even though it would feel really good to unleash my wrath.

"I could ask you the same thing," he replies calmly.

Shifting my feet so I can look at him, I try to hide my surprise when I catch sight of a giant bruise covering his jaw, a shade of purple deeper than my bed spread.

"What do you mean?"

"A stranger, in your home. Really, Freya?" he quips, one thick brow arching in a way that tells me he's unimpressed, just in case his gun show hadn't made it obvious enough.

Irritation sizzles beneath my skin. I inhale and exhale slowly before responding. "I thought you said you ran a background check?"

"I lied."

"What?"

"I never ran the background check. I stopped at his name." He looks away briefly, muttering under his breath, "I should have known better."

Why the hell wouldn't he run a background check after going all alpha-hole on me?

"What's an alpha-hole?"

Crap. I said that out loud.

"Why didn't you?" I ask, changing the subject.

He shrugs and says what I least expect from someone like him. "Because you wouldn't have wanted me to. I figured I need to trust your judgment if I want you to trust mine."

And just like that, he throws me for a loop.

Avoidance is probably the best way of handling things considering I'm confused and angry—two things which are a terrible combination. Planning to go to my room, I pause at the bottom of the stairs and take in the state of his face again.

"What happened?"

The dimple in his cheek pops up out of nowhere. "Even Batman bruises sometimes."

Rolling my eyes, I leave him behind. I'm halfway up the stairs when I turn back, feeling like I need to justify why Duane was here. I'm not quite sure why.

"For the record, we were studying. I have a quiz coming up that I was probably going to fail if Duane hadn't helped me."

He frowns. "Do you kiss all your study partners?"

It's a legitimate question—one I choose to ignore, retreating to my room.

***

The next morning, I go downstairs to make breakfast before Mom comes home and find something sitting on the kitchen counter, decorated with a small purple bow.

The words *Business for Dummies* glare up at me. Maybe Agent Price has a sense of humor after all.

"What's that?" asks my mom from behind me.

I startle. She's home earlier than usual and I didn't hear her come in. I grab the bow, scrunching it in my hand and hiding it in the pocket of my jacket.

"A book I left at college." I lie. "I need it to study and wanted to go back and find it last night. Agent Price must have had someone get it for me."

She arches a brow. "That was kind of him."

"Yeah." I wonder how kind she would think he was if she knew he'd bought it for me. I'm still trying to figure out the meaning behind the gesture myself.

It takes me by surprise when she pulls me into a hug. I inhale the smell of waffles and bacon that always lingers on her uniform when she's finished. "I've missed you. I feel like I never see you."

"That's because you don't," I reply, pulling away.

The hurt in her eyes makes my stomach twist, but she's going deeper and deeper down whatever dark hole she's found herself lost in. Working longer hours. Starting earlier, finishing later—in the morning, that is. We haven't seen each other in days, and I wouldn't even know someone else lived in the house with me if it weren't for the plate of food I set her out each morning being missing when I get back. When she gets like this, a sharp dose of reality is sometimes needed to make her realize what she's doing. It's never easy, but it helps.

"I'm sorry," she says quietly, sitting on a stool at the central island.

I sit beside her. "Has something happened?"

Her eyes water as she stares down at the counter. "Your brother called."

On the rare chance they manage to contact each other, Mom always ends up in a tailspin. I should have known.

"What did he say?"

"He's recovering from his accident, and he's met someone."

My stomach sinks, but I keep my expression neutral. I should be happy for him, but there's a niggle of jealousy I can't ignore, especially when I think back on the disaster that was last night between Duane and Agent Price.

"Then what's wrong?"

She sniffs. "He's holding himself back from having a future ..."

"And you blame yourself." She nods. "Mom, you can't keep doing this. None of this is your fault."

"But it is."

I shake my head firmly. "No. It's not. Michael and I are both capable of making our own choices and living our lives the way we choose. Even if we do have to adapt more than most."

"Your lives have been shaped by my mistakes ..."

"Believe me," I reach over and grab her hand, "our lives could be much worse. At least we still have you. Everything happens for a reason." Seeing her so broken, feeling like Michael and I are holding ourselves back only solidifies my decision to live my life. Perhaps just with less risky choices involved. "I've met someone too," I admit.

Her head snaps up and she looks at me with eyes wide with disbelief. "Really?"

"Really. I made a mistake though."

"What kind of mistake?"

"I invited him here to study. I'm sorry, I got carried away."

"It probably wasn't the best idea," she squeezes my hand when my expression drops. "But we all make mistakes. I know that better than anyone."

I think back on how Duane ran out of here and how I haven't heard from him since. "It doesn't make any difference. He probably doesn't want anything more to do with me."

Mom frowns. "Why wouldn't he?"

"He met Agent Price," I reply with a grimace.

Her face twists. "Ah."

"It was a disaster," I groan. "He flashed his guns."

Mom snorts. I probably could have expanded on that statement.

"If this guy likes you and he's worth the effort, he will give you a chance. Why don't you do something with him outside of the house?"

"Like a real date?"

"Is that what they're still called?" She chuckles. "I wouldn't know."

"You could date too, you know."

Her chuckle turns into hysterical laughter. "My dating days are over."

"Mom ..."

"Freya, we're talking about you, not me. Unless I meet a man that makes the world stop turning and would do anything for me, which I seriously doubt will happen, I'm done. Now back to you."

"Agent Price will probably say no."

"If Agent Price is against it and thinks there's a risk, then why doesn't he go with you? He's used to going undercover. He could just be there to scope things out, seeing as he's here each night anyway, watching over the house. It's merely a change of location."

"Right," I scoff. "Like he's going to agree to that."

"Freya, we're under no direct threat. We need to live our lives where we can and seize normality when it's offered to us."

"And what do I say to Agent Price?"

"Technically, he can't stop you from doing anything. But just tell him the truth. Tell him you need this."

***

Judgmental eyes burn through my clothing when I step outside to lock the front door.

Duane was surprisingly okay when I texted him, considering what a disaster last night was, and more than up for a second shot at our date—no studying involved. I picked a restaurant in one of the busiest areas in DC, where the odds of something happening would be slim. I figured there's no time like the present, so we arranged it for tonight.

Two dates in twenty-four hours. Maybe things really could go somewhere.

"Where are you going?" asks Agent Price. It doesn't come as a surprise that he's already standing behind me like a tall dark shadow in his usual black pea coat. With the length of his legs, it probably only took a few strides for him to get to me from his SUV.

"I have a date," I reply.

He frowns. "Would this date be with your study partner from last night?"

I turn and smile sweetly. "Not that the details are really any of your business, but yes, it is."

"The details are my business, Freya, because I'm trying to keep you safe."

Mom's right. If I stand a chance of him agreeing, I have to tell him the truth. I have to let him in.

97

"I need this. Please." My voice cracks and his face softens from its usual scowl. He looks away. I can see the cogs turning in his mind. There's a chance I could win him over with some reinforcement. "I need to feel normal, for once. Please, Evan."

Chocolate-colored eyes snap back to mine and he holds my gaze. My pulse races, waiting for his answer.

The muscle in his jaw ticks. "Fine."

"Yes! Thank you, thank you, thank you!" I close the distance between us, wrapping my arms around his surprisingly solid middle, before darting off to my car.

"I'm coming with you," he calls after me.

"I knew you would," I call back.

Nothing can dampen my mood, not even him lurking in the background, watching Duane's every move, most likely with a gun in one hand and a steak knife in the other, ready to pounce.

It doesn't take as long as I expect to get to the restaurant. For once, traffic is on my side, so much so I'm early and find myself counting down the minutes until Duane is due to arrive. Nerves kick in when it gets to seven thirty and he still hasn't arrived. My phone lights up with a message from him saying he's sorry, but he's running a few minutes late. I rub my clammy palms against the short plum t-shirt dress I'm wearing, feeling a little out of place with the funky lace tights and Doc Martin's I paired it with. This place is Agent Price kind of fancy. I'd be better suited to the middle of a mosh pit.

My nerves refuse to settle, especially knowing Agent Price is a few tables back, watching me behind his menu. God, I hope Duane doesn't see him, or I'm never going to be able to explain who he is without it being seriously awkward.

The restaurant door opens, and I hold my breath, expecting Duane to walk through. I'm disappointed when it's just a delivery guy. I watch him because I have nothing better to do while I wait. He talks animatedly to one of the waiters, who then looks in my direction, looking confused. He takes a long, thin box from the delivery guy and starts to walk toward my table.

The hairs on the back of my neck prickle and Agent Price appears beside me.

"Freya Becket?" asks the waiter.

I nod and he places the navy box down on the table, being careful not to knock the glass wear. Agent Price steps in before I get a chance to open the box. He lifts it carefully, then when he seems satisfied, gives it a gentle shake. There's no sound. A couple of people from other tables keep looking over, adding to the feelings of unease swarming through my body when he sets the box back down and lifts away the lid.

Sitting inside is a single white lily.

"Get up," he says darkly, setting the lid back into place and picking up the box. "We're leaving."

I glance up, heart hammering in my chest. I don't know the true significance of the lily, but whatever it is, it has Agent Price's eyes narrowed to slits.

"What about Duane?"

"I don't give a damn about Duane. We need to leave. Now."

There's an urgency in his voice I've never heard before, which is why I don't ask any more questions. I stand and grab my coat and bag. Agent Price is glued to my side when we walk quickly out of the restaurant.

"Freya!" I cringe at the sound of Duane's voice as we step out into the night.

"Ignore him," snaps Agent Price.

"But—"

"I said ignore him, Freya."

When I dig my heels into the sidewalk and shake my head no, he grabs my arm and drags me along the sidewalk toward his SUV. "We don't have time for this."

"Then tell me what's going on!"

I hear Duane shout, "Hey! Let her go!" in the background.

He's too late. I'm already being shoved into the passenger seat, with the door slammed shut after me. Agent Price races around to the driver's side, tossing the box onto the back seat. He doesn't wait for me to put my seat belt on, firing up the engine and tearing into the road at such speed I scream.

"Where are we going?"

Agent Price doesn't answer, instead taps the touchscreen on his dashboard a couple of times. Ringing fills the car.

"Price?" answers a male voice.

"We've got a problem."

"What kind of problem?"

He gives me a sidelong glance before answering. "A Belmer-related problem."

A shiver runs down my spine. It can't be.

"Where are you?" asks the man on the line.

"Heading out of state."

"Okay."

There are no other questions, no challenge.

"We need Angela Becket covered at all times, extra security. I'll be in touch when I can."

"Call for backup if you need it."

The call ends, and the only noise is the hum of the engine. Buildings whizz by and I grip onto the hem of my dress so tight my knuckles go white, praying we don't crash.

"Where are we going?" I ask eventually, not really wanting the answer.

"Somewhere no one will know you."

"Which is?"

"Vermont," he replies bluntly, as if him stealing me away and disappearing into the night is a normal occurrence.

Seven

Evan

I shouldn't have taken Freya out of the state, I should have taken her out of the country. Placed her on another continent or in a far corner of the Earth where no one could find her.

Vermont is my attempt at buying us time. How much we need, I'm not sure. It's a temporary fix.

Two warehouse stops and car changes later, we pull to a stop outside a modest, white, ranch-style home on the outskirts of Montpelier. I expect Freya to fall asleep during the journey, but she stays awake the whole way, watching the roads like a hawk. We arrive early morning when the sun is rising and making the out-of-season frost sparkle on the lawn.

"What is this place?" she asks.

I pull out my keys and jump out of the vehicle. "Come on. I'll answer your questions inside."

She follows, albeit reluctantly. The house is cold, spring's late arrival isn't just isolated to DC, and I spend a few minutes turning on the heat. When I'm done, I find Freya still in the entryway, looking awkward.

"Make yourself at home."

"Is that what this is now? Home?"

I drag a hand down my face and gesture into the living area. "Let's sit."

It feels like the right thing to say. I hope it's the right thing to say. What little progress we've made with regards to communication has been lost. It feels like we've taken ten steps back and I'm struggling to figure out how we do this. This thing that feels weirdly personal.

In the living area, everything smells musty. It's been over five months since I last came, and I make a mental note to pick up some cleaning supplies. And food. And clothes. I didn't think through the details.

When I opened the box and found the lily, one word sprang to my mind: run.

"Why are we here?" Freya asks tentatively, perching on the end of the bottle green couch.

"I need you out of the way for a while."

Her eyes widen. "Alone?"

I shake my head. "I'm going to arrange for your mom to follow when the dust has settled. We can't chance moving her straight away in case someone follows."

"What dust, Agent Price? What's going on? All this because of a flower?"

She doesn't know the truth and she needs to know all of it, otherwise how can she know what she's protecting herself from? "What do you know about Eugene Belmer?"

"Enough," she sniffs, "but nothing too specific. Mom never wanted me to know the details and I guess I stuck my head in the sand."

I bite back a groan of frustration. "Understandable. But from now on, I need your head out of the sand. You need to be aware of everything going on around you at all times."

"Why?" Her throat bobs when she swallows, waiting for what's about to become her grim reality.

"Belmer would send lilies right before killing his victims. Whoever's doing this is coming, Freya, and you have to be ready."

Her face remains blank, and then she laughs. Fucking laughs. Words might not be my thing, but I've never been lost for them like I am now. When she catches her breath, a switch flips and she shakes her head angrily, making her sandy blonde hair sway around her shoulders.

"I finally start making a life for myself and this happens."

"I'm sorry." And I am. Every case I've ever dealt with, I've managed to keep a wall up and never let my personal feelings become involved, and there's a reason why. Guilt is tearing me apart inside at the thought of taking away everything Freya has worked for. It will take a few days for the reality of the situation to set in, and when it does, it isn't going to be pretty. She's going to have to give up everything for a third time. At least, until we have our copycat safely behind bars with Belmer. Last night has reinforced what we thought to be true—she's at risk.

But Mara was right, she's a fighter, she can do this.

Her face says otherwise. "Is there a bed I can use? I'm tired."

Defeated would be the word I'd have chosen, because that's how she looks.

"Along the hall, third on your left."

A rogue tear escapes, trailing down her cheek as she stands and moves out of the room. It settles itself deep inside a part of me no one has ever managed to get at before, but not as deep as the next words she murmurs.

"I should have kept myself replaceable."

Listening to her footsteps pad away, I make a promise, not to myself, but to her, that no matter what it takes, I will keep her safe.

***

A week passes. A long, silent week.

Freya spends most of her time hiding in my room, the one now designated as hers. I give her the privacy she needs. It's all I know how to do; this isn't exactly my forte. The only thing we do together is visit a couple of stores, buying her enough clothing until her mom arrives and a stockpile of food. A couple of agents from the bureau join us two days in, taking some of the pressure off me and preparing to take over when I return to DC.

It's my second-to-last night in Montpelier and I should be using the time I have spare to catch up on my other cases. All I can think about is the petite blonde, with a vast collection of black band t-shirts and, ironically, a thing for cats.

Accepting I'm going to get nothing done, I decide a peace offering might help her adjust to this temporary set up a little bit better. I let Rogers and Grey know I'm going to pick up some pizzas, and they place their own orders before I leave.

Forty-five minutes later, I return with three huge boxes.

"Take the night off," I say to my colleagues.

They don't need to be told twice, snatching two of the boxes and hurrying to their rooms before I can change my mind.

I knock on the door to what has become Freya's room and wait for an answer. I don't get one, so I knock again.

"It's just me," I call out.

105

The door swings open, and giant green eyes stare up at me. "Who else would it be?"

She has a point. "I got pizza. Best in the city."

Her eyes light up and I give myself a mental high five for brightening her mood. "Thanks."

It's not much, but it's better than nothing.

She walks past me and I follow her into the kitchen, where she heads to one of the cabinets and pulls out two plates.

Two, not one.

I didn't think the plan all the way through. I wasn't expecting us to spend time together. Sirens sound in my head, warning me this is too personal.

"It's just pizza," Freya comments, reading my mind.

She's right and my stomach grumbles at the smell of cheese and pepperoni. I place a slice on each of the two plates she slides across the counter, then take a huge bite of my own to avoid the awkward silence.

Searing heat fills my mouth, making the skin on the roof of it bubble instantly.

"Motherfu—" I hiss, waving a hand in front of my face. My mood sours and my thin wire of patience from the past few days snaps. "Freya, you know we're not friends, right? I'm here to keep you safe."

Well, that's one surefire way to piss her off. I regret the words the second they're out of my mouth. She gives me a disappointed look, grabs the box of pizza, and silently walks into the living area. Meal for one it is. I take another bite of my slice, but it's like chewing on cardboard. My appetite is in another room with someone it has no right to be with.

Against my better judgement, I mutter, "Fuck it," under my breath and follow her.

She's sitting sideways on the couch, back resting against the arm, with her pajama-clad legs stretched out in front of her. The box of pizza remains untouched on the coffee table while she stares at the TV, ignoring me. I wrack my brain, trying to come up with something to say. Each time I open my mouth, I come up with nothing.

"Why are you nervous?"

I clear my throat. "I'm not nervous."

She looks over at me, pursing her lips. "Then why are you sweating?"

"I'm not." I'm actually sweating like a pig, but I refuse to admit that to her.

Why is this so hard? Because you don't do relationships of any kind, the little voice in my head answers. I interact with the people I work with and my parents. There's been the odd girlfriend over the years, but it's never worked out because I'm married to my job and the thought of never being married to me didn't appeal to them.

"Hmm." She grabs a slice and focuses her attention back on the TV.

"I'm sorry," I blurt out.

"That wasn't so hard, was it? Pizza?" she says, gesturing at the TV like I haven't just acted like a grade-A prick. "We could watch a movie."

My brain yo-yo's back and forth with one moral dilemma after another. "No."

"Why not?"

I rub the back of my neck. "It's not protocol."

She calls out softly, "Hello? Is anyone else here?" Of course, there's no answer, because Rogers and Grey have called it a night. She smiles for the first time in days. "I won't tell."

"Why do you want me to stay?"

"You want the honest answer?"

"No, I want you to lie," I deadpan. She rolls her eyes. "Why else would I ask?"

"I'm lonely." My personal radar flashes red, warning me to walk out of the room to somewhere I can safely keep an eye on her without crossing any lines. "It's just pizza and a movie."

I shouldn't walk to the couch and sit down, just like I shouldn't share a pizza with her. But for one night, I let myself not care, because misery loves company. She's not the only one who's lonely.

"What do you like?" she asks, the remote hovering in mid-air as I get myself comfy on the opposite side of the couch.

"I like mysteries, thrillers, that kind of thing," I answer, reaching over and grabbing a slice.

She laughs. "You're kidding, right?"

"Why would I be kidding?"

"It's a bit cliché."

I don't have a clue what she's getting at. "Cliché how?"

"Please tell me you're not that oblivious?"

"Okay, I'm not." I remove my eyes from hers and focus on the TV screen.

"Agent Price, do you ever let yourself switch off?"

"From what?"

"Work. Do you ever let yourself switch off from work? Who are you outside of the FBI?" Grabbing the control from her with my free hand, I start scrolling through the menu. I settle on a light-hearted romantic series, which is the complete opposite to the answer I just gave. "I know what you're doing."

I keep my eyes trained on the screen. "I'm watching a shitty program and eating shitty food. That's what I like to do when I'm not working."

"Whose house is this?"

Her question catches me off guard, and I reply without thinking about my answer. "Mine."

Her eyes widen. "Why do you have a house in Vermont?"

I shrug. "It's where I come to take a break."

"And how often is that?"

"Not often enough."

"Mind if I make an observation?"

I pick up another slice of pizza, having finished my last in record time.

"Shoot."

"Won't whoever is doing this be able to link the property to you and come looking for me?"

"The property isn't in my name. Call it a precaution."

She frowns. "Oh." We both sit watching the screen move. I don't know about her, but I haven't got a clue what's happening. Freya isn't done with her million and one questions, though. Note to self, 'let's watch a movie' is code for 'let's get to know each other'. I'm out of practice with all this communicating with people in the real world, and it shows. "Why not just add extra security to me and my mom in Silver Spring?"

"It would be a prison sentence in the making," I answer truthfully. "Here, you have the freedom to step outside and live a somewhat normal life, as long as Rogers and Grey are following."

"Okay," she breathes, shifting and grabbing the box of pizza, placing it on the couch between us without another word.

We steadily work our way through it while watching one crappy episode after another. It's the most basic of nights, but it's the best I've had in years.

***

Distant chiming creeps into my subconscious telling me I need to open my eyes. Before I do, I inhale the scent of wild rose and vanilla, imprinting it in my mind. Taking in the bright overhead lights and flickering TV in front of me, I look down and my stomach drops when I find Freya curled up against me, her chest rising and falling steadily.

Shit.

My phone starts ringing again. I shift carefully, lying Freya down on the couch, then pull out my phone from my pocket, catching the time in the top corner of the screen.

One-thirty in the morning.

Double shit.

"Hello," I whisper, tiptoeing from the room so I can speak without waking her.

"Price!" snaps Hewson down the line. "Why the fuck haven't you been answering your phone?"

"I was asleep," I grumble. "What's wrong?"

"He's out."

I frown. "Who's out?"

"Eugene Belmer."

I laugh. "Funny. What's really going on?"

"I'm not joking, Price. Sing Sing called. He disappeared hours ago."

His words sink in, and I pace back and forth. "That can't be possible. He's isolated, under maximum secur—"

"Are you going to keep wasting time listing things we already know? We need you back here ..."

He continues speaking, but I don't hear any of it, my mind working at a million miles an hour, trying to figure out how what he's saying could be possible. There's no way. Belmer would have to be a goddamn genie to get out of that place.

"I need to go," I say.

"Wait. Don't hang up, there are things we need to do. It's—"

I hit the red button before he can finish.

"What's wrong?" Freya asks, standing in the doorway to the living area, rubbing sleep from her eyes. I don't answer at first, opting for taking in the ridiculous oversized pajamas swamping her frame. "Evan?"

I flinch at the sound of her using my name. To avoid it happening again, I say, "Eugene Belmer has escaped Sing Sing Correctional Facility."

She pales and wobbles in the doorway, resting a hand against the frame to steady herself. "Escaped?"

I nod. "I should get going. There are things I need to do."

Like making sure her brother isn't lying in a ditch somewhere because he's the only Becket we don't have eyes on right now. I don't say that part out loud.

"Wait!" She grasps my arm and we both look down. I take a step back and her hand drops to her side. "Go where?"

"I need to go back to DC. Rogers and Grey will look after you."

I don't think about what I'm doing. I'm in a daze and halfway through the door when she says after me, "Promise you'll stay safe."

A long time ago, I learned not to make promises I couldn't keep.

"Goodbye, Freya."

Walking out into the dark early morning, I brace myself for the shit storm that's about to hit.

***

Shrill rings fill my SUV as I speed down the highway.

"Come on," I grumble, staring at the road. Streetlights strobe as I soar past.

Finally, she picks up. "Price?"

"Mara."

"Price, it's not even seven AM," she grumbles.

"Thanks for pointing that out, I wasn't aware," I snap, getting agitated with small talk we don't have time for.

"You're the one waking *me* up, therefore it should be me who's crabby, not the other way around."

"I need you to meet me at the unit."

"When? Aren't you in Vermont?"

"In a few hours. I'm on my way back, but I need you to do some things before I get there."

"Seriously? What's so important it can't wait?"

"Eugene Belmer's out."

A clatter fills the car and a loud "Fuck." There's rustling I assume is Mara climbing out of bed to retrieve her phone. "That's not possible."

"Apparently it is."

"Are the Beckets, okay?"

"Some of them are. I can't get in touch with Michael."

She doesn't make a comment about how I suddenly need her help after being a dick and shunning her off cases left, right, and center.

I'm grateful when she says, "What do you need me to do?" I rattle off my list and she promises to go into the unit and get to work before hanging up.

Breaking almost every speed limit from Montpelier to DC, I walk into the main unit a little after nine.

Mara raises a brow at me and tuts. "You'll be no help to anyone if you're dead."

"You're not paid to comment on my driving skills," I retort. "Can you pull up all the security footage from Sing Sing for the past twenty-four hours?"

I'm about to move over to my desk, but stop in my tracks when her lips form a tight line. She shakes her head. "The systems were down."

I close my eyes and tilt my head back while pinching my brow. "What do you mean the systems were down? For how long?"

She swallows. "Sixteen hours. The longest they've ever been out."

Years I've watched this case. Years. Since the Beckets first reported their sightings back in Jacksonville, I've always kept an eye out. I've been waiting, deep down knowing something was coming. I just never guessed it would be something like this.

I clench my fists at my sides, so hard I almost draw blood.

"Price?"

"So, there's nothing?" I say, exhaling long and hard, trying not to lose my shit. "Nothing at all?"

"Do you not believe me?"

"I don't know." Trust isn't something I give lightly. Ignoring the look of disappointment on Mara's face, I grab my phone. "I'm going to try Michael Becket again."

I dial Michael's number, the one only the two of us know exists. Still, I get nothing; it keeps going to voicemail. Mara digs and finds his main number, which also goes through to voicemail.

I'm on my fourth attempt when he finally answers. "Hello?"

"Thank fuck! Where have you been? Why aren't you answering your other phone?"

"Evan?" How'd you get this number?"

"Do you really need to ask that question?"

"Why are you calling?" His voice falters.

"I've been trying to call you all night," I snap.

"My phone died," he explains, "and I couldn't get to my charger."

"Great fucking timing," I grit out.

"Are you there?" Michael asks when I go silent, struggling to find the right words.

"He got out," I say quietly.

He hesitates, telling me that he knows exactly who I'm talking about despite the fact he says, "Who got out?"

"Don't play dumb," I answer. We spend the next few minutes going over the details and then I ask, "Where are you right now?" while calculating how quickly I can get to Jacksonville to scope things out.

"I'm in New York." I almost drop the phone.

"You've got to be kidding me!"

"I shouldn't have come back," he groans.

"No, you fucking shouldn't." Of all the times he chooses to go back to New York, he picks now. He may as well offer himself to Belmer on a platter for how close he is to Sing Sing. It hits me I'm taking out my frustration on him when he goes silent. "He would have found you wherever you were. Be on alert. I'm coming to New York. You can't be on your own right now."

The line goes eerily quiet.

"I was with someone last night ..." he says. "We had an argument, and I left her alone. I haven't heard from her since and now I can't find her."

"Dammit," I hiss.

Neither of us needs to say out loud what we think has happened.

"Why would he take her?"

Revenge.

He's using Michael's weakness to find Freya.

"To try and get to you," I answer.

***

Right before I leave the unit, Mara catches a figure in a black hooded jacket on CCTV, climbing out of a car a few blocks from Michael's girlfriend's apartment. The plane touches down in New York and I pray Michael has listened after I informed him and hasn't done anything stupid.

I quickly find out he's done exactly what I'd have done had it been Freya in this situation when I arrive at Britney Shaw's apartment, expecting Michael, only to be greeted by Britney's work colleague. She informs me he's left, and she doesn't have a clue where to. A sixth sense, along with a report of a gunshot in the area, has me firing orders for backup and updating Hewson.

"Can you drive any faster?" I ask.

We're en route to the Beckets' old apartment, where for them, the game began, and for Eugene Belmer, the game ended.

The officer beside me shoots me a look of disapproval, then focuses his attention back on the streets of New York, whizzing by dangerously. "If you'd like to get there in one piece, no."

"Fine." I tap my fingers against my thigh impatiently.

We swerve when a car blows through a stop sign straight in front of us. I grip the leather of my seat to the sound of tires screeching and horns blaring.

"Was that really necessary?" I ask as the car straightens and we pick up our pace again.

"I told you going faster would be dangerous."

The car comes to an abrupt stop outside an old, red-brick apartment block. My hand shoots out,

115

slamming against plastic to stop my head colliding with the dashboard. I arch a brow and open my mouth to say something, stopping when the street flashes blue in the disappearing evening light as police cars swarm in.

The S.W.A.T. team is already at the door, ready to enter the building when I clamber out of the vehicle. They disappear and I hold my breath, waiting for clearance to follow. A radio close by crackles to life.

"All clear." Crackle. "They're here." Crackle. "No sign of Belmer."

A bulletproof vest is tossed my way and I slide it over my head before heading into the building. Charging up one floor after another, I dodge holes in the steps and broken pieces of furniture. Torches flash all around. When we get to the right floor, a S.W.A.T. team is standing, guns raised, outside the door to the apartment.

Mold and rotting wood fail to mask the sweet, metallic scent of blood I'd pick up anywhere as I walk through the hallway and step into what I assume is the living room. The boarded windows and rapidly diminishing light make it difficult to be certain.

"Lights?" I call out.

"Powers out," someone responds. "They're coming up with LEDs."

Within a minute, the whole apartment is illuminated so bright satellites would be able to pick us out from the glow of New York City.

"Are they *all* necessary?" I snap. "The apartment's barely one-hundred square feet. We're not in a damn football field."

"Sorry," mumbles a local officer, dimming the lamps.

My eyes adjust and I find Michael unresponsive on the floor, with deep red marks around his neck and a gun beside him.

"How is he?" I ask the female officer checking his pulse.

"His pulse is okay." She turns her head to the side. "It's the female I'm worried about."

I turn to where she's looking. Zip ties are being loosened from the wrists and ankles of a female I assume is Britney Shaw, unconscious on a chair. She's only a few years older than Freya and her tangled hair, whiter than the lights flooding the room, is a stark contrast to her silk dress, covered with blood.

"Paramedics!"

The apartment becomes a flurry of activity while Michael and the blonde are placed onto stretchers and taken away. I'm standing close to where Michael was positioned, setting down a marker on the ground when Hewson barges into the apartment. He tosses a forensic torch my way and turns on the one he's kept for himself.

"What have we got?"

I glance around the room, digesting every detail. "High velocity impact spatter on the wall with a bullet hole." I carefully step around a large puddle of blood, close to where Michael was moved from. I walk the length to the front door of the apartment and back, shining the torch on the floor as I go. "Huh."

"Is 'huh' a technical term?"

I turn back. "Huh, means there's no blood leading out of the apartment."

Hewson's brows draw together. "Wasn't Michael lifted onto a stretcher? Could that not explain it?"

I shake my head. "I don't think this is Michael's blood."

"Could it be Belmer's?"

"Possibly," I answer. "Forensics have already taken a sample to run it for DNA. If it is Belmer, he must be a magician."

Hewson cocks his head to the side. "How so?"

I look down at the blood by our feet, already darker and thicker than when I arrived.

"This amount of blood suggests he's badly injured. But like I said, there's not a drop outside this area bar the spatter."

"What are you suggesting? He levitated out?"

"I don't know." I drag a hand down my face, wishing the day could be over. Unfortunately, I have a feeling this day is going to merge into the next, and many more after that. Sleep won't be on any of our radars in the imminent future, not unless Belmer and his copycat are safely behind bars.

"Helpful."

"I should get to the hospital and make sure Britney and Michael are okay," I say, sliding my gloves off.

Hewson nods. "We have all our free agents, as well as local enforcements, searching the city. If he's injured to the extent the blood suggests, he won't go far. We'll find him."

Famous last words, because like so many before us who have tried to take down Belmer, we find ourselves chasing a ghost.

Eight

Josie

I haven't heard from Agent Price in a week when he texts.

I'll be back in an hour.

No, 'Hi, how are you?'
No warning.
I'm quickly learning he does things his own way and is totally unforgiving in doing so. He could be considered an ass if it weren't for the fact he's out saving the world. It's getting late, and I make my way around the house, turning on all the lights and closing the curtains as I go.

Rogers and Grey made the mistake of following me and switching them off twice before figuring out the meaning behind it all. There's now an understanding between the three of us, and without Cat One and Cat Two to keep me company, the lights stay on all night.

I'm in the kitchen with my AirPods in, dancing to Muse and making a peanut butter sandwich, when my eyes skim over a figure in the doorway. I scream, dropping the jar. The smash echoes through the house and shattered glass covers the black tiles.

"What the hell?" My heart is racing so fast I'm contemplating taking a trip to the emergency room.

Agent Price starts to walk over to me. When he gets closer, he reaches over, pulling one of the AirPods from my ear.

"If you didn't have your music so loud, you would have heard me say hello." He scowls and his eyes darken. "Three times."

"Sorry," I say, disgruntled.

"I'm serious, Freya. You need to make sure you're aware of everything going on around you at all times. This ..." He waves the AirPod in front of my face. "Could have you killed in seconds."

"I get it, okay," I grumble. I step back, wanting to put some distance between us, yelping when a shard of glass pierces the bottom of my foot.

The next thing I know, I'm elevated and set on top of the kitchen counter.

"Don't move." Agent Price removes his hands from my waist and moves three cabinets over, glass crunching beneath his shoes as he goes.

Opening a door, he reaches up, effortlessly retrieving a first aid kit from a shelf I'd stand no chance of getting at, even with a step. He shrugs his coat off and crouches, before holding my foot and inspecting the wound.

I close my eyes and groan melodramatically. "Is it bad?"

His chuckle passes through his fingertips, vibrating against my skin and soothing the sting where the glass has penetrated. "It's only a small piece. You'll survive with a bandaid."

He's being playful. Interesting. This is a side to him I haven't seen before. Along with the dimple and sense of humor he sometimes reveals, I could almost be convinced he's less grumpy, more sunshine. Holding up a pair of tweezers, he counts down before pulling the glass out. I bite down on my lip. It might be small, but it hurts like a motherfucker, even more so when he sweeps an antiseptic wipe across it. He secures a bandaid in place, then stands to his full height, towering over me, despite the fact I'm perched on the counter.

"Let this be a reminder to be more aware. Wait there."

Scrap the sunshine. He's totally grumpy.

He rolls his sleeves up, then rummages in a low-level cabinet until he finds what he's searching for, then begins sweeping up the sparkling shards of glass from the floor with a dustpan and brush. Once finished, he leaves the room. I jump down from the counter and move back to my half-prepared sandwich.

"Bummer," I say to no one in particular. Only half of the bottom slice is covered, and it's skimmed if that. Everyone knows peanut butter needs to be layered thick to reach its full potential. I look up when Agent Price returns with two brown paper bags filled to the brim. "You brought supplies!"

"Not enough," he mutters. I know what he means. The other two agents living under his roof with me have an insatiable appetite. With another added to the mix, we're doomed.

He steps back, and I empty the contents from each bag. Luckily, I find a new jar of peanut butter, and surprisingly, the ingredients of the sandwiches I prepared for him when he was sick.

I arch a brow. "Swiss cheese?"

"Please."

I guess that means he wants one, so I lay out the ingredients in the order I need them, finding every step of my sandwich preparations under scrutinization.

"Mustard," he comments, brows furrowing. "Who knew?"

"Dijon, to be exact," I say, adding a thin layer to the top slice of bread.

"I've been trying to figure out what it was I was missing."

"And now you know." I smile, placing the mustard-coated bread on top of the perfectly structured sandwich. Slicing it diagonally, nerves kick in when I pass it over, wondering if it will be as good as he remembers.

He takes a large bite and my heart thuds when he starts to chew. I'm not sure when his opinion of my food started to matter, but it does. When he groans, I exhale, cursing to myself for caring so much, especially when his expression turns blank, and he becomes lost in thought. I could ask what's wrong, but I'm starting to learn when it comes to Agent Price, you don't ask. He tells when he's ready. I busy myself clearing up instead, my own sandwich long forgotten.

I'm up to my elbows in bubbles, when he finally says, "Why did you study business?"

Did, not do. Past tense. My education isn't something we've discussed. In fact, we've discussed nothing apart from the fact the figure of my nightmares, who is supposed to be safely behind bars, could be anywhere.

"It's a sensible choice," I reply, rinsing the chopping board and setting it on the drainer.

Silence settles between us, and I focus back on cleaning while Agent Price finishes his sandwich.

A few minutes later, he sets down his crusts. "For what?"

I make a show of dipping the cloth I'm using into the water in the sink before rinsing it through under the faucet, hoping it will distract him from my answer. "I want my own restaurant one day." A minute passes and he doesn't respond. I wish I'd never said anything. "It's a stupid idea. Forget it."

A hardened stain on the counter becomes offensive and I scrub at it frantically.

"What kind of restaurant?" he asks, and I look up. I expect to find him smirking or something along those lines, as if my answer is ridiculous. What I find is him looking thoughtful.

"I'm not sure."

Truthfully, I'm not. It's something that probably won't ever happen, and it feels like a dream which is too far-fetched for me to ever need to be specific with the details.

Even my dreams are replaceable.

Agent Price reaches over and squeezes my hand. "You can fly, Freya."

A chill covers my skin when he stands and leaves the room without saying anything else. I'm not sure if it's from the loss of contact or the effect of his words. Whatever it is, it's quickly replaced with annoyance when I realize he's left his crusts for me to clear away.

***

"Freya."

Agent Price's rough voice floats toward me. We're sitting across from each other in my old kitchen back in Jacksonville while he critiques one dish after another, which I've painstakingly prepared.

123

"Freya," he says, more firmly this time. His voice sounds like it's coming from somewhere else. "Freya."

Finally, I stir, prying one eye open at a time. When I find him towering over me, fully dressed, I grumble to myself and bury my way into the warmth of my sheets, trying to block out the lights.

"Wakey, wakey, sunshine." He pulls the sheets back just enough to expose my head. Loose strands of hair obscure my vision. I shove them out of my eyes and find him smirking down at me. "Nice hair."

He's most likely referring to the nest that tends to attach itself to my head during the hours of sleep. Just one of the perks of being as restless at night as I am in the day.

"What time is it?" I mumble. "And why is it so bright?"

"Just before six. And it's bright because every light in the house has been on all night."

"Right."

"Get dressed. We have somewhere we need to be."

That has me coming round fully. "We're going out?"

I'd go out in the middle of the night if it meant I could get outside these walls. The reason I'm here is so I can live a somewhat normal life. However, even with Rogers and Grey, two fully trained FBI agents at my side, I find myself freezing whenever I go to open the front door. I'm trapped inside my own head.

The image of the lily sitting in the box stops me every time. I'm living on borrowed time, and only Agent Price manages to calm the storm of fear.

"Yes," he replies, as if it's normal to wake someone abruptly and demand they leave the house before the sun has risen. "Up."

He disappears from the room, and I lay, blinking. The crack in the curtains shows a hint of daylight finally lightening the sky. It doesn't just feel unseasonably cold; it feels unseasonably dark. The seasons are playing games with us as well.

I jump out of bed and head into the shared bathroom before anyone can steal it. A shower later, I feel refreshed and ready to take on the day. I'm lacing up my Docs when Agent Price shouts for me to get my ass moving in a few less fruitful words.

"Coming!" I call back, grabbing a gray hoody to wear under my parka. Apparently, the weather is supposed to be getting warmer—only a month and a half late—but if yesterday is anything to go by, the weather reports lie. It's still freezing.

I find Agent Price waiting for me at the front door, looking all dark and brooding as per usual. The fancy dancy black car waiting outside is the kind you see in the movies that looks like the wheels don't move and levitate over the road instead.

"I thought we were flying under the radar?" I say, following him.

He glimpses at me over the roof, and with a shrug, says, "I needed a different car, so I thought I'd treat myself."

"What are we doing exactly?"

"You'll find out soon. Get in." He opens the driver's door and climbs in, never taking his eyes off me.

I slide into the passenger side and let out a whistle at all the gears and gadgets. "It's like the Batmobile."

His grumpy façade cracks. "I'm a super-secret agent, didn't you know?" I match his playful side with a grin. He tenses and faces out the front window. "Seatbelt."

Oooookay. I do as he says and leave him to stew in whatever bad mood has suddenly taken over.

We're forty-five minutes into the drive when I become bored of the silence. I reach forward to play with some of the dials in the hope of finding the radio. I'm about to turn one when Agent Price's hand shoots out, stopping me. I wait with bated breath for him to snatch it back, like the mere thought of touching me is revolting, but he doesn't. A couple of seconds tick by before he lifts my hand away from the console, setting it down in my lap, all the time never taking his eyes off the road.

"No touching."

"Can we have some music on?" I ask, my heart pitter-pattering at the thought of what his answer will be.

In true Agent Price style, there's no answer. I'm learning he's a man of few words, which suits me fine. I've always thought actions speak louder. They're the true voice of a person's soul. He taps the screen a couple of times and Alexisonfire fills the car. I keep my eyes focused out the window, watching the trees fly by as the morning gets brighter and the scenery we pass gets clearer. The next song that comes on is by Nine Inch Nails.

"You like rock music?" I ask, and he nods. "Since when?"

"Since you were in diapers."

"Right." I frown at his not-so-subtle reminder of the gap between us. I don't know why he's suddenly throwing it about. It's not like it's relevant in any way and it isn't even that big.

Another thirty minutes pass, then he pulls up on the side of a long, winding road. Thick woodland surrounds us, and I look around, confused.

"Erm, we're in the middle of nowhere."

"Observant of you," replies Agent Price.

"So, what are we doing here?"

"Walking," he answers, climbing out of the car.

I scramble after him, tugging my parka tight around me, wishing I'd brought a hat and gloves. He powers into the thick line of trees, and I struggle to keep up, my chunky Doc Martens weighing my feet down into the forest floor. We walk for what feels like an hour, but is probably only twenty minutes, and I spend the whole time trying not to break an ankle.

"Do you trust me, Freya?" Agent Price asks, finally slowing down.

My heart thuds hard when I think back on everything he's done for my family and the risks he's taken to keep me safe. A feeling I'm not willing to acknowledge ripples through me.

"Of course," I reply.

Because I do.

I trust him more than anyone.

I trust him with my life, something I've only just become aware of. Like, right this second.

He spins around so fast I barely register what's happening. Metal bites my skin when his gun presses against my forehead. The click of the safety being turned off bounces around the trees.

"Wrong answer."

***

Evan

I prayed the plan wouldn't get to this point. I wanted Freya to demand to know where we were going, to be more assertive. She did the complete opposite, and like putty in my hands, she got in the car and one response to one question was all it took for her to go happily wherever I was taking her.

I'm furious at her, but I'm more furious at myself for putting us in this situation.

I hold the object in my hands perfectly still, blocking out what I'm doing, trying to forget that I'm holding a gun to her head. The comforting smell of pine surrounds us in a situation that is anything but comfortable.

"What are you doing?" She barely breathes the words. Emerald eyes wild with fear.

"I could ask you the same thing." To my own ears my voice sounds like that of a stranger. I hate it. But for a few short seconds, I need to make her believe I could turn on her. She needs to understand that in order to keep herself safe. She can't trust anyone, not even me.

Our eyes remain locked and her lip quivers. "I don't understand."

"First lesson: don't trust anyone. Not even the people you think you can trust the most."

Her stance relaxes. Not the reaction I was going for. "So, this is a lesson. You're not about to kill me?"

"I don't know, you tell me," I challenge, pushing the gun harder against her skin. "Do you trust that I won't?"

"No," she croaks.

"Good."

"Okay", falls from her lips with a harsh exhale.

"This is what death looks like when it's staring you in the face. If you're going to come out of the other side of this, you can't fear it."

A nervous giggle escapes her. I push the gun harder, narrowing my eyes. The giggling stops and she swallows. "How is that possible?"

My first big case was a disaster, one that Hewson and I brushed to the side and refuse to talk about. The odds weren't in my favor with a Glock nineteen shoved in my mouth; the metal scraping against my teeth. It was a harsh lesson, like for Freya now. But when death is ready to knock on your door, you have no choice. Fearing it only holds you back.

"If you fear death, you can't win. *It* will be in control. You can't stop it from coming. To not fear death, you need to accept that it's inevitable. When you do, the power is in your hands."

"And how exactly do I do that with a gun pointed at my head?"

Even in a near-death situation, she has the same sass that had me regrouping and wondering who I was dealing with years ago. Freya Beckel is like no female I've met before—she's one on her own. Gentle, smart, kind, but feisty as fuck should the situation arise.

"Stop. Focus on what it feels like to be alive. Keep yourself grounded. Only you have control over your body and your mind. You, no one else, Freya. Breathe." I step forward once, twice. Our bodies almost touch and I move the gun to her temple, then drag it along her skin. When I force it under her chin, her head tilts back. A moment passes between us, the rising and falling of her chest steadies. Everything becomes calm. "Only you decide what happens next. So, who's going to be the winner?"

A cool breeze passes between us. "Me."

Her arm shoots up, chops down against the bend in mine. The gun drops from my hand and then she drives her knee up to my crotch. I hit the ground. The air escapes me with a gush. She smiles down at me curled on the floor. I've never felt prouder, despite my dick feeling like it will never function properly again.

"Was that what you had in mind?"

"Yes," I wheeze. She holds out a hand to help me up, but I shake my head no. "I need a minute." When I manage to get to my feet, I brush pines needles and dirt from my usually pristine coat. "Where did you learn to do that?"

She shrugs and makes a show of observing her nails. "TV."

I look up to the sky, biting back a groan. "I want to say a lot of things, but I can't, because that was actually really good."

"And you said I watched too much Netflix ..."

I laugh and grab my gun from the ground, placing it back in its holster where it belongs.

Freya looks at me expectantly, as if the past five minutes haven't happened. "So, what next?"

"Gun practice."

"Seriously?"

"You need to learn, Freya. Knowing will keep you safe."

"And then what? I get my own gun?"

"Yes," I reply. I have one in my bag ready for her.

Her mouth drops open. "I'm not keeping a gun. What if I set it off by accident? I'm more likely to shoot myself!"

I roll my eyes. "Stop being dramatic, and yes, you are keeping it. I can't always be there for you."

"When you're not there, I have Rogers and Grey." I stare into the distance, watching a squirrel scurry about in the foliage, and my jaw ticks. She places her hands on her hips. "What aren't you telling me?"

"What drives a serial killer is obsession." The squirrel starts to run through the forest, its movements rustling in the otherwise still atmosphere. "That's what it comes down to. An obsession to achieve a certain outcome."

"And if someone stops them?"

"Given the chance, they'll do whatever they can to finish what they started."

Freya's face hardens. "Teach me how to win."

***

We walk further into the forest to a spot I tend to come to whenever I'm in Vermont and need to clear my head. Firing a gun provides a feeling of control in what are otherwise uncontrollable situations. The deeper we go into the trees, the warmer it starts to get. Like promised, spring is finally arriving. When I come to a stop, I slide off my coat and loosen my tie, opening my top button to let in some air. Freya does the same, discarding her coat over a fallen tree on the ground.

"We're deep enough that no one should be around to hear."

"Okay." There's uncertainty in her voice. I'd be more worried if there wasn't. Learning how to use a gun isn't something that should be taken lightly, and only adds to the increasing urgency of this case.

I set down the backpack I've been carrying on the ground and pull out a couple of tin cans.

"Just like in the movies," Freya murmurs.

"Apart from it's real. Wait here."

With a tree stump in the distance as my target, I leave Freya behind, taking the empty cans with me. When I have one positioned where I need it, I head back over to Freya, crouching down for a second time and pulling out a gun from the bag.

"This is yours," I state, standing back up to my full height.

She stares at the black object in my hand. "Mine? You were being serious?"

"Keep it with you at all times. I need to know you're safe."

"What do I need to do?" she doesn't take her eyes off the gun.

"Come here."

"Where?" she squeaks.

I roll my eyes and chuckle. "Here," I say, grabbing her arm with my free hand and pulling her effortlessly toward me. She stumbles and I spin her around, so her back is flush with my front. My arm holding the gun loops around, so it's now right in front of her. "Take it." I look down, watching her chest rise and fall dramatically. For a second, I wonder if she's about to have a panic attack. Leaning down, I stop when my mouth is close to her ear. "I've got you. You can do this."

Her breathing settles, and she takes the gun into her shaking hand. I stay as close to her as I can, enveloping her with my calm.

"Good." All she does is nod in reply.

My other arm comes around her front. I help to position the gun. My fingers gently move those of her right, dominant hand, so her thumb is around the grip and her index finger on the trigger. When her other fingers seem like they're comfortably sitting just below the trigger guard, I move my hand away.

"How does that feel?"

"Okay," she barely breathes.

"You're doing great."

"I'm fucking terrified. Why am I so bad at this? The movies make it look easy."

Fighting back a laugh, I reply, "Because you're holding an object that could take someone's life away in a second. Now, you need to bring this leg forward."

I tap the outside of her left thigh and she does as she's told. "Settle your weight between both feet. Keep yourself grounded." When I notice she's unnaturally still, I add on, "And don't forget to breathe."

She lets out a long exhale and this time I do laugh. Taking hold of her left hand, I raise it in the air, encouraging her to raise the hand holding the gun at the same time. When she's in the correct position, I go to step back so I can talk her through everything else.

"Don't leave me," she says quietly. "Please."

My heart thuds hard in my chest. A slight breeze stirs around us, and I'm hit with the overpowering smell of wild rose and vanilla, something I didn't know until this second that I will always associate with Freya. I don't move away, giving her what she needs.

"There are two points," I say, close to her ear again as I look over her shoulder, focusing on the can. "One at the front and one further back." She nods in understanding. "You need to make sure the top of both points is level with each other and that the rear is centered within the notch of the front point. Got it?" She nods again. "Focus on the can with your more dominant eye. Block out everything else around you."

"I've got it," she says after a couple of seconds.

"Good. I'm going to turn the safety off." She stills with the click. "Don't forget to breathe. Now, take your time. Focus on nothing but where you're going to shoot, then when you're ready, pull back on the trigger. The gun's going to recoil when it fires. Don't fight it. Let it happen, then focus on remaining as still as you can."

"Can you count me in?"

"Sure." I rest my hands gently on her waist, leaning my body back to give her the space she needs. "Three. Two. One."

The sound of the bullet leaving the gun fills the forest. Freya misses the can completely.

"Damn."

"Again." She stills. "Breathe evenly. Block everything out. Three. Two. One."

This time the can wobbles when the bullet skims by it.

"I missed again," she groans.

"But it was better. Do it again." When both Freya and the can are still, I count down once more.

This time she hits the can dead on. She remains standing, watching the now empty spot on top of the stump.

"Maybe thrice is my lucky number," she comments.

"Let's hope." I pull my hands from her waist and step back. "Don't forget to put the safety on."

She does as she's told. "And now?"

I grab my backpack from the floor.

"We eat. Come on. I have somewhere I want to show you."

***

Josie

When Agent Price said we were going to eat, I thought he meant straight away, not after a massive trek that leaves me panting and sweating.

"Where are we going?" I moan.

"You'll see. We're almost there."

He doesn't slow down, and I race to keep up with him, making a mental note to start incorporating some kind of exercise into my routine, because I've never felt more unfit in my life. Ten minutes later, the breath is stolen from me when we break through the trees and stand on a large rock, hanging over the sparkling water.

"Where are we?"

"Lake Willoughby," Agent Price answers, walking to the edge of the rock face and setting down his bag.

He sits with his legs hanging over the edge and I eye the spot next to him dubiously.

He looks back, arching a brow in amusement. "Scared?"

Remembering everything we've done this morning and the point behind it, I shake away my fears and answer, "No," then sit down beside him. "It's beautiful."

And it is. It's the perfect day. As the sun makes its way further up into the bright blue sky, the air around us begins to warm and my skin tingles, drinking in the rays that have been missing for what feels like the longest winter there's ever been.

"I like to come here when I need to clear my head."

I watch him out of the corner of my eye as he looks at the water.

"Why?"

He nods for me to look where he is. The water is as still as the air around us and when I look down, a small gasp escapes at the image of a skull lying on its side, reflecting up at us.

"It's called Devil's Rock. There's one painted down on this side." He gestures to his right. "You can see it from below or across the water."

"But why do you come here?"

He shrugs. "When you deal with some of the things I do every day, sometimes facing the devil head on helps."

I smile, remembering the first time he met Cat One and Cat Two. "If you can't beat them, join them."

A hint of a smile plays on his lips. "Something like that."

My phone vibrates in my pocket, and I pull it out, finding a message from Duane asking how I am.

Agent Price frowns out at the water. "Have you spoken to him?"

"I just let him know I'm okay. He wants to know when I'll be back. He was worried after watching you drag me to your car."

"I did what I had to in order to keep you safe."

"I know. Thank you." Any anger I had because of what he did disappeared the second he explained his reasoning when we first arrived in Montpelier. I'm learning that everything Agent Price does is to keep me safe, and I put my frustrations to bed a while ago, accepting this is the way things need to be.

He opens the backpack and pulls out two sandwiches, layered thick with peanut butter and jelly. My favorite. I bite the inside of my cheek, fighting the grin threatening to take over my face. I sigh with relief when he pulls out a flask, unscrews the cap, and the rich smell of coffee reaches my nose. My body instantly craves the caffeine hit.

"Thanks," I say, taking a small cup from him.

We sit quietly, eating and drinking. When I feel more human, I ask, "Do you come here a lot?"

"Not as much as I'd like. Work doesn't let up often."

"But you're here now ..."

"We needed to do this."

"To keep me safe. I know." I try to ignore the feeling of disappointment that he's only here to teach me how to use a gun, not because he might want to spend time with me.

This is his job, I remind myself, then I echo the words he said to me what feels like forever ago in my head.

We're not friends.

"Why replaceable?" Agent Price asks for a third time.

"People always leave," I answer without thinking. "Them and me. If I keep things replaceable, they don't feel like they matter as much."

At least, that's what I try to convince myself.

"But you leave the lights on all night now?"

I wasn't aware he knew I left the lights on at all, but I should have known. "Cat One and Cat Two kept me company at night. They made the dark feel less scary."

Finishing his sandwich, right down to the crusts, Agent Price wraps them back up and shoves them away in the backpack. He's never struck me as the type to feed wild animals his scraps. Everything he does is measured. Minimal risk involved.

"What happened to your father, if you don't mind me asking?" He says it as if he hasn't already fired one question after another at me as quick as he can probably fire his gun.

"He died of cancer when I was five. Surely you'd know that from my file?"

"I only read the parts I really need. I try to avoid the personal bits where I can."

"Why?" I ask, turning the questioning back around on him.

"I prefer to get to know people the normal way. Not abuse my position."

"Like you did with Duane?"

"I made a mistake. I let my feelings get in the way."

Feelings. The word lingers between us. The one word that shouldn't, and we both know it.

I shrug and change the subject. "People always leave. It's just the way it is."

"Sometimes they come back."

"Rarely," I scoff, shuffling on the rock so I can get to my feet. "Can we go? I'm getting tired."

"Sure."

We're about to head into the forest when Agent Price catches my arm in his hand. My eyes settle on where his fingers skim against the bare skin of my arm, feeling warm beneath his touch.

"I have to leave later today. I don't know when I'll be back. We can't chance someone following me if I come too often. Your mom is arriving the day after tomorrow."

I try to smile, but my stomach sinks. I pull my arm from his grip and disappear into the trees, not wanting him to see the disappointment on my face and ask more questions. I don't want to answer and tell him that even though he says we're not, he feels like the closest thing I have to a friend.

If I do, then he won't be replaceable anymore.

Nine

Evan 4 months later

The doors to the unit slide open and Hewson storms in, his face an unnatural shade of red.

Mara stills at her desk, sinking down and focusing on her screen. "Incoming."

Months ago, her comment would have pissed me off, but as time's gone by, we've figured out a dynamic that works for the two of us. It helps that she's also one of the most hard-working people I've ever been partnered with, something her flowery personality disguises. Her comment isn't out of place either. In the months since Belmer's escape, he's been ratty, to say the least. Expected, considering our searches have come up with nothing. Not a scrap.

He's making a mockery of everything we believe we are, and the work we put in. He made his escape from Sing Sing seem as easy as walking out the front door, and we still don't know how he did it. The only saving grace is that the rest of the world is still unaware he's out.

"Turn on Channel Five," Hewson barks, striding to my desk.

He hovers behind me while someone in the room does as he asked. The voice of a news anchor fills the unit, and we all listen.

"... a source close to the investigation has confirmed a shocking FBI coverup. Four months ago, convicted murderer, Eugene Belmer, also known as The Cat, managed to escape the maximum-security prison, Sing Sing. It is still unknown how the inmate managed to escape while under strict surveillance ..."

Shit. So much for the world not knowing.

I keep my attention focused on the news report. A woman in her mid to late twenties with fiery red hair, fills the screen. Her name is sitting at the bottom of the screen, beside the name of the magazine she works for. It's the same magazine who made our lives chaos when they started outing Michael Becket's past and leaked a sex tape, putting a target on his head. I have no doubt they're largely responsible for the crap we're dealing with now.

"The public need to know the risk they're at with this monster on the loose again. They shouldn't be covering it up. How can we protect ourselves if we don't know people like this are out there?"

"Who the fuck is Leigh Clarke?" snaps Hewson. "And how the fuck does she know we have a fucking killer on the loose?"

"Want to say fuck any more times?" mutters Mara under her breath.

Not quiet enough, because steam billows out of Hewson's ears and he turns his attention on her. "I'll stop saying fuck when we find out where the fuck Eugene Belmer is."

"Sorry," she says.

I stare at the huge screen that fills the main wall of the unit, watching the red-head carry on speaking animatedly.

"Price?" Hewson snaps. Apparently, it's my turn for his wrath, but I'm too focused on her name. Leigh Clarke. It feels significant. "Price!"

It hits me, and I turn to Mara. "Bring up Britney Shaw's statement from the hospital." She doesn't move, just sits and waits. I roll my eyes and let out a huff of air, feeling Hewson's gaze darting between the two of us. "Please."

A couple of minutes later, Britney's statement is on the screen.

"Want to enlighten us all about what you're thinking?" asks Hewson.

I hold my hand up while reading, getting to the part I need. "Wait a second."

My eyes scan over each line, drinking in the early details Britney mentioned that seemed irrelevant at the time.

"Dammit!" I hiss, reading over the part that has been tickling my subconscious, telling me we missed something. Something big.

"What's wrong?" asks Mara.

"Leigh Clarke worked with Britney Shaw."

"We already know that. Why is it relevant?" says Hewson, leaning in to read some of the statement himself.

"Because Britney Shaw claimed Leigh Clarke set up the whole media scandal Michael Becket was a part of."

"And?"

"And she claimed Leigh was in touch with a source who helped them set everything up. The same source met with them in Jacksonville and supplied Leigh with drugs. Here," I point at the line we need on the screen. "She states she saw the exchange take place between Leigh ..."

"... and a figure in a black hooded jacket." Hewson's eyes widen as his own words sink in. "Fuck! How did we miss this?"

"It can't have been Belmer, though," says Mara, looking confused.

"No," I agree, "but it could be our copycat, and right now we have one killer, and one potential killer out there. It doesn't matter which we get first, just that we get one, hopefully before the world finds out we have two."

"If this Leigh Clarke," says Hewson, waving his hand at her huge face now frozen on the screen, "has worked with this source, she could help us ID him." His voice is urgent, but his face less angry and red thanks to our breakthrough. "I want this woman found by the end of the day. She needs questioning before she can do something stupid like disappear, the way everything does with this goddamn case."

He powers out of the unit, most likely to inform his superiors, who will be breathing down his neck now we have the media watching our every move.

Swiveling my desk chair, I face Mara. "I need you to do some hacking."

She looks at me, face blank. "One does not hack, Price. That's a terrible way of speaking about my craft." With a sniff, she goes back to staring at more numbers on her screen than I gave attention to in the entirety of high school.

I clasp my hands and watch her blatantly trying to ignore me. "Mara, you're a hacker. Say it as it is."

"I don't know what you're talking about," she sniffs again.

I call her bluff. "So that means you can't do it." I wait for a reaction, but she doesn't bite. "Fine, I'll ask Anders from CTD."

Pushing my chair back, I start to stand, getting ready to leave the unit, but Mara grabs my arm and drags me back down before I can.

"Anders is a prick," she snaps. "I can do whatever you need, but remember, I don't hack. I hate it when you call it that."

I chuckle. "What exactly do you do then?"

"I peruse."

"Peruse ..."

"Yes, peruse." Her thick, perfectly lined black brows draw down in the middle. "Hacking makes it sound cheap and nasty."

"Believe me, there is nothing cheap about your salary," I say under my breath.

"I heard that," she snaps. "Knowledge is power, and power costs money."

"Shit loads." I grin.

She rolls her eyes. "What do you need?"

"Leigh Clarke's number. It'll be quicker than going through the gatekeepers at the magazine where she works."

"On it." A few minutes later, she whisper-shouts, "Bingo!"

I type the number into my phone and hit call, raising it to my ear. Mara watches, knee bouncing. Five rings in, someone answers.

"Hello?" comes a wary voice down the line.

"Leigh Clarke?"

Pause. "Speaking ..." She sounds hesitant. I would too after her performance on national TV.

"This is Agent Price from the FBI."

"Oh, erm, okay."

"Are you free to speak?"

"I guess so," she says with a wobble in her voice. "Am I in some kind of trouble?"

"No. I just have a couple of questions for you."

"To do with ..."

"A job you completed with Britney Shaw a couple of years ago."

"Oh," her voice falls flat.

"She mentioned you had contact with a source for some drugs. Can you confirm this?"

Another pause. "It depends. What happens to me if I do?"

Anger flares inside me at her vague response. The last thing we need is her messing around. "I have bigger things to worry about than whether you have a nasty drug habit, Ms. Clarke. Now, did you or not?"

"Yes."

I grip my phone tight. "The source. Did you see their face?"

"Yeah, kind of."

I clench my jaw, stopping myself from snapping again. "Kind of?"

"I mean, they were wearing a black jacket and had their hood up. Weird, considering it was the middle of summer." I refrain from saying those kinds of behaviors are standard practice when dealing with drugs.

"Do you think you could ID them if I brought some images for you to look at?"

"I guess I could try. It's been a long time though ..."

Ignoring the reluctance in her voice, I jump at the opportunity to meet with her before she can change her mind. "Are you free tomorrow?"

"Wait? Seriously?"

"Yes. Can you give me your address?"

"You're in the FBI. Don't you already have it?"

"It would be better if you gave it to me willingly."

"Right. I'll text it to you."

"Great," I exhale.

"So, I guess I'll see you tomorrow?"

"You will."

With a newfound determination, I go about booking flights to New York for myself and Mara the following day. I spend the rest of my time praying Leigh doesn't do anything stupid, like leave the country before we get to her.

***

Our car pulls to a stop outside a building in the Meatpacking District, and Mara sniffs with disdain. "So, this is what being a deceitful bitch pays for. Nice."

We climb out, and rain hammers off the sidewalks, bouncing high and soaking my trousers as we run. Thankfully, it's not the kind of apartment block where a code is needed to get in, but the kind with security in the foyer. At least we're out of the rain.

I walk to the security guy and hold up my badge. "We're here to see Leigh Clarke."

His eyes widen and he doesn't ask any questions, just points at the elevators.

"Was that really necessary?" says Mara as we walk over to them.

I press the call button before answering. "If you want to get this done without any issues, yes."

The elevator doors slide open, and we step inside.

Mara presses the button for the fourteenth floor. "Even the elevator's fancy," she says to herself.

She's not wrong. It's the kind with spotlights, perfectly polished mirrors and marble flooring, and glides upwards so smoothly you wouldn't know you were moving. The transition to stopping is flawless, not even a jolt. I follow Mara out and we turn left, then walk down a long corridor.

Eventually Mara stops outside a door. "This is it."

She suddenly looks nervous, and I remind myself she doesn't do this often. She hides behind her computer any opportunity she gets. I tap my knuckles against the door. I knock again when there's no response and we wait another couple of minutes. Everything remains silent. Mara looks up at me and I can see in her eyes exactly what I'm thinking.

Leigh has pulled a fast one.

I pull out my phone and bring up the number I called yesterday, hitting call. I raise it to my ear and hear it ringing. Mara looks at me, confused.

"Wait," she whispers. "I can hear something." The call cuts off and I drop my phone to my side. "Ring the number again."

I do as she says, but turn the volume on the handset down. We both still when we hear it. It's faint, but it's there. Ringing inside the apartment. When the call cuts off, just to be sure, I hit dial one more time and, like clockwork, the ringing starts again inside the apartment.

"What are you doing?" asks Mara when I start walking back toward the elevator.

"Getting security. We need that door opened."

She scurries after me. "Don't think you're leaving me behind with this freaky shit."

Ten minutes later, we're back with security. Thank fuck for the master key in case of emergencies. The lock clicks open, and the security guy steps back. The door swings open, and Mara digs her nails into my arm. We peer in from where we're standing, finding the apartment empty, and by the looks of it, not a thing is out of place. When I manage to prize Mara's hand off me, I call Leigh's phone again, walking to the kitchen counter in the small open plan apartment. The brightly lit screen stands out against the dark marble. I pull out two pairs of gloves, handing Mara the first set and sliding the second set on myself.

"Put them on. I need you to peruse," I say over my shoulder.

Her eyes move to the security guard, and it registers what I mean. She takes the phone from me, grabs her bag, and pulls out her laptop, setting it on the counter, then fires it up.

"Is there WiFi?" she asks the guard sweetly.

He gives her the code, and she copies it to her computer. After a few minutes, she picks up the phone and taps the screen. I watch the way her expression changes.

"Price," she murmurs, holding out the phone with a slight shake to her hand.

I take it from her, look down, and read the message.

It's time to play a game.

"What does it mean?"

I slide the phone into an evidence bag, then take off my gloves. There's no point in us being here any longer. "It means he got to her first."

***

Three days pass without any sign of Leigh.

Hewson ambles over from the other side of the unit. "Any news on the Clarke girl?"

Mara and I both shake our heads. "This fucking case," he mutters. "It's going to be the death of me."

"I'm going to take a trip to Vermont. Check things over and give Rogers and Grey some time off."

"Be careful," says Hewson. "We've got two at it now, the last thing we need is someone following you."

"I need to go to the Becket's home before I leave. I need to pick something up. Well, two things."

Mara brightens. "Does this mean I'm off duty?"

"Your special job is complete."

Hewson looks at us, bemused.

"Cats," I explain.

His reaction is the same as mine when I first met them. "Of course, there are cats." He shakes his head and grumbles to himself while walking away. "Cats everywhere. If I didn't know better, I'd think I was losing my mind."

"Want me to come with you?" Mara asks.

"Nah. I'll be fine." I glance at the time on my watch, finding it's later than I thought. "I better get going. I'm going to keep them at my place so I can leave before it's light."

"So it's easier to spot if someone's following you, right?"

"Right."

"I'm getting better," she beams.

"You are. Keep searching the forums for any sign of Leigh Clarke. Britney said that's where she met the source, and with her line of work, it seems likely she uses them a lot. They're a dirty source for information. If she's flying under the radar, she'll still be using them. People like her don't take time off."

"I'll let you know if I find anything."

I'm almost packed up when I look over at Mara. "Thanks for looking after them."

She shrugs. "I did it for Freya. She shouldn't have to lose her pets on top of everything else."

"Yeah …"

"Have you spoken with her? How is she getting on?"

"Briefly. I think things improved once her mom joined her. That's what I gathered from the couple of texts she sent."

"Is she still studying?"

I shake my head, ignoring the stirring of feelings inside me I can't put my finger on. "No. It was too risky."

"Then what's she been doing?"

I grab my laptop and slide it into my bag, zipping it up after. "She's been working in one of the local diners with her mom. Rogers and Grey have been watching them while they work."

"At least she's getting to do something normal. It was nice of you to take them there. You didn't have to." There's a hint of something in her voice. Mara doesn't just like to peruse computers, something I quickly learned when we first began working together. She likes to peruse people's lives as well, and she's far more observant than she lets on.

"I did what was right," I reply. "I'll see you in about a week. Figure I might as well stay there a bit longer."

"If anything happens with Leigh, I'll let you know."

***

I pull up to the Becket's home an hour later. It seems strange, the house being unlit in the darkness. I became used to it being the brightest on the street whenever Freya was inside. Ironic, considering they were meant to be hiding.

Before getting out of my SUV, I send Freya a message telling her to expect me tomorrow.

She replies instantly with a shocked emoji face, followed by a woman dancing in a red dress. I smile to myself and put my phone back in the inside pocket of my suit jacket, then climb out. I unlock the front door with my spare key and step into the house. Everything is eerily quiet when I listen out for any sign of movement.

I don't bother turning on the lights. The last time I did, Cat One and Cat Two scattered and it took three visits for them to appear again. We don't have three days to spare. I head into the kitchen where I know their things are and go straight into the pantry. I remember seeing two stacked cat boxes when Freya asked me to pull out some ingredients while she was cooking once.

Finding them straight away, I grab them and walk back out, freezing when I find four eyes staring at me in the dark from the kitchen counter. Lifeless.

Clapping fills the room. I go to pull my gun from its holster, stopped when something collides with the side of my head, hard. Pain shoots through my skull, along with the sound of glass shattering.

"Ooof." I stumble, catching myself before I hit the countertop.

Spinning around, I find a figure in a black hooded jacket. I squint, trying to make out the face in the shadows. It's no good. I dart forward, ready to drive my shoulder into their stomach. They step to the side effortlessly. I fall forward, wobbling when I try to stop myself from hitting the ground. The head injury affects my balance, and I face plant the floor, hard. It takes a second for me to bring myself round and be able to roll onto my back.

A gloved fist smashes against my face. Then another. And another. The punches rain down. I feel dampness on my skin I know will be my blood. Stars shine brightly behind my eyes. I'm not sure if I hear or feel when a booted foot smashes into my ribs. Pain takes over and everything tilts. A final fist to my face, and the sound of my nose crunching, sends me over the cliff, hurtling into darkness.

The world slips away with the figure, leaving me behind with two dead cats and a single white lily.

Ten

Josie

My heart skipped a beat when Agent Price texted yesterday to tell me he was coming. Four months is a long time not to see someone. Especially someone who is having as much of an influence as he is starting to have in my life.

It was a couple of weeks after he left when my mom called me because there was something waiting for me. The 'something' was more than a little something. More like a big something. It was a Pottery Barn explosion in the living room, with boxes upon boxes of pots and pans, and every kitchen utensil I could ever hope for.

It was the note that came with it all that set off the first traitorous butterfly, and once it spread its wings, there was no stopping it.

Practice makes perfect.

Swarms of butterflies followed, and ever since, I've found myself over-analyzing every moment we've shared, every gesture. Agent Price will always be a man of few words, and the few he gives are putting me back together, with the potential to tear me apart in a heartbeat. It's terrifying. He's no longer replaceable in my life.

It's ten PM and I haven't heard anything from him.

"I don't think he's coming," says my mom, walking into the kitchen where I've been waiting for hours with my new sandwich experiment sitting on a plate beside me.

"Yeah, I gathered," I huff, unable to keep my bad mood at bay.

The problem with letting people in is it opens you up to a world of disappointment, like I'm feeling right now. If you don't let people get close, you don't need to expect anything from them. Maybe that's the way things need to be. It feels safer for my heart, which feels heavier with each minute that passes.

"I'm sure he has an explanation." She smiles, but it doesn't reach her eyes.

"It doesn't matter. We're not friends." The words don't sound convincing to my own ears, and the way my mom purses her lips tells me she believes me as much as I believe myself.

"Okay. I'm going to bed. I'll see you in the morning."

One of the perks of Montpelier. No more night shifts. It's not really out of choice, there aren't any diners open twenty-four hours. So, unfortunately for my mom, she's stuck inside these walls with me. For the first time, we're facing our demons together.

I wait up another half hour before leaving the sandwich behind on the kitchen counter, along with the small part of myself I poured into it. When I come down the next morning, it's still there waiting.

Agent Price never turned up. He didn't even bother to text.

***

Evan

"You look like you've seen better days." Hewson towers over me, looking a mixture of concerned and angry.

Mara stands by his side, twiddling her hands and looking paler than normal. "Can I get you anything? Water?"

I don't shake my head. It hurts too much to move. "I'm fine. Can you sit or something? I can't look up."

Neither of them asks why, for which I'm thankful. Pride plays a big part in who I am and I'm the first one to acknowledge it. I'd be on my deathbed before I'd admit to needing help.

"What happened?" asks Hewson. I take a small breath, digging my nails into the sheets when pain sears through my rib cage, so strong a wave of nausea hits me. "Price, you're looking green. Are you sure you're okay?"

"I'm fine," I barely manage to say.

Mara watches me, eyes narrowed. "I'll be right back." She disappears before I get a chance to ask where she's going, returning a few minutes later with a nurse by her side. "Why aren't you taking your pain meds?"

"He's been refusing them since he regained consciousness," comments the nurse. Traitor.

"I don't need them," I state.

This time, Hewson is the one to watch me, a look of understanding crosses his face. "Leave us for a minute." The nurse starts to walk out, but he stops her before she exits the room. "Leave the pills. Please."

She sets them on the table beside my bed, then she and Mara both leave.

With them gone, I really take in Hewson. He looks older, tired. The deep lines around his eyes and the way his skin sags against his cheekbones make it clear this case is taking a bigger toll on him than most.

"Why aren't you taking the medication?"

"I don't need it," I reply, gazing out the window, not wanting to meet his eye.

"You have a broken nose, ribs you're lucky aren't broken and enough bruising to make even Tyson's eyes water." When I don't respond, he goes straight for the jugular. "You're not your mother, and you won't turn into her. Don't put yourself through unnecessary pain to prove a point."

My gaze moves from the window, finding his face full of concern. "What if I lose control like she did? What if I wind up dead in a gutter because I'm too strung out to see what's happening around me? I can't help anyone if I'm dead."

"Her death isn't your fault. You're one of the strongest people I know."

"If you fall, we'll catch you." My eyes dart to Mara. I didn't hear her come back into the room. "We're a team."

Hewson nods. "Give yourself a break, Price. For once. No one will think any less of you."

They both stare straight at me, gazes unwavering. My resolve crumbles when I suck in a breath too hard, and pain radiates from my ribs to every limb.

"Can you help?" I ask Hewson.

He walks over, popping the two pills from the blister pack and placing them on my tongue, before picking up the glass of water and holding the straw to my lips for me to take a sip. I swallow the pills down and my heart races painfully, anxious for what's to come. I promised myself I would never do this, go down the same path as her. But Hewson's right. The circumstances are different, and the world won't end. I'm not like my mother. Not my biological one, at least.

"The nurse said you should only need them for a few weeks," says Mara. "Just until the bruising around your ribs heals."

"When can I get back in the field?"

Hewson's lips form a flat line. "That's irrelevant. But, because you're a workaholic, I'll allow you to be on desk duty on two conditions. The first is that your doctor says it's fine, the second is that you take three weeks off to recover."

My eyes almost pop out of my head. "Three weeks?"

Hewson chuckles. "You can barely move. You're no good to anyone like this."

"Fine." An idea hits me. "I want to go to Montpelier when I'm discharged. Mara can drive me."

Hewson frowns. "Are you sure?"

"I can work the case from there for a while. That's where I was heading, anyway."

"Speaking of," says Hewson. "We need to log what happened. Do you feel up to going through it?"

I don't hesitate before starting, knowing if I don't do it now, someone will be back later. "I went to pick something up for Freya Becket. I was coming out of their pantry when something smashed over my head."

"A vase," states Mara.

"Right," I reply. "I didn't stand a fucking chance with the room spinning. There were three of everything."

"It was a really big vase," Mara comments again. I scowl at her, not needing the reminder. "Sorry."

"Do you think it was Belmer?" asks Hewson.

I pause, thinking back. "I don't think so. The frame was smaller, less bulky, more agile. Plus, why would Belmer be going after me? He would be fixated on finishing what he started. The MO doesn't fit."

Hewson grimaces. "The cats. Sick fuck. Who decapitates an animal?"

"Two ... animals, that is ..." Mara trails off when Hewson throws daggers her way.

A weight sits heavy in my stomach, anticipating Freya's reaction when she finds out something else has been taken from her. Two more things added to the ever-increasing list.

"So we think this was our copycat?" asks Hewson.

"It's likely," I reply. "The actions are more volatile. Less measured and precise. Messy. It's a warning."

Hewson nods, his face twisting in a way that tells me that wasn't what he wanted to hear. "We need to take extra precautions going forward. We have two killers trying to claim the same identity."

Mara bites her lip. "What does that mean?"

"It means if we're not careful, we could have a bloodbath on our hands," answers Hewson. "When you go to Vermont, make sure you're not followed. Whoever attacked you knows you have a connection to the Beckets."

"We'll swap vehicles a couple of times like I usually do, but change the pickup and drop off spots." I turn my attention to Mara. "We'll both need new phones while we're there."

Mara's eyes widen. "You think whoever's doing this can hack our phones?"

"Belmer. No," I reply. "The copycat? Yes."

"How do you know?"

"Because in Britney Shaw's statement, she mentioned their source was on one of the forums they use. They've been in the shadows a long time, waiting. We can't treat anything as coincidence." I face Hewson. "Any updates from Sing Sing?"

"They've finally released their manual sign-in sheets for the forty-eight hours each side of the time they think Belmer might have escaped. There's nothing suspicious, though. We have nothing else to go off without CCTV footage."

"There's nothing at all on any cameras in the areas surrounding the facility?" I ask Mara.

She shakes her head. "Nothing. I've checked every camera within a mile radius. If he was on foot or in a vehicle, he knew where every camera was."

I stare down at the bed sheets. "Or he swam."

"What?" says Hewson.

I look up, beginning to feel the effects of the painkillers kicking in when things become hazy and slow. "There's no way a camera wouldn't have picked something up, somewhere. There are more in the areas surrounding Sing Sing than there are in the bureau. The Hudson is our best bet. Mara, I need you to see if there are any blind spots he could have used. It won't change anything, but at least we will know how he managed to get out without being picked up."

Mara grins. "I can do that. And I can take you to Vermont. But only when you're discharged."

"Thanks." My eyes start to grow heavy.

"We'll leave you to get some rest," says Hewson, and he and Mara both stand up.

"Great," I slur.

I'm already in a painless sleep before they make it to the door.

Josie

With my eyes closed and feet planted on the mats, I tune into everything around me. Above the steady hum of the refrigerator, deeper in the house, I hear a barely there shuffle, then feel a brush of air, so slight, I could almost be convinced it was in my head. My eyes open and Rogers is in front of me. He lunges forward and my arms shoot up, under his. I twist him round with his arm locked in my grip. With his front against my back, I squat down. Within a second, I roll him forward. His back slams down onto the ground with a loud thud. Just like he taught me.

"Excellent," he groans. "I don't think we need to practice that again."

My mom claps while I stand up straight. At the same time, a deep voice I could never not recognize fills the room and I freeze. "Careful, Rogers. With moves like that, she might be replacing you."

My skin bristles. I'm still upset he didn't show, without so much as a text to let me know he was okay. He doesn't owe you anything, I remind myself. It's those ridiculous butterflies confusing things, making what should be really simple, really complicated. This is his job. Nothing more, nothing less.

"Holy shit!" exclaims Grey, looking over at the front door. "I heard you'd taken a beating. I didn't realize it was by a fucking bulldozer."

I spin around and gasp. Agent Price couldn't look less like Agent Price if he tried. My eyes trail upward from his feet, taking in the sneakers, gray sweatpants and oversized hoody, along with his hair, which looks soft and fluffy compared to it usually being perfectly styled. Our eyes meet across the room. In his deep brown ones is a silent apology, one that isn't needed. The second I turned around, I realized I should be the one apologizing to him. I doubted him and I shouldn't have. He's never given me a reason not to trust him. Well, apart from when he had a gun pressed to my head, but that was a much-needed lesson that has stayed with me and will probably keep me safe.

A striking woman with jet black hair—not much older than myself—helps him shuffle to the green couch we've pushed back against the wall. It's standard practice whenever my mom and I have our self-defense sessions with Rogers and Grey. As are the mats.

I'm at a loss for words. Even more so when he winces as he lowers himself down. His nose is clearly broken, his whole face a mixture of shades of purple and black, so swollen he's barely recognizable apart from his eyes. He looks up and gives me a weak smile. I open my mouth to say something, then close it again.

My mom clears her throat. "If we'd known we were having more visitors, we would have prepared. I think a trip to the store is in order," she says pointedly to Rogers and Grey.

Grey never takes a hint. "We went this morning," he says, clueless.

"And we can go again," replies my mom with a roll of her eyes. "Agent Price, what can I get you?"

He moves his eyes away from me to talk to her. "Things that are soft, please."

A burning sensation builds behind my eyes. I hate seeing him like this. I want to take whatever pain he's feeling away. "Do you want a drink?" I ask, needing a distraction.

He nods and I leave the room, busying myself in the kitchen. I hear my mom demand that Rogers and Grey leave with her immediately, then a set of footsteps head in my direction toward the kitchen. I look up from where I've been staring blankly at the kettle and find the random woman watching me.

She smiles and gives me a little wave. "I'm Mara, Price's partner." My face drops, then, realizing my mistake, I school my expression. It's none of my business if he's in a relationship. My blunder doesn't go unnoticed, because Mara clarifies, "At the bureau. Work partners."

"Ah." My cheeks warm with embarrassment.

I decide I like Mara when she ignores my little tell and waves a plastic bag in the air. "These are his pain meds. He needs to take them, even if he says he doesn't." She glances at her phone. "He's actually due some now. I'm going to get his things from the car and then leave you guys. Which room should I put his bags in?"

I pause. Every room in the house is taken. "Along the hall, third on the left. He can have mine. I'll take the couch."

Mara smiles again. "I'll be out of your hair in a bit. It was great to finally meet you, Freya."

True to her word, she's a whirlwind, moving in and out of the house with Agent Price's things. I'm finishing up making his drink when I hear her saying goodbye. I wait until the front door closes before moving back into the living room, picking up a straw and the bag of meds on my way.

"Thanks," Agent Price says, when I hand over his coffee. He goes to set it on the coffee table and winces again.

"Sorry," I mumble, taking it from him and setting it down.

Things get even more awkward when I hand over his pain meds and he looks at me expectantly. "Could I have some water, please?"

"Sorry," I mumble again, cheeks blazing, as I power back into the kitchen. I'd make a terrible nurse.

Inhaling deeply with the cold water running, I tell myself to get it together. This is Agent Price, the same Agent Price I've known for what feels like forever. Something's changed though, and I don't know why. Maybe it was the pans. Or perhaps it's been there all along, simmering under the surface, ready to boil over. It's most likely the fact that beneath his grumpy exterior is a whole other person I've barely gotten a taste of, but could become addicted to if I was given a chance to take a full bite. He's not for everyone, but I've always preferred unique flavors, ones that give a dish depth and help it to stand out from the rest.

Lost in thought, the water pours over the sides of the glass and I curse, turning off the faucet. I pour some out and dry the outside with a towel, then make my way back into the living area. I hand it over and, after Mara's hint that he doesn't like to take them, watch Agent Price like a hawk as he swallows down the pills. With a face mashed like his, I wouldn't be sitting upright. He's probably in more pain than he's letting on.

"How have things been?" he asks, handing me the glass. "It looks like your self-defense is coming on well."

"Yeah, Rogers and Grey are good teachers," I reply, placing the water next to his coffee.

"Your job at the diner?"

I shrug. "It passes the time." I brighten a little when I add on, "The owner has agreed to let me help out in the kitchen and learn some of the ropes."

He smiles. Like, actually smiles. "That's great."

Seconds tick by, and I don't know what to say again, so I go for a good old reliable, "Yeah."

Agent Price glances around the room. "When Rogers and Grey come back, they can move the couch so I can rest. That drive was a killer."

I frown. "Why don't you just go to your room?"

"Because it's now your room."

"No. It's your room and you're injured. I'm fine on the couch."

"Freya ..." he sighs. Obviously, he's still stubborn while injured; like I'd expect anything less.

"Agent Price," I reply, holding my chin up high and narrowing my eyes, making it clear there's no way I'm backing down on this.

"Fine." He gives in. "But only until I'm feeling better."

"Okay."

Thankfully, my mom's trip to the store was quick, and she bustles into the house, arms filled with two large brown paper bags. Rogers and Grey follow behind, their arms full as well.

"Freya!" she squawks, a woman on a mission. "Come help me cook."

She doesn't need to ask twice. I dart out of the room, leaving Agent Price and our whole bunch of awkwardness behind.

Eleven

Evan

A hand waves in front of my face, and I startle. Freya hovers at the side of my bed, then leans down and pulls out one of my headphones.

"What happened to always being aware?"

I pull the other headphone out. "Is everything alright?"

"It's your favorite time of day." She holds the plastic bag I loathe in the air. "I remembered your water this time."

"Thanks." I flinch when I try to move. Damn bruising. I've Googled too many times how long it takes to heal. Not quick enough, is the answer I keep getting.

"Want some help?"

That question sounds so wrong coming from her. It's supposed to be the other way around. Not a lot is working in my favor at the moment, which is why I say, "Sure."

Chewing on the inside of my cheek, I try to ignore the pain when I reach up and wrap an arm around her shoulders. Her hair falls forward and tickles my face, making the bruising feel like it's on fire.

"Sorry," she says, tucking it back behind her ear, leaving a trail of perfume in her path.

Together, we somehow manage to shift my body back, so I'm leaning against a small pile of pillows and the headboard. Freya leaves the room and quickly returns with more, propping them behind me. My muscles relax as I sag into them, the small bit of exertion exhausting. I'm a useless mess.

She sits beside me on the bed. "Can I ask you a question?"

"Sure," I reply, because I know she'll ask anyway, regardless of my answer.

"Why don't you like to take your pain meds? I mean, they're to help, right?"

Mara and her goddamn mouth. I never should have left them alone together. Two people who probably have my best interests at heart shouldn't be allowed in the same room. It's a recipe for disaster. There's no way I'm getting out of this without replying, so I go for a vague version of the truth.

"I don't like to feel out of control."

Freya ponders my answer. "I get that. Especially with your job." She looks like she's contemplating saying something else, but thankfully, doesn't.

What she does do is linger, in the way someone who's lonely and doesn't want to go back to their empty space does.

"How have things really been?" I ask, watching her face for any sign she's lying when she replies.

She bites down on her bottom lip. "Pretty crappy."

I arch a brow. "Just crappy?"

"Okay, fine. They've been shit."

"Why?" I figure the more questions I ask her, the less she can ask me. Ridiculous, considering I crossed every metaphorical line there is between us when I bought out Pottery Barn.

"I miss Silver Spring," she admits, playing with a loose thread on my sheets. "Something I never thought I would say. But I was starting to build a life for myself there and now it's all gone, again."

Her phone vibrates. I shouldn't look down at the screen, but I do, catching the name Duane before she picks it up to read the message. Whatever the message says makes her face break out in a wide smile that I've never seen before. Something that feels a lot like jealousy rushes through me and I still. What the hell was that, and why the hell am I getting jealous over a text? Freya has every right to have friends or whatever she wants to call Duane—it's none of my business.

I'm here to do one thing: my job.

"You still talk to him?" I ask, instantly regretting it when she looks at me, alarmed.

"Is it a problem?"

"Not if you don't give away where we are. Otherwise, you'll have to move again."

She lets out a huff of air. "He's a nice guy."

"I wouldn't know. But it could be a while until you get to return to see him ... if that's what you want."

Our eyes lock. Sadness swirls in the depths of her emerald irises. For the first time, I notice the ring of yellow around her pupil. That's why they're so bright. Central heterochromia. Her eyes are rare, like her nature.

She swallows. "I don't know what I want any more. Each time we leave somewhere, I feel like I leave a part of myself behind." My stomach twists with guilt, knowing I'm responsible for two of the times. "Does it sound melodramatic if I say that sometimes I wonder if it might be easier if he found me? At least then this would all be over."

Ignoring the stabbing pain in my ribs, I reach over and squeeze her hand, crossing another one of those lines I shouldn't. "You're stronger and more capable than you give yourself credit for. Don't let him win."

Watery eyes stare back, and I pray a tear doesn't spill over, because I don't know if I'd be able to stop myself wiping it away. The sooner I recover, the better. It will mean less chance for meaningful moments like this. Moments which shouldn't happen, even though deep down, there's something stirring inside me that wants them to.

***

Two weeks pass in a blur.

"What is it?" I ask, wrinkling my nose at the dish in front of me.

Rogers and Grey sit on either side of me at the dining table, stirring the contents of their bowls dubiously. Freya and her mom watch us all in amusement.

"Corn chowder," answers Freya.

"I'm not a corn fan. It looks like someone puked in my bowl," says Grey.

Freya rolls her eyes. "Try before you judge."

Reluctantly, I pick up my spoon and raise it to my lips, trying not to focus too much on the pale, mushy liquid with the occasional yellow kernel and fleck of red.

"Stop being a baby and just try it," laughs Freya, watching me.

The word baby is a challenge I refuse to back down from. I put the whole spoon in my mouth and wait for the urge to spit it back out. It never comes. It's one of the best things I've tasted in a long time, not that I'm about to tell her that.

167

She looks at me eagerly, waiting for my verdict. "So?"

I place the spoon back in the bowl and shrug. "It's okay for soup, I guess."

"That's because it's not just soup. It's chowder," she chimes.

"What's the difference?"

"Lumps."

"It is very lumpy," comments Rogers, leaning forward and sniffing.

Angela Becket tuts. "Anyone would think we have children in the room, not FBI agents. You take on killers and you seem more afraid of a bowl of chowder."

Grey and Rogers both pick up their spoons and scoop the chowder into their mouths.

"Huh," says Rogers.

"It still looks like baby food," grumbles Grey. The content of his bowl disappears within a minute, and he refills it straight away.

I catch Freya's eye across the table, and she gives me a knowing smile.

It's just a look, barely a glance, but for some reason, in this messed up dynamic we've found ourselves in, my heart starts to race, and I forget how to breathe.

***

Josie

I thought I was safe in Montpelier. I should have known better. I'm safe nowhere.

I race through the house. Feet thud behind me at a steady, eerie pace. He doesn't rush. Every move he makes is calm, collected, confident. He knows that eventually he will get what he wants.

When I look behind me, he's gone. A scream of terror lodges in my throat. I turn to run, smashing face first into a hard fist. I hit the ground hard. Eugene Belmer climbs over me. He grabs hold of my shoulder and pulls it back so hard it almost dislocates, slamming me back against the floor.

"Why?" I croak, as his hands slide around my neck.

He starts to press down, holding me in the position so many have found themselves in before. His face moves in closer. So close, I can taste the stale coffee on his breath, and I almost retch.

"Because I can."

A strong pair of arms engulf me.

"Freya, it's okay. You're safe."

I blink, trembling. Even the light can't get rid of the darkness.

Without thinking, I lean into my only source of comfort, the side of my cheek resting against warm skin, inhaling the scent of sandalwood and citrus.

Agent Price.

I pull back, realizing he hasn't just got his arms around me. I'm sitting in his lap on the couch while he's half dressed.

"I'm sorry," I say, remembering he's injured. I go to climb away, but he keeps me wrapped tightly against him.

"You're fine."

I bite my lip and lean back into him carefully, trying to keep as still as possible while my heart settles. I focus on the wall, because each time I close my eyes, Eugene Belmer's face is still there. Minutes pass, and calm washes over me.

"You good?"

"I think so." It feels weird having a conversation like this, but I don't move away. He doesn't ask me to either.

"Do they happen a lot? The nightmares?"

"Only since we arrived in Montpelier."

"You're safe here, Freya."

"I know. I guess I miss Cat One and Two." Agent Price shifts slightly, letting out a pained breath. "I can move if I'm hurting you?"

He ignores my question and asks, "Is that why you leave the lights on, because they aren't here?"

I think back on my little furry friends and how they used to snuggle up against me in the dark. The world would think I was mad if they knew I found comfort from the one thing I should fear.

"Yes," I sniffle.

I've tried not to think about them, because even though I've always told myself they're replaceable, when it comes down to it, I miss them. And without them by my side, the nightmares have started to creep back in, which is why we're here now. Agent Price has only been here a couple of weeks and already he's witnessing me falling apart. I don't know when I started crying, but a tear drips from my chin onto his chest. It takes a steady path down his skin, drawing my attention to his injuries.

I frown, wipe my cheeks and pull away, sucking in a sharp breath when I take in the bruising covering his ribs. It's deep purple, and in parts turning a tinge of yellowy-green where it's beginning to heal. I've never seen anything like it, not even when my brother used to come home with football injuries. It covers his whole side, wrapping around his ribs from underneath his armpit, round to the front, tucking just beneath his pectoral muscles and down to his stomach. It looks like someone's tried to crush him. Next, I take in his face. He looks more himself now, less swollen, but still wearing a mask of bruising.

A lump forms in my throat. "What happened?" His chin drops and he diverts his eyes. Reaching forward, I carefully cup his jaw, encouraging him to look straight at me when I say more firmly, "What. Happened?"

His throat bobs, and his eyes fill with regret. "Please don't ask me again."

"Why?"

"Because I don't make promises I can't keep, and I promised myself I'd never lie to you."

Whatever it is he's hiding; it can only mean one thing.

My time in this bubble is running out, and when it pops, everything and everyone around me will come crashing down. I can only hope I'm strong enough to survive the fall.

***

Evan

Four little paws pad up and down my legs. When they stop, claws bite my skin, and a purr vibrates through my thighs. Grey smirks when I hold the brown ball of fluff in the air to inspect. It meows, and I set it back in my lap. I really don't like cats. Pets period.

"So, you found her cats dead and now you're buying her new ones?" he states.

"Yes," I reply.

"You're taking the whole 'going the extra mile for your job' thing to a whole other level." I know what he's getting at, and I ignore it. He doesn't let up.

"She's special, that's for sure. And single. I wonder if when all this is done, she might be up for a da—"

"Stop it," I snap, giving away what I'm not ready to acknowledge myself. I exhale and say more calmly, "I know what you're doing."

Grey opens his mouth to respond, but stops when one of the store assistants walks over with another kitten.

"One Russian Blue. You're lucky, they're hard to come by. The breeder dropped her off this morning." I give her a terse nod. "What made you choose this one?"

"It reminds me of someone I know," I reply, ignoring Grey's stare burning into the side of my skull.

The assistant hands over the second kitten. Bright green eyes surrounded by dark fur stare up at me. It lets out a big yawn and I find myself warming to it just a little. It has a sweet temper to match its soon-to-be owner. I read somewhere black cats are lucky. We need all the luck we can get. I also read somewhere they're associated with evil. We're already knee deep in the worst kind there is. Shit can work whichever way you spin it, so I'm anchoring for the more positive vibes.

Now I just need to figure out how to tell Freya that these are her replaceable replacements.

***

A few hours later, feet thunder along the hall. The door to my room, that became Freya's and is now my room again, flies open. Freya storms in, the two new kittens clutched against her chest. Her lip wobbles and I can't meet her eye. There's a painful stabbing

172

feeling in my chest that has nothing to do with the bruises that have almost healed.

"Where are Cat One and Cat Two?" I don't answer. "Evan," she bites out. "Where are they?"

No Agent Price. This is as personal as things get. How do you tell someone that something they loved was taken from them in the most brutal of ways to purposefully hurt them? The answer is simple. You don't. You cover it up and bury it deep, praying it will never be uncovered.

"I fucked up. I'm sorry."

"What happened?"

I've already prepared myself to answer whatever questions she throws my way.

"I forgot to feed them." Mara and I were actually on a daily rotation making sure the exact opposite happened, but I'm not about to tell her that.

"You forgot?" She clutches the kittens closer to her chest, as if she's scared them merely being around me might put them at risk.

I shrug and say what I know will seal the deal. "I had more important things to deal with."

"Right." The look of disappointment in her eyes has me feeling like the biggest prick to walk the face of the earth. With an ounce of venom in her voice, she calls over her shoulder as she walks out of the room, "Thanks for the replacements."

Grabbing the remote, I turn on the TV and stare at it, not taking anything in. I spend the rest of the day reminding myself that when someone means something to you, like Freya is starting to mean to me, you do whatever you can to protect them.

Even if it means they hate you for it, you need to be the villain to protect them from the devil.

***

173

My three weeks of leave are up, and Freya hasn't said a word since I gave her Cat Three and Cat Four.

Another pair of replaceables.

The thought of going back to DC with her still mad at me doesn't sit right, which is the reason why I'm hovering outside the living area like a lovesick teen, watching her play with the kittens.

"Are you going to stand there all day?"

Busted. I straighten my tie, tug on the cuffs of my shirt, then walk into the room.

Freya glances over while tickling the belly of Cat Four. "I see the Bat Suit has made a return. Does that mean you're leaving?"

Even under the circumstances, she's acting like a bit of a bitch. It sets me on my back foot. The last time she showed animosity like this, she was a teenager, sitting on her window seat, hating the world. Now, it's clear all she hates is me.

I'd have her hate me a thousand times over if it saved her from the truth.

"I'm breaking it in," I reply. The joke falls flat. "I have to go."

"Will you be back?" she asks, staring down at the fluff balls.

"Not straight away." She stills. "Freya. I can't."

"Why?"

"Because each time someone comes and goes, it opens up more opportunities for him to find you."

"And?"

"And I'd avoid you for a lifetime if it meant you'd be safe."

"Evan ..."

"Freya ..."

Defiant eyes gaze up. "Do you think if the circumstances were different, you'd call me by my real name?"

Against my better judgement, I take a step forward, crouch and wrap my hand around the back of her head. Pulling her in toward me, I place the briefest of kisses against her forehead, then stand and walk away.

I'm halfway out the door when I glance back.

"Under different circumstances, I'd call you by whatever name you asked me to."

Twelve
Evan 3 months later

I once watched a movie about a cop who was married to his job. He was the loneliest person I'd ever seen, and despite it being one of those ridiculous Hallmark movies, I found myself drawn to him.

I now know why. Because I am him. I don't let anyone in and it's starting to take its toll.

"Price!" snaps Hewson, breaking me from my thoughts. "It's been almost nine months and we've heard nothing from Belmer. Nothing at all. Why?"

Leaning back in my chair, I click my pen, then click it again. "He's lying low. He knows we're going after him with everything we've got. He's not an idiot, far from it. He isn't going to do anything with so many eyes looking for him. It's too risky."

Hewson lets out a cross between a sigh and a grumble. "Leigh Clarke?"

"Nothing," I reply.

"Then what do we have?"

"A blind spot," says Mara, and everyone looks at her. "Price was right. The Hudson is how he got away without being seen."

"So, we have a killer who is an expert at hiding and also an Olympic swimmer." Steam blows from his ears. He's pissed. We all are. It's not unusual for cases to go stale and things to take time, but the pressure is on and the world's watching our every move, only there's no movement. "Could we draw him out?"

I straighten, narrowing my eyes. "No."

"Price, she would be safe. We'd make sure of it."

Even though my chest is constricting to the point it feels like it's going to cave in on itself, I manage to keep my voice calm. "What are you suggesting? We have Freya Becket dangling on a string, ready for him to play with?"

"That's not what I'm saying, and you know it."

"It sounds like it," I reply, clenching my jaw so hard I almost break a tooth.

"Then come up with another solution, because we're sitting ducks right now and it's only a matter of time until he starts killing again. We all know this. We're working on borrowed time and the longer he's out, doing nothing, the worse it's going to get."

With those parting words, he leaves the unit and us behind, trying to figure out how you find someone who's an expert at never being found. The one time he was, he was at the hands of the youngest Becket. I refuse to make it a second time. There has to be another way.

"Well, he's in a delightful mood as always," says Mara to her screen.

"He'll get over it," I reply.

She looks over when I start packing up my things. "You're still going to Vermont?"

I shut down my computer. "Yeah."

"Would it have something to do with it being a certain person's birthday?" Her voice comes out light, and she glances everywhere apart from directly at me, her telltale snooping sign.

I grab all the case files and slide them into my bag. "I just want to check everything is okay."

"You haven't spoken with her?"

"Not since I left."

"But I thought …"

My eyes snap up. "You thought what?"

She shrugs. "I don't know. She seems to care about you, and you seem to care about this case more than the rest."

"Because it's been going on a long time. Years too long."

"You seemed like—"

"Whatever you're about to say, don't," I hiss, glancing around to check no one is listening. "I could lose my job."

"You don't have to shut people out all the time, you know," she mutters. "Having friends and opening up to people doesn't make you weak. And if you have feelings for Fr—"

"We're not friends, Mara." Hurt flashes through her eyes. That's the second time I've upset someone with those words.

Usually, I wouldn't give a crap, but since spending more time with Freya, I've found myself caring about how my words affect people. It's annoying as hell.

"I'm sorry."

Mara snorts while typing. "She really has got a hold on you."

I guess if there's anyone I can admit to crossing a line with, it would be the person who's crossed about a hundred herself without batting an eyelid. The main reason she's in the bureau is to pay her dues.

I groan, admitting defeat. "I want to take her out for her birthday." Mara's brows shoot up. "You're a woman, right?"

Mara looks down and starts talking to her lap. "Hey, Vee! Am I woman?" She cups her ear. "I am? Oh great, thanks for letting me know."

I seriously need to assess how I communicate with the women in my life. "I don't know what to do. Maybe you could give me a woman's insight. That's all I meant."

After a minute of pondering, her face lights up. "How about you let her decide?"

I scratch my head. "I was thinking I could surprise her with something."

"Hear me out. If she's missed out on pretty much her whole life 'cause of all this, I'm guessing she'll have a list longer than you of the things she wishes she could do."

I think over what she's saying. "You're a genius. A 'yes day'."

She snorts. "You watched *Yes Day*?"

"With Freya," I admit.

"Of course you did. Anyway, I thought you were leaving?"

"I am."

I grab my bag and walk out of the unit with a spring to my step that symbolizes how screwed I am.

***

Josie

It's hotter than hell and there's no chance of sleep. I've been tossing and turning for an hour already when I decide to give up and head to the kitchen. I find a late-night baking session always helps an overactive mind.

I'm almost at the kitchen when I hear a noise coming from the living room. Assuming it will be Rogers or Grey, I'm surprised when I find Evan sprawled across the couch, snoring lightly. The night he left, I found myself calling him by his real name in my head—one of the main reasons why I haven't contacted him in the three months he's been gone. He's become the most permanent thing in my life and too many times I find my mind wandering, picturing one scenario after another where something bad happens to him because of his job. Or because of me. I didn't message or get in touch, scared that if I did, he'd come back and put himself at risk. I'm a ticking time bomb and when I explode, everyone around me will be collateral.

Even in sleep, there's a troubled expression on his ridiculously handsome face. The line between his brows is as deep as his thoughts. He shouldn't be the one for me. He's probably too old. Definitely too uptight. With a job that makes him too dangerous. If we survive this ordeal, there will be another following close behind, because that's the nature of the life he's chosen. The sacrifice he's made to protect others. I'd forever have a target on my head. But somewhere along the line, I've fallen into whatever this is and I'm in so deep I don't think I'll ever find my way back out.

He murmurs in his sleep and throws his arm back. It causes his shirt, already untucked, to lift, revealing a toned abdomen with a trail of dark, coarse hair that travels beneath his suit pants. Heat courses through my veins like wildfire. I'm glad he isn't awake, or he'd see the evidence of this little crush I've developed blazing on my cheeks. Ice replaces the heat when my eyes skirt to the side, landing on the coffee table, which is covered in sheets of paper and images. Files are piled haphazardly on the floor.

I check Evan is still lost in sleep before tip-toeing over. I wish I hadn't. These are things I shouldn't be looking at, images that could be me. Facing my reality, seeing with my own eyes what I'm hiding from, is too much to take in. The worst part is when I catch one of the images on the far edge of the table. My heart splinters, taking in two sets of little eyes I'd grown to love, staring up, dead. Next to them is an image of Evan laid in a hospital bed, his face swollen to the point of being unrecognizable, covered in blood.

A strangled sound climbs up my throat, one I can't stop escaping, too loud to muffle with my hand. Evan's eyes fly open, and he darts up from the couch at the same time I'm hit with an overwhelming wave of nausea. I run for the bathroom but realize it's too far away, so sprint into the kitchen. He hisses "shit" behind me at the same moment I empty the contents of my stomach into the sink. A pair of hands swoop round, pulling my hair back away from my face as I continue to retch. When I finally stop, Evan rubs my back gently. I look down, finding my Nirvana t-shirt covered in vomit. I don't know which feels worse, the horror or the humiliation.

"Go get cleaned up. I'll sort this."

A part of me wants to put my foot down and say no, it's too much, but I don't have it in me. Whatever inner strength I had is swirling down the plughole with my dinner.

"Okay," I croak, making my way to the bathroom.

Ten minutes later, smelling much cleaner, I make my way into the kitchen, finding it empty and spotless. I don't turn on the oven, baking is now the last thing I want to do. I find Evan back in the living room, not a picture in sight. Sitting down next to him on the couch, I'm careful to put as much space between us as I can.

"I'm sorry. I shouldn't have looked at them," I say, feeling guilty for prying into an area of his life I had no right, even if it does involve me.

"No. It's my fault. I shouldn't have left them out. It was careless of me." He gives me a side-on glance. "I never wanted you to see any of that."

Staring down at the table where the image of Cat One and Two, or what was left of them, sat previously, I swallow over the lump in my throat. "What happened?"

Evan gives me a pained look, but he doesn't say no or tell me that he can't say. He considers his words first. "I went to get them so I could bring them here …"

He doesn't expand, and just that snippet of information is enough. I don't need him to. "I got mad at you for not turning up when you said you would," I admit.

"I should have text. At first, I couldn't, because I didn't have my phone. When I did, I didn't know what to say."

Cat Four jumps up into Evan's lap. He startles, and I chuckle. "She likes you," I say, watching the way the black kitten purrs and settles in his lap.

"I seem to have a thing for connecting with what I shouldn't."

My heart skips a beat. "Why are you here?"

Evan smiles down at the kitten, tickling it behind its ears. "I wanted to do something for your birthday."

"Tomorrow?" I ask, confused.

"Yeah. Is that going to be a problem?" He looks uncertain. "I mean, do you have plans?"

"Who exactly would I have plans with?" I laugh.

"True," he replies with a sheepish smile that makes his eyes crinkle in the corners.

"I didn't take you to be the spontaneous type."

He holds a hand to his chest and mocks looking offended. "I'm as spontaneous as it gets."

"The most spontaneous I've seen you be is leaving the top button of your shirt undone."

He shrugs. "Fine. I like routine."

"Why?" I pry, wanting to take from him whatever details I can get. It feels like he knows everything about me, yet I know nothing at all about him.

"My job is unpredictable. Working with criminals can take its toll if you let it. I like my life to be in order, because it helps to keep me grounded. When everything is chaos, it helps me to breathe."

"I get that." A comfortable silence settles between us that I'm reluctant to break. The giant yawn I fail to hold back does the job for me.

"Go to bed. I need you fresh for tomorrow."

"Are you going to tell me what we're doing?"

"It's a surprise." I frown and he smirks. "Now who doesn't like being spontaneous."

I yawn again and decide I really do need to get some rest. Taking Cat Four from him, I start to walk out of the room. "Night, Evan."

The butterflies in my stomach refuse to settle and a perma-grin sits on my face until I eventually drift off to sleep.

For the first time, he smiled when I called him by his first name.

***

Evan

I wasn't this nervous about finding out if I'd got in the bureau. Freya's 'yes day' has sent me into a tailspin. It's the deviation at the end, something I've had in my back pocket for a few weeks, that I didn't tell Mara about, which has me worried. I think she'll like it. I hope she will. I'll feel like an idiot if she doesn't.

Freya's awake before me, and I hear her bustling in the kitchen from my makeshift bed on the couch. As predicted, I find her dancing around, lost in her own world, while preparing enough food to feed Rogers and Grey—almost. The guys are tanks and would give a football team a run for their money with the amount they pack away. My stomach growls at the sweet smell of pancakes sizzling in a pan. Luckily, Freya has her AirPods in and doesn't hear. She isn't even aware I'm in the room. I slide the sheet of paper I prepared last night after she went back to bed, onto the counter, then leave the room before she turns and sees me.

I grab a quick shower and get ready for the day before returning to the couch. I turn on the TV, flicking through the channels until I find football reruns. My phone vibrates in my pocket, and I smile when I pull it out and find 'F' on the screen.

F: *Are you for real?*
Me: *Yes.*
F: *You're giving me a 'yes day'?*
Me: *Yes.*
F: *Stop saying yes.*

Three dots appear again before I have a chance to start texting her back, so I hold off replying.

F: *Actually, don't stop saying yes.*
Me: *Yes?*
F: *You're infuriating sometimes.*

I laugh out loud, imagining the look she'd be giving me if she were in the room.

Me: *Thank you. I think.*
F: *Are we legit having a 'yes day'?*
Me: *Yes.*
F: *I'm doing an excited dance right now.*
Me: *I always thought people that wear black and worship the devil didn't get excited?*
F: *I'm rolling my eyes at you.*
Me: *I wouldn't expect anything less.*
F: *What do I wear?*
Me: *Anything you want.*
F: *I'm so excited.*
Me: *Get ready, otherwise there won't be anything to get excited about.*

I go back to watching the old Jacksonville Jaguars game. Michael's in his prime, flying across the screen with the ball tucked under his arm. The other team doesn't stand a chance. He dances around the stadium like he owns it. He's as unreadable on the field as off—no one can predict his next move.

A throat clears behind me. Freya walks into the room and stands directly in front of the TV before setting her list down on the coffee table. Sitting up straight, I lean forward and drag it close so I can read what it says.

A normal day.

That's it. No long list we need to work our way through. My heart, which hasn't felt a thing for anyone ever, aches at the simplicity of her request.

"Is it okay?" she asks, tucking some of her hair behind her ear.

"Fine." Realizing how off my voice sounds, I smile and try again. "This is great."

"Is what I'm wearing okay?" She tugs at the hem of her acid wash Guns and Roses t-shirt, which is paired with a black mini-skirt and fishnet tights. With her long, sandy blonde hair tousled and eyes smokey, she looks breathtaking.

"When was the last time you went out somewhere besides working at the diner and going to the store?"

"Back in Silver Spring."

"Freya ..."

She shrugs. "What did you expect?"

Exactly this reaction, I don't say out loud. The last thing I want on her birthday is to bring up reality. Today is meant to be escapism and I plan to keep it that way.

Keeping hold of the not very listy list, I stand, fold it, and slide it into the pocket of my suit pants. "So, what would you like to do first?"

"Shopping." There's a glint in her eye. She's up to something.

I hesitate. "Okay."

"You're meant to say yes." She smirks.

"Yes," I chuckle, stepping around the coffee table. I walk over, lean down close to her ear and say, "You look beautiful," leaving her behind with her mouth hanging open. "Come on, Birthday Girl, let's go have a normal day."

***

My brows draw together. "This is your day. You remember that, right?"

"Yes," Freya replies.

"You're sure you want to go in *here*?"

"Yes."

"Stop saying yes."

"Not so funny when the shoe is on the other foot, is it?" she sasses, backing into the store and wiggling her finger for me to follow. "Come on, Agent Price, it's time for you to be Evan for a day."

Because I have an inability to say no to her, regardless of the 'yes day', I step inside the store and take in my surroundings, tapping my foot to the rhythm of Six Seconds to Barcelona. It's the kind of store I'd have expected younger Freya to hang around in if she'd grown up like other teenagers her age. The walls are lined with rows of rock band shirts, skateboards, and trainers. Random rock memorabilia are scattered around, and the store floor is filled with stands holding variations of the clothing I've seen her wear.

I'm hit with a wave of panic when I look to the side and she's gone. Quickly scanning the store, I find nothing. Instinctively, I place a hand on the gun sitting beneath my suit jacket. My eyes dart around, trying to find her in the clothing chaos.

"Freya?" I call, trying not to draw any unnecessary attention.

When I don't get an answer, I call her name louder. Still nothing. How can this be happening? We've not even been out for an hour and I've lost her. I cover the full floor of the store, sagging against one of the clothing stands, when I finally find her in the back right corner. She points at one of the shirts hanging close to the ceiling as a store assistant stands on a ladder trying to get it down.

"What size are you?" she asks, trailing her eyes over my chest, oblivious to my minor freak-out. "You look like you're a large."

"Don't wander off like that. I couldn't find you," I answer through gritted teeth.

"Small people problems," she says, taking the shirt from the assistant. "Put your hands down by your sides."

"Rule for the day, you don't move out of my sight."

She holds the shirt up against me and nods her approval. "Unless I need the bathroom."

"Fine, unless you need the bathroom. Freya, what *are* you doing?"

Ignoring my question, she passes the shirt back to the assistant. "How tall are you?"

"Six-four."

The assistant nods, and Freya throws another question my way. "Shoe size?"

I look back and forth between them, trying to figure out what's going on. "Twelve and a half."

"Oh wow! You know what they say about big feet, it means you've go—"

"Freya," I growl.

"Hands, Evan. What did you think I was going to say?" She winks and says to the assistant, "Twelve and a half in the checkerboard, please. I'm not sure about the pants. I'll let you decide. If we can have the fitted black denim, that would be great."

The assistant bustles off and Freya focuses her attention back on me.

"What are you doing?"

"Getting you new clothes," she replies, giving what I'm currently wearing the stink eye.

I go to say no, then realize I can't. "Why?"

She gives my tie a playful tug. "You need to unwind. You can't do that in a suit."

"I could go home and change."

"You could." She grins. "But this is more fun."

The assistant returns with the clothes and shoes Freya requested bundled in her arms and I reach to take them from her. As I do, my suit jacket falls open, putting my gun on full display. She gasps, and her eyes dart around the store in panic.

Clearing my throat, I reach into my jacket for my badge. "FBI."

My explanation does nothing to appease her. She throws the items at Freya and runs to the checkout, where she talks hurriedly to one of her colleagues.

Freya passes over the clothes, acting as if the past minute hasn't happened. "Changing rooms are on your left."

Five minutes later, I reluctantly step back out.

"Nice to meet you, Evan," she preens, scanning every inch of me.

"I feel like I'm about to audition for an Avril Lavigne video," I deadpan.

She gives me a blank look. "Avril who?"

I turn toward the changing rooms, ready to put my suit back on. Freya's hand flies to my arm, stopping me before I can walk away. My skin buzzes under her touch and when she looks up, her eyes seem even greener under the bright store lights. I struggle to look away.

Freya snatches her hand back. "You look great. Non-work attire suits you."

"I'll go pay." We need to get out of this store and away from whatever moment that was.

We walk to the checkouts together and the store assistant hands over a bag for my suit, appearing more relaxed.

The words 'have a great day,' float behind us when we exit the store.

Thirteen

Josie

Evan in a suit is a sight to behold. Evan in a black Nine Inch Nails t-shirt, black fitted jeans and a pair of Vans is what my teenage dreams are made of. Walking with him by my side, eyes skirt our way, and I know they're not looking at me. The females all around us seem to be appreciating his new attire as much as I do.

"What do you want to do next?" he asks.

"Coffee," I reply, walking along the street to one of the best coffee houses in Montpelier. Their selection of roasts is superb, their selection of syrups … next level. When I'm not home, I'm a mocha or syrup gal.

Evan walks at my side. The stride he takes to keep my pace is barely an effort for him. When we get to our destination, he holds the door open for me. I shift my backpack further up my shoulders and walk through, reading too much into it and swooning like a schoolgirl. I'm hit with the smell of coffee beans; the noise of the grinder fills the room, along with lounge music and chatter.

Standing in line, I eye up the cake counter. There's one with four layers, creamy white frosting and covered in multi-colored sprinkles that holds my attention. I'm hit with a sugar coma just looking at it. Evan watches me all the way to the front, and I wonder what he must be thinking. I don't ask, because I don't want to darken what has already been the lightest day I've had in a while.

"What can I get you?" asks the server.

"Black coffee, please," replies Evan.

I fight back a snort and go to place my own order. "Pumpkin Spice latte, full fat, cream, extra shot, and can you throw a few marshmallows on?"

The server chuckles and writes down my order.

"You'll be hyper," says Evan. "You're also setting yourself up for a heart attack in later life."

"You're more likely to go before me with the amount of stressing you do," I wink, sliding my bag off one shoulder. I unzip it and search for my purse so I can get some money to pay, struggling with the amount of crap there is inside. When I finally find it, I look up and watch Evan tap his card against the card reader. "I could have bought my own."

Evan shrugs. "Let's grab a table."

We move deeper into the room. I gravitate to one of the back corners where there's a low-level table and huge, squashy leather chairs. It's the perfect setup to lose yourself in a good book and I make a mental note to come back for this exact spot another day. Dropping into one of the chairs, I let out a long, satisfied exhale. They're even comfier than they look.

Evan folds in half, his knees almost touch his shoulders, and he couldn't look more uncomfortable. For once, being small is working in my favor.

"Sorry, I didn't think," I say, trying not to laugh at how ridiculous he looks.

"It's fine." One of the servers comes over with our drinks, setting them down on the table.

Evan says thank you, but I'm lost, staring at the giant piece of cake with multi-colored sprinkles and a single candle. A lump forms in my throat.

"Happy birthday." Evan grins. It's a smile that could light up an entire city and my heart hammers against my chest. For a second, I let myself become lost in eyes the color of warm chocolate.

He's ruining me for all other men, and he isn't even mine.

I swallow harshly. "Thanks."

He pulls a lighter from the pocket of his coat and reaches over. Something sparks to life deep inside me with the wick of the candle.

"Make a wish."

Holding back my hair, I lean forward and close my eyes. The thing about wishes is they open a world of possibilities, but I only want one thing. I open my eyes and blow the candle out; my hope disappears with the flame when I take in Evan's troubled expression, and tension sits heavy around us. Trying to ignore it, I grab a couple of sticks of sugar and dump them into my already sugary drink.

Evan watches in disbelief. "When I came back down from getting ready, Rogers and Grey had eaten everything I made," I explain. "This is a meal in a cup." I pick it up with my hands wrapped around the ceramic and inhale the sweet, spicy combination. After a few sips I set my sights on the cake, placing my drink back on the table. "Want some?" I ask, picking up a fork and tucking into the cake.

We've only just got past the plain chicken and rice stage, so when Evan picks up the other fork and takes a giant mouthful, I'm shocked.

"Who are you?"

"Evan Price," he laughs.

I light up when I figure out how I can make this 'yes day' work in my favor. "Tell me about him. Who is Evan when he isn't out saving the world as Agent Price?"

He hesitates. "What do you want to know?"

"Hmmm. Favorite movie?"

"*Snatch*."

"Never heard of it," I reply, taking a sip of my drink. It's as sweet as the cake. Heaven.

Evan's eyes widen in excitement. "You've never heard of *Snatch*?" He clears his throat, and then, with a terrible cockney accent, quotes part of the movie, about a getaway driver called Tyrone. When he's finished, he creases over laughing, then eventually he wipes at his eyes. Whatever he's referring to, it's tickled him *that* much. "Tyrone gets me every time. It's a classic. We should watch it."

My stomach becomes a flurry of butterflies high on sugar. He said *we*. Not you. *We*.

"Where did you grow up?" I ask, moving on before he can do any more terrible impressions.

"Santa Monica."

"No way."

He frowns. "Have I said something wrong?"

"I wouldn't have put you down for growing up in a sunny place. Not with the whole dark, broody thing you have working for you."

He arches a brow. "And where exactly would you have me come from?"

"Washington. State, not city. Somewhere without much sunlight. Like that Forks place."

"So, you think I'm a vampire?" I wouldn't have guessed he'd know I was talking about *Twilight*.

"Rarely sees sunlight. Check. Skulks in the darkness. Check. Tall, handsome and brooding. Check, check, check."

God, I just called him handsome out loud. I sniff my coffee again, wondering if they might have laced it with a birthday shot.

"For the record, I'm actually from New York."

"Seriously?"

He nods. "I'm adopted. I might have inherited my broodiness from the city."

I'm tempted to ask more about the bombshell he's just dropped, but there's something in his eyes that tells me not to. Perhaps we're more alike than I realize, and some of the darkness he tries to control and keep at bay isn't just from his job.

I want today to be a normal day, though. Agent Price and Freya are at home, waiting for when we return.

"Can we go to the movies?" I ask, changing the subject to something safe.

"Anything in mind?"

I smile. "There's a really good rom-com that just came out."

Evan groans, but he doesn't say no.

***

I couldn't tell you what the movie was about. I spend the whole time hyperaware of the FBI agent sitting next to me, trying not to combust each time his arm brushes against mine. Of course, he's the epitome of cool. He could be sitting next to my mom for how unaffected he seems. This 'yes day' is a bottle of gasoline, firing up my crush. I should stop it before it gets out of control, but I can't. No, not can't. I simply don't want to.

A couple of hours later, we walk out into the bright, early afternoon light. I've definitely had too much sugar. I'm more wired than an energizer bunny. Evan is the one to lead the show this time. He doesn't know what I want to do next, but he stalks along the sidewalk with purpose.

"Where are we going?" I ask.

"My car." My stomach drops at the thought the day might be over already.

"Why?"

"We're taking a trip to Burlington." My backpack bounces against me as I struggle to keep up with him. We make it to his car in record time.

I move around to the passenger side door. "What's in Burlington?"

"A change of scenery," he replies over the roof of the car. "It's a fifty-minute drive, if that."

"Okay," I reply, climbing in.

We sit in an amicable silence, apart from me humming along to S.C.A.R.A.B.'s latest release, while Evan drives. My stomach sinks when the song finishes, and the radio presenter talks about their tour of the East Coast. So close, yet so far away. Seeing them is on my bucket list, but the knowledge it probably won't ever happen, like a lot of things, puts a dampener on what's so far been a perfect day.

True to Evan's word, we arrive about an hour later.

"Erm, Mister Safety, it looks a bit shady round here," I say, peering out the window at the last place in the world I'd expect him to park.

"We'll be fine. Come on, we've got the rest of the afternoon to fill."

"'Til what?" I ask, clambering out.

"A surprise. What do you want to do before then?"

I smile mischievously. "I've always wanted to get a tattoo." Evan goes pale. "You can't say no."

His nostrils flare. I can see the letters 'n' and 'o' forming on his lips.

"Come on," I quote him. "We've got the rest of the afternoon to fill."

Pulling out my phone, I do a quick Google search for the best place in Burlington to get a tattoo, finding somewhere on the other side of town. I pray the whole way, with Evan scowling behind me, that luck is on our side, and they have some last-minute availability.

***

"I can't believe I'm letting you do this," Evan grumbles beside me in the tattoo parlor.

Disappointment is an understatement for how I felt when we arrived and they said they didn't have space. I was halfway out the door when the woman behind the counter miraculously changed her mind. It probably had something to do with the badge Evan was sliding back into the pocket of his pants when he thought I wasn't looking.

Now, we're standing in the waiting area until it's my turn. I can feel the sterile environment seeping into my pores. Unfortunately, it does little to cleanse me of the unwholesome thoughts I keep having about the man at my side. The smell of green soap burns my nostrils and will probably stay with me well into next week.

"Freya?" calls the woman behind the counter.

I step forward, excited. I've already picked out what I want and where I want it. Doing this has been on my bucket list for a long time.

"Want me to come with you?" asks Evan.

"I'll be fine," I smile. He frowns and looks around, dejected. I remember his comment from earlier about not wanting me out of his sight. Apprehension prickles the skin on the back of my neck. We might be out having what appears to most to be a normal day, what feels to me like a normal day, but we're as far from normal as it gets. It's easy to forget it's all an act. "Why don't you stand by the door?" I suggest.

His jaw unclenches. "Okay."

The woman behind the desk leads us through to the back of the building and I enter one of the empty rooms, getting settled on the chair. Evan waits at the door. Almost the whole way through, he faces away from me, only glancing over occasionally to check I'm alright. Thanks to the tattoo guy positioning himself expertly, all he can see when he does look over is my head. The process takes hardly any time at all, and around half an hour later, I have a tattoo, something I've dreamed of getting for years.

"Thanks," I say to the tattoo artist, pulling my shirt down, trying to ignore the burning across my ribs while I tuck my bra into my backpack.

"No problem. What about your friend?" he asks, looking over at Evan.

I chuckle. "He won't want one."

Evan turns around, his face is unreadable. "What did you get? Can I see?"

"Nope," I reply, adding an extra pop to my 'p'.

"Why not?"

"It's personal." I refuse to admit that I don't want to show him because of where it is.

If his face was unreadable before, it's like the morse code now. He shrugs his coat off and says to the guy behind me. "Sure, I'll get one."

All I can do is stare while he shows the guy what he wants on his phone.

I always thought I knew who Evan was. Montpelier has taught me that what I thought I knew was just a glimpse of the person beneath the bat gear. The truth is, all I've ever really known is Agent Price, and I'm somewhat grateful, because the parts of Evan he's finally let me see have crawled beneath my skin and worked themselves in so deep, I don't think I'll ever be able to get rid of them.

This ridiculously grumpy, broody man has become my light leading me through the darkness, and without him, I don't know if I'll be able to find my way. What's more terrifying is the thought that I might not want to if he isn't there walking at my side.

All my life-affirming thoughts drop to the floor with Evan's shirt. My mouth hangs open and the small flame that lit with the candle in the coffee shop turns into a raging fire, coursing through my veins and pooling low in my core. I knew Evan would be fit, but seeing him under the unforgiving overhead lights, looking like every muscle has been expertly carved, is something else.

He glances over at me and twirls his finger in the air. "Turn around. No looking."

I stick my tongue out, then grin at the blank wall when I've got my back to him. It's a relief to know his assholeishness is still there. Perfect people are intimidating as fuck.

Evan's tattoo takes longer than mine. Like, an hour longer. Impressive considering we walked in without appointments. I spend my time pondering what else we might be able to get away with if he flashes his fancy badge around.

"That looks great," comments the tattoo artist.

"Can I turn around?"

"One sec." I hear shuffling and then Evan says, "Yeah. You can now."

Sadly, his shirt is back on, and my ovaries weep. I look for any sign of where his tattoo might be, but can't figure it out. When my eyes move up to his face, the corners of his mouth are lifted in a smirk. "You won't find it."

"I'll show you mine if you show me yours." Evan's brows shoot up into his hairline and I slap a hand over my mouth, wishing the ground would swallow me up.

I need to work on my filter. Saying things without thinking is a Becket family trait. Mom and I have kind of got it under control, but my brother's the worst for it, which is where his bad rep has come from, along with his temper. My stomach twists thinking about him, and I'm hit by an overwhelming sadness.

The tattoo guy saves the day and starts taking us through our self-care routines. I hope he might slip up and let me know where Evan's tattoo is, but he doesn't.

"What's another thing you've always wanted to do?" asks Evan as we step back out into the world.

I tap my chin and a flashing neon sign in the distance catches my attention. "Go to a bar."

Holding my breath, I wait for Evan to say no. He doesn't flinch or give anything away when he pulls out his phone. Standing in the middle of the sidewalk, I watch him hold it up to his ear, trying to figure out what he's up to.

"Grey." He pauses. "Everything's fine. I need a favor." Another pause. "No, I can't stop Angela Becket rationing your portions if she's the one who's cooking the food." He pinches his brow and looks up at the sky. "Because technically it's hers. Stop being a lazy prick and cook it yourself."

I smile, picturing what has become an every-other-day occurrence back in our new home: my mom cutting off Grey and Rogers food supply when they devour whatever we make, and them then bitching about it for hours after. Thanks to our forced proximity, we've all gotten far too comfortable with each other. They're like having two extra brothers in the house. One's who carry guns and wouldn't hesitate in killing someone to keep me safe. Pretty much like my actual brother.

"I need you to come out to Burlington later tonight. I'll text you when I need you to leave." Pause. "My car's fine." He lets out a frustrated groan. "You don't need to know what I'm doing. Just come when I text. Bye." Looking back at me, he almost snaps, "Let's go."

Alrighty then. I could tell him to chill out, and that whatever Grey has been saying is nothing less than what I've had to deal with for almost nine months, but I choose not to. He's already tiptoeing the line of being grumpy and challenging him will probably push him over. Something, quite frankly, I can't be bothered to deal with. Instead, I scurry next to him as we head to the bar.

When we reach the door, I hold my breath. This feels like it could be one of those life-affirming moments you read about or see in the movies. We step inside and the smell of stale beer manages to overpower the lingering green soap scent stuck up my nose from the tattoo parlor. The bar itself is dark and dingy. It's a total dive with a few old guys sitting on high stools chatting to the bartender, ass cracks on show.

Not life affirming at all. At least I know I haven't been missing out on anything.

Evan walks to the bar. I follow, and when we get there, he glances down. "What would you like?"

"A Long Island Iced Tea."

"You know what's in that, right?" He watches me for any sign I might not know what I'm ordering.

"Everything," I grin. "That's the point."

He catches the bartender's attention and says, "Two Long Island Iced Teas, please."

"You're drinking?" I ask, surprised.

His foul mood from speaking with Grey shifts and he smiles. "Can't let you have all the fun."

It dawns on me that he carries around a dangerous object with him all day, every day. "Are you even allowed to drink when you have a gun?" I hiss.

He crouches low, and his lips almost touch my ear. His breath on the soft skin makes tingles shoot everywhere. "Chill, *Miss Safety*. I left it in the car."

I ignore his mocking, too focused on a not so minor detail. "You don't have a gun with you?!"

The older guys look at us dubiously.

"Would you like to say it any louder?" Evan mutters.

"Sorry," I cringe. "I just thought you always had it with you."

"I do," he confirms, picking up our drinks after paying the bartender. "But it's not safe having it with me for what we're doing next."

We walk over to one of the tables. I stop three times on the way thanks to leaving my shoe behind when the sole bonds with the floor. Like I said, total dive. Even the chairs are uncomfortable, made of hard, shiny wood, most likely so whatever gets on them can be wiped off. Gag.

Evan watches me when I pick up my drink and take a sip through the straw. It tastes fine until it hits the back of my throat and I choke, struggling to keep it down. I've had this drink before, but it's never been this strong. Dives have their perks, after all. Evan discards his straw and goes straight in, mouth around the rim of the glass, taking a large drink. I watch him swallow and wait. He doesn't even cough.

He gives himself away when he clears his throat a couple of times before speaking. Even he isn't immune to the drink's potency. "So, what else is on your bucket list?"

"The Cappadocia Balloon Festival in Turkey. Skiing. Seeing S.C.A.R.A.B. live. Go to Paris. Fall in love. Cooking school. Open my own restaurant, but you know that one. Go to a dance."

Of all the things I rattle off, it's the last one that catches his attention. "A dance."

"I've never been to one," I explain.

"Why?" He picks up his drink and takes another large gulp. His is already half gone.

I try to catch up, which results in me coughing for a few minutes. I laugh it off thanks to the alcohol in my blood. "Sorry. Yeah, so dancing. I've never been to one." He gives me a puzzled look, so I explain further. "I wasn't really interested when we were in Jacksonville. Well, I was, but I never had anyone to go with. I was only just starting to figure out who I was and who I wanted to be friends with when we had to move. After two moves, I decided it was better to keep things—"

"Replaceable," he finishes.

A shy smile plays on my lips. "Sad?"

"Not in the pathetic way you're referring to." His brown eyes bore into me, and everything slows around us. "One day, you'll get to do everything on your list."

"I thought you didn't make promises you couldn't keep?"

Evan downs the rest of his drink. "I do a lot of things I shouldn't when it comes to you." With that, he slides back his chair and stands. "Another?"

"Please," I breathe, not taking my eyes off him all the way to the bar.

I don't let my brain explore all the possibilities that could come with his words, because I lied before. I do have one friend who's been with me since I was a little girl. She goes by the name of Disappointment. We parted ways a while back because she became a bad influence in my life. Now, I don't let myself believe or hope for things I shouldn't. It's easier and less painful.

Before Evan returns with my next, I focus on finishing my drink.

He comes back and sets mine on the table. I notice he's already had some of his when he sits down in his seat. Seeing him like this is … refreshing. I could almost believe he's a normal person. That's when I remember Batman was never an actual superhero. He was a man with a flawed past who wanted to help make the world a better place.

"What's with all the Batman references?"

Cringe. I really need to work on the whole saying what I'm thinking out loud thing.

I bite my lip.

"Don't lie, Freya."

Dammit. With a swig of tea for Dutch courage, I say, "Because you're like him. Well … actually, at first, I thought you were like Christian Grey, but then you didn't strike me as the type to have that funny room with all the paddles and whips …" Evan's eyes bulge and he sits with his drink hovering midway to his lips. "But you had the whole Alpha/macho/grr thing going on. I figured with the way you brood and like to save the world; you were more Christian Bale. So yeah, Bale, not Grey. All you need is one of those voice changing things and you're good to go."

Christ. I hold my glass in the air and inspect it. What the hell is in it?

All I need to do now is tell him I masturbated while thinking about him a couple of weeks ago and I might as well hand myself over to Eugene before embarrassment takes me first.

Evan splutters on his drink and looks at me in shock.

Fuck. My. Life.

"I'm just gonna go to the restroom!" I squeak, darting away from the table before I can say anything else he shouldn't hear. Now I know what people mean when they talk about drinking going wrong.

Perching on one of the toilets, trying not to think about what might be lingering on the seat, I lower my head between my knees and take a few deep breaths. The door to the restrooms opens and slams shut, but I focus on my breathing. When I have it under control, I stand and leave the cubicle, slamming straight into a hard chest that smells like Evan.

Because it is.

"What are you doing?" I go to pull back, but Evan's hands take a firm grip of my upper arms.

He walks me backward, and I hit the cubicle partition. "I told you not to leave my sight."

"Apart from the bathroom. In case you hadn't realized, that's what we're in."

My attempt at a joke falls flat and I glance away, taking an interest in the sinks because this all feels too much, and my brain can't catch up.

Evan's hand skims up my arm, leaving a trail of goosebumps behind. He cups my jaw and pulls my head back so I'm facing him. His thumb finds its way to my bottom lip, and he drags it down. A groan crawls up his throat and vibrates through me.

"No more drinking."

"Why?" I croak.

He steps back. "Because it's like truth serum with you, and if you keep talking about how you think about me when you touch yourself, I won't be able to stop myself from showing you how good it can be when I'm the one to actually make you come." He walks to the restroom door. "Come on, it's time for your surprise."

I sag against the cubicle, clinging on for dear life. Maybe I was wrong. Maybe Evan has a bit of Christian Grey in him after all.

Fourteen

Evan

I almost kissed her.

Given half the chance, I would have done a lot of other things. I blame the tea. Whoever called a drink like that such an unsuspecting name had deceit on the brain. If they're dead, they'll be looking down laughing at all the major indiscretions their concoction has caused.

The feelings I have for Freya are growing out of control, and I don't know what I'm doing anymore. At first, I thought it was merely a need to protect her. Now, when I look back, I'm not so sure. The gift sitting perfectly wrapped in my bag back at the house is evidence of that. How did she become this woman? So passionate, driven and caring despite her circumstances? Each time life throws her a curve ball, she swings and smashes it out of the ballpark.

At times, she feels like an enigma. Reserved, patient and considerate, but then there's a kooky side that makes me question if I'm with the same person.

Where most would crumble, she stands strong, proving what can happen when life pushes hard. You can become a diamond under the pressure. And like a diamond, she's beautiful in every sense of the word, wearing her scars on the razor edges of her exterior, threatening to cut anyone that gets too close.

The overcast sky darkens as we walk through Burlington.

"Come on, we're going to be late," I grumble, feeling out of sorts after what happened in the restroom.

"Late for what?" pants Freya, struggling to keep up with me. "You remember I'm small. Like, seriously small, right?"

I shorten my strides. "Sorry. We're almost there."

When we turn a corner onto a new block, we're hit with noise. We both blink, taking in the large, white one-story building, the word S.C.A.R.A.B. plastered on the side. It's chaos. Freya grabs my arm and starts jumping up and down excitedly.

"No fucking way! You did not do this!"

I can't help beaming down at her. Her mood is infectious, and that smile ... I'd take her to every S.C.A.R.A.B. concert, then go back in time and take her to all the ones she's missed, if it meant I could see her looking at me like she is again. Like a normal person loving everything life has to offer. I pull the tickets out that have been sitting in my coat pocket all day and wave them in the air. Freya stops jumping and just stares. When her eyes start to water, I reassess and try to figure out if somewhere along the line I've messed up.

She steps forward, eliminating whatever distance is left between us and wobbles on the tips of her toes. A kiss on the cheek makes my heart beat in a way I thought it had forgotten.

"Thank you."

A gust of icy wind blows her hair across her face, and it sticks to her lip gloss. I shouldn't, after what happened at the bar, but I can't stop myself from reaching up and pulling it away, tucking it behind her ear. The noise and everything around us disappears. My eyes lock on where her hair was stuck a second ago. I've never wanted to do anything more—not join the FBI, not feel every part of her in the restroom before—than I want to kiss her now. The moment isn't fueled by chemistry. It isn't hormone, sex driven or whatever Alpha Christian Grey crap she was going on about in her Long Island Tea induced state. It's an earnest moment. One where your heart settles into a different beat that it only knows for one other person in its lifetime. A beat which tells you the person standing in front of you is the one.

Typically, my heart wants the one person it can't have.

Wanting her could get me fired. Needing her could get her killed. If not now, then somewhere in the future, and I'd never be able to live with myself for it.

But that's the thing about soulmates. They don't know logic. They don't know reasoning. They don't make things easy. What they do is make life worth living, no matter how dark and messy things get. They're *your* person. They're *the* person. The one who, when you feel like giving up, reminds you why you have to keep going. Because when the storm passes and the clouds part, they're there shining, brighter than the sun and the moon. They are and always will be everything, and not experiencing life with them would be a tragedy.

That's the moment when I see her for who she really is. I see her without the mask. The second I see Josie Miller standing in front of me, not Freya, I know nothing will ever be the same.

I point over at Higher Ground. "We really are going to be late."

She nods, and neither of us says a word as we cross the road. Only when we're standing at the entrance does she look excited again.

"I can't believe we're doing this," she squeals.

We find our way into the crowds. Outside was chaos. Inside is carnage. Freya looks like she wants to pinch herself and check she isn't dreaming. I follow her in a daze, but for completely different reasons. If at some point I wake up, I won't be disappointed, because it's been a damn good dream.

Freya gestures for me to get closer and I dip my head so I can hear her over the noise. "How did you know I would want this on my 'yes day'?"

"I had a feeling," is all I reply.

She doesn't get a chance to psychoanalyze my answer, because it goes dark, and the overhead stage lights pan down on S.C.A.R.A.B. The crowds around us go wild, with cheers that almost bring the roof down. We stand together, jumping and taking everything in as the music floats around us. A feeling of euphoria hits me. For the first time, together, we each forget the pasts that haunts us.

***

Josie

"Did you have fun?" asks Evan.

I literally skip beside him, high on life. "Yes! Can we do it all again?"

"Soon," he replies. "Grey is almost here. I just need to get a few things." By things, he means his guns, but neither of us says that out loud. "I'll come back tomorrow for the car."

It's a good idea considering the super strength cocktails we drank earlier, which I still feel hazy from.

We stop a handful of steps before his latest car, and he shoves his hands into the pockets of his new jeans. "Today was fun."

"It was," I reply.

He looks boyish, like he doesn't have a care in the world, until he shifts his weight and takes a step back. Glass crunches beneath his foot. We both turn, taking in the broken back passenger seat window.

"I told you it was a shady area," I joke, even though nothing about this situation is funny.

Looking down at the ground, all I can see is red glass. Evan peers through the broken window. Whatever he sees makes him visibly pale in the poor lighting.

He reaches to pull his gun from the band of his pants, then, remembering he left it in the glove box, mutters, "Fuck," under his breath. Unlocking the car as he goes, he races to the front passenger side, flings open the door and reaches inside. This time a louder "Fuck!" fills the night. Righting himself, he stalks toward me. My skin prickles like a thousand tiny ants are skittering across it.

He grabs my upper arm and drags me away, pulling his phone out in the process. Before we clear the car, my eyes trail to the right. I raise a hand to stifle a scream.

Evan pulls me into his side. "I know you're scared, but we have to get away from here."

His words break through my fear. "It's him, isn't it?"

"Can't be certain," he replies as we race along the sidewalk.

That's Agent Price code for yes.

When we get into a steady flow of movement, he lets go of my shoulders and grabs my hand, increasing his stride as he taps away on his phone.

He raises it to his ear and when someone answers, says, "Where are you?" He waits for a second. "How much longer will you be?" Pause. "Can you get here any sooner?" Pause. "We have an issue."

The issue being hundreds of dead mice in the back seat of his car.

He carries on speaking heatedly, then confirms a place for us to meet. Ten minutes later, a black car swerves up alongside the curb.

"Get in the back, quick," Evan snaps.

The warmth of the car is a welcome reprieve when I scramble inside, helping to relieve the glacial chill after what's just happened.

"Hey, Frey," says Grey, his voice distant.

The car screeches into the night, and Evan and Grey speak in hushed voices in the front. I stare out the window, barely able to make out what they're saying. The only clear word I hear is 'mice', which leaves me feeling sick remembering the bloodbath. His phone starts to ring, and the tension in the vehicle increases tenfold.

"Hewson?" he answers.

From where I'm sitting, I can see him grind his teeth while he listens. "You're sure?" He lets out a long exhale. "Leave it with me. I'll catch a flight down there first thing tomorrow."

Disappointment overrides the fear inside me. He's leaving.

"Everything okay?" asks Grey.

Evan turns his phone in his hands, over and over. "When it rains, it pours. Leave it at that."

Grey doesn't ask any more questions. Forty minutes later, we pull up outside Evan's temporary, come our semi-permanent, home.

"Wait here," says Evan, before jumping out of the car and walking up to the front door and letting himself in. The stealth he displays has me panicking. He's on high alert.

"He's just going to check everything is safe inside," says the Grey.

"It looks more like he's going to check there hasn't been a massacre."

Grey flinches, but I don't feel guilty. Inside that house is my mother, my world. If Eugene, or whoever the hell is pretending to be him, has taken her from me after all this time, I'll take down everyone in my path to make sure I get justice.

Evan walks back out. He doesn't look like he has a shit ton of murders on his hands, which can only be a good sign.

"Freya."

"I'm coming," I say, climbing out of the vehicle, less than gracefully.

I wobble once upright, and Evan steadies me.

"Easy," he murmurs. It's a relief to hear his voice softening after the past hour. "I'm having a hard enough time keeping you alive as it is." He drops to my eye level. "You good to walk?" I nod.

Inside, I don't see my mom anywhere, and assume she's in bed, hopefully oblivious to whatever is happening. When we get to what is my room, but is really Evan's, he holds his hands up animatedly. "Wait there."

"Wha—" he's down the hall before I can ask what he's doing.

Rather than waiting at the door, I move into the room, kicking my Docs off at the foot of the bed and hanging my coat over the back of his desk chair. A couple of minutes later, he reappears with a small package in his hands. My heart rate increases when I take in the pristine wrapping and small bow. It's so

Evan, he can't even let packaging go without it being done to perfection.

He holds the package out, and it hovers in the air between us.

"This is going to be kinda awkward if you don't take it."

I glance between the object in his hands and his face. "You got me a present?"

His voice drops to a level that does funny things to my insides. "It's your birthday."

"Do all super-secret agents get the people they're trying to protect presents?"

He shakes his head no, and with a small smile, I take the present and sit on the bed. He walks over and sits beside me, closer than he should.

"You could have used less scotch tape," I say, struggling to open it.

He chuckles, and the movement causes our arms to brush. I focus on my breathing and what I'm doing, which feels like an impossible task. I finally manage to get a black box free of the gift wrap and pause.

"Open it," he urges.

His head is so close he could rest his chin on my shoulder. My cheek warms from his breath and my stomach somersaults. I lift off the lid and find a black rope bracelet wrapped around a small, silky white pillow. Resting on the top are a pair of wings.

"It's a charm bracelet."

I smile and remove it from around the pillow. "I know what it is. Why did you pick it?"

"It's for when you work through the rest of your bucket list, to remind you of the things you've achieved when this is all over."

"You sound certain it's actually going to be over."

Evan takes the bracelet from my hands, undoes the clasp, and fixes it around my left wrist. He toys with the wings and his fingers skim my skin. "What are they for?"

"They're for when you feel like you're falling. A reminder you can still fly."

My head snaps up. He remembers the poster.

He cups my face and his thumbs brush over the damp skin of my cheeks. "This wasn't the reaction I was going for."

I hold my breath when his eyes fall to my lips. The air crackles between us.

"Why does it have to be you?" he murmurs. I lean in toward him and my eyes close. "Dammit, Freya." His words brush against my lips, and I wait for his mouth to follow.

The slamming of a car door outside startles us both. My eyes fly open and all I find is regret.

Evan stills, then pulls back, shaking his head. "I'm going to Jacksonville tomorrow."

His hands drop away from my face, but I still feel them everywhere.

"For how long?"

He stands and I toy with the charm on my bracelet, scared of what his answer will be. Today has been the best but most torturous of days. A small part of me, the part that knows deep down Evan has the potential to break my heart, wishes I didn't know what it was like to walk with him toward the light. It hurts knowing how things could be if we were two different people in a different reality. Ignorance really is bliss.

"I'm not sure."

And just like that, my heart, which at times I've thought might be made of stone, takes a hit. The damage could be seen as minimal, a hairline fracture, but one that runs deep.

If I keep letting Evan in, I might never recover.

"Okay."

He rubs the back of his neck and looks around the room. It's like today, the past nine months haven't happened. We're back to being Agent Price and Freya, two people who can never be together. I don't know why I ever thought we could. I've been a fool, letting schoolgirl fantasies get in the way and affect my judgement.

"I should go?" he says, backing toward the door.

My heart thuds heavily. I predict when Agent Price walks out, I might never see him again. It would be the best thing for both of us after today, because being around him and trying to convince myself I don't feel the way I do would be living a lie.

Before he leaves, I decide I need one last thing from him. A truth only he can give.

"Was I the reason Eugene Belmer went after my brother and his girlfriend? Is it me he wanted all along?" Agent Price's lips form a flat line. "You said you'd never lie."

And what happens when water gets inside stone? It runs to the core. And when it freezes, it expands, destroying everything around it.

"I think so," he replies, not meeting my eye.

His words linger between us and my heart shatters, knowing I'm why everyone is at risk. People are in danger, people have almost lost their lives because of me.

"Goodbye, Agent Price."

He opens his mouth to say something but stops himself, choosing to walk out without so much as a backward glance.

This game we've been playing together is a losing one, and I was wrong. Evan never stood a chance at breaking my heart, because all along the darkness has been there, ready to take down anyone in its path, and now it feels like it could swallow me whole.

***

Evan

Mara once described me as cool, calm, and collected. She was being nice. Grey hit the nail on the head with a more fruitful description when he called me a grumpy fuck.

I worked my ass off to get into the FBI. Some of the things I had to do to get to where I needed to be weren't easy. Not everything came naturally, so self-control and restraint are how I've excelled. But in all my training, there was one thing I overlooked. That everyone has a weakness. I now know mine goes by the name of Freya Becket.

I've never felt more of a prick than I do now, with her standing in front of me, huge green eyes full of pain. After what Hewson revealed on the call earlier, and what's happened tonight, her safety has never been more paramount. How I'm starting to feel about her will get her killed, and I need to walk away. When she's around, my judgement isn't just clouded, it's non-existent.

I don't have it in me to say goodbye when I leave her room, because I don't want to admit this is it. Saying goodbye means drawing a line under the best thing to ever happen in my life. So, I don't. I leave things open, praying to the big man above as I go, hoping that someday we might get a second shot. Maybe when we're the only players on the board.

I'm at the front door, about to leave, when Grey catches me. "Why do you look like the world's about to end?"

Because it feels like it might.

"Don't," I answer.

He shrugs, but for once, he does as I ask and leaves it. "What did Hewson want?"

I stare straight ahead. "There's a possible error in Britney Shaw's statement."

"What kind of error?"

"She used the word *they*."

"Huh. What could it mean?"

"I'm not sure. We need to know if it's right first. I'm going to catch an early flight to Jacksonville tomorrow."

"We'll keep Freya safe."

I give him a weak smile. I'm rattled to my core. "Thanks."

I'm about to open the door when Grey clears his throat. "Price, I don't know what's going on between the two of you, but can I say something?"

"Will it piss me off?"

"Probably, but when do I ever not?"

"True. Hit me with it."

"You're a good guy, don't forget that." I raise a brow. "I see the way you look at her ..."

I narrow my eyes, having had enough of the day. "Where are you going with this?"

"Sometimes rules are made to be broken." And there it is.

"See you around, Grey," I say, opening the front door and leaving everything I don't want to behind.

I might not have broken the rules and kissed Freya, but what I did feels worse. I began to want to, more than I've ever wanted anything else.

Fifteen

Evan

So, this is how the other half live.

I'm sitting outside Michael Becket's home, which looks more like a palace. I know NFL players get paid a lot, but I'm obviously in the wrong profession. Trying to clear my head of all thoughts related to Michael's sister, I grab the report from the passenger seat and scan over it a final time. One-word glares at me. They.

Climbing out of the car, I walk to the front door and knock. I look over my shoulder, counting the seconds as they tick by. The lock turning brings my attention back to the door. When it opens, Michael's huge frame fills the space. The television screen doesn't do his size justice.

My eyes move to the knife in his hands at the same time he says, "Evan, hi?"

He looks at me uncertainly, and I don't blame him. The times our paths have crossed, it's never been for a good reason.

"Can I come in? I have a few things I need to go over?"

He shrugs, and the knife glints as he lowers it. "Sure."

He leads the way into a huge kitchen and Britney Shaw glances at me like I'm the last person she wants to see. Thankfully, she looks better than the time we met in New York, after Michael sent me a message asking me to check on her.

I've barely eaten since yesterday, so when Britney mentions joining them for food, my growling stomach wins the battle. If I didn't already feel like I was overstaying my welcome, a diamond catching the light when Britney goes to pass me the salad seals the deal. I pray to God it didn't just happen and I'm interrupting their celebratory meal. Michael explains it happened the night before, and I feel less like an intruder.

Having consumed more than my fair share of the spread of food, my eyes settle on the time on my watch. I swallow my final mouthful and decide I need to get things moving if I stand a chance of catching the last flight back to DC.

Reading my mind, Michael asks, "So, what did you want to clear up with me?"

He's not going to like what I'm about to say, and I don't blame him. He probably wants to protect his fiancée from all of this, as much as I want to protect Freya. "It was actually Britney I came here to talk to."

"Okay?" says Britney.

"It's nothing bad." I smile at them both. Michael looks ready to ask me to leave. "My admin picked up on something in your statement and I have to clear it up. Part of the process. Sorry."

Michael goes to protest, but before he can, Britney says, "It's fine, just let me know how I can help."

"It's simple." My phone starts ringing on the table, and I frown when I read Grey's name. Freya should already be home from her shift at the diner. Deciding he can wait, I mutter, "Sorry," and silence it. "In your statement, there was something flagged up. I'm really sorry, Britney, I'm going to have to talk about part of it with you again. Is that okay?"

She takes a deep breath. "I'll answer whatever questions you have."

"So, I just need you to confirm something from the beginning, where you recollect first coming around. You used the word *they*. I just need you to confirm that I can change it."

Pausing, she frowns. "There's nothing to change."

That wasn't the answer I was expecting. "What do you mean, there's nothing to change?"

She doesn't even blink when she replies, "The word *they* is right."

"But you said there was only one person there."

She nods. "The rest of the time, yes. But there wasn't at that point. I heard two voices."

"You're sure?"

"Yes," she says, staring at me blankly.

I rub a hand across my jaw, trying to ease some of the tension. "It doesn't make sense," I say to myself, as I go over every detail quickly in my head. Details I've read so many times I know them almost word for word.

My phone lights up on the table and I read a single 'F'. I look up and catch Britney glancing at the screen. If she puts the pieces together, she doesn't say anything. Michael doesn't notice, too busy trying to break one of the serving bowls with his glare.

"Excuse me a moment." I smile tightly and pick up the phone, opening the message.

I'm sorry.

My stomach churns with a feeling that something isn't right. I need to get out of here and check Freya is okay. I place my phone face down on the table. It starts ringing. I snatch it up, expecting to see an 'F' flashing on the screen. Instead, I find Grey's name again. I hit reject, only for the shrill rings to fill the room instantly.

I look between Michael and Britney. "I'm sorry. I'm going to have to take this."

Walking away from the kitchen table, I raise the phone to my ear, feeling Michael's gaze burning my back as I go. "Hello."

"Why the fuck haven't you been answering?" shouts Grey.

I hold the phone away from my ear. The sounds of sirens in the background almost pierce my eardrum. I start pacing the kitchen at the same time the doorbell rings. I glance back to the dining area, catching Britney's white-blonde hair flowing out behind her as she leaves the room to answer the door. Michael's gaze remains lasered on me.

"What the hell is going on up there?" I hiss.

More sirens are added to the mix. "Rogers is en route to the hospital."

"What?"

"Freya's shift ran over. We couldn't get a space close to the diner and had to park a few blocks over ..." he tails off and I hold my breath, waiting for what comes next. "We left her for a few minutes. We were walking toward our car when Rogers spotted the lily. He went to go check it out. The fucking thing exploded when he lifted the window wiper up."

"Freya?" Silence. "Grey. Where's Freya?"

There's a hint of panic in his voice. "I had to call for backup and make sure Rogers was okay. He was on fire! When the paramedics got to the scene, I ran to where she told us she was parked straight away ..."

"And ..."

I hear him swallow. "I'm sorry, Price. She's gone."

The world tilts. "What do you mean, she's gone?" I roar. "Find her!"

"Becket!" Britney shrieks.

Michael races out of the room, and I don't know whether to follow or finish the call.

"I have to go." I'm about to run through a list of things he needs to check for when he clears his throat. "Yes?"

"There was a lily on the front passenger seat along with her phone."

My blood runs cold. "I'll call you back." I race through to the entryway, grabbing fists full of my hair not caring if I look unhinged because right now, I feel it. "It's Josie ... she's gone."

Neither Becket nor Britney pick up on my use of the wrong name. They both stand, staring at the floor. I look down and find a piece of paper covered in bloodstains.

Fool me once, shame on you.
Fool me twice, shame on me.
Fool me thrice, shame on us both.

I slide my phone into the inside pocket of my suit jacket, then retrieve an evidence bag and gloves. When I've ripped the gloves from their packet, I kneel and carefully pick up the paper, putting it in the bag.

"Where's Freya?" asks Michael.

I don't answer until I've sealed the evidence and I'm standing. "I'm sorry."

"What for?"

Britney looks between the two of us with worried blue eyes.

"She's gone." It seems to be all I can say.

Michael looks confused and smaller than his six foot plus frame. "Gone where?"

"I don't know," I reply, unable to meet his eye and struggling to process the information myself.

"Belmer?"

"Maybe."

"But he was here? How can he have been there as well?"

The pieces slot into place after what Britney revealed, a few minutes that feel like hours ago. We're not dealing with a copycat, we never were.

"Because The Cat, as the world likes to call him, isn't one person. He's two."

***

Josie

I hold my hand to my mouth, trying to stifle a scream.

Freya,
What a beautiful name. It's a shame it's not your own.
Fool me once, shame on you. Fool me twice, shame on me. Fool me thrice, shame on us both.
There won't be a thrice.
Run, Josie, run.
This game is coming to an end, and only one person can be the winner.

Before I have a chance to second guess myself, I grab my bag and clamber out of the car, disappearing into the night, quiet as a mouse, leaving Freya behind.

With lead feet weighed down with terror, I struggle to put as much distance between me and the vehicle as I can. I've been walking for a couple of minutes when a bang ripples through the night. I fight to increase my pace, glancing over my shoulder. The hairs on my arms stand on end. The shadows creep in.

I crash into a figure and topple to the ground. All I see is black.

"Watch it!" a woman in a long black coat snarls before hurrying off.

Paralyzed, I watch her retreating form. The world flashes bright blue when four emergency vehicles fly past, followed by two cop cars heading in the direction of the bang. Their sirens startle me back into action, and I jump to my feet. My ass aches from the impact, but I don't have time to stand and feel sorry for myself. Checking the area is clear, I dart away.

After a quick detour to the drug store, I step inside the bus terminal half an hour later. Walking over to one of the ticket desks, I pull my purse from my bag as I go.

"Evening, Ma'am." I offer a tight smile and my eyes move to the side, taking in the people around me. "Where would you like to go?"

I weigh up my options. "Where's the next bus going?"

The woman behind the desk stares at the screen in front of her, unphased I don't have a destination in mind. "Las Vegas, in an hour."

"One ticket, please."

"Round trip?"

"No."

She taps the keyboard. "One hundred and forty dollars."

Shit. I rummage through my backpack, thanking the big guy above when I find the envelope with the cash Mom gave me for my birthday. Five hundred dollars "for things," she said. I'm not sure this is what she had in mind, but I have no choice. A quick calculation has me wincing when I figure out all I have left to my name is three hundred and sixty dollars. I have cards, but I can't use them, not if I plan on being invisible.

Ticket in hand, I make my way to the restrooms with just under an hour to spare. I grab one of the extra-large cubicles, the kind that have their own sink and mirror, locking myself inside. Dropping my bag to the ground, I open the paper bag from the drug store and pull out a pair of scissors, a box of hair dye, and shampoo.

I stare at my reflection while holding the scissors.

My confidence wavers. I want to go back to Evan's house, where I feel safe. But I'm not safe. I never am. And neither is anyone around me. This isn't for me, it's for them. If he can't find me, then maybe he will leave them alone. It's a risk, but it's one I'm willing to take.

Pulling the elastic band from the messy bun on top of my head, my hair tumbles around my shoulders. I tease it with my fingers, then raise the scissors and start to chop in line with my jaw. The first cut is the worst, watching the locks fall. A few minutes later, my old hair is a pile on the floor. Next, I open the box of dye. The restrooms are quiet and the few people who do pass through seem unbothered by the chemical smell floating from my cubicle.

With my hair covered, I perch on the toilet seat and wait the forty minutes it takes to develop. When the times up, I angle my head in the sink and run my hair under the water, rinsing away the dye before I give it a quick shampoo. Finished, I squeeze the water as best I can from my now short locks. I stand straight and stare. The baby blue material of my dress has the odd smudge of black, and the occasional drip of water from my hair adds further dark splatters.

After clearing my hair off the floor, I pick up my bag and unzip it, pulling out the bus ticket. My heart falters when the reality of what I'm about to do and everything I'm going to leave behind hits me. I almost stop myself from going through with it. Almost. But then my eyes catch on a small piece of paper next to my foot. I bend and pick it up. I stop breathing.

Only one person can be the winner.

My face hardens, and I slide on my black leather jacket. With only ten minutes until the bus is due to leave, I hurry out of the bus terminal, dumping the bag from the drug store in a trashcan as I go.

A few minutes later, I settle into my seat and wait. The doors close and the bus pulls away, leaving every part of me behind.

***

Evan

Freya's been missing almost twenty-four hours when I finally manage to get back to Montpelier.

I leave Angela Becket at the house with Grey. She's beside herself and won't come out of her room.

Crime scene tape greets me when I walk along the sidewalk toward Freya's car.

"Price!" calls Hewson. He powers over with Mara at his side. They each give me a grim expression.

"Anything?" I ask.

Mara shakes her head. "No sign of forced entry into the car. No prints."

"Like magic," I mutter to myself.

I refuse to believe he has her. I won't let my brain go there, because if it does, every worst-case scenario will start to appear, and if I'm going to find her, I need to keep my shit together.

"How could he have known she was here? I thought everything was locked down," says Hewson. "Could we have a leak?"

"Not he," I correct Hewson, "They."

His brow furrows. "Excuse me?"

"Britney Shaw's statement was correct?" asks Mara in disbelief. "What does that mean?"

"It means," I say, staring through the window of Freya's car, "One killer is hard to catch, two working together might be impossible."

"Wonderful," spits Hewson. His phone starts ringing and his shoulders slump. "Excuse me while I go explain to the powers that be that, along with an exploded car and an agent in the hospital with second-degree burns, we also have two killers working together, and two missing females." He starts walking away and calls over his shoulder. "Let's see if while we're searching for Freya Becket, we might be able to find Leigh Clarke, yeah?"

Mara whistles through her teeth then shoots me a side on glance. "You good?"

"Why wouldn't I be?" I bite back. She gives me a look that tells me I'm making it clear how not okay I am. I exhale long and hard through my nose. "I'm fine."

"I'll start going through CCTV," she says. "It might take a while."

"Thanks. Anything at all on Leigh Clarke?"

It's been months. She's most likely dead. Neither of us say it out loud.

Mara's lips form a tight line. "Nothing."

Shit.

"Go do what you have to. *Whatever* you have to."

I watch her walk away and drag a hand down my face. The weight of the case presses down on my shoulders, and inside, not knowing if Freya really is okay, I feel dead.

Where the hell are you?

***

Josie

Forty-eight hours in Vegas and I've run out of money.

With nowhere to stay, I had no choice but to book a room in a hotel. The second night has bled me dry.

Sitting in the cheapest diner I can find, I drown my sorrows in the final cup of coffee I can afford. A stray tear drips against the table and I wipe my cheeks. How am I supposed to eat? Where am I supposed to sleep?

I have no clothing, nothing to a name that's never been my own.

Belmer can have me. I'm done fighting.

"Penny for your thoughts." I glance up and find a scantily clad brunette woman, around mid-thirties, watching me with a smile. "Mind if I sit?"

I should say no. Mom taught me never to talk to strangers. But I don't know who I can trust anymore. I don't even trust myself.

"Sure."

"Bill!" A burly guy wanders over. "Bring my usual. Plus, one more."

Bill disappears into what I assume is the kitchen. The smells coming from it are as questionable as the stains on his shirt.

"Are you here alone?"

228

I would have thought it's obvious I am, but I don't say that. "Yeah," I admit.

"First time in Vegas?" I nod. "So, what is it?"

"I'm sorry?"

"With eyes as sad as yours, there has to be a story."

I hold her gaze. "What's yours?"

She leans back against the booth. "A mild coke dependency and an ex-husband with a too happy fist."

There's something about this strange woman that has me giving her a glimmer of the truth. "I have a dark past."

"Honey," she snorts. "*Vegas* has a dark past."

"Why?"

She gestures for me to lean across the table, holds a hand up and whispers behind it. "We're in the home of the devil. It's where everyone comes to play." She's bat shit crazy and I have a strong suspicion it's to do with the coke dependency that probably isn't as mild as she claims. "I'm Eve."

I say the first name that comes to my mind. "Bella."

Bill wanders back out, balancing a large black tray on his shoulder. He decants two omelets that look surprisingly good, and two cokes.

I grab the glass, take a giant swig, and choke.

"Gah!"

"That will be the vodka."

I place the glass back on the table and wipe my mouth with the back of my hand. "I figured."

Eve tucks into her omelet, and I watch. My stomach grumbles, and I decide I'd eat garbage right now; this can't be much worse. I'm surprised when it's good. Really good.

When we're both finished eating, Eve raises her hand and asks for the check.

"I don't have any money to pay."

"I know," she replies, the corners of her lips turning up into a smile. "Come with me."

"Where?"

"To a place where money won't be an issue."

Eve dangles the forbidden fruit in front of my face. Leaving me with no choice but to take a bite, I follow her all the way to Fremont Street.

Later that night, getting ready to step out and dance, my stomach twists, remembering how Evan said when it all became too much for him, he liked to face the devil head on.

I wonder what he'd say if he knew I'd sold my soul to him.

Sixteen

Evan 6 weeks later

*T*he sky flashes vivid blue against black. Rain pours in torrents, cascading down my skin. I stare up at the dark building in front of me.

"Price, we haven't got all night," snaps Hewson, his face a blur. My feet splash against the saturated tarmac. "Price! Come on."

One, two, twenty, thirty-eight. Sixty. That's how many steps it takes to get to the top.

I open the door and step inside my home in Montpelier.

Cats Three and Four run across my feet while I walk carefully through a sea of mouse carcasses, the floor smeared in blood.

Clapping comes from somewhere in the house. I follow it.

Water floods beneath the bathroom door. When I open it, there they are.

Freya and Leigh in the bathtub. Lifeless eyes surrounded by bloated blue flesh.

Hidden in plain sight before being replaced by a figure in a black hooded jacket.

It stands, sweeps toward me. I almost see its face before it steals me away into the darkness.

My eyes fly open, and I suck in a sharp breath, pulse racing. Sitting up, I give the bottle of Scotch discarded on the floor, next to the couch, a dubious look, before grabbing my phone and calling Hewson.

He answers after three rings.

"What couldn't wait until the morning?"

"I know where Leigh Clarke is."

"And?"

"We need to be on a flight to New York in the morning."

***

I've watched countless crime movies and shows where a significant moment happens, and the weather reflects the scene. I chuckle every time at how cliché it all is.

With Hewson and Mara by my side on the bank of the Hudson River, stormy clouds hang above us, so dark and low, the line between them and the walls of Sing Sing is barely distinguishable.

We're standing in the blind spot Mara found, watching, waiting for the dive team to come back.

The water rolls dangerously. Even the elements don't want us to find her.

I let out a sigh of relief when a hand breaks through the water and there's no signal.

But then a finger is raised. One body.

Another is raised. Two bodies.

The world crashes down harder than the waves breaking at our feet.

***

"Price, you have to eat," says Mara.

We're back in DC waiting for the bodies to be identified.

"I'm fine."

"You're not fine. You look like shit. When was the last time you slept?"

"I'm fine Mara," I bite out. I'm not in the mood for her game of a hundred questions.

"You can't shut the world out every time something bad happens," she mumbles, going back to working at her computer.

Stewing in my mood, I bring up the image of Sing Sing so it's enlarged on the screen. It sits beside the water like a palace holding the royalty of the underworld. The walls surrounding it so high they pierce the sky.

How did you get out?

I drag the list of sign ins from the day Belmer escaped across my desk, because it's all we've got to work with. Normal names in an abnormal situation. Nothing stands out, but I can't help feeling like I'm staring at Eugene's escape plan.

"I've found her!" exclaims Mara.

I'm at her side faster than a greyhound. At the same time, Hewson walks into the unit. He heads in our direction, but I take no notice of him. Mara points at the screen and there she is. Freya standing in Montpelier bus station. Adrenaline surges through me and my hand trembles. She's alive. At least, she was the night she disappeared. It's easy to see why Mara could have missed her all the times she's been searching. With her hair short and black, she looks like a completely different person. I want to jump into the screen. I'm torn between the need to hold her and never let her go or shake her and ask what the hell she was thinking.

"Follow her." Mara nods and walks us through the CCTV footage right up to the point she climbs on a bus. "Find out where that bus was going to."

I turn to Hewson, holding my breath.

"We've got another body." Shit. Mara glances up at the two of us with a sad expression and a slight shake of her head. "We're just waiting for confirmation on some of the details from the local enforcements so we can be sure that it's linked to this case."

"What do we know so far?" His expression turns grim. "That bad?" He nods.

Since Freya's disappearance, Belmer and whoever's working with him have been on a killing spree. We've never seen anything like this apart from killings en masse.

"It's safe to say that the change in MO is probably linked to Freya's disappearance," I say. "Any news on the bodies?"

"We've got a positive ID for Leigh Clarke."

A lump forms in my throat. "And the other body?"

"There was a hole in the bag. The water decayed it to the point it's impossible to ID through facial recognition. They're running it for DNA."

"If it's decayed that much, it can't be Freya, right? Plus, this killing spree they're on, it's most likely them lashing out because things haven't gone to plan."

Hewson holds a piece of paper in the air between his fingers.

"What's this?" I ask, taking it from him.

I blink, not quite believing my eyes. It's an image of Freya. Freya standing on a stage with her pixie haircut in the tiniest pair of pants, and a top almost as small. Even with the poor lighting, I catch sight of black marks sitting beneath her breasts, but the image isn't clear enough to make out what they are. Now I know why she didn't want me to look in the tattoo studio.

"This flagged up on a social media site. Someone must have snuck a phone in."

"Lucky us," I murmur.

"The profile it was found on didn't have location enabled. We're running the image through the systems to see if we can find where it was taken," continues Hewson.

"She's in Vegas," states Mara. "That's where the bus was going."

"I'll go tell admin to book you the next available flights," says Hewson.

"Flights. As in plural?" asks Mara, eyes wide. She's done more jet-hopping in the past two days than she has in the whole time she's been my partner.

"Yes, Mara," says Hewson as he walks away. "You're going to Vegas. I suggest you pack a bag, because from the looks of it, Freya Becket doesn't want to be found."

I look back down at the image sitting in my hands, wondering who's going to be standing in her place when we get to her.

***

Three hours into the almost six-hour flight to Vegas and I'm losing my mind. There's a tightness in my chest that, no matter how deep I breathe, won't ease. My leg bounces high, colliding with the fold-down table, causing water to spill over the sides of a small plastic glass.

"That's it. I'm done with this," hisses Mara, unfastening her belt and walking along the aisle toward the back of the plane.

She returns a couple of minutes later with her hands full of small bottles that look a lot like Sc—

"Scotch," she explains. "You need to chill the hell out."

"Turning up wasted isn't going to help."

She snorts. "But it might stop you freaking out. Seriously, if you turn up like you are, Freya's going to run in the other direction." She opens a bottle and when she's poured it in a glass, starts on the next. Three bottles in, the glass is almost full. She raises it in the air and all but pours it into my mouth. "Drink."

"I have to drive." I pin my lips together.

"No. You don't. I can. This is you being a control freak and not trusting people."

"I like things done a certain way."

"I know, which is why Freya's good for you."

"How have you figured that one out? You met her for thirty minutes, if that."

"Because she's got you by the balls."

An older woman behind us tuts.

I turn and apologize, then look back at Mara. "Seriously, tone it down."

"No. Have the Scotch and you won't care." She narrows her eyes, and reluctantly, I raise the glass and take a large drink, almost finishing the glass in one. "As I was saying," she continues, opening another couple of bottles and topping up my glass. "She's got you."

An air steward moves past with the snack cart, interrupting her flow. Mara orders a day's wage in junk, leaving her tray full of colorful packets, next to mine, which is filled with empty liquor bottles.

"Got me how?" I ask when the steward moves onto the next row.

"Six weeks of malnutrition and sleep deprivation doesn't suit you, Price. I seriously hope when we find her, you accept how you feel."

She's more perceptive than I give her credit for and has an eye like a goddamn eagle. But if there's anyone I can have this conversation with, it's her. Where Mara comes from, rules have no meaning.

"I don't feel anything," I reply, wishing it were a vat of Scotch in front of me.

"Having feelings isn't a bad thing. Especially when you're married to your job, like you are."

"It can't happen," I reply, tapping my finger against the plastic table.

"Why?"

I stare at the back of the seat in front, going over all the arguments I've convinced myself are right since Freya Becket re-entered my world and turned it upside down. "I'm too old for her."

Mara snorts. "You're hardly Hugh Hefner. You're what, ten years older, at most?"

"I've lived my life. She's barely started hers."

"I wasn't aware thirty-four meant you were already one foot in the grave. I better arrange my funeral."

I move onto my next point. "My job would put her at risk."

"More than the serial killer who already has a mark on her head?"

Final argument. "I could lose my job."

This one has Mara pausing. "Would it be the worst thing in the world? There's more to life than the FBI. And anyway, screw the rules. I could bring up a ton of emails and texts to show you who is fucking who. I know for a fact that Jules from reception sucks—" A guy in front clears his throat. "Sorry," she calls to him. "All I'm saying is that you're miserable at the best of times. And if we're not happy in life, then what's the point?"

I pick up my Scotch and take another long drink. Memories flood in—ones I've shut in a box for weeks. I've been afraid of reopening it. Afraid of what would happen if I did and then I could never see her again. I lied to Mara. I don't not feel anything, I feel *everything* when it comes to Freya, and these weeks of not knowing if she was alive have been torture. I blame myself for not keeping my guard up. I let my feelings for her get in the way of my judgement, which has led us to this point.

But even punishing myself doesn't change the fact that when Freya's around, life seems brighter. She gives it a meaning and a purpose besides chasing the monsters that come after us in the night.

I love being with her. I love being around her.

I love her.

The thought hits me like a sledgehammer to the chest. There's no coming back from it.

I drain my drink and look at Mara through glazed eyes. "I think I need another drink."

***

Josie

Everyone makes mistakes. Vegas is mine.

Before I realize it, I'm too far in, struggling to keep my head above the surface.

Each day I hide from a figure in black. Each night I dance to hundreds of shadows under the bright stage lights.

"Want some?" asks Eve, perching on the edge of my dressing table, waving a bag of coke in my face. Like she does every night, she's wearing red. Apparently, it makes the men hornier, and she gets better tips.

"No," I answer. "But I'll take some vodka."

She disappears and I focus on trying to finish my make-up with a shaky hand. It never gets any easier. Hence the vodka.

"Are you sure everything's okay?" she asks, returning with a huge bottle. I grab it from her and unscrew the cap, drinking it like water before offering it back. She shakes her head. "It's yours. You look like you need it. Sure you don't want a line?" My grimace is her answer.

I watch as she shakes a small pile of powder onto the dresser. She lines it up with a card that appears out of nowhere, then leans over and snorts it like a pro. I don't judge. As I suspected when we first met, there's nothing mild about her dependency, and after our shift one night, she clarified why. Her ex-husband's fist wasn't the only too happy part of him, even when she said no.

When I asked her why coke, she replied, "Everyone has a place they need to escape to. This helps me get to mine."

None of the other girls have pushed to know my story. We're kindred spirits, literally dancing around each other, doing what we can to avoid our pasts. Weirdly, in the six weeks I've been here, I've felt more accepted than I've ever felt before. We don't need to know each other's details. The fact we're here says enough.

"You know I'm here anytime you need me." Eve stands to leave, but before she goes, throws the bag of powder down on the dresser. "For when the vodka isn't enough."

Her performance is next, mine after, meaning I have five minutes to spare. I pass the time drinking more vodka than I should and giving my appearance a final once-over. Shrugging one of the silver bra straps up my shoulder, I barely recognize myself. It's looser than a few weeks ago. The cups billow at the front and my cheeks look almost as hollow. Eve lets me stay at her place with a discount, but the money doesn't go far.

One of the girls called in sick earlier and, with dollar signs in my hopeful eyes, I found myself volunteering. An hour later, I'm three dances down and wobbling on skyscraper heels with more tips than I made in the whole of last week. Maybe things are looking up after all. I take a breather in the dressing room and eye up the vodka again. I hate it, but the alcohol masks the humiliation.

As I wipe my mouth with the back of my hand, another girl gives me a concerned look.

"Bella, we need you out there again," someone calls from outside the dressing room. I carry on touching up my make-up, oblivious. "Bella." The owner of the voice taps me on the shoulder. "Bella."

I look at them through the mirror. "Sorry." I smile. "Daydream."

I stand and make my way on stage, shielding my eyes from the bright lights. The music starts, but I stop. Apparently, you can have too much of a good thing, because I'm so wasted I'm struggling to remember my routine.

Eve comes to my side. "Improvise," she whispers in my ear.

The beat vibrates through the floor, and my hands skim over my body. With each spin and drop, black dots fill my vision. When I crawl across the stage and flip my head up, I know I've drunk too much.

My eyes connect with a pair as dark as cocoa. One's I dream about every day.

And then I black out.

***

A wave of nausea hits me, and I bolt upright, looking around frantically.

"Bucket's on the floor."

I don't have a chance to analyze the situation I'm in, because vomit shoots up my throat and I lurch over the side of the bed, luckily finding my target. A few minutes of retching pass before I feel like I'm safe to sit and take in my surroundings. When I do, I almost pass out again.

"Evan?" I pinch myself. He's still in front of me, sitting in a chair in the corner of the dimly lit room. "What time is it?"

"Almost five ... AM." His voice comes out darker than I've ever heard it before.

My eyes widen, and I dive off the bed, searching for my things. "Shit!" I'm having heart palpitations at how badly I've messed up. Eugene Belmer and his partner in crime are the least of my worries right now.

Evan remains seated with his hands clasped in front of him. "Where are you going?"

"I have to get back to my shift!" I snap, panicking. I've heard enough rumors to never want to miss one.

"It's the early hours of the morning, Freya." He scans me up and down and I shrink in on myself, realizing I'm still wearing my 'uniform'. I never wanted him to see me this way. "You're not going anywhere. Not like this."

241

Folding my arms across my chest, I hold my head high, reminding myself that I'm here for a reason. A damn good one. "I don't have a choice."

He stands and moves toward me. Suddenly, he's so close, nothing in my head makes sense. "Dammit, Freya." The disappointment in his eyes has another wave of nausea surging through me.

"Where are my things?"

Evan reaches out and strokes a hand down my face, wiping what I'm almost certain is vomit away. He steps forward again and my heart stops. Why does he have to make me feel like this? He's making it so much harder to walk away, to remember why what I'm doing is right.

The door to the room rattles. Evan steps back at the same time it swings open, revealing a familiar raven-haired beauty with a tray of coffees and what looks to be a bag of clothing hanging from her arm.

"Oh good! You're awake!" Mara chirps.

Spotting my backpack down by the chair where Evan was sitting, I dart forward and grab it while he's distracted, then rush to the door, pushing past Mara. She grabs my arm before I can disappear.

"These are for you," she says quietly, her eyes focused on my face.

I've lost most of my dignity already, but I'm thankful she's helping me keep a grip on what little I have left. I take the bag from her without a word and leave them both behind.

Seventeen

Josie

The following night, I walk into the club hesitantly. I'm terrified of what the fallout will be. When I get to the dressing room, Eve's waiting by my dresser, wearing her usual red but extra sparkly today.

"Am I in trouble?"

"No. Your knight in shining armor saved the day."

"What?"

She smirks. "Some tall, dark hottie swooped in and got you before anyone else could. Stormed out with you in his arms like he owned the place. He came back ten minutes later, and went straight to one of the back rooms, pulled out a gun and threatened to out the club for dealing if anyone laid a hand on you." My mouth falls open. "Who is he?" asks Eve, dropping her voice.

The chatter from the girls in the background and the music filtering in from the club blocks our voices somewhat. I go to explain, then remember what Evan told me about not trusting anyone.

"No one." I fumble with my bag, the adrenaline of the past twenty-four hours still firing.

Eve doesn't accept my answer. "Old fuck buddy?"

The reference of Evan and fuck in the same sentence is too much for my already fragile nerves, and I drop my bag. The gun Evan gave me back in Montpelier slides across the floor and Eve's eyes widen in shock. She bends over and quickly puts it back in my bag, then bundles it into my arms.

"What the hell are you doing with a gun, Bella?" she hisses.

"It's nothing."

"Firearms are not nothing. *This* will get you into serious shit." She watches my bag as if she expects the gun to jump out and start firing itself.

"It's to keep me safe."

"I don't need to know," she says, holding up her hand. "But you can't bring it in here again. If the bosses find it, your safety won't be a worry anymore." Eve's eyes move away from my bag, and she straightens. Pushing her chest out, she gives whatever has caught her attention a satisfied look. "Although you might not need to worry, because your friend is back."

Evan.

I don't turn around. Instead, I focus on applying my make-up, as I'm already running late.

"Somebody enjoyed the show," says Eve when he walks over to us.

My stomach flutters at the sight of his frame behind me in the mirror. I finish applying a layer of foundation Eve gave me. It's a shade of orange that shouldn't be classed as a skin shade.

"Not really," says Evan.

"Last night wasn't our best," Eve admits. "We don't usually have dancers passing out on stage. Right, Bella?" She places a hand on my shoulder and squeezes hard.

"*Bella* wasn't fit to be on stage." Evan shoves a hand in one of his pant pockets and the movement causes his suit jacket to fall open. I catch a glimpse of his gun and start to sweat. One in the room is bad news, two means we're screwed.

"She was tired. It was a long night," Eve explains, playing with his tie. "I can give you a private performance to make up for it."

I don't get a chance to be jealous, because Evan grabs her hand and places it down by her side. "That won't be necessary. Strippers aren't my thing."

Every pair of eyes in the room focuses on the three of us. Only the clink of glasses and chatter from the club can be heard. My pulse starts to race. I'm already in trouble and him making comments like that isn't going to help matters.

"We're dancers, not strippers," says Eve, a coldness to her voice I haven't heard before.

"Right," chuckles Evan, poking the bear with a stick. "Whatever you say."

Eve tuts and spins on her heel, strutting away.

I turn in my seat and look up at Evan. "What the hell was that?"

"I'm here to take you home," he replies, his face unreadable.

I turn back to the mirror, pick up my eyeliner and apply a thick line around each eye before grabbing my mascara. "I am home."

His brows draw together and his jaw ticks. "Last night proved you're not even safe with yourself right now."

Ignoring the sting, I say what I hope will have him turning and walking out the door. My heart aches as the words leave my lips, because it's the last thing in the world I want him to do. "You don't need to babysit me. You can leave. You're off the hook."

Pushing him away is the only answer, because the second we start to discuss this like adults, I'll follow him out the door, and following close behind will be a figure in black, ready to kill us both. I'm biding my time until the end, because it's coming, and neither of us can stop it. I'm terrified of death, not just for myself, but for everyone around me.

He crouches down and stares at me through the mirror. "Your mom has been worried sick, and your brother. They miss you."

I wait for him to say, 'I miss you', but it never comes.

A flurry of noise travels along the corridor. I spin around at the same time Evan does, and five bouncers charge into the dressing room. A large man in an expensive suit follows them, his movements slow and controlled. I've only met him once when I first interviewed for the job, and I'm grateful I haven't seen him since.

Flanked by his crew, he points at Evan. "You need to leave. I put up with your shit last night, but I won't do it again. Out."

Panic explodes in my chest. Evan looks down, his eyes pleading, "Come with me."

I shake my head and glance at the crowd behind him. There's no way they'll let me go, not until I complete the contract I signed.

Evan's expression turns grim, and he says under his breath, "I can't fight for you if you're not willing to fight for yourself."

"I won't ask yo—"

"I'm leaving!" snaps Evan without an ounce of fear. He shrugs the guards off when they go to grab hold of him. "I can see myself out."

The room empties and when they're out of earshot, one of the girls whistles through her teeth.

"Honey, I would not be letting that man leave without me by his side."

"I don't have a choice," I sigh.

She swipes some gloss across her mouth, then smashes her lips together, finishing with a pop. "We always have a choice."

Her words are like the sun breaking through the clouds on an overcast day. I stare at my reflection, taking in my bloodshot eyes and cheap make-up. My hair hangs limp, and even with the orange foundation, my complexion is sallow.

If you fear death, you can't win. It will be in control. You can't stop it from coming. To not fear death, you need to accept that it's inevitable. When you do, the power is in your hands.

I make a choice. If I'm going, I refuse to let it be in this hellhole. I stand, pick up my bag from the floor and hook it over my shoulders, then pull up the zipper on my jacket, making sure I'm as covered as possible. I scurry out of the dressing room and down the corridor before anyone has a chance to ask me what I'm doing. Turning left, instead of my usual right, I find the group of guards congregated in front of the back exit.

"He's in the dressing room!" I shriek. "He has a gun!"

Luckily, none of them are bright, and they race past me. I'm through the fire door and halfway along the dark alleyway when I hear one of them scream from inside the building to go after me.

I sprint away from the club. My feet pound against the hard concrete; the street ahead in sight. When I reach it, it's somewhat of a relief to be out in the open. Shouts approach from behind and I decide I need crowds. I turn right, pumping my arms back and forth, trying to move faster, my bag slamming against my back. At the end of the block, I make another sharp right and then another, looping back on myself.

Straight onto Fremont Street.

It's a risk passing the front of the club, but tourists have flooded the place. The glare of the neon lights from each side makes my hands change color. The LED canopy overhead, filled with moving images, reflects against my face. I can't decide which is worse, being hidden where no one would ever know I'd disappeared, or being lit up like a Christmas ornament for everyone to see. As I dart through the crowds, people jump out of my way. I can still hear the guards behind me, but as we delve deeper into the chaos, the gap between us increases. Lactic acid pools in my muscles; the burn becomes unbearable. Cramp threatens to take over. I push harder.

Do not stop, no matter what.

My lungs feel incapable of drawing in enough oxygen. Sweat runs down my back. I'm almost at the end. The darkness of the night gets closer with each stride, but the guards aren't backing down. I pray the detour has fatigued them as I dart over the threshold of Fremont Street and hang a left.

A block of buildings in the distance become my target. I focus on nothing but them. Then, suddenly, I'm being dragged sideways. I go to scream, but a hand slams over my mouth. Another moves around my middle, skimming against the exposed skin of my midriff where my jacket has risen. I'm about to bite down, but sandalwood and citrus make me stop.

"Shh, it's just me," whispers Evan, pulling us back into an alleyway. "Stay quiet."

He moves further into the shadows, but it's not enough, because darkness is never truly dark in Vegas. The guards are about to race past and they're going to see us. I hear them approaching, and as their voices get louder, my pulse picks up its pace. Evan must see the wild panic in my eyes, because he pins me against the wall and the bricks bite the skin on my back through my jacket.

"You can trust me," he murmurs, placing his right arm against the wall next to my head.

He leans down, tilts his head to the side and his mouth seals with mine. The world slips away and just a single brush of his lips has me forgetting the fear, too focused on the little flame that's sparked inside me—a light in the darkness. Somewhere in the distance, I hear the guards. Their voices get terrifyingly close, but are replaced with the sound of wolf whistles as they pass by.

I barely register what's happening, too focused on one thing. Evan, and the fact he's kissing me. But the kiss isn't the kind I would expect from him. His lips are gentle; his movements soft. It isn't a real kiss. He's protecting me from the world, but I don't want him to be my shield. The next time he kisses me, I don't want it to be a performance. I want him to kiss me like his life depends on it, like the world would end if he didn't show me how he felt through the touch of our skin. That's if he feels that way at all. As far as *we're* concerned, Evan is still a closed book. Unfortunately for me, the butterflies swarming my stomach make it perfectly clear that the weeks we've spent apart have done nothing to dull how I feel about him.

Silence lingers around us, signaling the guards are gone, for now. Evan pulls away, and for a second, his eyes linger on my lips. I want to lean back in and finish what we've started, but make it so much more. The moment disappears when he blinks away whatever is playing on his mind.

"Where do you live? We need to go back and pack your bags."

"There's nothing to pack. I'm good to go." I smile, trying to lighten the seriously depressing moment where I reveal how shit things really have been, in case he wasn't aware when I was spewing up my guts in barely any clothing.

"Why are you making this so easy?" Evan asks with a frown.

"I never should have left," I admit.

"I never wanted to," my mind screams.

Everything that has happened in my life has always felt out my hands, but this, me being here with Evan right now, is my choice. Not one forced by my circumstances.

With a swift nod, he pulls out his phone, tapping the screen a few times before slipping it back away. "Come on."

My stomach sinks at the thought of leaving Eve without so much as a goodbye. But I know if she were here, she'd tell me to get away while I can. I also know this isn't the first time she's done this dance, and there will be more after me, dancing in the light, hiding from the dark.

He walks in the opposite direction of the way he dragged me into the alley, and I follow. We're almost at the end when a car pulls up. Evan opens the back passenger door and I climb inside.

As we leave Vegas, the words, *we always have a choice*, play on repeat in my mind.

This is my choice. I'm ready to fight, and I want to do it with Evan by my side.

***

Evan

Around an hour into the journey, Freya is fast asleep. Not surprising, considering it's the middle of the night.

"You sure you're okay driving?" I ask as we fly along Route 66. There's nothing enjoyable about the journey; no tourist sights to take in, being that it's pitch black out.

"I'm a night owl, didn't you know?" Mara replies to the desert through the window screen.

I'll be the first to admit it's eerie as fuck, driving through in the dark like we are. It feels like we're soaring straight into a black hole of nothingness and I'm trying not to read too much into it—trying to ignore the niggling thought in my brain that maybe we really are. Occasionally, the headlights catch on a wild animal darting across the road, or a cactus at the side. It's the stars above that are something else, and I find myself more than once being all poetic and astounded by their beauty.

Mara breaks the silence when she says, "I'll book a flight back to DC for tomorrow night."

"I was thinking maybe you could book a room close by, 'til we're ready to leave."

With her hands squeezing the steering wheel tight, she looks at me briefly, like I've lost my mind. "And why would you want me to do that?"

I shrug and gaze out the window. "We're partners. And right now, I need my partner's help."

Mara grins and opens her mouth to say something, but Freya starts to move behind us. We both still.

The slight movements turn into thrashing and then she cries out, "No. No! Please, no! Stop!"

I turn around at the same time she bolts upright, eyes wide and wild, yet vacant.

"Pull over," I say to Mara, and she does as I ask without missing a beat.

Ignoring a howl from somewhere in the distance, I climb out, slam the door, and climb into the back. Freya is still sitting looking lost. I don't care that Mara is in the front, about to witness what I do next, because apparently, she knows more about me than I do myself, if our conversation on the plane is anything to go by.

Reaching forward, I gently pull Freya toward me, swallowing over the lump that forms in my throat for what I'm about to say next. Because the person sitting beside me isn't Freya Becket, it's the little girl who lost herself the night she stopped a monster to save one of the people she loved the most.

Stroking a hand carefully over her hair, I tuck her trembling body into my side. Her body relaxes into mine when I drop my head, pressing my lips to hair and murmur, "Shh, Josie. I've got you."

Mara pulls back onto the road without a word and around the fourteenth 'I've got you', Freya's nightmares are replaced with dreams, and she settles peacefully with her head in my lap.

***

Josie

The sun filtering through a crack in the curtains wakes me. I sit up, scrubbing my eyes. Panic sets in when I look around, not recognizing anything. The last thing I remember is leaving Vegas in the back of a black SUV with Mara and Evan in the front.

The room I'm in is huge, with a king sized, perfectly positioned bed overlooking the ocean. There's something about how everything has its own place, like back in Montpelier, which makes me believe wherever we are now, this is Evan's room.

I spend a few minutes taking everything in before getting up in the same clothing from the night before. There are two doors along the wall to the left of the bed. I go for the one closer to the floor to ceiling windows, hoping it will be a bathroom. Luck's on my side and I sit, taking in the bath which sits beside another huge window overlooking the ocean, while on the toilet.

When I'm done, I open the other door and walk out into a modern hallway. There's lots of glass and lots of white; it's incredibly beautiful. Nerves swirl in my stomach as I make my way down a set of floating, dark wooden stairs, remembering how Evan said he grew up in Santa Monica. Judging by the pier I caught in the distance, that's where we are. Which also means we're in his parents' home. For someone who doesn't do personal, it doesn't get more personal than this.

The smell of eggs is my path and I wander through the house using my nose to guide me. When I get to the kitchen, I stand hesitantly in the doorway, finding Evan next to a much older woman at a central island which puts ours in Silver Spring to shame. I watch them chatting quietly for a while as they're oblivious to my presence, then take the time to absorb the incredible kitchen. It even has a rack which comes down from the ceiling. A selection of copper pans hangs from it; the kind I could only dream about owning.

"Hey, Sleepyhead," says Evan, drawing my attention away from the pans. The playfulness of his words throws me. Evan doesn't do playful, like ever, and the fact he's doing so in front of the person I think is his mother is even more mind blowing.

"Hey," I reply quietly.

"I don't bite," says the woman at his side. I take that as my cue to move further into the kitchen.

She walks around the island, meeting me on the other side, holding out her hand. "Kate Price."

I take it, expecting her grip to be firm like her words, but her touch is gentle, reassuring. I wonder how much Evan has told her about the strange young woman standing in her kitchen.

"Freya," I reply. Her eyes flicker in a way that tells me she knows exactly who I really am, but she doesn't say anything.

She doesn't look at all like Evan, not that she would being that he's adopted. Kate reminds me of a younger Meryl Streep, like the one in The Devil Wears Prada, with short, white, gray hair, piercing blue eyes and cheekbones that mean business.

When I chuckle to myself while glancing around the room again, Evan asks, "What's so funny?"

"Everything is very white." That sounded more logical in my head. Evan arches a brow in amusement, and I feel the need to explain. "You're the last person I would expect to grow up in a white home, you know, 'cause of the whole dark suits, broody face thing you have going on. I was expecting more gothic mansion."

"Well, you did reference me to *Twilight*, not *The Vampire Diaries*."

"Well, dip me in mustard and call me a hotdog. How do you know the difference between the two?"

Evan shrugs, and Kate throws her head back and laughs at the two of us. "I like this one. You should keep her around."

"Mom," Evan says, grinding his teeth as a faint blush creeps across his cheeks.

"I've made breakfast," says Kate, oblivious to the embarrassment she's caused her son.

She picks up a pan from one of the hobs and places it in front of me.

"Mom makes mean eggs," confirms Evan when he catches me drooling over the contents of the pan.

"I can see," I say eagerly. I can't remember the last time I ate something that didn't come out of a packet with a four-year shelf life. My stomach growls, and it's all I can do not to snatch the pan up and inhale them in a second.

"They're all yours," says Kate. "Sourdough or spelt?" I give her a confused look. "Toast."

Of course, they have a selection of bread. I bet they have gluten-free as well. This home is what my dreams are made of. I'm hit with guilt, remembering my mom and her simple waffles, always served with a healthy dose of love. That's the real dream, being with her, safe. I need to ask Evan if she's okay, but I don't want to do it with Kate around.

"Sourdough, please."

As if she can read my mind, Kate goes to leave the room. "Evan will make your toast. I have a couple of things I need to do."

When we're alone, I wait until the bread has popped up from the toaster before I broach the subject.

Clearing my throat, I ask, "Is my mom okay?" Evan doesn't answer. "Don't lie to me."

"As well as can be expected, considering she thought you were dead." His face twists as if he's in pain. "Freya we al—"

He doesn't get a chance to finish whatever he's going to say, because Mara barrels in with bags upon bags. Evan butters my toast while she walks over to me.

"These," she grins, "are for you."

I frown. "Me? Why?"

"You have no clothes, silly," she laughs. My expression softens. There's something about her which draws me in. If I ever had an older sister, I think she'd be like Mara.

Evan loads a plate up with toast and eggs and slides it across the counter before opening a drawer and grabbing a fork. He walks around the island, following his mother's footsteps, only he stops at my side, close, with the fork in his hand. His head drops and his lips are so close he could press them to my skin without barely moving. Such a simple action draws a riot of emotions from me, and my cheeks burn, knowing Mara is right next to us, witnessing whatever the hell is going on.

I fight to hold back a shiver when his breath tickles my temple. "You okay if I leave you with Mara for a few minutes? I need to make a call."

All I'm capable of doing is nodding. One corner of his mouth lifts, the side with the dimple which is now forming on his cheek. And then he's gone, and I instantly wish he was back.

Mara clears her throat, drawing my attention to her. "As I was saying, these are for you."

She shakes the bags, but I'm too tired to explore what's inside, so instead I ask, "How did you know what I'd like?"

"I didn't. I was sent with a very specific list." She bends over and starts rummaging around in the bags, huffing when she can't find what it is she wants. Eventually, she rights herself and waves a box in the air. "Here you go. I thought maybe you'd like a change from the black. You know, a fresh start."

Staring at the box of hair dye in her hands, I don't need to ask how she knew which to pick.

I smile to myself. Never once have I told Evan my favorite color is purple.

***

Early afternoon, I walk back downstairs with freshly dyed hair and brand-new clothing, which is on the roomy side. Something which becomes apparent won't be an issue when I make my way into the kitchen and find Kate preparing another spread while Mara works intently at her laptop. At the rate Kate's cooking, I'll be rolling out of here.

I groan when I've demolished three plates, leaning back against the stool. "That was amazing. Thank you."

"No problem," says Kate. "You're welcome anytime. I'm just sad we're leaving. Evan's father and I have a trip booked to Mexico."

"It's fine. I'll be out of your hair later anyway," I reply.

Mara snickers and Kate laughs. "Not if Evan has anything to say about it." I give her a confused look. "He's taken some vacation time," she explains. "I don't think he plans on you leaving anytime soon."

Evan and vacation are two words I never thought I'd hear in the same sentence. He's the epitome of a workaholic.

"Oh? Right," I stammer, not sure what else to say. Kate starts clearing some of the plates away and I jump down from my stool. "I'll do this. You've done enough."

I grab my plate and go to scrape it in the trash can when she shouts, "Freya, no!"

257

It's too late. I've already opened it and seen what's inside. I suck in a sharp breath, staring at the huge bunch of lilies laying on the top.

"I'm so sorry," she babbles, coming beside me. "They're my favorite. As soon as you got here, Evan made me throw them away. I should have taken the trash out."

Like I suspected when we first met, she knows my history.

Even though my heart is hammering in my chest, I say, "It's fine." Mara watches me, concerned. I try to smile at them both, but all my lips manage to do is form a tight, flat line. I'm ready to escape up to my room when I clock the wraparound terrace facing the ocean, just outside the dining area. "Do you mind if I go outside?"

"Of course not," says Kate.

I feel both her and Mara watching me as I walk toward the terrace. When I open one of the doors and step out, I take in a deep breath, filling my lungs with warm, salty air. I head straight over to the rails and rest my arms on top, watching a family playing in the sand. After a couple of minutes, I close my eyes and tilt my chin up at the sky, enjoying the afternoon sun warming my skin. Then, all I do is listen. Waves break against the sand and laughter floats on the breeze from the pier further along the beachfront.

Without opening my eyes, I know Evan is near me. "I haven't been to the beach since we moved from Jacksonville. I forgot how much I missed it, and the endless skies. I used to play games with my mom, imagining what was on the other side of the ocean. Before the figure started reappearing, we'd have whole days, from first thing in the morning, and not come home till it was late, living off hot dogs and ice cream."

"They sound like good memories," he replies.

I remain standing with my eyes closed. "Michael got burnt once when he refused to put lotion on and walked around with shade marks on his face for weeks." I snicker. "He spent each day after that lying outside with one of those foil things women in the eighties movies used to have."

I start to laugh so hard my stomach hurts, remembering how ridiculous he looked and how pissed he was every time I pointed it out. At some point, the laughter turns to tears. I can't open my eyes; I don't want to see Evan's face. He pulls me against him, his arms tightening around me.

When he rests his chin on my head, I cry harder. "I miss them. I'm sorry," I sob into his chest. "I'm so sorry."

He pulls back and lifts my chin. I pull down my sleeve and wipe the snot away, trying not to think about how gross I must look after my spell of ugly crying.

"Why did you leave, Freya?"

"You said it was me he wanted. I thought everyone would be safer if I wasn't around. I was trying to protect you all. Sometimes I think everyone would be better off if I weren't here at all."

Evan lets out a strangled breath and presses his forehead to mine. "We all ..." Stopping to correct himself, as he does, his body tenses. "I thought you were dead," he croaks. "Don't ever disappear on me like that again." Pulling back, his eyes hold mine. "Please. I can't go through it again."

Taking a page out of Evan's book, I don't reply, deciding not to make a promise I can't keep.

If it meant I could keep him safe, like I expect he would do for me, I'd disappear again.

But that isn't the reason I don't promise.

Unfortunately, what he's asking from me, I don't think I have any say over. My fate has most likely already been decided.

Eighteen

Evan

With Freya napping peacefully up in my room, I call Hewson from out on the deck. "Is she safe?" he answers.

"For now," I reply, unable to keep the tension from my voice. "Any developments?" Hewson doesn't answer straight away, and his silence is unnerving.

I scowl at the ocean. "What aren't you telling me?"

The door opens behind me, and Mara steps out looking pale. Whatever he's about to tell me, she already knows.

"We got the DNA results on the other body."

I hold my breath. "And?"

"The second body is Eugene Belmer."

Well, damn. I wasn't expecting that. My brain instantly kicks into action, trying to figure out what this new cluster fuck of information means.

Mara rests her arms on the rail beside me, and I set the call to speakerphone. "Mara's here."

"Hi," she says with less finesse than normal, clearly shaken by the news. Usually she's an optimist, even with those who don't deserve her optimism. A few more years in the bureau will stamp it out of her.

We all remain silent; the weight of Hewson's words hanging thick in the air and tainting every beautiful thing around us. Eugene Belmer is dead. Dead, as in, not living anymore. Dead, as in, will be buried in the ground, no longer able to kill innocent women. Widows who were never able to mourn in peace. He fucking deserves his ending, but the moment is bittersweet, because it means the case has become more complicated than any of us could have predicted.

"I guess Michael Becket's shot in New York was fatal," I say.

"Looks like it," agrees Hewson. "Why would whoever was working with him hide it?"

"Because they didn't want us to know," I reply, then pause. "If Belmer did die that night in New York, that means he wasn't around the night Freya went missing."

Mara watches me, brows drawn together.

"What's your point?" asks Hewson.

"My point is, we had two incidents at exactly the same time, in different states, hours away from each other. Which means if there's no Belmer, there has to be someone else involved."

"Three killers?" asks Mara, looking skeptical.

"No," I reply. "I don't think so."

"Then what are you suggesting?" asks Hewson.

"That our cat has some mice he's playing with."

***

I spend an hour making plans for the next few days with Mara and Hewson. We all agree Freya needs time out before I take her to Jacksonville. We moved her mother there to be reunited with her brother right after she went missing. He has a tighter security

262

system than what the bureau has to offer right now thanks to how stretched our resources are. I haven't told Freya yet, though. I don't want to overwhelm her with the news of a grand reunion.

When we're finished on the call, Mara decides to go down to the beach before the sun starts to set, and I go inside, expecting to find Freya awake. When I don't find her in the dining area of the kitchen, I make my way to the sitting area, my heart rate picking up a notch when I find she isn't there either.

"She's still sleeping," calls my mom from her office.

"Thanks," I walk in, finding her sitting at her desk, working at her laptop, glasses perched on the end of her nose. "I was just checking."

"You were worried," she replies, reading something on her screen. Awards fill the walls behind her, won by the private law firm she and my father run. They're known for their work in the community, and after my rocky start in life, they made it their mission to take on more pro-bono cases than any company in the state.

"I wa—"

"Worried," she repeats. Her eyes move away from the screen. "Are you sure you don't want us to stay?"

"I think we could both do with the space and some time to just breathe."

"Okay." She stares at me.

"Yes?"

"How do you plan to navigate your position with how you feel about her?"

My stomach twists. Of course, she knows. She's more perceptive than Mara, and she knows me better than anyone. "Is it that obvious?"

"I saw the two of you on the terrace. You showed more emotion with her than I've seen you do with anyone."

I find myself going backward. It's my go-to reaction. Saying no and not putting my heart on the line feels safe. "It can't happen."

"If she means what I think she does to you, you'll find a way."

She stands and walks around her desk to the door.

"I'd lose what I've worked for," I say to her empty chair.

She leaves me to reflect on her final words. "Evan, sometimes in life we have to lose something to gain everything in return."

***

Josie

I can hear a voice, faint from somewhere, but I can't quite grasp it. My eyes flutter open and I find Evan perched on the edge of the bed.

He scans my face. "You good?"

The warm cocoon I've made in the blankets has me smiling, content. "I'm good."

He carries on watching me, before shaking his head and breaking himself from whatever he's thinking. Turning away, he grabs something from beside him on the bed. He hands over a box and my eyes widen when I take in the image of the newest iPhone, which has probably cost him a fortune, along with everything else he had Mara buy me earlier.

"I ordered this. You left your old one behind, and it's safer to have a new one, anyway."

"I have money. I can pay you back." I don't know why I feel so embarrassed about him buying me things, but it draws something out of me. A feeling of not being able to look after myself and stand on my own two feet.

"I don't want it," he refuses. "They're a gift."

I open my mouth to argue with him, but stop when I see guilt swimming in his eyes.

What does he have to feel guilty about?

Reaching over, he tucks a piece of rogue purple hair behind my ear. "I shouldn't have said what I did. That you were the reason Belmer was around."

He blames himself for me leaving.

"Evan, I—"

"If you died, I never would have forgiven myself."

Something akin to torture crosses his face as he gazes at me. I recognize it, because for years it's the same kind of look my mother wore whenever she watched me or talked about Michael. That's the thing about misplaced blame directed at oneself. It knows no rhyme or reason. When the seed is planted, it festers and clouds your judgement, warping every truth there is. How Evan must be feeling right now is probably similar to how I felt when I left Montpelier, and that was a very dark place to be—one I don't plan on letting him visit.

"Turn around." He frowns at me. "I need to get out of bed, and I have no pants on."

Heat flashes through his eyes, and they drop to my lips just for a second, before he blinks and turns away. I climb out from under the covers and quickly pull my jeans on before walking over to my backpack. I pull out a small piece of paper, tucked safely away in the very bottom next to my gun.

When I walk back over and go to pass it to him, he eyes it warily. "What's this?"

"The reason I left," I reply.

He straightens his back and opens it. His face remains emotionless. It's Agent Price reading, not Evan. The only telltale sign of how he feels about the words on the paper is when he cracks his neck.

"Yes, your words hit close to home," I admit, "but I had no intention of leaving. Not until I got this."

"When did you get it?"

"Literally the night I left. I ran. I didn't know what else to do."

"Rogers and Grey's car exploded," he says.

My stomach drops. "Oh my God, are they okay?"

"Rogers spent some time in the hospital, but he's recovering." His eyes stay focused on the paper.

"I heard something when I was running. I didn't know it was them. If I had, I'd have gone back."

"You did the right thing. This and the lily prove that."

He looks up and my breathing falters at what I see in his brown eyes. Suddenly, I want to climb over him, push him back into the bed and forget our realities. I want to hide away and pretend we could be together. It's a silly fantasy, considering I don't even know how he really feels about me.

"Thank you for the phone, and everything else," I say, needing a break from the current subject and the feelings his eyes are drawing from me.

Evan doesn't let up. He's one big ball of intensity when he stands. "I'm sorry for something else."

He sucks every bit of oxygen from my lungs when he steps into my personal space. "What?" The word comes out raspy, betraying me and giving away everything I'm thinking.

Cupping my jaw with his large hand, his thumb pulls down on the bottom lip I didn't know I was biting, and his eyes remain lasered there.

"For making the alley our first kiss." He leans in and presses his mouth to the edge of mine. The small flame I felt last time was nothing compared to the fire now roaring through my veins. "I promise when I kiss you next, you'll forget everything about the last one."

With that, Evan steps back, leaving no more uncertainty in my mind as to whether he wants me.

***

Evan

Heart pounding so hard my ears ring, I make my way back downstairs.

I could have kissed her, but I didn't. It wasn't the right moment, and I meant what I said. The next kiss we have, I want it to be her first. Next time, I want to erase every feeling she's ever had for anyone else, and with just my lips against hers, embed myself so deep inside her heart she'll never be able to feel for anyone the way I want her to feel about me.

Avoiding my feelings for her has proven to be a losing game. I never should have gotten on the board, because I never stood a chance, not when green eyes like hers make me forget who I am and everything I was before she walked back into my life. The next time I kiss her, I want to make her feel about me the way I feel about her. I want there to be no uncertainty; something I can't do with my parents and Mara sitting in the kitchen.

Back on the ground floor, I follow the sound of chatter into the kitchen, finding Mara sitting at the island with my mom and dad on the other side.

"You look a lot brighter," smiles my mom off to my side. "And I love the hair color."

Feeling Freya behind me before I see her, the hairs on the back of my neck raise in awareness.

"Thanks," she replies with a hint of shyness. "Evan picked it."

"I bet he did," Mom hums. I'm surprised she doesn't wink. She isn't known for being subtle. "This is Evan's father, Owen."

Dad walks over to Freya and offers out his hand, beaming. "It's nice to meet you, Freya."

"It's great to meet you too," she replies, shaking his hand.

When the formalities are done, she sits next to Mara at the island and my parents chat between themselves. Standing on the outside, it's hard to grasp the situation we've found ourselves in. But despite every fucked up thing that's brought us to this point, I feel content for the first time in a long, long time.

"I'm sorry we have to go," says my mom. "We've got a late flight to catch. If we'd known earlier that you were coming, we'd have cancelled our trip."

And that's the reason I didn't tell them. I love my parents, but them third-wheeling on what little time I have with Freya isn't appealing.

"It's fine, Mom," I say. "Go. Have fun."

She twiddles her hands in front of her, looking like the last thing she wants to do is leave. "The fridge is full and if you need anything el—"

"Mom, seriously." I all but push her out of the room. "Go."

"Okay," she replies reluctantly.

My dad grabs their things and they both say goodbye to Mara and Freya. I walk them to the front door and give my mom a swift kiss on the cheek.

"Remember what I've taught you," she says.

I wiggle my eyebrows. "Always practice safe sex?" I receive a swat around the head, but her eyes shine with amusement.

She turns back when my dad is out of earshot and drops her voice. "When all you're surrounded by is darkness, remember who you are and what you're fighting for. Let it be your light."

With a swift nod, I shut the front door, staring at the white wood for a few seconds, digesting what she said.

And then there were three.

I turn, trying to figure out a polite way I can get rid of Mara for the next couple of days, but she's behind me and I almost jump out of my skin.

"Christ, a little warning next time," I snap.

She chuckles. "Whatever. I'm out of here. Thanks for the hotel room. I have a date with a bottle of wine and a movie."

Before she leaves, something hits me. "Mara, wait." She turns back. "I know we're technically on vacation, but I was wondering if you could do something over the next few days?"

"Shoot."

"Look into any people who might have had personal ties with Eugene Belmer. Family members, close friends, old work colleagues."

"Sure, why?"

"The murders while Freya was missing have a different meaning now we know he's dead. That's why the MO didn't fit them, because it wasn't Belmer's. But if our new unsub has personal ties to him, then the motives could be worse."

Her jaw tenses. "Hell hath no fury like someone scorned."

"Right," I say, choosing not to correct her.

But she's right, and this has the potential to turn into more of a massacre than it already is. Unlike with Belmer, whose actions were always pre-measured and precise, revenge fuels something deeper, and the person we're dealing with could become more volatile than they already are, lashing out at anything in their path.

There's a likelihood whoever it is we're after won't stop until we're all in hell beside them.

***

Josie

I hear the front door close and wait. Evan's footsteps pad into the room and my pulse quickens with each one. My heart is in my throat by the time he's standing in front of me.

"So ..." I say, cringing inside at how awkward I sound.

"So ..." echoes Evan, the corners of his mouth lifting. "Mom's right, the purple suits you."

Heat covers the back of my neck. "Thanks."

"Hungry?" After how he left things in the bedroom, all I'm capable of doing is nodding like one of those dogs you see on the dashboard of cars sometimes. If I look ridiculous, Evan doesn't comment on it. "We can order in, or I can see what I can scrape together?"

I sit a little straighter. "I could cook?"

"Really?"

"Yeah!" I'm dying to cook something. I haven't touched a pan since leaving Montpelier, and it feels like something is missing in my life without it.

Evan smiles and steps to the side, revealing the cooker. "Be my guest."

I race over to the fridge with a little squeal. Excited is an understatement for how I'm feeling, even more so when I open the fridge. I gaze at the contents. It's so full I'm surprised it hasn't burst open. "What's it all for?"

"Mom got carried away when you were sleeping this morning."

Glancing over my shoulder, I recall the time in Montpelier he burnt porridge to a pan so bad we had to throw it out and had the windows open for days despite it being sub-zero outside. The memory is burned into my brain after having Grey bitch and moan the entire time, while walking around dressed like he was ready to trek across the Arctic.

"And *you* were planning on cooking?" I ask with an arched brow.

He rubs the back of his neck, causing his shirt to rise, revealing enough taut skin to have my mouth running dry. "I was hoping you'd assist."

I laugh off my raging hormones and fill my arms with ingredients, spinning back around and dumping them on the counter before grabbing the utensils I need from the hangers on the wall. Evan reaches up and pulls down the copper pans I request, laughing when I grab hold of them and squeal again. I try to explain why they're so special, but all he does is comment on how ridiculously expensive they are. At some point, he turns on a playlist of all my favorite songs, and I dance while stirring the sauce I'm making to go with the pasta.

When the song gets to my favorite part, I spin around, using the spoon as a mic. Evan watches me with a weird look on his face.

"What?"

"Nothing," he mumbles.

Setting the spoon down, I walk around the island, then lean against the counter beside him. "Is everything okay?"

His shoulders sink. "I missed you. I missed this. Us, together like this."

I blink slowly at his admission, not wanting to believe what I'm hearing, to then be brutally disappointed when I find out it's a joke. Luckily for me, Evan rarely jokes, which is why I whisper, "There's an us?"

Deep brown eyes lock me in. They're the only dark things in the world I'd willingly lose myself in.

I don't get a chance to find out his reply, because he sniffs deeply. His eyes widen when he stares over at the cooker. "Your sauce is burning."

"Sorry, what?"

He points at the pan where gray smoke is rising. "Sauce. Burning."

"Crap!" I run over, finding the sauce burnt to the bottom of the pan. A quick taste test confirms it's inedible. Pouring a bit of water in to help cool it, I say, "I guess I'm rusty. Maybe you'd have been better cooking after all."

Evan grins. "I think there's some Swiss in the fridge."

I flick a spoonful of sauce at him without thinking. My mouth forms a shocked O when it lands on his forehead and trails a steady path down his nose, dripping onto his white t-shirt.

He jumps down from his stool and stalks around the counter, his mouth twisted in a playful smile. "That was a bit immature."

I smirk. "Sorry, Daddy."

His eyes fill with a promise of something that has an ache between my legs building. I'm a puddle, like the one forming at my feet when water pours over my head and in front of my eyes.

Evan places a now empty glass down on the counter. "I'd like a Swiss cheese sandwich waiting for when I get back."

"Asshole," I call after him, shoving sopping wet hair from my eyes.

Nighteen

Evan

When I return downstairs, there's no sign of a Swiss cheese sandwich. Or Freya.

What there is ... a pile of ingredients and a list of instructions how to make it. I could be a little pissed if it weren't for the sass spilling off the page in some of the little comments she's made, proving that after the past couple of months, she's still the Freya I know. As much as she might have seemed it in the photo Hewson presented me with before we found her, she's not lost.

Lying awake in one of the guest rooms, sleep refuses to come. I'm torn between wanting to reveal parts of myself I haven't to anyone and fucking her senseless for ruining one of my favorite shirts. There will be no fucking, I keep reminding myself, every time my mind starts to wander. She's more than just a quick round in bed.

A thud coming from the direction of Freya's room has me bolting out of the room and flinging open her door without a second thought. My chest tightens with panic as I take her in, sprawled face first across the floor. And then she giggles.

"Sorry, did I wake you?"

"No," I reply, omitting the not so minor detail that I've been up for hours thinking about her and was prepared to murder whoever I thought I might find in the room. Freya gets up, then contorts her body into a weird position, looking like a human pretzel. "Erm, what are you doing?"

"Yoga," she replies, as if it's a normal thing to be doing in the middle of the night.

"It's midnight."

"Fine," she lets out a long breath and sweeps her body into another position I didn't think was possible. "Midnight yoga."

And just like during the 'yes day', the clouds part and her sun shines through.

Midnight yoga. I roll my shoulders and somehow find my hands planted on the ground next to hers, struggling to get my body into the same position.

Freya's head turns toward me upside down, face red from acting against gravity. "What are you doing?"

"Joining in."

Her lips twitch. "You're doing it wrong."

"Is there a right way to do this shit?"

"Please don't cuss during yoga, Evan. It gives it the wrong vibe."

She manages to detangle herself, but I find myself well and truly stuck.

"Wow, you're really getting into it," she comments.

"I can't move."

Midnight yoga is a load of cr—

"Want some help?"

Embarrassment burns my cheeks, which I can thankfully pass off for hanging upside down too long. "Please."

Freya tries to untangle my legs at the same time I move my arm. I fall back, taking her with me, and hit the ground with a loud 'oof'. Laughter vibrates through me thanks to Freya's body being plastered against mine. She raises her head, purple hair falling in front of her face, and without thinking, I brush it away. I want to pull my hand back, but I can't. The skin on my palm burns and heat soars to parts of me I didn't know existed.

Her expression turns serious and emerald eyes pierce into me. "I was wrong the night I said I was lonely." She doesn't need to confirm which one, because every moment I've spent with her is etched clearly into my brain. "I'm never lonely when I'm with you."

The words 'I love you' flash through my mind, and my heart constricts. We've barely kissed, and it doesn't seem possible. But maybe that's why I've never fallen in love before, because there was never all the other stuff beyond the physical, not like with Freya. The moments you cherish with the right person and look back on, wondering how you functioned before them and how you'll ever function again if they're not there. I knew how I felt on the flight to Vegas. I just wasn't ready to accept it. I realize now though, it wasn't about accepting how I feel, it was about accepting how I'd feel if it all got ripped away, when there's a strong possibility it might. I'm screwed either way.

I glance over at the bed. "Fancy some company?"

The tinge of pink that creeps across her cheeks makes my stomach flip. "Sure."

When we've managed to scramble onto the bed, we both lie back flat, a good distance between us, staring up at the ceiling. "Want to see something cool?"

"Yeah."

"Turn out the lights." Freya hesitates. "I've got you."

Understanding flashes across her face, and she gives me a swift nod before reaching for the switch behind her. When we're lying in darkness, I reach down next to my bed, where I know I'll find what I'm searching for. Suddenly, the sound of mechanisms grinding fills the room. Clearly, it hasn't been used in a long time.

Freya laughs. "This isn't something kinky, right?" I roll my eyes. "Stop rolling your eyes."

The blinds above us finally retract back into the rest of the ceiling, revealing glass.

"I didn't even know it could do that. It's pretty cool." I know the moment it registers what I'm trying to show her, because a little gasp comes out. "Oh my God. It's beautiful."

Thankfully, it's a clear night, and the stars above us shine brightly, even with the glare of Santa Monica beneath. We lay in silence for a while, taking it all in, until I clear my throat, ready to tell her something no one knows apart from my parents and Hewson.

"There were complications after my birth mom had me." Freya tenses at my side. "After one too many operations, she was addicted to pain meds and pain meds led to everything else." I take a breath, ready to re-open the deep wound and reveal the festering flesh beneath all the badly healed scar tissue. "I was two the night she took me out to the store. She was so high she forgot me." A hand finds mine on the sheets, covers it and squeezes. The warmth of her skin against mine is like a soothing balm, making everything I'm telling her a little less painful. "We lived in the kind of neighborhood where everyone minded their own business, and I wandered the streets for hours until the cops picked me up. They found my mom the next day in an alleyway, beaten and stabbed to death. I was placed in the system but found a family quick. I was one of the lucky ones. I got dealt a good card.”

“Evan …”

“The reports said it was a crime of passion. An ex-lover or some shit like that. A string of murders identical to hers in the months after makes me believe it was otherwise.”

“You looked into her file?”

I nod up at the sky. “Until I knew the truth, I thought she didn’t want me. Kate and Owen didn’t want to tell me the truth until I was old enough, which is understandable. For years, I felt like I was unworthy of someone wanting me. I thought she’d just left, and that I was someone else’s second best. So, I pushed everyone around me out, kept things impersonal. There was a careers talk one day in school and there was an agent there from the FBI. His name was Hewson.” I chuckle. “He’s been a pain in my ass ever since.

“When I looked into my mom’s file, it sparked something inside me. It drove me to the unit I’m in now. I felt a need to protect others from what I went through. I wanted to prevent things from happening, not just solve cases. Then Hewson dropped your family’s file on my desk. I wanted to say no. There was something about it that hit too close to home.”

I pause and the stars twinkle above us.

“What happened to your mom … you could have been me. Which is why the day we first met, I made a promise to myself to keep you safe. You did what most wouldn’t have the courage to do. You fought back, Freya. You have so much fire, so much potential. You deserve the world and I promised myself I'd help you get it."

"I'm sorry." The sincerity behind those two words is blinding.

"Mom had this ceiling fitted at a time when I was really lost, and I didn't know what I wanted from my life. Whenever things felt like they were too much, she'd tell me to dump it into the universe, then reach for the stars that shine the brightest, because they're filled with the most promise. At the time, that was the FBI for me. My job is who I am. But now, sometimes I think it's not enough."

"Why?" Freya breathes.

When I tug her hand, she raises up from the bed and I pull her in, tucking her into my side. With her head on my chest, I rest my chin in her hair. Surrounded by wild rose and vanilla, I find the brightest star in the sky.

"Because I'm tired of being lonely."

***

Josie

Enveloped in warmth, I could stay asleep forever. Sadly, the sun blaring against my face, threatening to burn my skin if I don't move, has me stirring. But there's nothing sad about waking up when my face nuzzles against a firm chest, stirring the swarms of butterflies in my stomach that are never really asleep with him close by. I breathe in everything Evan, scared to open my eyes in case he disappears.

"Hey, Sleepyhead."

My eyes fly open, and I find him staring down at me, brown eyes bright, like he's been awake for hours. And then I remember last night. I remember everything he told me and how my heart broke a thousand times over for everything he never should have been through.

Awe. That's what I feel, looking up at the man watching me.

"Hey, Batman," I reply, because that's what he is, grumpy persona and all. I wouldn't change one part of him, because all those parts create the perfect mixture, filling the cracks in my heart, cementing it back together. I wince in the bright sunlight and glance up at the ceiling. "This was epic last night, but it's not very practical in the day."

Evan chuckles and the vibrations work their way into my chest, awakening a deep ache. If someone asked me what I'd want if I ever got to the end of what's happening, my answer would be that I just want him. I want every part of him. I never want to let him go. Staring up at the stars, when he told me he didn't want to be lonely anymore, my heart connected with his, and for one night, we let them dance together in the universe, where nothing could get in the way and ruin the beauty of what's become us.

"What are you thinking?"

"That I'm happy," I answer without thinking.

"Good," he hums.

We lay for a while. Not in a tense, awkward silence. An amicable one. One filled with understanding. Two kindred souls.

After a while, Evan clears his throat. "Go on a date with me."

I pull back and stare at him. "Seriously?"

"I mean, we can't leave the house, but yeah," he looks a little sheepish. "If you want to."

"I really want to."

His eyes move down to my lips and for a second, time stops.

While the world pauses and refuses to spin, I take in every part of him. Thick brows and tousled brown hair, sticking up in a way that would send him into a tailspin if he caught sight of it. Stubble lining his jaw that I wonder what it will feel like between my legs. And then there are his eyes. Eyes that, when he's happy, are a soft brown, warm like the colors of autumn, but darken and become a lifeless abyss when something threatening is around.

"I want you," I whisper, scared of saying it too loud, in case he doesn't feel the same way.

Heat pools in his eyes and I think he might kiss me. He doesn't though. Instead, he pushes me back against the bed, so my head settles in the pillows, and pulls back the sheets. His eyes roam over me, leaving heat everywhere, drinking in the exposed skin surrounding my black shorts and vest from midnight yoga.

I'm not sure when he became shirtless between now and last night, but I'm all for it—every perfectly defined part of him. It's mesmerizing watching each muscle in his arms and chest tense and flex with even the slightest movement.

And then my eyes settle on the only tattoo he has. A diamond sitting above his heart.

He looks at where my eyes are focused.

"What does it mean?"

"It's a reminder of someone special," he replies cryptically.

Briefly, my stomach twists, trying to second guess who it could be. My questions disappear as quickly as they appear when Evan sits upright. The sight of him in crumpled black sweatpants sitting low on his hips is something else. He leans back on his haunches and grasps my foot. His fingers press firmly against my flesh as he raises it in the air.

His lips skim the inside of my ankle and electricity sizzles beneath them. "I want this." When they skim the inside of my knee, I feel every single goosebump raise on my body. "This." His lips move higher, leaving a path of fire wherever they touch. Head hovering between my thighs, he watches me hungrily, then leans in, his stubble bites the soft skin on the inside of my thighs. He places a kiss against the material of my shorts, not close enough to the place I'm aching for him the most. "Definitely this." Then he stares at where my chest is rising and falling. He spreads himself over me, then drops his head and sucks one of my nipples over my sports bra, then moves over to the other to do the same. "These are a given."

I snort and start to laugh, stopping abruptly when my eyes meet with his again, and what I find steals the oxygen from my lungs.

"I want you, Josie. I want every part you're willing to give."

I freeze when he shifts, settling himself between my legs. "You called me the wrong name."

His nose strokes mine. "I called you the right name."

I shake my head. "I thought you didn't do personal."

Right before our lips brush, he says. "Well, *Josie*. I guess it's growing on me."

The kiss that follows is the one that should have been our first. It's not slow or languid. It's not soft or hesitant. Our lips clash, then mold together like they were created for this sole purpose. Evan's hand entwines in my hair and tugs down, causing my head to tilt and my mouth to open. Letting him in, our tongues dance in rhythm with our racing hearts. It's the kind of kiss you'd expect if the world were about to end. A kiss that sparks a fire, destroying anything in its path. Kissing him feels like the beginning of something great, with the risk of it being the end of everything before it.

And while my heart pounds so hard I think it might burst through my chest, I know that I'll never be able to feel about anyone, the way I feel about Evan.

***

Evan

I never want to move from this spot. If I could spend a lifetime with Josie's legs wrapped around me, just kissing like we are doing, I'd die happy. But we've been like this for well over an hour and it's becoming unbearable.

Each breathy moan against my lips is hard-wired to my dick. I'm trying to do what's right and take things slow, but the only thing my brain seems to think is right is exploring exactly what we've been missing out on. Slowly, I remind myself, fighting the urge to circle my hips, which proves a hard task when she presses her heels into my lower back and encourages them to grind into where they shouldn't.

Josie draws my bottom lip between hers and bites down.

Fuck this. I spring back, adjusting myself as I go. And what does she do? She smirks at me. It's infuriatingly hot and even though I didn't think it was possible, I get harder.

"I have some things I need to do." I lean back in and place a brief kiss on her lips. Anymore, and we'll be back where we started.

"Work?"

I kiss her again, lingering a second longer than the last. "I won't be long. I have a few other things I need to do as well."

"What time later?" The hesitation in her question tells me she feels the same as I do, like this isn't real and we're living in a dream.

"Five? In the kitchen."

"It's a date."

She grins, and my heart kicks painfully against my ribs. I frown, not wanting to pull away.

Josie picks up on the change in my mood. "What's wrong?"

"I don't want to go."

One of her hands reaches up and drags through my hair, then moves down to the back of my neck. She pulls me in, and right before our lips connect, she says, "Then don't."

Another hour later, I'm finally sitting in my mom's office with the door closed. I hit call on Mara's contact and wait for her to answer.

"Hey?"

"Any updates?"

"Nothing. Price, I'd have called if there were."

"Right," I reply vacantly, staring at one of the awards hanging on the walls.

"Is Freya okay?"

"J—Freya is fine." Mara doesn't comment on my little blunder. "Could you pick me some things up from the store?" I have an idea for our date later, but I can't leave Josie alone. The distance between us right now is as far as I'm willing to go.

"Sure," replies Mara. "Send me over a list."

Half an hour later, I send her everything I need, then settle down into the tons of work hanging over my head. Vacation, my ass.

***

Josie

At first, I think I'll struggle to fill the morning, but then I remember my new phone and all the details I need to input. I backtrack, settling on the bed and catching up with a world I've willingly blocked out, my trusty friend Netflix keeping me company in the background. In true Evan style, there's a list waiting for me inside the box with the phone with all the potential contacts I'll need. Among them are two I never expected.

The first is my brother. Surprising, considering we've spent God knows how long being incognito with each other, as any form of contact has never been on the green flag list.

The second is Duane. It's Evan's way of letting me choose.

When I've inputted all the contacts, minus one, I head downstairs, avoiding the office where I know Evan will be, not wanting to disturb him while he's working. I make my way into the kitchen and try to figure out what food I can prepare for later. We agreed I'd cook, and Evan would organize something else, which he was adamant he wanted to keep a secret. Not wanting to end what is probably going to be a very short-lived honeymoon period, I agreed. It's hard to decide with a fridge so full and cabinets bursting with every herb and spice, but eventually I settle on something I know Evan will like and go about prepping what I need.

When I'm done, I wander around the large living area aimlessly with my new phone clutched in my hand. There's something niggling at me. During my six-week hiatus, I've heard nothing from Eugene Belmer following the threat I found on my car. I might have done a good job at hiding, but that's never stopped him before, and I want to know why. Curiosity gets the better of me and I settle in one of the plush armchairs perfectly placed by the windows with a direct view of the beach. The beauty surrounding me feels at odds with what I'm about to do.

I type 'cat' into Google, knowing that's what the world refers to him as, and all I get are images of cats and a Wikipedia list of all the different breeds. Next, I type in Cat Killer. The search engine takes a second or two to load, and I sit in shock when the results fill the screen. I tell myself not to, that the headlines are enough, but my finger taps the top search result, and I hate myself when I read the article.

Holding a shaky hand over my mouth, I try to stifle a sob as I read about the victims who have found themselves at his hands since I left. It's only been a few weeks, yet there are so many women gone and it's all my fault. When the walls start to close in around me, I step out onto the terrace, gasping for air. It's no good. Powering back through the house, I fling open the front door and race out, not caring what happens, not caring that I don't have any shoes on my feet.

All I know is people are dead and I might as well have done it myself. I was the catalyst. I feel his hands wrapping around my neck as I race along the street. The mid-afternoon sun beats down, causing sweat to bead on my forehead, increasing my distress. I charge down a path toward the beach, moving my feet faster with each step I take. When I get to the end, I stumble and fall to my knees in the sand. A family close by looks over in alarm, but I barely see them, scrambling up and racing toward the ocean.

Somewhere in the background, I hear someone calling my name, but it's like I'm not part of my own body and as I continue to gasp for air, black spots creep across my vision. When I get to the water, I step in, the cool wet swirling around my feet does nothing to bring me out of my state of panic. I lean over with my hands planted on my thighs, choking. I'm going to die and all I can think about is them and how they felt when they took their last breaths. Did they have families? Partners? What were their dreams? I feel myself starting to fall when a strong pair of arms swoops around me. They pull me in and hold me up.

I press my face into his chest, scrunching my eyes, trying to block out the victims' faces I saw. I'm still gasping when sandalwood and citrus hits my nose. I inhale it greedily, filling my lungs until I start to relax. I drink in oxygen and lose myself in Evan.

"What's wrong?" he whispers against my ear, stroking a large hand across the back of my head. His fingers tickle the skin on the back of my neck when he toys with the ends of my hair.

"Is it my fault?" I say into his chest, not wanting to pull back and face the world.

"Is what your fault?"

I sniffle and finally pull my head back, needing to see his eyes to know the truth. "Are all those victims my fault?"

Evan swallows, and what I see in his eyes is something I don't expect. He looks as lost and as broken as I feel. His hand moves to my back; my nerves settle more with each stroke it makes up and down.

"I ask myself that question every day." He turns his head and looks to the horizon. The muscle in his jaw ticks. "I ask myself if I were better at my job, if I worked longer hours, if I searched harder, if I didn't miss clues, if I were one step ahead, would they all still be alive?"

"Evan, this isn't your fault."

He turns back, and this time his eyes are filled with resolve. "And it isn't yours, either. The only person to blame in all of this is the monster who takes those lives."

"How do you keep going every day, doing what you do? How do you live with guilt that isn't your own?"

He gives me a lopsided smile which has my heart leaping in my chest. "The oak fought the wind and was broken. The willow bent when it must and survived."

I smile, blinking through tears at his obscure words. "And that means?"

"Don't let the sorrow break you. Feel it, bend with it, and when the storm passes, stand stronger. You didn't kill them, *he* did. Don't ever forget that."

A warm breeze circles around us, and Evan pulls me back into him. We both look across the ocean.

"When all this is over, I want to see what's on the other side."

He places a kiss into my hair. "And you will."

We're walking back up to the house hand-in-hand when Evan stops abruptly. His brows furrow in the way they do whenever he's about to do or say something he doesn't want to, and I start to feel uneasy.

"Why do you look like someone just told you the FBI isn't real?" I joke.

His frown only deepens. "I need to tell you something."

"Go on."

"I have flights booked for us tomorrow afternoon."

I swallow. "Where to?"

"Jacksonville." Straight after the word has left his lips, they form a flat line, and he tenses.

It takes a moment for what he's said to sink in, and when it does, that's the moment I realize I might love this kind, selfless man.

I jump into his arms and wrap my legs tightly around him.

"Is this a good reaction? Are you happy?" he asks, his voice muffled in my hair.

Pulling back, I take in the dark brown of his eyes, which turn the color of whisky, when I say, "Thank you."

And then I kiss him, pouring every part of myself into it, not caring who's watching.

His chest rumbles with laughter when I grumble as he sets me back down on the sand. He presses a small kiss to the corner of my mouth and fireworks spark inside me. "Later. I have things I need to do."

"Like what?" I bite my lip, suddenly feeling nervous.

"You'll see. Go get ready."

Inside, we go our separate ways, although I'd glue myself to him if I could. Now I know what it feels like being with him, I don't think I'll ever be able to let him go.

Twenty

Josie

Light kisses find the crook of my neck, and I struggle to keep my attention on the herbs I'm chopping when the buttons of Evan's shirt brush against the exposed skin on my back.

His fingers toy with the scalloped lacy strap of my dress, and he spins me round. Dark eyes roam over the black silk V that dips between my breasts, ending just above my belly button, then move to the slit surrounded by gun-metal gray taffeta that finishes in-line with my pelvis, barely hiding my thong.

His throat bobs. "I'm going to kill Mara."

"I should have known you wouldn't have picked something as exquisite as this."

I grin and spin on the spot, letting the soft material of the gothic style dress fan around me. Evan stops me and pushes me back against the counter. Every inch of our bodies presses together.

"I'd prefer you in a sack. Now all I can think about is taking it off, and I promised myself I'd take this slowly."

"Slowly?"

"Yes, Josie, slowly. As in, clothes will be remaining on."

After our hot and heavy make-out session this morning, the ache between my legs has been unbearable and my inner sex goddess screams with disappointment at the news. I had high hopes for how the night was going to end, but it would appear Evan and I weren't on the same wavelength.

"Oh."

"Stop pouting. It isn't helping," he grumbles.

The scowl on his face is ridiculous, and it hits me that he's also a super grump when he's horny. I laugh and the movement makes my body connect with his. I feel exactly how turned on he is and need pools low in my pelvis. Evan's nostrils flare and he leans in, making me dizzy with his cologne.

"Keep looking at me like that, and the kitchen will be your favorite place for a completely different reason." Teeth nip my earlobe and then the words he hums shoot straight to my clit.

Goodbye, Bale. Hello, Mister Grey. As much as I love all things superhero related, tonight I don't want Evan to do the right thing. I want him to do every wrong thing he can think of.

He pulls away and starts to walk out of the room.

Dammit.

"Did I say that out loud?"

"Yes," he grunts. "I'll be back in a minute."

Ten minutes later, he returns, conveniently, when I'm setting the food out on the table.

"Sorry," he mutters, not meeting my eye.

"It's fine," I smile, because I'm as much to blame. I'd have jumped on him in a second if he let me.

He gazes down at the table and his eyes light up. "Chicken and rice?"

"I thought I'd pass on the chowder for one night."

Originally, I wanted to go fancy and practice my skills, make him a meal he'd never forget. Then I decided I'd rather make him something he enjoys. I don't mention that I marinated the chicken for hours in herbs he's never heard of and infused the rice to give it an extra bit of flavor. There are some things he just doesn't need to know.

"That was incredible," he says, leaning back in his chair when he's finished.

"Really?"

"The best meal I've had." He winks—something I never thought I'd see him do—and my stomach somersaults. "Don't tell my mom." He stands and starts clearing the table. I go to help, but he shakes his head. "I'll do it. There's wine if you want some?"

Surprised after how he found me in Vegas, I say, "You trust me?"

He walks into the kitchen and places the plates on the counter with all the other dishes. "Things are different here." When he turns back, he's magicked two glasses that look almost as expensive as the copper pans. "So?"

"Sure," I croak. I can't take my eyes off him as he moves around. The fitted black shirt he's wearing, with the top two buttons open and sleeves rolled up to his forearms, is doing funny things to me.

"White or red?"

"White." I need something to cool me down.

He walks back over and places a glass on the table in front of me. I pick it up and take a long drink. Sweet, citrus flavors coat my tongue. It's not my go-to drink, but I'd take anything to calm the riot of emotions building, making me feel like I'm going to combust.

Instead of sitting across the table from me, like he did while we were eating, Evan takes a risk and sits beside me. I play with the stem of my glass, alcohol starting to flow through my veins, and watch him take a drink of his own wine.

"I thought super-secret agents only drank Scotch or beer?"

He sets his glass down and his face twists. "Yeah, I don't like wine. I was trying to be fancy."

I chuckle at how the word 'fancy' sounds coming from him. "Me neither."

"Beer?"

"Please." He disappears to the fridge and returns with two bottles. He looks more relaxed and like himself when he takes a long drink. "Better?"

"Yeah."

He's acting weird all of a sudden. Nervous. Evan is never nervous.

"So, why the fancy outfits?"

He drains his bottle. There's definitely something up.

"Come with me," he says, voice strained.

He jumps up and grabs my hand, then pulls me out onto the terrace. I don't get a chance to walk hesitantly, because he's too busy tugging me behind him. A shiver shoots down my spine when we step out into the night, and I giggle nervously.

"I hate to break it to you, but I've been out here before."

"Ah ..." He wiggles his eyebrows, like, actually wiggles them. I'm about to ask him if he's high, but he carries on speaking. "But have you been to this part?"

He starts walking and turns left, leading me around the side of the house to where the terrace opens out into what can be only described as the most tranquil place I've ever seen. Filled with foliage, it's green and lush, with a pergola covered in bougainvillea which will create a hot pink blanket in the summer. String lights trail back and forth overhead, twinkling against the dark sky, covering the terrace in a warm glow. The sound of waves crashing on the shore adds to the magic of it all.

"Wow." I inhale, trying to catch my breath. "What's this for?"

Evan walks backwards, a playful smile on his face. He pulls his phone out of his pocket, taps it a couple of times and then music drifts through the air, combining with the faint lull of the water like they were made to work in unison. After he sets it down on a small metal table, he rubs the back of his neck and looks over at me. Uncertainty flashes through his eyes, then he reaches into the pocket of his pants again and pulls something out, keeping it tight in his grip.

I narrow my eyes suspiciously. "What is it?"

"Come and find out."

There's no demand behind his words. In true Evan style, he asks a question without actually asking one. It's another choice. Everything is always in my control. He gives me options. A chance to decide if it's a yes, or a no.

With him, I'd say yes, every time.

My palms start to sweat when I move over to him. Walking along the cliff, tiptoeing at the edge, I find myself with another choice to make. Do I jump, and if I do, will there be rocks at the bottom?

He twists his hand so it's facing up. When I lift his fingers, one by one, there, in the middle of his palm, is the charm bracelet he bought me for my birthday.

My head snaps up. "You found it?" He nods. "I thought I'd lost it. It must have fallen off when I was getting out of the car tha—"

He doesn't let me finish what I'm saying and I'm glad, because if I had, it would have ruined a perfect moment.

"I found it in the footwell."

I pinch the new charm between my fingers. "What's this one for?"

A sheepish smile transforms his face while I take in the tiny dancer. Gesturing with his arms at everything around us, he says, "It's a dance." When I look at him, confused, he scratches the side of his temple. "Kind of. I had to improvise."

"My bucket list?"

He nods and walks back over to his phone. Coldplay's "Yellow" starts and he holds out his hand.

"Dance with me."

Because the exhilaration when we fall is sometimes worth the risk, I jump, praying that when I hit the water, I don't sink; I swim.

I take Evan's hand and he pulls me into him, wrapping his arms around me and settling his hands on the small of my back. His thumb strokes my skin while we sway, and while he sings the lyrics in barely a whisper, I question how far he's willing to go to protect me.

***

I don't know how long we stay outside, but it could never be long enough. Eventually, I prize myself away from Evan and my body misses the contact instantly.

"I'm pretty tired," I lie, remembering what he said about wanting to take things slow.

I want to take things as slow as my galloping heart, and my body is so charged I feel like I've drunk a gallon of coffee.

"Yeah," he agrees. "We should probably get inside."

We stand staring at each other, neither of us moving. I gesture behind me. "I'm gonna go."

"Right," he nods, his throat bobbing as he swallows.

I take a step back, expecting him to stay where he is, but he follows with a step forward. I take another back, and he follows again.

"Evan, what ar—"

He reaches forward, grabs my hand, and tugs me back into him. The air is sucked out of me, and my limbs turn to jelly when he dips his head and presses his lips against mine. His hands grip my hips tight, and his frame remains rigid, at odds with the slow, sensual movements of his mouth.

All too soon, he stops, stepping back and dragging a hand through his hair while I'm left disorientated.

"I'm gonna go," I say for a second time, blushing furiously.

This time, Evan doesn't follow.

Inside the kitchen, I decide I'm too hyped up to go to bed. My eyes catch on all the dishes there are still to do. I grab my new phone off the counter and set some hardcore rock music playing, the kind that has no sexual vibes whatsoever, to try and distract my wandering mind. With the music blaring from the table and the water running, I don't hear Evan come in or the door shut.

I look up from the sink and almost jump out of my skin when I find him standing in front of me, brown eyes watching intently.

"Christ! Give a woman a warning next time!"

"Sorry," says Evan, sounding anything but. "What are you doing?"

"The dishes," I reply, keeping my focus on the soapsuds.

"Why?"

I look up. "Because they're dirty."

"You could have left them 'til the morning."

"Well, I haven't."

"Leave them, Josie," he says, "Please."

"Fine." I grab a towel and dry my hands, then walk over to the dining table to get my phone.

I switch the music off, and tension hangs heavy in the silence. Chills run over my skin, and I feel Evan watching my every move. With a deep breath, I turn and he's still standing in the same spot.

Somehow, I end up in front of him, the tips of my toes kissing the ends of his shoes.

"So ... slow ..." I look up and my mouth goes dry. Lava floods my veins when my eyes lock with his.

The air crackles around us. "Go to bed, Josie."

"I'm going." My hand drops to the side and slaps against the counter.

"Right."

Evan's hand falls on top of mine and fire shoots up my arm, burning every part of my body. We both stare at where our skin connects. I can't look away.

"Screw it," hisses Evan, pulling me in.

Our lips clash and teeth smash together, then he tilts his head, and his tongue moves deep into my mouth. This kiss is different from all the others. It feels like there won't be an end. I moan against him, fisting his shirt, trying to pull him closer. When he slams me back against the island and thrusts his hips against me, I whimper. Any rationality I have flies out the window and I can't think about anything apart from how I want to tear off his clothes.

The sound of black buttons bouncing against marble fills the room.

"You ripped my shirt?" Evan frowns at the kitchen floor. "That's the second piece of clothing you've ruined."

"I'm so sorry." Mortified, I raise my hands and cover my face.

He tugs them away and says, "Get on the floor." Then he shakes his head as if it's dawned on him what he's said. "Please."

"Why?"

I draw in a breath when his head lowers, and he nips my neck.

"Because I don't want anyone watching when I fuck you."

Not needing to be told twice, I drop to my knees and, without thinking, unbutton his pants. The scraping of his zipper opening might as well be his fingers on my clit with the effect it has on me, and I clench my thighs together. Evan groans when I tilt my head back and smile, then lick my lips as I eye the erection tenting his boxers.

"Floor, Josie."

Him using my real name is like catnip to my soul. I lie back and rest on my elbows without arguing, taking him all in. He looms over me, black shirt falling open, face broody. He's Batman, Christian Grey and all those vampires on Netflix packed into a giant orgasmic package.

He's on his knees, crawling over me when he arches a brow. "Orgasmic package?"

Deciding to roll with it, I stroke him over his boxers and his dick throbs against my hand. "Very, very orgasmic."

His eyes darken. "Say orgasmic one more time ..."

The challenge there in front of me, I take it. "Orgasmic."

He collapses and steals my breath away with his mouth. My legs wrap around his waist and only a few thin layers of material sit between us when he grinds up against me. When my nails dig into his back, he stills and pulls away, letting out a harsh breath and gazing down.

"We can still take this slow." The way he gazes down at me through hooded eyes makes it clear it's the last thing he wants to do.

I circle my hips. "No, thank you."

"Josie," he groans against my lips. "I mean it."

Sweeping my tongue through his mouth first, I then tilt my head back and hold his gaze. I refuse to let my lashes even flicker, not wanting him to find any reason to stop, because I'm in too deep.

"I know." He shakes his head, and his eyes move to the side. The moment's slipping out of my grip, and I refuse to let go. "I don't want slow, Evan. I just want you."

His eyes move back to mine. "You're sure?"

"The surest I've ever been." I grin.

He kisses me quick. "Wait there."

I watch in horror as he starts to move away. "Where are you going?"

"To get a condom."

I clear my throat when he's on his knees, ready to stand. "I'm covered. And I'm clean." He watches me. "Evan, nothing happened at the club. I know what you think you saw, but it wasn't that."

"Covered?"

"Implant," I confirm with a wink. "Momma Becket was adamant."

If I thought his eyes were dark before, it's nothing compared to when he understands what I'm suggesting. He climbs over me and pushes me back against the cool marble. His mouth moves to just below my jaw, and I lose myself in the moment, moaning when he sucks down on my neck. He moves lower, alternating between biting and sucking the tender skin and I arch my back. Nothing's ever felt this good, and I have a feeling it never would unless it was with him.

Rough fingers from one hand trail up my arm while he leans on his, watching everywhere he touches.

"This dress ..." he growls, tugging down the strap and taking my nipple in his mouth.

I feel it everywhere, and I swear I could come just from him teasing it with his tongue. When he moves his mouth away and blows, a chill sweeps over my body and I almost do. I shift beneath him and pull the other strap down, but when I go to drag the dress lower, he stops me.

"Keep it on." He gets up onto his knees and moves the middle panel of my dress away, then grips my hips over my thong. His eyes focus on my center, and I know it takes every last bit of restraint he has, when for a final time he says, "You're sure?"

Taking him by surprise, I sit up and grip the waistband of his boxers. "Are you sure?" He swallows hard and nods. I lower the material, freeing his dick, and I can't take my eyes away from it. "I solemnly swear that I, Josie Becket, want you to screw my brains out."

Evan shuffles his knees further into my parted legs and lowers himself over me, cupping my jaw with one hand as we lie back down. "No screwing, Josie." He kisses me slowly, then drags one side of my thong down and I lift my leg through. He doesn't bother pulling it off completely, and I don't care. "This isn't just a quick fuck."

All the humor disappears, and the backs of my eyes burn. "I know."

Nothing about us has been quick. It's been the slowest form of torture getting to this point. But the best things in life take time to grow and nurture so they can become something beautiful. What sizzles between us isn't lust. It's love in its truest form.

My breathing grows heavy when he grabs the base of his erection and a bead of pre-cum glistens in the light, right before he guides himself inside me. True to his word, he doesn't screw me. He moves every inch in at an excruciatingly slow pace until he's buried deep inside with both of us still half clothed. He closes his eyes for a second, and when they re-open, they're black. The first time he thrusts, his jaw ticks. It clenches when he thrusts the second time. On the third, it turns to granite, and somewhere between thrust seven and eight it looks like it's about to crack. Each time, he hits the perfect spot, and I moan against his mouth, scraping my nails against his scalp and pulling at his hair.

He doesn't fit the perfect mold; he does things his own way, making love to me on the kitchen floor with the promise of fucking me senseless in the bedroom later. And as I fall apart beneath him and he follows, jumping off the cliff right behind me, black buttons embed themselves into the skin on my back, leaving a reminder of exactly how perfect we can be.

Twenty-One

Evan

Josie squeals when I grip her ass and squeeze. It might only be twenty minutes since I pulled out of her, but it already feels like too long ago. When I lift her up, her legs wrap around my waist. Gray taffeta hides where she rolls her hips against my erection. I stumble toward the stairs with one destination in mind, but with the blood surging around my body—down to one place in particular— it's looking likely we won't get there.

There's a risky moment when her breasts in my face make me forget what I'm supposed to be doing. My mouth drops to one, and I suck her nipple hard, making her hips buck, the friction against my dick making me miss a step. With no fear for her safety, she cackles, and somehow, I manage to get us to the second floor in one piece.

Only the light from the hallway spills into the room when I drop her onto the sheets. She spreads herself out across my bed with a soft pink flush covering her pale skin. I should have known she'd be like this since the moment she revealed the lack of filter she has when it comes to her dirty thoughts.

That's why I'm not surprised when she trails a hand across her chest and teases one of her breasts. I'm happy to stand watching until her hand dips beneath the slit in her dress and her head tilts back with a moan.

Something in me snaps, and I grab her ankles, dragging her along the bed so she's closer. As much as the dress she's wearing does funny things to me, I want it off. Seconds later, it falls to the ground, and she's in front of me, naked, thanks to her underwear being somewhere on the ground floor.

Josie watches as my fingers trail across the intricate tattoo sitting across her chest, just beneath her breasts. All the words I'd use to describe her stare up at me. *Fearless, sexy, divine, unbeatable, creative.* I'm halfway through when I realize they're lyrics and I stop at the word love.

Our eyes meet.

"Isn't this a TikTok song?"

"Aren't you too old to know what TikTok is?" she quips. "And it's not just a TikTok song. Emmy Meli is a genius."

"It's ... different," I comment.

She grins. "What can I say? I like a bit of pop music as much as the next person."

I chuckle. "Josie, your favorite song is called Zombie Crew and one of your favorite bands is Ice Nine Kills."

Laughing, she reaches over and grabs my pants, which are still hanging open, pulling me in and dragging us back against the bed.

"The lyrics are empowering."

I move down, settling between her legs and trace over them with my lips. "They're perfect." When I get to my favorite part, I look up and find her watching me, emotion swirling in her startling green eyes. "So?"

"So, what?"

"Am I in line?" I ask.

She pulls my head into her, so my lips press against her skin. Goosebumps tickle my lips, tempting the words *I love you* to come out.

"You're right at the front," she replies, gasping as I tease her entrance with my fingers. She moans her disapproval when I pull away. Ignoring her, I lean over and flick on the bedside lamp. There's no way I'm missing a second. "Evan," she breathes when my face hovers above where I'm dying to taste her.

I hold back and glance up, taking in the thick lashes that fan across her cheeks. "What do you say?"

"Please," she pants.

A growl climbs from deep inside my chest, watching how she almost comes when I've barely touched her.

"Don't move." Of course, she doesn't listen. She never does. She bucks when my tongue connects with her clit. I press her hips down into the mattress. "Don't. Move."

As my tongue circles against her, I glide two fingers in, feeling her walls tighten when my teeth graze against the bundle of nerves I'm learning drives her mad. I grin and lick until she's writhing beneath me and almost throws us off the bed. When Josie shatters into a thousand pieces, I drink up every part of her orgasm, then shrug off my pants and boxers before climbing over her. It's the first time we've been completely naked together and my skin feels like it's on fire wherever hers touches mine.

Trying to slide in slowly, I bottom out when her tongue darts around the outside of my mouth, licking away the last bit of evidence, giving away how much she enjoyed having my mouth between her legs. "I think I've found my new favorite flavor."

It's painful pulling back, and I grind my teeth. "I'm trying to be good here."

Innocent eyes captivate me, but once again, Josie proves she's the one running the show. "I don't want you to be good, Agent Price. I want you to fuck me."

Pulling out with lightning speed, she squeaks when I flip her over. "On your knees."

I'm greeted with a shit-eating grin over her shoulder, surrounded by wild strands of purple hair. "What do you say?"

Tingles shoot to the base of my spine, and I almost come all over her back from four words.

"Please."

In a daze, she does as I say, and I trail my hands across her skin before thrusting in deep and Josie cries out. The headboard rattles against the wall each time I drive inside her, then pull out at an excruciatingly slow pace. My legs burn, but I don't hold back, completely lost in the moment.

"Dammit," I hiss.

I don't think I'll ever last long enough with her. She begins to shake, and ringing starts in my ears when I slam back inside her.

All I hear is "Evan," before she buries her face into the pillows and falls apart, taking everything she can from me. My balls tighten, and I come harder than I did in the kitchen. Something I didn't think was possible.

"I think you've broken me," I say, struggling to stay upright and squinting against the light.

She giggles, and the movement makes my dick grow hard again. She looks at me. "Seriously?"

I shrug. "You've unleashed the beast."

Dropping back against the bed, she covers her face with the sheets and wheezes. "You did not just say that."

Falling beside her, I take a few minutes to come back down to earth. Josie nestles into my side, and her breathing settles into a slow, peaceful rhythm. I flick the light off and stare up at the stars, finding the one with the most promise and imprinting this moment into it. My last thought before I fall asleep is thank God we didn't take it slow.

***

Just over a year ago, I thought I had my life sussed, and that I had things in order. I understand now that my life was, in fact, lifeless, until mine and Josie's paths crossed again. My heart thumps harder when she's around, and it's the little things that bury themselves deep within it. The way she dips the spoon back in whatever dish she's preparing after tasting it, which drives me crazy. Her obsession with the one thing she should be scared of ... cats. And how she hums along to heavy metal like it's one of Adele's bestsellers.

There was a moment in the night when I rolled over and watched her sleeping, and I felt like maybe I wasn't good enough. It hit me soon after that *the one*, your person, shouldn't care about your flaws. Josie takes all my bad parts and helps to make them better.

Before, I thought everything in my life was right, but nothing could feel as right as her mouth around me. My balls tighten when she swirls her tongue around my tip, then takes me so deep, I hit the back of her throat. That's all it takes to finish the job, and I fist her hair as she swallows every last drop.

I shake my head and chuckle when she presses kisses up my stomach, settling herself back under my arm. She trails her fingers through the rough hairs on my chest and I pull the sheets up around us.

"Can I ask you something?" she says, outlining the tattoo on my chest.

I place a kiss in her hair and trail my fingers up and down her spine. "Anything."

"You probably won't like the question."

"I don't like a lot of things."

She tilts her head and grins, but then her smile falters. "Have you ever killed anyone?"

"Yes," I reply without hesitating.

"How many people?"

"Six."

Her eyes widen, and she looks back at the diamond. "Do you regret it?"

My hand stills on her back and I look over to the window where the sky is becoming a mixture of soft blues and yellows above the ocean. "I regret two things. Not doing it sooner and saving innocent lives. Not doing it sooner and saving those left behind from the pain they'll endure for the rest of theirs."

I feel her swallow. "Is it easy?"

My eyes move back to hers. "You've held a gun, Josie. All it takes is one pull of the trigger. But the consequences of that one small action live with you forever. When you pull it, you need to be certain it's the right thing to do. You need to be sure that the darkness that follows that small action is worth it."

"Okay."

We don't talk anymore about guns, or about how likely it is she'll need to use one soon.

What we do is spend the rest of the morning in bed together before our flight to Jacksonville, and I show her with every small touch that the thing I'm most certain of is her.

Only when she's in a slumber at my side, and I press a light kiss to her temple, do I admit another certainty to myself. That I love her so much, I might not be able to survive without her.

***

Josie

The butterflies I've become used to with Evan around are swapped for nerves, churning up what little I've managed to eat as Evan drives us through Jacksonville. It's been years, and the streets we pass through have changed as much as I have.

"You good?" asks Evan, reaching over and squeezing my knee before turning his attention back to the road.

"Nervous," I admit.

"You've got nothing to be nervous about. I've got you."

My blood warms and I squeeze his hand while biting my lip and glancing out the window. The last time I saw Becket, as he's now known to the world, I was about to turn fifteen. Nine years is a long time and when we parted ways, it wasn't on the best of terms. Think shouting, foot stomping, door slamming. The usual sibling issues all heightened by a serial killer lurking in the background.

We sit in silence for most of the journey and occasionally I glance over at Evan. He seems distant, and the way he keeps tapping his finger against the wheel is a dead giveaway that he isn't as calm as his face makes him appear.

"Is everything okay?" I ask when the silence gets too much.

He swerves the car to the side of the road and a horn blares when a car passes by; the driver giving Evan a not very nice salute.

"Assh—" My string of curses is silenced when Evan's mouth collides against mine and he kisses me like the world's about to end. My heart doesn't know whether to swell or constrict at all the emotion behind it.

When the skin on my lips feels raw, he pulls back and lets out a shuddered breath. "It is now."

The dimple in his cheek pops and his gaze lingers on my lips. His nostrils flare and he leans back in, kissing me again.

"I really did unleash the beast," I laugh against his lips.

He pecks my nose, then settles back in his seat, checks the mirrors and pulls into the road. "I should have booked the flights for in a few more days." A hungry gaze is thrown my way, and he grins.

"I wish we could have stayed in Santa Monica forever," I sigh.

"Yeah," he frowns. "Me too. Mara's meeting me at the motel for us to drop off our things. I figured you all might want some time alone together."

The nerves come back full force when we pull into a ridiculously expensive gated neighborhood.

Evan grabs my hand while continuing to drive and brushes his lips against my knuckles. I give him a sad smile and pull my hand away. We haven't spoken about how we're going to handle the real world; both of us trying to stay in our bubble until the very last second.

"Ready, Freya?"

"As ready as I'll ever be, Agent Price."

All too soon, Evan says, "We're here," and stops the car.

"So, this is what the NFL gets you," I say, peering across his lap at the gigantic white building.

His eyes follow mine. "Don't forget, I've got you. Always."

I give him a final smile. "See you on the other side."

We climb out, and when we get to the front door, Evan presses the doorbell.

I hear it ring through the house and my mom's voice shriek, "Coming!"

My heart turns into a stampede of a thousand horses while we wait. The door flies open, a hurricane of sandy blonde hair barrels out and then my mom holds onto me for dear life, her sobs sounding out for the whole of Jacksonville to hear. Eventually, she pulls back, and only when she reaches over and wipes away my tears do I realize I've been crying too. I look up at Evan, and mouth thank you. It's a thank you for him not giving up and bringing me back to the two people who are my home.

"I'm sorry," I say sadly.

"None of that now," she replies, waving her hand in the air. "It doesn't matter what or why. I learned a long time ago not to dwell on the details. All that matters is you're here. Now, there's someone that's been more excited to see you than I have."

Evan hovers at my side longer than he should, and my mom glances between us with a faint smile on her lips. Realizing he's supposed to leave, he clears his throat and returns to his charming agent self.

"I'll be back later," he says abruptly.

Fighting the urge to turn and watch him go, I follow my mom inside. The huge entryway is empty and the rest of the house silent. "He's in the living room," she says, nodding toward one of the doorways. "I'll give you both a bit of time alone."

I linger for a few minutes, my stomach churning. Ringing in my ears starts when I take my first step. It gets louder and my heart beats harder with each one that follows. When I enter the room, I find a figure, even larger than I remember, pacing back and forth in front of a TV as giant as he is. I don't think he hears me, because he keeps his gaze set on the hardwood floor, lost in his own world.

I clear my throat. "Hey, you."

The pacing stops and his head snaps up. Green eyes identical to my own find me across the room. The ringing in my ears stops and I hold my breath.

"Hey, José," he says, smirking at the name he used to tease me with when I was younger.

I quirk a brow. "Still busy being an asshole?"

"Would you expect anything less?"

"Obviously not."

His smirk falters, and he opens his arms. "Come here." I race across the room, and he engulfs me. Time slows, and we stand together for I'm not sure how long. Eventually, Michael lets go of me and stares down as if he can't believe I'm with him. "You've got smaller."

"Or you've got bigger." I poke his chest. "Steroids?"

He throws his head back and laughs at the same time a blonde female walks into the room.

She smiles over at us both. "Don't inflate his ego anymore. We can barely get him through the door as it is." I look her up and down, and it hits me who she is. She's even more stunning in person. She holds out a hand and says, "Britney Shaw."

I narrow my eyes. "You put us all in danger."

Memories of the tape and media scandal she helped create linger between the three of us like Britney's outstretched arm.

I stare up at Michael, waiting for some kind of explanation as to how he could trust her after how she betrayed him. When he glances over at her, I get it, because what I see in his eyes is what I see in Evan's when he looks at me. Sometimes you don't have to know the details of a person's journey, you just have to respect and understand that the choices that get them to where they are, are theirs.

Taking Britney's hand, I give her a tight smile. "Freya."

Our hands snap back. It's not much, but it's enough, for now.

Mom walks into the room, beaming. "We're having a welcome home meal later. Some of Michael's friends are coming over."

I catch Britney shake her head out of the corner of my eye. Clearly, she isn't a fan of whoever's coming.

"Great."

"Agent Price will be coming." She watches me, and I watch her back, refusing to give anything away.

"His partner will be as well," says Michael, oblivious to our mom's not-so-subtle prying.

"Great," I say, turning to him. "Mind if I freshen up?"

"Sure." He shrugs. "Whatever." I fight back an eye roll. He communicates as well as Evan.

We all head out of the living room, and I grab my bags as I go.

Mom has a strange smile on her face, and when I walk up the stairs, she calls after me, "Your room's the third on the right. All your things are in there."

I find the room she said was mine and step inside. True to her word, my things are everywhere, but I don't feel how I always thought I would whenever I'd dream about returning. I just feel flat.

Dropping my backpack on the ground, next to the small case Mara bought me, I collapse back on the bed, and for some reason, I start crying. There's something about having my things around me here. We've come full circle to mine and Evan's beginning, which could very well be our end.

My heart stops when something falls off the dresser, hitting the floor with a loud bang. And there, sitting on it like it's her throne, is Cat Four. When Cat Three jumps onto the bed and nuzzles against me, purring, I fall back into the mattress and close my eyes, believing for a short spell of time that this could be home, not just a brief visit.

Twenty-Two

Josie

A shower and change of clothes usually make things feel better, but they do nothing to improve my mood. Unease crawls deep inside me, darkening every bit of lightness in its path. There's only one person that can stop it from taking over.

Evan.

The past few days have confirmed he is *the* person—*my* person. How the hell we're going to get through the meal is beyond me. I don't feel ready, but I drag myself downstairs in search of my mom. I'm passing the living room when I hear hushed voices. I find her standing off to the side of the room with a huge, overbearing man, built like the house we're standing in, wearing a cap on his head with the Jacksonville Jaguars logo.

There's something about the moment, about the way they're talking, just a little bit too quietly and standing a little bit too close. When I almost catch his face beneath the cap, I feel like I recognize him, but I can't figure out from where. And just when I'm about to move away and leave them to whatever moment they're sharing, he tucks a piece of hair behind her ear and gives her a sad, lopsided smile.

Biting the inside of my cheek, I tiptoe away and walk further into the house, my stomach rumbling as I follow the smell of cooking. In the kitchen, I find Britney sitting at a medium-sized table, typing behind a laptop. I don't acknowledge her straight away, because I'm not sure what our dynamic is supposed to be. Instead, I source the fridge and head over to it, praying there's orange juice. Luck's on my side and I do a little happy dance because there's no pulp. I hate the way it gets stuck in your teeth and the only time bits are acceptable is when the orange is still whole.

Then there's the issue of a glass. Trust my brother, who used to be one of the messiest people I know, to have a kitchen that's so pristine, with everything hidden away, that it barely looks like anyone lives here. His kitchen is more flash than Evan's parents, which is saying something. I look at the cabinets aimlessly and opt for the good, old method of opening each one and hoping for the best.

I'm four cabinets in when Britney says, "Left by two."

"Thanks," I say quietly. She doesn't say anything back. My head is in the cabinet when I remember how my brother looked at her earlier. Deciding sometimes in life you just have to move on, I peer around the cabinet door. "Would you like a glass?"

Taking the olive branch, she closes her laptop and grins. "I thought you'd never ask."

I fill two glasses and walk over to the table, sitting directly opposite her once I've placed them down. We sit looking at each other and she smiles again.

"You look just like him. Well, apart from the purple." She gestures at her own hair in explanation.

"I can't decide if that's a good thing or a bad thing," I joke.

"Well, to me it's good." She wiggles her eyebrows and I choke on my juice.

"Gross."

"Only as gross as you and Agent Price." She trails her fingers absentmindedly along the table.

My eyes widen and then I cringe, realizing I'm giving the game away. "I don't know what you're talking about."

A compact mirror and stick of concealer slide across the table. "Little tip. Next time you turn up with a gorgeous FBI agent at your side, make sure you cover up the hickey."

I grab the mirror, and my cheeks blaze when I find the evidence of the crime peeking just beneath the collar of my Rolling Stones t-shirt dress. There's no point in denying it. Britney's got me. Which is why I don't hide what I'm doing when I slide my phone out of my pocket, flip the camera and take a selfie of my neck. I send the image to Evan, and he replies instantly.

Agent Price: *Looks like you met one of the Salvatore brothers.*

Three dots appear again.

Agent Price: *Or was it Edward Cullen?*

Another three dots.

Agent Price: *;-)*

"Fucker," I hiss, locking my phone, then grabbing the mirror and concealer. Too lost in post-orgasmic bliss, I forgot to check how I looked in the mirror. My stomach drops when I remember my mom giving us one of her knowing gazes at the front door. Now I know why. She's not the problem though. The oddly loveable, football-playing oaf somewhere in the house is.

"Does my brother know?"

Britney laughs and leans back against her chair, rubbing her stomach affectionately. "Don't worry. He's oblivious to *everything*."

My mouth drops open and she holds a finger up to her lips, then picks up her juice and takes a small sip at the same time my brother and mom walk in, the ball-cap wearing stranger towering behind them. Mom wanders over to the stove and goes back to preparing the food. Meanwhile, Michael and the tall stranger wander over to the table. Michael stands at my side and rests a hand on my shoulder, giving it a small squeeze. Britney watches the subtle interaction with a smile, and something I could almost call contentment rushes through me. It all feels ... normal.

Michael grabs my glass and downs my juice in one. "Hey!"

He looks at me, a mischievous twinkle in a familiar field of green. "Oops, sorry, Sis. Was that yours?"

The now only stranger to me in the room chuckles, and I look over. He must pick up on the question in my eyes because he smiles, although his face is still covered in shadows. When he takes off his cap, I bite down on the inside of my cheek. This time so hard I almost draw blood. I know him, but not for the reasons I should.

"Coach Langford."

"I know who you are," I reply, swallowing hard. Michael looks between us, confused. I blink and plaster a smile on my face. "My brother's coach."

He nods and I look over at my mom. She stares for a second, wariness in her eyes. Clearly every person in this room, apart from my brother, is hiding something, and shortly we're going to add more people to the mix. Tonight should be exciting.

There's a knock at the front door and we all still, united by one thing. Fear.

"That's probably Evan," says Michael.

Mom becomes a flurry of activity, and her voice comes out shrill. "Well, go and answer the door then! In fact, everyone out so I can get things ready. You're crowding my space."

We all glance around at the cavernous kitchen-diner that could hold the Jaguars, but no one makes a comment. The sound of scraping chairs fills the room, and we leave her before she can get herself more flustered. In the entryway, my heart starts to pitter patter in my chest when I watch Michael walk to the front door. He swings it open, and the darkness from earlier is replaced by light.

My eyes connect with Evan's, and all the feelings of unease and uncertainty from the past few hours wash away. The corner of his mouth twitches before he focuses his attention on Michael. I stand back, watching them, and Mara gives me a little wave. It's then that I notice another female, and I remember Mom earlier, saying *friends*. I also remember the change in Britney's mood, and when I look at her out of the corner of my eye, the happy-go-lucky blonde from in the kitchen is nowhere to be found. Interesting.

Mom rushes out of the kitchen and tuts when she finds us all standing around aimlessly with our guests still outside. "Useless," she mutters, brushing past me and Britney. She's at Michael's side in a flash, and considering she's as small as I am, pushes him out of the way effortlessly. "Agent Price, Mara and ..." she tails off.

"Lola," says the other woman.

"Lola," continues my mom. "Come in, we have Champagne!" She turns on my brother. "Can I leave you to get everyone a drink?" Michael shrugs and she rolls her eyes, which then settle on me and Britney. She points a finger my way. "Sort the Champagne, Freya."

"Okaaaay," I say under my breath.

"This way," says Michael, sounding less than impressed as he leads us all into a dining room that would better be described as a dining hall.

"Are we celebrating something?" I ask my mom as I walk past her.

"That you're home and safe," she grins, bouncing on her feet and clapping her hands.

"Safe, right," I reply, deciding not to point out that she's getting ahead of herself.

"Ooh Champagne!" chirps Britney, wandering over to the table.

She retrieves one of the many bottles sitting on ice and hands it to Michael to open. I'm about to walk over and help when awareness runs through me. I hold my breath and focus on watching Michael as he struggles to figure out how to open the bottle. Coach Langford, like my mother, is nowhere to be seen, and Mara and Lola are both watching my brother, laughing. Evan stands behind me, not close enough it would look suspicious.

"Did you bump into a vampire while I've been gone?"

I turn and narrow my eyes at him. I open my mouth to say something, stopping when I catch the faint outline of his dimple. Whatever witty response I had disappears, and the dimple deepens.

Dammit.

I blink and walk over to Michael, holding out my hand for the bottle.

He smirks and hands it over. "Be my guest." I take it from him, and less than thirty seconds later, we're all greeted by the sound of the cork popping. Michael scowls. "Beginner's luck."

I ignore him and start filling the glasses on the table, opening another bottle when we've run out. I'm about to take a drink when Michael snatches the glass from my hand.

"What are you doing?" I snap, taking it back.

"You're too young to drink," he replies, stealing the drink from me.

I take the glass again and hold on to it, tight. "No. I'm not."

The evidence of too many missed years sits between us in the form of a glass of alcohol. Eventually, Michael looks away and picks up a glass for himself. With a feeling this is a sign of things to come, I take three long drinks in quick succession, draining the glass and dropping it to my side while no one is looking. Britney sidles over and swipes it from my hand, replacing it with her full one. I receive a wink as she wanders off. When I turn, I find Evan watching the interaction, intrigued by the spectacle starting to unfold.

I slowly raise the new glass of Champagne to my lips, letting out a small moan of pleasure when the cool liquid travels down my throat. The previous glass is already soaring through my bloodstream, making me feel bolder than usual. Licking a rogue droplet of liquid from my bottom lip, I look up and my eyes connect with Evan's over the glass, taking in his dark expression.

"Is something wrong, Agent Price?"

He's saved from answering, because my mom screeches through the house. "Food's ready. Everyone sit down."

We all find a place at the large table, and I smile across at Evan as Mara drops into the chair beside him—Lola Fisher into the one on the other side. Michael sits at the very end of the table, of course. When my mom, Coach Langford and Britney have finished bringing the food through and setting it down in the middle, they also sit. Britney between me and Michael, my mom at the opposite end to Michael, and finally Coach Langford between me and my mom.

An awkward silence fills the room until my mom clears her throat and throws daggers across the table at my brother. He stares at her, oblivious, and I bite down on my lip, trying not to laugh. She taps her glass and Michael's eyes widen.

He clears his throat and raises his. "Thank you for coming, everyone. You're all welcome anytime."

I snort, while my mom shakes her head in despair and Britney says under her breath, "Not everyone."

Her words sink in, and I look over at Lola Fisher sitting next to Evan. Another familiar face, and I can't put my finger on why. Then it hits me.

"Wait, aren't you the one from the sex tape?"

Michael cracks his neck, and Britney's knuckles turn white around her glass of water.

"Thanks for that," says Michael, sounding the opposite of thankful.

Lola gives me and my mom a tight smile. "We're friends."

"When it suits," says Coach Langford under his breath.

An expensive shoe taps my leg, then settles between my bare feet. I freeze, quickly glancing at Evan. His face remains blank. Meanwhile, Mara looks around the table like Christmas has come early.

Having had enough, my mom says loud enough that her voice can be heard over all the tension, "Let's eat before it gets cold. And everyone, please get more Champagne." Everyone does as they're told and starts tucking into the food she's prepared. When she thinks we aren't listening, I hear her add on, "Lots more Champagne."

Evan's foot remains where it is and I decide to have a little fun beneath the table, needing a break from what's happening above it. Making sure I keep perfectly still above the table, I skim my foot up and down his calf, while concentrating on my plate of food. My mom continues trying to make the meal less of a shitshow, firing questions at us all, left, right, and center. When I dip my toe beneath the hem of Evan's trouser leg and our skin connects, I start to feel warm and shift in my seat. And that's pretty much how the rest of the meal goes.

"Have one of the last rolls, Freya," says my mom. "They're your recipe. Agent Price, you need to try them."

I reach forward to grab one at the same time Evan does and our hands clash. Sparks shoot across my skin. We might as well have our own firework display announcing we're together.

"Sorry," I say, like a normal person would—one who hadn't had him inside them for the majority of the past two days.

"So," says Michael. "Did you get up to anything fun in Santa Monica?"

Evan stills and I trail a finger over the area where he left his not very subtle mark on my skin, while looking over at my brother. "I spent most of it in bed."

Britney snorts and Mara's fork clatters against her plate. Michael grabs his glass. Still oblivious.

I take a bite of my roll and groan. They're really, really good. My eyes flicker over to Evan, and I catch the slight flare to his nostrils.

"How are they, Freya?" asks my mom.

I give her a sweet smile. "Orgasmic."

She purses her lips and jumps to her feet. "Time to clean up. Coach Langford, you can help."

Evan's chair scrapes along the floor as he slides it back. "I'm just gonna go to the bathroom."

"Yeah, Man," says Michael, sounding like a total jock, "there's one straight across from here."

"I'll help clear up," says Britney, standing. She leans down to take my plate and whispers so my brother can't hear. "Naughty. Welcome home, Freya."

I follow her out of the dining room and linger in the entryway. Before she reaches the kitchen, she looks over her shoulder and gives me a knowing smile. Now I know why my brother loves her. She's probably the only person in the world able to take him on. Faint chatter flows out from the dining room, and when I'm certain the coast is clear, I walk carefully over to the downstairs bathroom. I start to press down on the handle, but don't get far. The door flies open, and Evan drags me inside. He shuts the door behind us and when he spins round, his eyes are full of promises I hope he keeps.

"That wasn't a very fair game."

"I'd say it was about as fair as this," I reply, pointing to the mark on my neck. Even with concealer, it's obvious it's there and how no one has commented on it is beyond me.

My eyes move down, taking in his suit, which now, knowing the man beneath it, has a whole new meaning.

"Stop looking at me like that," he says, moving in closer.

I can't take my eyes away from where his trousers sit perfectly around his thighs, the charcoal material highlighting a very obvious bulge.

"Like what?"

"Like you want me to screw you senseless."

Our eyes clash and I shift, the ache between my legs unbearable after the past couple of hours.

I blame the four glasses of Champagne for when I say in a deep voice, "No screwing."

Evan laughs and pulls me into him. I can feel exactly how much he's been enjoying our game. "You're playing with fire, Josie Becket."

Grabbing his tie, I stand on my tiptoes and whisper close to his ear. "I've already been burned, Agent Price."

His hand darts up and he grabs my jaw, his other, my hip, then walks us back and presses me into the sink. His lips make a path from the crook of my neck up to my ear and then back down. So close, but never touching.

"Evan," I moan in a whisper.

He does it again and I roll my hips forward, desperate for any contact I can get.

"The last time I kissed you here, you told me off."

His warm breath tickles below my ear, sending a shiver through me. His free hand moves from where it has a firm grip on my hip, dropping and reaching round to just below where my dress has risen. When one finger skims beneath it against the back of my thigh, I moan his name again.

"What do you say?" he croaks, giving away that I'm not the only one lost in the moment.

"Please," I whimper. The word is a match igniting the fire between us. His lips crash down on mine and my head swims when his tongue dives in, taking everything from me and more. The hand on my chin drops and he lifts me, so I'm perched on the sink. My hands tangle and tug at his hair when he starts kissing my neck hungrily. "I need you," I breathe into the room.

He stills and pulls back, eyes full of so much emotion I stop breathing.

"Josie, I—"

I wobble dangerously, and my hand flies back, colliding with the faucet. Thanks to Michael having the house kitted out in fancy everything, it starts spraying cold water all over my back. I scream and jump against Evan, who goes to set me down at the same time the door to the bathroom flies open.

"What's wro—"

The words are stolen from my brother's mouth when he takes in the sight of me with my dress practically over my hips, my legs wrapped around Evan, who, thanks to my literal handy work, looks like he's been dragged through a hedge.

"You're fucking my sister?!" he roars.

I yelp when Evan involuntarily drops me as the NFL's biggest quarterback dives at him. Evan might be big, but my brother is a giant.

They tumble out of the bathroom, and I scream, "Michael, no!" right before his fist collides with Evan's face.

Michael raises his trunk of an arm in the air, ready to go in for another punch, when a small hand grips onto him, stopping him in his tracks.

"Don't," says Britney.

"She's right, Son," says a low voice. Coach Langford is standing in the background, concern all over his face. "Don't go down that path. You're better than this."

Michael drops his arm, but his shoulders continue to rise and fall. Evan's shirt is still in his other hand. Evan's eye is already bruising and swelling and there's a gash with blood trickling down his cheek. They stare at each other and, eventually, as if the storm has passed, Michael's face becomes less angry and red.

He blinks. "How did I miss this?"

Britney steps in front of him. "Probably for the same reason you missed that I skipped my period."

The silence somehow gets more silent. Michael turns and gapes down at where her hand rests on her stomach.

"We're having a baby?"

She nods, and he pulls her into his arms, burying his face in her hair.

Britney winks at me over his shoulder and I give her a small smile back, thankful she's taken the edge off mine and Evan's grand reveal. When they eventually pull apart, Michael turns back to Evan.

"Get out."

Blood smears across Evan's cheek when he tries to wipe it away. He nods before walking over to the front door. Mara follows him, and the door closing echoes around us all as we stand, each trying to process what the hell has just happened.

***

I want to text Evan, but I'm not sure what to say. What happened downstairs is his worst nightmare, and the reality of what it could mean for his job, if Michael says anything, looms around me.

Cat Three and Cat Four are keeping me company while I contemplate what to do, when there's a knock at the door.

"Hello?"

It opens and my fellow secret-keeping mother walks in.

"How are you doing?" she asks.

"Fine."

She sits on the bed and takes Cat Three from me. The little hussy dribbles all over her when she starts tickling under its neck. Then she gives me the look; the one only mothers give.

"How are you really?"

"Concerned," is all I reply.

"Why?"

"In case Michael says something and gets Evan in trouble."

She smiles. "Your brother won't say anything."

"How do you know?" I ask, arching a brow.

"Because he knows he will have me to deal with if he does."

I sit up straight and rest my back against the luxurious velour headboard. "You're not mad?"

She shrugs. "I mean, you could have been a bit more discreet." Heat covers my cheeks. "But of course I'm not mad."

"Why do you not seem surprised?"

Her eyes settle on my collar. "The hickey gave it away, but I had my suspicions. It was the look over the chowder that did it. Anyone who looks at someone like Agent Price did you, while being challenged to eat lumpy soup, is definitely in love."

A lump forms in my throat, remembering how he was about to say something in the bathroom.

"He isn't in love with me."

My mom throws her head back and laughs. "Freya, that man would die for you."

Her words give me a chill.

"And you and Coach Langford?"

She stands and then leans over and places a kiss on top of my head. "You know better than anyone that sometimes we find love in the most unexpected places." Almost at the door, she looks back. "Freya, go find Evan. Don't take the opportunity you've been given for granted. Make sure you tell him how you feel ..."

The end of her sentence is left behind, unsaid.

"... in case you don't get another chance."

Twenty-Three

Evan

I thought my spell of taking shots to the face was done. I'm praying Michael Becket's fist was the grand finale, because it hurts. A lot.

Mara stopped by the liquor store on the way back to the motel and picked up two bottles of Scotch. When she gave me one, and I asked what it was for, she said, "To numb the pain. Consider it medicinal." When I asked what hers was for, she replied, "It hurt to watch."

I'm a couple of glasses—that aren't helping—down, when there's a knock at the door. I walk over warily with my gun. Mara called it a night a couple of hours ago and she's the only person who knows where I am. When I look through the peephole, I find a distorted version of my favorite, purple-haired, small person.

I fling the door open and pull her into my room. "What are you doing here?" I ask after closing and locking it. She holds up a bag of ice and I frown. "Did you come on your own?"

"No. Michael's security team brought me." She walks to the table and puts down the bag, before shrugging her backpack off her shoulders and setting it on the floor underneath.

"How did you know where I was?" I ask, placing my gun on the desk.

"Mara."

"Of course." She walks into the bathroom, and I call after her, "What are you doing?"

She returns with a damp hand towel and holds it up by way of explanation, then opens the bag of ice. I watch as she adds a pile of ice cubes, then twists the towel, so it creates a bundled package. She walks over to me and holds it up.

"Can I?"

I nod, unable to take my eyes off her. The few hours we've been apart have been hell. Santa Monica has well and truly messed with my head, and now I don't want to be without her. When she isn't with me, all I can think about is being back by her side.

The ice filled towel connects with my cheek, and pain surges across my face. I wince.

"Sorry," Josie says, pulling her hand away.

I reach up, covering it with mine, and guide it slowly back. Our eyes meet, and even in the poor lighting, I can see the ring of yellow close to her pupil. I stand. Stare. Transfixed.

Josie looks down and her eyes settle on my bare chest, then move over to the diamond.

She swallows. "Who does it remind you of?"

"You," I answer, without missing a beat.

Her eyes snap up, wider than I've ever seen them. "Me? But I thought ..." She stammers, then becomes lost in thought. She shakes her head, and with more confidence, says, "But I thought you said it reminds you of someone special?"

"You are my someone special," I reply, the words coming out strangled.

I don't feel the towel and ice knock against my smashed face as I walk us across the room, only stopping when Josie's back is against the wall.

"Why a diamond?"

I reach up and cup her face with one hand. "Because the most beautiful things are created under pressure, and I'm in love with the rarest diamond there is. You, Josie."

Her lip trembles and she sniffs. When she doesn't respond, I feel sick, questioning whether I've said the wrong thing. But then she looks up and I see how she's really feeling swimming in her eyes and pouring down her cheeks.

"There have been so many times when I've wondered if it was all worth it. The running. The hiding. Living. There were times when I'd forget why I was fighting to stay alive. Until ..."

She tries to look away, but I hold her head in place. "Until ..."

"Until you came back into my life. I am so in love with you, Evan. It scares the hell out of me."

I move her hand holding the ice down to her side, needing nothing to be in between us, then lean in so our lips almost touch. "You've got nothing to be scared of."

"I have," she croaks. "Losing you."

Going against the one rule I've always followed, I whisper, "I promise you won't lose me. I love you."

Her body goes slack, and I press her against the wall, holding her in place, kissing her with everything I've got to give. The ice drops to the floor with a thud as she sighs into my mouth. When her hands creep over my shoulders, nails bite the skin on my back. I lose it, because loving her is all-consuming, and when we're together, I feel like I can't get close enough.

Battling with her dress, I drag it over her head. Her bra and pants follow a few seconds later.

"I love you," she moans into my mouth when I skim her nipple with the pad of my thumb.

I pull back. "Say it again." A shy look crosses her face, and she bites down on her lip. "Say it again, Josie."

"I love you."

She doesn't ask what I'm doing when I pick her up, walk away from the wall and lower her onto the bed. She watches intently when I climb out of my pants and boxers, then move over her on the mattress. *I love you*, are the only words that fill the room when I spend the rest of the night showing her exactly how much I do.

Later, exhausted, she curls into my side, and I pull the sheets around us, smiling at the small breaths that escape when she drifts to sleep.

My phone bleeps on the nightstand and, being careful not to wake Josie, I reach over and grab it.

Becket: *Is my sister with you?*

She's safe, I reply, before giving in to sleep.

***

"What would you do if you weren't in the FBI?" asks Josie.

"Hmm, let me think about it." I trail kisses up and down her neck, then move away, and with the most serious face I can manage, say, "You."

Laughing, she shoves me off the top of her and settles onto her side, snuggling under the sheets. "I'm being serious."

Flopping back onto the bed, I stare up at the ceiling. "Honestly? I'm not sure. I've never really thought about it."

"Do you think you'd ever leave?"

I turn on my side. "Do you want me to leave?"

"No. I want you to do whatever makes you happy."

I lean in for a kiss. "You then."

A few minutes later, she ends the kiss, cheeks flushed. "What are we?"

I should have guessed this was where the conversation was going, and the anticipation all over her face that my answer would be anything other than what it is, is adorable.

"A couple. I thought that might have been obvious when I told you I loved you." I climb over her, settling between her legs and thrusting my hips with just enough amount of pressure to make her squirm. "Or when I screwed you on the kitchen floor."

"I thought we didn't screw," she smiles, eyes becoming heated when I sit back on my knees.

"Roll over."

"What? Why?" she asks, looking confused, but she does it anyway. I lift her hips and she settles on her knees, then I cover the back of her body with mine, and reach round and circle her clit with my fingers. She falls down onto her arms, and when I start peppering kisses down her back, she moans, "What are you doing?"

Smiling, I graze my teeth against the back of her thigh, close to my target. "Reminding you why you're fighting to stay alive."

***

We've spent most of the morning in bed. Josie's just finished showering and walking out of the bathroom when there's a knock at the door. She pales and I hold up a hand for her to stay put. I don't hide my groan when I look through the peephole and see who it is.

"Open the door, Asshole," Michael snaps.

I swing it open, and his eyes dart between me, in just my sweatpants, and Josie behind me in the room, in just a towel.

"Seriously?" He looks around my shoulder at his sister. "You guys aren't even going to try and hide it?"

Josie tilts her head. "You already know. What's the point?"

I go to tell Michael we need to speak, stopping when he narrows his eyes. "Don't." He looks back at Josie. "I need you to come with me."

"Why?" she asks.

"I want to talk to you." I straighten. "Without him around." Josie and Michael stare daggers at each other. Figuring we're not getting anywhere; I go to close the door. "What are you doing?"

"Getting dressed, or would you like to watch?" He scowls. "Like I thought."

When the door closes, Josie sighs. "This should be fun."

"I can hear you," Michael calls through the door.

I grin and walk over to her, brushing my hands down her arms. "It will be fine."

"What are you going to do while I'm gone?"

"Catch up on some work."

We both get dressed quickly before her brother has a temper tantrum.

"I won't be long," Josie says, smiling against my lips.

Banging starts on the door. "Come on, José."

Josie grabs her backpack, then walks over and flings it open. She jabs Michael in the chest.

It's comical to watch when he rubs it and says, "Ouch."

"Stop being an asshole," she snaps. He waits for her to leave the room and walk first, but she shakes her head. "Like I'm going to fall for that one. You'll probably try to take another swing at him. Go. Now."

Michael throws me another dirty look before letting out a huff of air and does as he's told. Josie turns back and waves, before stepping through the door to follow her brother. I walk out and watch her go, reassured when I catch Michael's security team not too far away.

I'm about to go back into the room when Josie spins around and walks back to me. "What are y—" I'm cut off with a kiss that steals my breath. Michael makes gagging noises somewhere in the distance, but I couldn't give a shit. "What was that for?" I ask, when she drops down off the balls of her feet.

"Because I can. Oh, and I forgot to tell you something."

"Enlighten me."

"You were never the villain. You've always been the hero." She beams as she starts walking backwards and, in that moment, I love her more than I ever thought possible. "I love you, Agent Price."

"I love you too," I reply, watching her purple hair and checkerboard backpack disappear.

***

I've been staring at the same files for the past couple of hours when there's a hammering at my door.

"Price! Open up!" The urgency in Mara's voice has me jumping off the bed and opening the door within seconds.

335

I close it after her when she strides into the room. "What's wrong?" She waves her phone in my face, literally, and I have to take a step back. "What's this?"

"There was never a blind spot."

"Blind spot?"

"Outside Sing Sing," she pants. "I have a friend. Well, actually I have lots of friends, probably the kind you sho—"

"Mara," I say through gritted teeth, trying to get her back on track.

She starts pacing back and forth, her phone clutched tightly in her hand. "When I found it, it just didn't make sense, and it was bugging me. There are more cameras in the four-square miles surrounding Sing Sing than there are in the bureau and The White House combined, and that's a fact."

I frown. "What's your point?"

"My point is, why would there be a blind spot? There wouldn't. So, my friend looked into it, and this ..." she points at the phone, "is what they found."

She taps the screen so it starts to play, and I watch. It's dark, but the bank of The Hudson is familiar. Two figures in black hooded jackets move around on the ground. One points up at the camera and disappears, leaving the other alone. The lone figure turns and looks up, then a shadow crosses the camera, and the screen goes blank.

"They disabled it," I say.

"Rewind, zoom in, and watch again," replies Mara tersely. "Tell me who you see."

My brows shoot up at how abrupt she's being. Whatever she's found, it's got her rattled.

I replay the video, doing as she told me to and zooming in. I frown when the figure on the ground looks up.

"Wait a minute ..." I hit play again and watch the point before the video goes black intently. "That's ..."

"Lola Fisher," confirms Mara.

I pass her phone back. "Call Hewson and tell him to get a flight down here."

Mara does as I ask and walks over to the window. I grab my phone from the dresser, needing to hear Josie's voice.

"Evan?" she answers.

I hold the phone away from my ear, struggling to make out what she's saying over the noise in the background.

"Are you okay?" I ask.

"I'm fine, Evan. I can't hear you very well, though. I'll speak to you later."

The line goes dead at the same time Mara ends her call and faces me.

"Hewson's phone keeps going to voicemail. I'll try him again later."

I nod. "Go get your things."

"Where are we going?"

"To pay Lola a visit."

***

Josie

Michael picks a sports bar for our place to talk. I wouldn't expect anything less. When we're inside, it's crowded, loud, and impossible to have a conversation. It's also impossible to overhear one.

"We could have just gone for a drive," I comment as we grab two stools at the bar.

Michael barely acknowledges I've spoken, focused on the large TV screen hanging off the wall above the display of liquor bottles.

"I wanted to watch the game."

I shake my head and order a diet coke, head still groggy after the four glasses of Champagne yesterday, and forty-eight hours of almost no sleep, thanks to Evan. Michael orders a beer.

When he catches me watching him, he says, "What?"

"Are you allowed to drink? You know, being a super-duper NFL player and all."

He returns to staring at the screen and takes a long drink. "I'm stressed."

"About?"

He turns back to me, his expression hard. "Evan, seriously? What are you doing, Freya?"

For a second, I'm confused by the name he calls me. I've quickly gotten used to Evan using my real name. Too used to it, floating in a bubble, at times forgetting how we came to be together.

I look away and stare at the rows of liquor in front of me. "I could ask you the same question."

"What's that supposed to mean?"

I glance at him and raise a brow. "Britney? The woman who screwed us all over. I might have come around to her, but it doesn't change what she did, or the fact you chose to be with her after everything. How is this any different?"

"Because it's Agent Price! He knew you when you were fourteen, it's just, it's ..." he tails off and gets lost in thought for a moment. His voice drops a level. "Did he ever touch you when you were younger?"

I shake my head. "Please. This is Evan we're talking about. You wouldn't believe what it took for me to get him to touch me now."

Michael's eyes narrow. "I didn't need to hear that."

"He's a good man, Michael. You know that, I know you do. All he has ever done is try to protect me, and somewhere along the line we fell in love."

"Right," he scoffs.

I turn on him, but he looks up at the screen. "Look at me." He looks back slowly. "Newsflash, you haven't been around for over nine years. *I grew up, Michael.* Don't belittle my choices and make me feel like a child."

"I just want to keep you safe," he says quietly.

"Then you and Evan have more in common than you think. You don't have to like my decision, but if we stand a chance at making up for lost time, I need you to respect it."

After a few minutes, he backs down. "Okay."

I smile. "Really?"

"I'm not saying I like it, but maybe I'll come round to it over time."

"Thank you," I say, reaching over and giving his giant hand a squeeze.

He picks up his drink and drains it. Feeling like a weight has lifted off my shoulders, I signal for the bartender to get us two more drinks. This time, I go for a beer as well. I'm all for celebrating victories, no matter how small.

I'm onto my third and feeling fuzzy and content, when I say to Michael, "So, you're going to be a dad …"

He grins at the screen. I'm not sure if it's because of what I said or the touchdown that was scored, but when he looks over at me with sparkling eyes, I decide it's the former.

"I'm scared."

"You don't need to be. You're going to be great."

He rubs a hand across his jaw. "Hopefully." He gets off his stool and says, "I need to piss."

Delightful.

As I watch my brother walk away, my phone vibrates in my pocket. I pull it out and the name on the screen makes me smile.

"Evan?" I answer.

"Are you okay?"

The room fills with cheers.

"I'm fine, Evan. I can't hear you very well, though. I'll speak to you later." I don't catch his reply, so I hang up.

A few minutes pass, and I finish my beer, deciding I could use the restroom myself. Grabbing my bag from the floor, I locate them at the back of the bar at the end of a long, dark corridor. I hear Michael humming to himself in the men's room when I pass. When I enter the restroom, the door bangs shut behind me. I'm tempted to call Evan, but decide against it. Maybe I can convince Michael it's time to go, and surprise him back at the motel.

Once finished, I wash my hands and grab a paper towel, tossing it in the trash can when they're dry. I step out of the restroom and start to walk back along the corridor. Michael must be back in the bar because I don't hear him humming anymore.

When my foot connects with something on the floor, I stumble. Using the wall to steady myself, I look down. The single light overhead flickers and my blood runs cold. Dropping my bag, I fall to my knees.

"Michael! Michael," I whisper, grabbing his face. "Michael! Wake up."

I go to stand to get help. The noise spilling along the corridor from the bar increases as the game finishes. Shouting, cheering and singing a world away. A hand comes around my face, covering my mouth.

Nothing comes out when I try to scream.

Something in me is triggered. I drive my elbow back and stomp down. Barely taking in the 'oof', I race forward. Footsteps follow. I'm tugged back so hard my hair almost rips out. My head hits the ground and I see stars. When they clear, they're replaced by a figure in a black hooded jacket. Fear trickles through me. I kick out and they fall back. Pulse racing, I scramble.

Nobody hears when I do scream.

Dragged back by my ankle like a rag doll, I follow the path of a cold, calculated laugh.

My nails scrape across the tiles, tearing from their beds.

We stop. My breathing stalls.

"What's wrong, Josie? Don't you want to play?"

I feel a prick to my neck, and then the world disappears.

Twenty-Four

Evan

A quick call to Michael Becket's home and we have Lola's address, thanks to Britney. She hands it over happily and her obvious dislike for Lola might not be unjust. I don't tell her that, though.

Just over an hour later, we stop outside Lola's house. Mara asks, "Ready?"

"Yeah."

We climb out of the car and walk to the front door. I knock hard and it swings open, revealing a disheveled Lola.

"Agent Price," she says, not quite meeting my eyes.

"Mind if we come in? We have a few questions." She backs away and holds the door open. We walk inside, finding a tidy home with coordinating interiors. Two couches form an L shape in the living room, with a large coffee table in the middle and a standard-size flatscreen TV. Everything looks normal. I do another scan of the room and Mara shifts beside me. "Is there anyone else here?"

"Just me," Lola answers. "Would either of you like a drink? Or something to eat?"

"No," I reply.

"I'm good, thank you," says Mara.

I gesture toward the couches. "Please, take a seat. This shouldn't take too long. We just have a couple of questions."

Lola perches on the end of one of the couches. Her knee bounces. Once. Twice. Three times. Her smile falters. "Okay."

Keeping my eyes fixed on her, I slide a piece of paper with a list of dates across the table. Nestled in the middle is our golden nugget. "Where were you on these dates?"

Lola looks down and reads, frowning. She trails her finger up and down the list, hovering on the date we need more than once. She starts recalling out loud where she was for each and when she gets to the only date we're interested in, she says, "I was visiting family."

Mara and I look at each other out of the corner of our eyes. She's lying.

"And where was that?" I ask, trying to keep my voice even.

Lola looks up. "New York."

The room is so silent, the car passing by could be in the room with us.

We've hit a roadblock and she hasn't bitten the way I thought she would. The naïve part of me thought as soon as we started questioning her, she'd crumble and reveal whatever it is she's part of. But she hasn't, and we need more evidence to take things further.

I stand, and Mara follows suit. Lola gives us both a tight smile and walks us to the door. She opens it and says, "I'm sorry I couldn't be of more help."

Mara leaves first and I follow. Before I've cleared the door, I turn back to say goodbye, but something in the background catches my eye. A closet to the side of the room, the door partially open. Inside hangs a black hooded jacket. Lola's eyes follow mine.

Before I get a chance to react, she turns and darts.

"Wait!" I shout, racing after her through the living room. When I get to the kitchen, it's empty. "What the?"

There's a loud thud and glass shatters. Pain shoots through my head and the room starts to spin. The last thing I hear is Mara screaming my name before I collapse.

***

Josie

I open my eyes and darkness spins around me.

A hand grabs my face, forcing me to look at a small screen. I can barely make it out. When my eyes adjust, I realize it's the only light in the room.

"And where was that?" My eyes widen. Evan.

"New York," comes another familiar voice. There's a pause. "I'm sorry I couldn't be of more help."

The next pause is longer. I try to look around, but the room tilts.

"Wait!" shouts Evan. Hot breath tickles below my ear, and I try to scream over the material shoved in my mouth. "What the?"

A ball of fear twists and grows in my stomach at the voice I hear next.

"Scream all you like, Josie. Nobody can hear you."

***

344

Evan

"You're sure you're okay?" asks Mara, giving me a concerned look from the driver's seat.

"I'm fine," I snap, watching the local police department drive away with Lola in the back of their vehicle. "Stop fussing over me."

"You had a vase smashed over your head ... again! Do not tell me I am fussing over you. You're bleeding, Evan. You need to get checked out."

"And I will, later." I ignore the unbearable pain in my head that I don't have time for. "Let's go."

Mara watches me for a second, then shakes her head and pulls away from Lola's home.

***

Forty minutes later, we're inside Jacksonville Police Department waiting to be taken through to question Lola.

An officer greets us, then leads us toward an interrogation room. We enter the stark space, finding her sitting on one side of a table positioned in the middle of the room with a lawyer by her side. Her tear-streaked face screams guilty.

Lola stares as we sit opposite her. When her eyes reach my hairline, crusted with blood, she looks down at the table.

"Twice in one day. Aren't we lucky," I smart.

A tear spills down her cheek. "I'm sorry."

Her lawyer turns his head away from us and says to her quietly, "I told you not to speak unless I told you to."

Lola raises her chin, throws her shoulders back, and says to him, "I'd like you to leave."

"You've made the wrong choice," he says, gathering his things. "I'll be outside if you need me."

He leaves the room and the three of us sit in silence.

I lean back in my chair and point at my head. "Thanks for this, by the way."

"I panicked, I'm sorry." She looks guiltily between me and Mara. "I'm not a bad person, I swear. I never wanted to be a part of this."

I press play on the recorder positioned in the middle of the table and introduce myself, then Mara, and finally, Lola.

"What exactly have you been a part of, Lola? Start from the beginning. And this time, no lying. We can only protect you if you give us the truth."

"No, you can't," she says grimly. "One day, I stepped out of my house and there was a black jacket on my porch. There was a note with it."

"What did it say?" I ask.

She bites her lip and looks to the side. "It's time to play a game."

I keep my expression schooled. "Why didn't you go to the police?"

"I was scared. After that, I'd receive random messages from unknown numbers telling me when and where to wear it and what to do. I thought they were just trying to freak Michael and Britney out. And then Brad told me about the kidnapping, and it all started to make sense. I searched for The Cat. I had no idea what I was part of, I swear. If I had ..."

"Is there anything else?" I finish.

When she shakes her head, I end the recording. Mara and I both say thank you and leave. The door shuts behind us.

"She's lying," I say.

"I figured as much," replies Mara.

I look at her in amusement. "And what made you figure anything at all?"

"She never told us the reason why she did what was asked. You?"

"We never told her this had anything to do with Belmer." I look back at the door. "They're two big slip-ups for someone trying to hide something."

"What are you thinking?"

I pull my phone out when it starts ringing in my pocket. "That she isn't trying to hide anything. She's either fucking with us or stalling. Probably both." Checking my phone's screen, I find Hewson's name. I hold up a finger for Mara to wait while I answer.

"Where are you and Mara right now?" he says before I get a chance to answer.

"Jacksonville still. Where are you?"

"I've just landed in Jacksonville."

Time slows as I listen, making a mental note of the address where he needs us to meet him.

"We'll be with you as soon as we can," I say, hanging up.

"What's wrong?" asks Mara.

"We've got another body."

***

The car pulls into the Ortega neighborhood, just South of downtown Jacksonville. It's the kind of neighborhood where shit like this doesn't happen. That's probably why most of the residents are standing on their front lawns, in front of their expensive homes, trying to figure out why the FBI is swarming the area, when we pull up outside the address Hewson gave us.

Their American Dream has been tainted by blood.

Mara and I climb out of the car and head to the forensics tent. When we're dressed in hazmat suits, we enter the large house.

"Can I make a comment?" says Mara.

"You will regardless ..."

"This looks a lot like Michael Becket's house."

I take in the entryway. It's almost the spitting image. "Yeah."

We don't get a chance to say anything else, because Hewson walks over.

"Second floor," he says before heading upstairs.

Mara and I follow, suits rustling as we move up the grand staircase and straight ahead into the master bedroom. Forensics scopes the scene in a flurry of silent activity.

My eyes zone in on the bed, and Mara stops in her tracks.

"Fuck," I mutter.

"Look familiar?" says Hewson.

Mara opens and closes her mouth. "Her hair ..."

"Cause of death?" I ask.

"Asphyxiation." Hewson's phone rings, and he signals that he's going to step out of the room to take it. "Hewson speaking."

Mara walks closer to the bed and leans over, inspecting the short purple strands spread out like a halo against the pristine white sheets. "They're the exact same shade."

Bile rises in my throat, and I remind myself that Josie's with her brother and his security team. I walk over to a large chest of drawers, taking in the images positioned on the top, all showing a woman with long, blonde hair. When Mara stands at my side, I don't take my eyes away from the photos.

"How did he know?" I ask myself.

"Do you think the unsub has been watching Michael's home again?"

"Michael's security has it covered. There haven't been any reports …"

"Unless it's related to Lola," says Mara, reading my mind. "I'm waiting on a few things."

I finally look at her, my interest piqued. "What kinds of things?"

"My guy said he might have some more information. He's supposed to be getting back to me when it's confirmed."

I stare at the body on the bed, then walk over to it when something red catches my attention on the sheets. Mara sticks to my side. I ignore the way my stomach twists when I catch green eyes focused on the ceiling.

"Has anyone moved the body?" I ask the room.

A member of the forensics team shakes their head. I lean in closer and find a small scratch on the skin, peeping out beneath the body.

"Do we have everything we need?" Forensics discuss between themselves, then answer yes. "Roll the body over."

We all stand, staring at the words etched into the victim's back.

Are you ready to play, Agent Price?

Hewson walks back into the room and comes to my side, blinking when he reads the message. "We need to go."

I take in the tight line of his lips. "What's wrong?"

He swallows, and the hairs on the back of my neck raise.

"Michael and Freya Becket are missing."

***

"Price!" screams Mara, holding onto her seat as I run a red. "Slow the fuck down!"

I grip the wheel tight, refusing to acknowledge her. My chest is so tight I can barely breathe.

Horns blare when I blow through a stop sign, and cars swerve out of the way.

"Price!"

I grind my teeth, focusing on the road. "Josie is missing, Mara. What do you expect me to do?"

She closes her eyes when the car drifts left and the tires screech across the tarmac. When the car straightens and we're flying down a straight—and thankfully empty—road, she reopens them.

"We can't find her if we're dead," she hisses.

I push harder on the gas.

Twenty minutes later, we screech to a stop in the carpark of the bar where they came hours ago.

I'm fine.

My vision tunnels, and my throat constricts. I press my head to the wheel.

"Evan," says Mara firmly. "Josie *needs* you. She needs you to be Agent Price right now."

I blink, coming out of the darkness. "Let's go."

The darkening sky flashes blue with the lights from a local police department vehicle. A couple of officers stand, talking to three huge guys, all of whom look disorientated. Michael Becket's security team.

Mara and I walk over.

"FBI," I state, holding up my badge.

One of the officer's steps to the side. "Someone walked past their car and found them unconscious and restrained inside. They called it in, and the bar owner came out to help. That's when we found out about Michael and Freya Becket."

I look over to the entrance of the bar, where groups of people linger outside.

"Is it empty?"

The officer nods. "The owner cleared it out."

"Has anyone been back in?"

"We're waiting for backup," he confirms.

"Right," I reply, clenching my jaw, trying to remind myself that he's following procedure and keeping himself safe so he can return to his family, while mine is missing somewhere.

Leaving the officer behind, I walk back to Mara. At the same time, Hewson pulls up and jumps out of the car he's in.

"We need to check inside," I say.

"We need to wait for backup," replies Hewson.

I pull out my gun, turning off the safety. "I'm not waiting for backup."

He holds my gaze, and I wait for him to argue back. Instead, he nods and pulls out his own gun. "Well then, let's go."

Mara's phone rings in the background as we walk toward the entrance of the bar.

"I need to take this," she calls after us.

I barely hear her, too focused on one thing—finding Josie. Hewson remains at my side when we step through the door and take in the empty room. The tables still have half-filled glasses and pitchers of beer on them. The TVs are still running one of the local sports channels; the sound blaring through the room.

"Would that back there have something to do with your relationship with Freya Becket?" Hewson asks, over the sound of our feet crunching against lost bar snacks on the floor. I give him a blank look. "Come on, Price. We're the FBI. You didn't think I'd figure it out? I've known you since you were practically a kid."

"Let's just find her," I grit out, moving through the bar.

There's nothing in the main room, so we move to the back, where there's a dark corridor. We're halfway along when my foot collides with something on the ground. I reach down to pick whatever it is up.

"What's that?" asks Hewson, coming up behind me.

"Freya's bag," I confirm, placing it back down because I need my free hand. There are doors everywhere. "You take the left. I'll take the right."

At the final door, I've almost given up hope of finding anything. I open it carefully, but it's darker and deeper than the rest. I skim my hand along the wall beside the doorframe until I find the light switch, flicking it on. It takes a second for my eyes to adjust. When they do, I find Michael on the ground in the back corner. Tape covers his mouth, and his hands and legs are restrained with cable ties.

"Shit!" I hiss, racing over, gun raised as I go.

With nothing keeping us company apart from bar stock, I lower my gun. Wide, terrified eyes find mine.

"You're okay," I say, then grip the corner of the tape. "You ready?"

He nods, then lets out a grunt when I tear it from his mouth.

"Where's Josie?" he rasps out.

I can barely meet his eye, riddled with guilt. "I don't know."

Hewson rushes in with Josie's bag in his hand. "There's nothing in the other rooms, but there's probably something in this."

Michael remains spread on the ground, watching our interaction. I almost forget he's there, focused on only one thing. Purple checkerboard.

"What is it?"

Hewson hands over the bag. "Take a look." My eyes skim over Josie's bag, then I open it, finding nothing. "Hidden in plain sight, Price."

I shut everything out. That's when I see it. A minor tear, right at the top of the strap by the seam. The bag is so old it's barely noticeable. I pull out the Stanley knife from inside my suit jacket and tear the strap apart. There, nestled in the padding, is a small, white, Apple AirTag.

"He knew where she was the whole time," I say under my breath.

"Looks like the Kraken Cartel weren't the only ones getting their use out of them."

I place the bag on the floor when my phone rings, answering when I see Mara's name.

"I need to talk to you," she says.

"Okay. I'll be right out." I hang up.

"Has she got something?" asks Hewson.

"I think so," I reply.

"Do I want to know how?"

"Probably not."

Hewson looks down at Michael. "I'll help him. You go find out what Mara has."

I'm almost out of the room when Michael croaks, "If you find him and he's touched her, will you kill him for me?"

I leave my *yes* in the room, unsaid.

Mara corners me outside instantly. "Lola Fisher doesn't exist," she says before I get a chance to ask her what she has.

"*Lola Fisher* is being held in Jacksonville PD," I reply.

She shakes her head. "Whoever is there isn't Lola Fisher."

Pain shoots through my head. I close my eyes and pinch my brow.

"Are you okay?" Mara asks.

"I'm fine." I open my eyes and blink. For a second, I struggle to take all three of her in. "Didn't you get an image of the sign-in sheet the day Belmer got out of Sing Sing?"

Mara nods. "Show it me."

She spends a minute scrolling through her phone and then, even in the dusky light, I see her pale.

"What is it?" She hands her phone over and I scan the list. My eyes lock on one name and I grip her phone so tight I'm surprised it doesn't shatter. "Lola Melber?" I crack my neck, muttering to myself about how she's taking the piss as I stalk over to the car. Mara climbs in after me as I slam my hand against the wheel repeatedly. "How the fuck did we miss it?"

"Price. Let. It. Go." Mara stares me down and my breathing begins to settle.

"This is the whole reason I never did personal," I snap, pulling out onto the road, heading back in the direction we came.

"You can't blame yourself for this. The whole reason Josie is still alive is because of you. If you hadn't been around, whoever it is would have got to her a long time ago. Don't forget that."

"Right."

"Loving someone is a good thing."

"Loving someone is a weakness," I reply, tearing along the streets of Jacksonville, because in this moment, my veins flooded with rage, I've never felt less in control.

Twenty-Five

Josie

A door groans and light spills in from above. Face flat on the ground, I daren't move. Goosebumps cover my bare body.

Stairs creak. Humming carries down with the thudding of feet. It's almost welcome, lulling me in and out of consciousness; an escape from the pain threatening to consume me. A pair of black boots leave the bottom step and hit the floor, then move toward me.

A predator stalking its prey.

I whimper, then fall silent. *'Run, Josie, run.'* Those were the words he wrote to me, and that's exactly what I did. And now, we're here.

A boot collides with my face, and the pain is almost blinding. I scrunch my eyes shut. I don't want to see him. I can't. My shoulder is wrenched to the side and my back flattens to the ground. He drops to his knees, straddling my waist.

He reaches forward with a gloved hand, and the material in my mouth is torn away. Clumps of hair go with it, and I scream. There's a whoosh of air and a crack echoes off the walls. My face goes numb. I'm not sure if it's blood or tears trickling down my cheek.

Kill me. I don't want to be here anymore.

Fingers trail back and forth along my tattoo, before moving up, skimming over places they shouldn't. When his hands press down on my neck, my eyes fly open.

"You," I choke. The pressure eases, and he cups my face affectionately. He smiles the smile of death, then leans in. His nose hovers close to my skin, and I can smell the sweat on his forehead. A bead drops onto my lips, slipping into my mouth. Salt coats my tongue and I retch. He inhales long and deep, groaning, before raising back on his heels. "Why?"

His hands press down again, harder. This time, he doesn't lift them away.

"Because I can," he replies with no remorse.

He sits and watches. Staring intently as my eyes bulge. My heart slows, struggling to pump what little oxygen is left through my veins, and consciousness starts to slip away. Just when I think I'm about to pass out, he pulls his hands back and strokes my face tenderly.

"No, no, no." He taps a finger against the tip of my nose. "It's not time yet." My head lolls to the side. He reaches down, bunches the gag in his hand, and shoves it back in my mouth. "I've been waiting a long time for this, Josie." He grins and his teeth sparkle. "So beautiful." His eyes settle on the mark on my neck and flash with anger. He grabs my hair, dragging it and forcing my head back. "I don't like it when other people play with my toys," he snarls against my neck.

His weight lifts off me, and he stands. I watch as he walks over to the unit where the small screen is sitting. I stare at it, praying to see Evan walk across it again, so I can see him one last time.

He picks up a knife and starts to hum. A shiver travels down my spine when I watch him pass it from one hand to the other, observing it. He drags it between two gloved fingers, and then the humming stops. He turns to face me, his eyes devoid of all emotion.

"You were never the villain. You've always been the hero. I love you, Agent Price."

My words fill the room on repeat. The most bittersweet of songs.

The knife drops to his side, and he walks back over. Acceptance washes over me when he presses the blade against my cheek. His other hand travels down my body, leaving not an ounce of skin untouched. The blade pushes harder, the pressure builds and then pops when the knife passes through my flesh like butter.

A faint *pat, pat, pat,* is the only sound beside his ragged breaths and my words, still playing in the background.

"It's time to get you ready," he sing-songs. "Now, which game should we play first?"

There's a clatter on the ground. His weapon replaced with much worse.

When his hands slide over me, it might as well be his knife. Like there's no one to hear my screams, there's no one to hear my protests. As he peels away parts of me that were never his to take, I close my eyes, and for the first time, the darkness becomes my friend.

The only calm glimmering through the storm raging inside me is the knowledge that he can't take my heart.

It's already being guarded carefully in somebody else's hands.

Evan

Powering through Jacksonville PD, all I see is red. Mara races behind me, struggling to keep up. I'm almost at the interrogation room where they placed Lola while I was getting changed, when she grabs my arm.

"Stop."

"Mara," I growl, trying to tug it away.

People pass, shooting us wary glances. I couldn't give a shit. I'd burn the place down in a second if it meant I could find Josie.

"Stop, Price. Breathe."

For a second, my muscles relax, my lungs expand, and I do what Mara says. I breathe.

"I can't do this," I admit.

"You already are." Mara's hand grips my arm tighter. "I've got you, Evan. Just like you've got Josie."

She drops her hand and mine grasps the door handle, ready to push as far as I have to in order to get to the truth.

"Wait!" shrieks Mara, waving her phone in the air, the screen flashing with an incoming call.

"We don't have time for this."

She narrows her eyes. "This guy has given us the most reliable intel yet. Wait."

I don't press down on the handle when she raises the phone to her ear.

"I'm here," she answers.

Almost five minutes pass, and I listen to her hum and tut. Finally, she hangs up and closes her eyes.

"What is it?" I ask.

"Come with me."

I stare back at the interrogation room desperately but follow. "What the hell is going on?"

"I'll tell you in a second." We stalk into the break room, which is thankfully empty. Mara spins around. "Lola never lied. She was visiting family in New York."

"Who?" I ask darkly. Mara taps her phone and then holds it up. The image that fills the screen makes my blood boil. "This is a joke, right?"

"Eugene Belmer had two stepchildren. Melber was an anagram. They must have changed their identities. And, just like Lola Fisher never existed, neither did Duane Jackson."

"Why?"

Mara shakes her head. "I don't know. But there's something else ..."

"Go on ..."

"My guy found all the security footage and electronic records from the day Belmer escaped Sing Sing. The system failure wasn't a failure. They deleted everything."

"Why?"

"To cover the fact they fucked up. Belmer made a suicide attempt that day and one of the attending paramedics w—"

"Was Lola Melber. It was a setup, and they covered it up because they wheeled him right out of there themselves. Shit!"

"Where are you going?" she shouts after me when I storm out of the room.

"Where do you think?"

The door to the interrogation room flies open, slamming back against the wall.

Lola straightens in her seat. "Agent Price ... daaamn. The whole SWAT vibe you've got going on? Much better than the suit."

She blows her mask away in the air along with her chef's kiss.

"Where were you the night Britney Shaw was kidnapped?"

"Visiting family." She smiles the kind of smile I'd happily tear off her face. "Like I said."

"Why did you sign in to Sing Sing with the name Lola Melber?"

She shrugs and makes a show of picking at her nails. "Whoops. My bad. I must have spelled it wrong. Melber ... isn't that a dessert?"

"Is your stepfather Eugene Belmer?"

Eyes filled with ice hold my gaze. "Was, Agent Price. Get your tense right."

My nails bite the inside of my palm.

"She's playing with you, Price," murmurs Mara at my side. "Don't let her win."

"Where is Freya Becket?"

"I'd like some water."

Ignoring Mara, I lunge toward the table, slamming my fists down against the wood. "Where is she?!"

Lola doesn't even flinch. "I don't know where Freya Becket is." Silence. "But I do know where Josie Miller is." She tilts her head innocently. "Is that who you mean?"

"I'm only going to ask you one more time. Where. Is. She?"

Lola curls her finger, urging me to lean across the table in close to her. I have no choice but to do it.

When she's right by my ear, she whispers, "Didn't mommy ever tell you not to ask questions you already know the answer to? Sometimes what we're searching for is right under our ..." Her finger trails slowly up my bulletproof vest, over my face, tapping the end of my, "nose." She grins. "Or our feet. Technicalities."

"You're going to rot in hell," I hiss, flying back.

Her final words follow me out of the room. "Be careful, Agent Price. We're at the grand finale and we all know they end with a bang."

"Where is she?" asks Mara, racing at my side.

Lola's laughter floats after us.

"She was with us the whole time. Hidden in plain sight."

***

Streets fly past the windows of the car in a blur.

I take a deep breath and my foot presses against the gas, putting some distance between us and the car behind. I take a second deep breath and check all the mirrors, making sure we're clear and everything is safe. When I take my final deep breath and exhale, I press hard on the brake suddenly. Mara flies forward and her hands slam against the dashboard.

"Price!" she screams. "What the hell?!"

I swerve to the side of the road, slowing steadily and pulling up alongside the curb. "Fuck! I think I hit a nail or something. Dammit!"

Mara eats it up, completely missing the fact that when you get a flat, everything slows, it doesn't speed up. "I'll check. Wait there." She unbuckles her seatbelt and jumps out, slamming the door behind her.

I activate the central locking system, and she looks up, walking back to the door. She rattles the handle when it won't open.

"Don't do it, Price," she shouts, looking terrified.

I mouth 'goodbye' and hit the gas, watching as she disappears through the rearview mirror.

***

The house is in complete darkness. My gut stirs. They're inside. I know they are.

Deciding the back of the property is the best way to approach, I pull out my gun. My only visibility comes from the streetlights behind, and I skulk through the shadows, being careful with my footing. Occasionally, I step on a twig, the snapping sound may as well be a snare drum announcing my arrival.

In the back garden, I glance to the side—a large greenhouse catches my attention. Tiptoeing over, my nostrils flare when I get close enough to see what's inside. A sea of white lilies glow in the moonlight, taunting me.

I grip my gun tighter, tempted to fire a round of bullets and bring the whole thing to the ground. Instead, I move toward the back door. Pressing down on the handle carefully, it swings open, inviting me to step inside. Quietly, I rummage through the kitchen drawers until I find a serrated knife. There's a faint humming from somewhere in the house. Then it stops. My eyes catch on an open door. I stand, tuning into every sound around me. A pipe gurgles. The refrigerator clicks. A floorboard creaks.

Adrenaline floods through me when the humming starts again. Holding my breath, I tilt my head back and listen. It's coming from upstairs.

I stare at the open door for a couple more seconds, then make a snap decision. It feels like I'm walking straight into a trap, but if Josie's sitting in the middle of it, I don't give a damn. I head over and open it fully, finding a set of stairs leading to a basement. I take each step with my feet as far to the side as I can, the weight as light as possible on the balls of my feet.

When I get to the bottom, my eyes land on Josie, laid on the floor. She looks peaceful, like she's sleeping, her skin shining red. She's so still and calm. Too still and calm. I lurch forward and fall to my knees beside her.

"Josie," I whisper frantically. "Josie. Josie."

Her face is swollen and bruised, a shade of purple that matches her hair. There's a cut just below her eye, already closed with a path of crusted blood leading to a much bigger, deeper cut. A purposeful slice. My eyes move down, taking in the rest of her injuries. When I find the ones on the inside of her thighs, my stomach rolls with a wave of nausea.

"Josie, please ..." I lean over carefully and place a light kiss on her mouth.

I'm not religious, but my lips linger close to hers as I hover over her and pray. A small moan climbs up her throat. I pull back and she moans again, louder this time. Her eyes roll and her lids flicker. Finally, they open.

She stares at me and croaks, "Evan?"

I hold a finger against her lips to keep her quiet. "Shh. It's okay. I've got you."

She starts to shake her head, and her eyes widen. "Evan, it's—"

In her panic, her voice gets louder and carries through the silence. I press my finger more firmly. "Shh. I know." I look down her bare body, taking in what I'm dealing with. Her wrists are locked together with cable ties, her ankles too. "I need you to keep still. I'm going to try to get you free."

A floorboard creaks above. I place my gun on the ground and raise Josie's hands in the air, moving my lips to her ear right before there's another creak.

"I'm going to cut the ties on your ankles and wrists underneath. I might not be able to do them both, but I'll try," I whisper. She nods, and her chest starts to rise and fall rapidly when there's another creak. "He's coming. Don't let him see what I've done. Don't move unless you have to." Another creak, louder this time. I pull the spare gun I brought from my holster. "Arch your back." She does as I say, and I slide the gun beneath her. "I'm going to try to cut the ties now."

I pinch the cable tie away from her wrist and slide the knife carefully against it. I pause when she shivers. I try to move quicker and press harder, being careful not to nick the paper-thin skin on her wrists in the process. Finally, the knife slides into the plastic, rather than over it. I keep dragging it back and forth, feeling the tension lessen the closer I get to breaking through. Her wrist's part, but then there's another creak, directly above us. I guide the knife away and place it in my pocket. Josie lowers her hands, and her expression turns blank.

"Lay flat," I whisper. She does. I give her a reassuring smile and mouth, "I love you," then reach up and make a show of stroking her face and comforting her, as if that's what I've been doing the whole time. Josie leans into my palm, her eyes saying a thousand words her lips can't.

We both still when a shadow casts over us from behind. The humming starts again, and feet hit the stairs. Only when his shadow threatens to swallow us whole, and Josie's eyes widen in terror over my shoulder, do I turn.

A hard object collides with the side of my face. It comes with such force my brain rattles inside my skull. Thanks to the injury I obtained from Lola earlier, everything starts to spin. I fall to the side and roll onto my back, struggling to focus. One figure in a black hooded jacket turns into three, and they make their way toward me, but I'm too disorientated to do or feel anything.

My vision starts to right itself right when he crouches down in front of me. The side of my face throbs, but I focus on only one thing—a pair of eyes glowing in the dark.

Duane smirks. "You finally came to play."

***

Josie

Cold laughter fills the room, turning my body to ice.

"Evan," I murmur.

He's leaning against a wall, holding his head. Each time he goes to move, he sways. Remembering what Evan said, I keep my arms perfectly still, trying to ignore the searing pain across my back that comes with every breath I take. I blink away tears, trying to hold it together.

Come on, Evan. I can't do this on my own.

As if he can read my mind, he straightens himself and stares at the black hooded figure in front of him. My muscles twitch in anticipation of what's going to happen next. I fight the urge to move.

Duane turns his head my way. It's a slight movement, but the split second is all Evan needs. He launches away from the wall, driving his shoulder into Duane's stomach. There's a loud thud when they both hit the ground.

I hold my breath and wait for them to start fighting. Nothing happens. Evan stills instead of jumping back up. He rolls off Duane and falls to the floor. I'm about to move my hands, but Evan catches my eye and shakes his head. He drags out his gun, but his movements are too slow. Duane kicks it hard, leaving behind the sound of bones crunching and the gun clattering.

365

Letting out a roar of pain, Evan jumps to his feet and lunges forward again. That's when I see it. A glint of silver hidden beneath Duane's sleeve. I scream and Evan's eyes widen in shock. Trembling hands frame the knife sitting low in his stomach beneath his vest. He falls against the wall and slides down, grimacing.

My heart stops. The gun Evan hid presses into my lower back. His eyes lock with mine, saying one thing: don't.

"Why?" hisses Evan.

"You're the one with all the fancy training. You tell me."

Something akin to understanding crosses Evan's face. "You were the child ..."

"... with a Mommy who liked to play some fucked up games," Duane chuckles. "Forget Daddy issues. He saved us. He was the only one who cared." He turns his attention to me. "And you stole him from us."

My throat grows tight when he walks over, drops to his knees, and wraps his hands around my neck. "You look just like her," he whispers. My feet kick the floor as I fight for oxygen. Evan tries to move to help but cries out in agony. "This is what justice looks like."

"It's not justice," groans Evan. "It's revenge."

The pressure eases when Duane dives at him, his fist colliding with Evan's face.

I suck in as much air as I can, relief filling my lungs. I glance up the stairs in desperation, trying to figure out a way to get out of this alive. Duane's busy raining punches down on Evan.

My body screams when I roll over and grab the gun from beneath me. I struggle to my feet with the ties still round my ankles and raise it in the air with a click as I turn the safety off.

The barrel of Evan's other gun points straight at me.

This is what death looks like when it's staring you in the face.

"It's not your turn to play," Duane sneers.

Keeping my arm as still as possible, my finger rests on the trigger.

When you pull it, you need to be certain it's the right thing to do.

I tilt my chin and search Duane's face, finding nothing.

You need to be sure that the darkness that follows that small action is worth it.

In the very periphery of my vision, I see Duane's finger start to curl.

Only one person can be the winner.

I press the trigger, and an ear-splitting bang ricochets off the walls. Duane's body slumps to the floor.

It's not an eye for an eye.

It's a life for those much more deserving of a place in the world.

Twenty-Six

Evan

Three long days pass. Days holed up in a hospital room, unable to do anything or see Josie.

Mara walks into my room with Hewson by her side. They each wear the grim expression I've been dreading.

Hewson clears his throat. "Evan, the test results came back ..."

I look away, and he doesn't continue.

"You were both lucky," the doctors keep saying. *"Your wounds will heal."*

Mine might. Josie's ... I'm not so sure.

At no point do any of them talk about the scars that are left behind—the ones the eye can't see.

***

Josie

The first day I sleep.

On the second, the nightmares come.

On the third, pain consumes me from the inside out.

On the fourth, it stops, and everything becomes numb. I remain in the darkness. Lost.

Light spills into the room, and my mom walks in, closing it behind her. I don't acknowledge her. Instead, I continue staring at the blacked-out windows. She walks over to the table at the side of the bed and sets down the tray like she has been doing three times each day. When she lifts the lid off a bowl, the smell of comfort reaches my nose, the food inside it filled with false promises.

Mom dips the spoon in the bowl, then lifts it to my mouth. I swallow down the warm liquid, but it does nothing to thaw my insides. When I'm finished, she places the spoon back down and takes the tray.

Right before she opens the door, I say my first words in days.

"I don't think I can do this."

***

Evan

In life, we're taught how to deal with the loss of those we love. We're not taught how to deal with the loss of ourselves.

The sun shines bright against blue skies each day, yet it's the darkest week of my life. My days are spent watching a room, waiting for Josie to walk out.

Hewson sits on the seat beside me in the hospital corridor.

"Mara and I have to go back to DC. We can't put it off any longer." I nod. "Will you be okay?"

I continue staring at the closed door. "I don't know."

Another two days pass.

"She won't turn on the lights," I say, when Michael sits down next to me.

He stares at the room. "I know." We sit in silence until he says, "I want you to come somewhere with me."

My eyes snap to his. "I'm not leaving."

Britney walks over and takes Michael's seat when he stands. "Don't worry, I'll stay here," she says.

I give the door a lingering look. A knot forms in my throat at the thought of leaving Josie behind.

Michael stands in my path, blocking my view. "This is important, Evan. Come with me, please."

I let out a ragged breath. "Fine."

"When was the last time you ate?" he asks, when I sway on my feet. I shrug and he shakes his head. "Wait there."

He returns with a wheelchair and a bright packet of something in his hand.

"I can walk," I inform him, eying the chair.

"You were stabbed, Evan. If you're going to stand a chance of helping my sister, you have to help yourself first. Now, get in the chair and eat."

The look he gives says it isn't open for questioning. "Okay."

An hour later, Michael's limo pulls up outside a run-down building. He climbs out with two large bags bundled in his arms and tells me to wait. A few minutes later, he pulls a wheelchair, borrowed from the hospital, out of the trunk, then wheels me inside the building. When we're in the middle of a huge room, he sits on the floor next to me and starts rummaging through the bags. I'm surprised when Coach Langford walks in.

Michael stares at my middle, where the bandages and dressings are hidden by my sweatshirt. "What have the doctors said?"

"The knife didn't hit any vital organs. A few more weeks for the wound to heal." I look around the room. "What are we doing here?" Michael waves a bottle of vodka in the air. I arch a brow. "No Scotch?"

Pulling out three plastic cups from the bag, he frowns. As he's setting them down on the ground and pouring us each a drink, his throat bobs. "Britney can't be around the smell. It's a trigger."

"I'm sorry," I reply, hit with understanding.

"She's like my sister," he says, passing my drink over. "A fighter. Which is why we're here."

He spends the next ten minutes explaining. Every now and then, Coach Langford speaks.

"I can't do this without you, Evan," says Michael, his voice cracking. "I can't hold them both up ..." He tails off. "Coach Langford is here to talk to you about Josie. I can't kn—. If I d—" He shakes his head and drags the base of his hands across his cheeks. He looks like a broken giant. "If I do, I'll spend the rest of my life trying to figure out how to bring that fucker back from the dead so I can kill him myself."

When he leaves the room, I stay sitting with Coach Langford. At first, neither of us says anything.

"I don't know Josie well," says Coach Langford, "but I know her mother." I eye him warily. "Michael doesn't know. I'd appreciate if you kept it that way."

"I won't say anything."

"I'm guessing you're scared for Josie right now, but I promise you, Angela Becket will hold her daughter up and keep her going, no matter what it takes. What I want to know is how *you* are doing?"

"Not great. I blame myself," I admit, spinning the cup in my hands. This is the first time I've spoken with someone about what happened, and it hurts more than when the knife pierced through my skin. "I wasn't there … I shouldn't have left her."

Coach Langford frowns. "You were doing your job, Evan. You were trying to keep her safe."

"It wasn't enough. It was a setup. I should have seen it coming." I tilt my head back and stare at the ceiling, wishing I could fly through the sky, somewhere away from all of this, with Josie by my side.

Coach Langford takes my cup, refills it, then takes a large drink from his own. "I've worked in the NFL for thirty years. The Beckets are one of many families I've seen affected by this kind of grief, although admittedly theirs is … more complicated." He clears his throat. "For a player to give their full potential on the field, sometimes it requires parts of them to be fixed, inside."

I lower my gaze, taking in the lines around his eyes. Deep lines filled with happiness, pain and experience.

"When I first took on the job," he continues, "I was naïve. I thought it was just football. Just teaching a group of guys to throw a ball around a field. I never imagined what would cross my path, or the demons I'd have to help my players fight. I've seen families fall apart with all kinds of grief. I've seen players lose their careers because they blamed themselves for things that were never their burden to carry. *You* are not to blame, Evan."

"I'm scared she'll break."

"And if she does, she'll have you there to help put her back together."

"What if she doesn't want my help?"

"Sometimes people don't ask for what they need. Sometimes you have to be there waiting to catch them in case they fall." The frown between Coach Langford's brow softens, and he gives me a small smile. "We're all flying through life, Evan, but some of us have our wings clipped, and we have to learn how to adapt."

"And what if I don't know how ... to be there for her like this?"

"Unfortunately, there isn't a textbook that can help. When things like this happen, *everyone* has to adapt, not just the victim." My shoulders sink, overwhelmed by the enormity of what's to come. "But you and Josie will figure it out together. At some point, you will learn to hold each other up, and what Michael wants to do here can help you both, and many more to come. So, are you in?"

I nod and let out a long breath, dumping every uncertainty I have in this room, so that when I leave, it will be left behind, alone, so it can destroy itself, not me.

"I'm in," I reply.

***

Josie

I wince when light fills the room. My mom stands from the seat she's been in beside my bed since the day I was admitted.

Britney clears her throat. "I was wondering if I could talk to Josie?"

My mom looks at me for my answer. "Okay." I swallow. "Mom, it's fine. Go," I say when she hesitates. She goes to squeeze my hand but stops herself. I don't speak again until we're back in darkness. "What do you want?"

Britney walks over to the bed and sits in my mom's seat. "I want to help you."

I let out a bitter laugh. "If that's all, then I suggest you leave, or you'll be disappointed."

She leans back in the chair and gets herself comfier. "I'm assuming Michael hasn't got round to telling you about my past ..."

"No?"

"May I?" For a second, I'm confused about what she's asking, then it hits me that she's asking if she can tell me about whatever is lurking behind her eyes. It's the 'whatever' that draws me to her, and why I nod for her to go on. "One of my mom's boyfriends, unfortunately, liked me more than her." I glance at her and hold my breath. "It started when I was thirteen."

"I'm sorry." And I am. In that moment, I forget my own pain.

Britney shakes her head. "I'm not telling you for you to feel sorry for me. This isn't a match to see whose scars are the worst. I just want you to know that on some level, I get it."

"What did Belmer do to you?" I ask, suddenly aware of how little time has passed since she was kidnapped. I find myself unable to comprehend how she's sitting talking to me like she is after what seems like no time at all.

A tear falls down her cheek. "Not what his son did to you, but it doesn't stop it hurting. I'm still healing, and I will be for a long time. As will you."

My lip wobbles. "What if I can't heal? What if I can't come back from this?"

Britney leans over and carefully holds my hand. "I'll be with you for whatever you need. We can heal together."

"Everything feels so dark. I don't know if I can do it."

"When we're stuck in the middle of a tunnel, we have two choices, Josie. We can go back through the pain that brought us to that point, or we can move forward toward the light. Only you can decide which way you walk, but whichever way you choose, you will have us all there, supporting you."

"Will you stay with me?"

"Of course," she smiles and settles back in the seat.

After a few minutes of us sitting in darkness, I say, "Can you do me a favor?"

"Anything."

"Please, can you turn on the lights?"

She does as I ask. When she turns around and sees me properly, she sucks in a small breath before walking back over and tapping the bed.

"Can I?"

"Yes," I whisper. She climbs on and stretches out at my side carefully. "What are you doing?" I ask when she reaches an arm around my shoulders.

The pain that shoots across my skin disappears when she whispers against my hair, "I'm holding you together."

Grief takes over like I've never felt before. Pain hits me, inside and out. It threatens to tear me apart. Strangled cries fill the room, and it takes me a while to realize they're mine.

When the last tear falls, all I'm left with are the wounds on my body.

Later, Britney helps me to bathe. She tells me that when the wounds heal, they will turn into scars, and they will become a reminder.

A reminder that, like her, and so many others, I'm a survivor.

***

Evan

I don't know what to expect when I get to Michael Becket's home. All I know is that Josie is finally ready to see me after a couple of weeks of nothing.

Michael greets me at the front door. Surprisingly, for someone who's known to the world as an asshole, he pats me on the back and treats me like family, reassuring me all the way up the stairs.

He doesn't linger when we get to Josie's room. All I get is one last pat on the back and then he disappears.

My pulse races and my palms go clammy when I knock.

The words, "Come in," make my heart skip a beat, and I brace myself for what I will find on the other side.

What I'm greeted with isn't quite what I expect. Josie in lounge wear, looking comfortable and relaxed on the bed. The wariness in her eyes and the sunken cheekbones are the only telltale signs of how she might really be feeling.

She looks up from playing with Cat Three and Cat Four and says two words that make me crumble. "Hey, you."

"Hey." My eyes and nose burn just watching her. Memories of that night threaten to surface. I blink and look away.

"Are you going to come in?" she asks, tilting her head.

I hadn't even noticed I was still standing in the hallway. Giving her a weak smile, I move inside the room, leaving the door open behind me. If Josie notices, she doesn't make a comment about it, and I wonder if secretly she's relieved.

I hover in the middle of the room, not sure what to do. Josie goes back to playing with the cats. Every now and again I catch her glancing at me through her lashes. My heart breaks for the thousandth time when she looks at me properly, and I see that her eyes are like the first time we met. Dull.

"I missed you," she says quietly.

"I missed you, too."

She points at the bed. "You can sit. If you want to, that is."

I frown. "What do you mean, *if* I want to?"

She bites down on her lip. "It's okay if this is all too much. I wouldn't blame you for walking away." She lets out a small laugh, one that's at odds with the tears streaming down her face. "I'm a mess."

When I walk over to the bed and sit down, she looks surprised. I pick up Cat Four, needing something to calm me down. Every emotion under the sun is firing, and I don't know how to handle them. I don't want to scare her.

"I would never walk away, Josie. You know that, right?"

"Evan, I don't want you to stay because you feel like you have to, as much as I don't want you to leave. I—"

"I love you, Josie. That hasn't changed." I eye her hand resting on the bed and swallow hard. "Can I hold your hand?"

She nods, and I reach over, lifting it to where the diamond sits on my skin, right above the organ that beats in my chest for her, and her alone. "This is yours. It always will be. I have no choice in the matter, because it's decided what it wants, and all it wants is you and whatever you're able to give."

"I've changed," she whispers.

"And I'll adapt," I say, echoing the lesson from Coach Langford, which has stuck with me through some of the dark times over the past few weeks. "Whatever you need from me, or don't need from me. I'll do it."

"What if it takes time?"

Carefully, I reach over with my other hand and lift her chin. "We have all the time in the world."

She holds my gaze. "Our foundations are pretty shitty."

"Even flowers have to grow through dirt," I reply.

"Well, we'll be the most beautiful flowers in existence," she chuckles.

That's when I know we'll be okay. I know that at some point, no matter how long it takes, we will figure things out. I know, because when the right two souls find each other, they slot together and become whole. United, they can overcome whatever life throws their way.

We sit for a while, watching Cat Three and Cat Four play, until Josie smiles and says, "Want to help me with something?"

"Sure," I reply. "What?"

"I want to name them. I don't want them to be replaceable anymore. I don't want anything in my life to be."

"What were you thinking?"

"Stars. The brightest two there are."

"Wait a second," I say, getting my phone out.

"What's wrong?" she asks, when I frown at Google's answers.

I scratch my head. "Sirius and Canopus?"

"They sound like something out of *Harry Potter*," she snorts. "Maybe not." Her eyes light up and she grins. "Swiss and Cheese."

"You're joking, right?"

"Nope. I'm a no joke zone. You've rubbed off on me, Agent Price."

When she winks, I have the urge to reach over and kiss her, but I don't. It's not the right time.

"We're going to be okay," she says later, when Swiss and Cheese are sleeping between us, and a Disney movie plays in the background—one with a happy ending.

"Yeah," I reply. "We are."

***

I don't see Josie for over four weeks, but we text every day.

Closing down the Belmer case—and the rest of my case pile—takes time. But like I told Josie, we have all the time in the world, which is what I keep reminding myself with each day that goes by. I don't tell her why I have to be away for so long, though, just like I don't tell her all my plans.

When I log out of my laptop for the last time, Mara sniffles at my side. "We made a beautiful team. I won't ever forget you."

"Mara, I've not died. You can pick up a phone and say hi if you want."

She perks up. "And you'd answer?"

"I'd think about it."

Hewson walks through the unit and looks down at my now ex-partner, who has gone back to being a sniffling mess. He rolls his eyes, then turns to me. "Ready?"

I grin. "Yeah. I think I am."

Most of the people in the unit have already said their goodbyes over the past couple of days, but when I stand at the sliding doors, ready to walk into my new life, I give them a wave.

Outside, Hewson and I stop by my vehicle. "Let me know when she asks. I'll have it arranged."

"Thank you," I reply. I've come to know Josie as well as I know myself, and even after what's happened, there's something I know she will want to do at some point in the future.

"Who'd have thought ... the whole thing was setup ..."

"From the moment Michael Becket got on that plane to New York two years ago. I know. Sometimes, I wonder what would have happened if he hadn't gone chasing after Abby West, where we'd all be."

Hewson's lips flatten. "That's like asking what would have happened if you hadn't done anything in life. I learned a long time ago not to question or second guess. We can't live in the past, Price, as much as we can't live in the future. All we can do is live in the here and now and make the most of what we've got."

"I'm going to miss it here."

"I'll miss you too." He winks, and I laugh. "I'm proud of you and how far you've come. Remember that over the coming months, because there will be dark times. It's inevitable. But you've already survived the worst. Now, you just have to learn how t—"

"To adapt." I open the driver's door. "I'll miss you too." Hewson sniffs, and I roll my eyes. "You're as bad as Mara."

"Don't even get me started on her. You've left me with the delightful task of finding someone with enough balls to handle her."

"She can handle herself."

"Bye, Price. Don't be a stranger."

"Bye."

As I pull away from the bureau for the last time, I don't feel sad like I expected I would. I feel hopeful about everything to come.

Twenty-Seven

Josie

The four weeks that pass without Evan are hard, but I learn it really is true what they say. Time heals.

What I've been through will take a lot of time, but I'm in no rush. I'm not taking it one day, one step, or even one minute at a time. I'm taking it second by second. And with each one I move forward from, I refuse to look back.

And each day is made easier thanks to the unbreakable force that is my family, and that includes Britney. She's become the sister I never knew I needed, and when a day is too dark, she pulls me through to the next.

"Your brother wants to take you somewhere," says my mom, bustling into my room, tutting when Cheese gets under her feet.

"Where?"

"He didn't say." She moves around, tidying my things into all the wrong places.

"Can I ask you something?"

"That sounds like a very serious question," she comments.

"Why did you never tell me Coach Langford came to visit you?" She walks to my door and closes it, then returns and sits on my bed. "I used to see him in the diner. He came to see you, didn't he?"

The way she watches me, I almost think she's going to lie, but then she says, "Yes. He did."

"Why didn't you tell me?"

She fiddles with my rogue sock. "I didn't want to upset you."

My eyes widen. "I wouldn't have been upset. I would have been happy for you."

"We connected the first time we met when he was trying to help your brother get scouted. I'd lost your father, and then after everything that had happened … and he'd lost his wife a few years before. I guess you could say we were kindred spirits." She doesn't need to explain what they are. I already know, because it's exactly how I'd describe Evan and me. "You were alone so much. I felt guilty about the times he came by, because I was already hiding away, working so much. I didn't want you to think I chose him over you."

"I'd never think that." I reach over, and she sucks in a breath when I squeeze her hand for the first time since that night. She squeezes back like she's holding on for dear life and never wants to let me go. "You, more than anyone, deserve your happily ever after."

All she does is watch where our hands meet. "I hate that you're having to go through this. If I co—"

I stop her before she can continue. "The world is full of ifs, Mom. Too many that we've lived with for too long. I don't want to be an if anymore. I want to be a certainty. I'm sorry for what you went through with me in the hospital, but I wouldn't change it. It had to happen, because if it didn't then, it would somewhere in the future."

"You're stronger than you give yourself credit for."

I offer her a watery smile. "I have a good example. And now, I'm ready to live out of the shadows, without being afraid."

She reaches up and strokes my face. "And you will. Finally."

***

An hour later, I pull up outside a large building with Michael.

I climb out of the car and look for a sign, but there isn't one.

"I'll explain inside," he says, then holds up a fob and the doors swoop open.

Inside the area is clean and professional. There's a reception area and a sign with a map of the building layout. I take in the words 'treatment and therapy rooms', then stare at the large block that covers almost the whole of the ground floor, with the word 'gymnasium'.

"Follow me," he says, scratching the back of his head and seeming nervous as he walks off.

He leads us away from what I assume is the reception area and through to an office. Waiting inside is Coach Langford, sitting behind a large desk.

"You can sit," says Michael.

So, I do.

"Where are we?" I ask, looking around for any sign that will give away where we are.

"The Becket Foundation," confirms Coach Langford.

I glance between the two of them. "And what is the Becket Foundation for?"

"It's to help survivors, Josie," explains Michael. "A safe space where they can receive counseling,

384

therapies, and, most importantly, learn protective techniques to help make them feel safer and more secure going back into the world."

"Why did you do this?" I ask, breathlessly.

"I've worked with survivors for years." Coach Langford nods, confirming that he's telling the truth. "A couple of months back, the place where I helped out with self-defense classes closed down due to lack of funding. The women I helped … they became a unit. A family supporting each other through the hard times. They understood each other like no one else in the world could. Not unless they'd been through what they had, like you and Britney.

"When I found out I couldn't help them anymore, it broke me. I was already trying to figure out a way I could help. I have enough money sitting untouched. I never played football for the money, Josie, you have to know that. It helped me feel connected to the world when I felt like I didn't belong."

"I get it," I say.

"And then," he continues. "That night happened. I can't change what happened. I wish I fucking could. But this here," he gestures around the office, but I know he means the whole foundation, "is for you, and Britney, and any other woman out there who needs help, so they can move forward and save themselves. It's a tool. A lifeline.

"Coach Langford helped with the logistics of it all because we all know I'm not good with that shit. And E—" He stops himself and I frown, wondering what he was going to say next. "What do you think, José?"

I don't answer straight away. I stand and walk over to him. Reaching up onto the tips of my toes, I kiss his cheek. "I think that the world doesn't deserve the real Michael Becket. Thank you."

Coach Langford stands and moves away from the desk. "I'll leave the two of you alone for a minute."

When he's gone, I focus on Michael. "I owe you an apology."

He looks confused. "For what?"

"For how I reacted when you quizzed me about Evan in the bar that night. I didn't know about Britney's history, and I'm sorry. I know why you were concerned about mine and Evan's relationship now."

All of a sudden, I'm engulfed in his huge arms. "Don't ever fucking scare me like that again. I thought I'd lost you, José."

"I'll try not to," I mumble into his chest.

Eventually, he lets go of me. "Do you think you'll use the foundation? You know … to help you deal with what you went through."

"Try to stop me." I smile, and he wraps an arm around my shoulders, tugging me along beside him. "Where are we going?"

"Somewhere I think you'll like," he replies cryptically. When we get to a door, he turns around. "Do you think you can close your eyes?" When I frown, he says, "I promise it's a good surprise."

"Okay," I reply, faltering. I go to close my eyes, but each time I try, I can't do it. "I'm sorry," I whisper, my eyes burning with disappointment.

But then, a rough voice fills the room—one I've needed to hear for weeks—providing a wave of calm. "It's okay, Josie."

Evan.

Michael smiles. "You're safe. Neither of us is going to let anything happen to you."

When Evan says, "I've got you," my eyes close and I focus on trying to keep my breathing steady. I feel him close behind me. "Can I take your hand?" A choice.

"Yes," I reply, reminding myself that I'm safe, even in the darkness.

A warm hand wraps around mine, and a small flame ignites. It's a sign that all hope isn't lost, because a small flame, if left to burn, can turn into a fire. It's the hope I need that maybe one day Evan and I will get back to where we were. And I have a feeling the new version of us will be even better.

"I want to take you into the room. It's okay. I promise." There's a pause. "Would you like to come with me?" Another choice.

"Yes," I whisper.

He guides me through to wherever it is, and each step feels like I'm walking on glass. It's painful. My lungs constrict and I feel like I'm about to pass out. When my fight-or-flight kicks in, I get ready to bolt.

"I've got you, Josie." His words calm me again, and my muscles relax. "Would you like to leave?"

"No," I reply.

"I want you to lie down. I know what I'm asking, but trust me, it will be worth it."

I nod yes and start to lower myself to the ground, with Evan guiding me. He never lets me fall. He helps me lie back on what feels like mats, and then I feel him lie beside me.

His hand holds mine, his thumb brushes over the back of it, and then he says, "Open your eyes."

I do, and what I find breaks my heart and puts it back together all in one go.

"Who are they?"

"Some of the women your brother helped when he volunteered. It's taken weeks."

"I can see why," I say with a smile, squeezing his hand harder.

I don't know how long we lay, staring up at the ceiling in what I learn will be the gym for teaching self-defense. I take in one of the most incredible murals I've ever seen. It's breathtaking. Women of all different ages, sizes, and nationalities look down. Half of their face sad, half smiling. Merging. United. Light with dark.

And in the middle of it all is a small girl, her back to the world, wearing a pair of wings. On the left, matching the women's sadness, is the word fall. On the right, matching the women's happiness, is the word fly.

"Was this your idea?"

"Yes. I wanted it to be a reminder that you're not alone."

Sitting up, I turn and rest my weight on one arm, gazing down at him. His warm brown eyes scan my face, and when I lean in, he holds his breath.

When our lips brush, it isn't much, but it's a start. It's another sign that, despite everything that's been taken from me, I'm not broken.

"I love you," I smile against his lips.

"More than anything."

***

Six months pass. I'd like to say they're perfect, but they're not—far from it. So many times, Evan and I are pushed to our limit, wondering if we have the strength to endure the journey.

Each day, when I wake up, I remind myself it's a fresh start and take a step forward.

I was shocked when Evan told me he'd left the bureau. I pushed; I challenged him; I told him to go back.

Every single time I got the same reply.

"Sometimes, you have to give something up to gain everything in return."

388

His belief in me during some of the darkest times never wavered. That's why I knew that when I asked him for the one thing I needed, he would say yes.

"Will you tell me their story?" I ask, rubbing the wings charm between my fingers as we both stare down at Eugene and Duane Belmer's graves.

Evan doesn't hesitate before giving me what I need.

Closure.

He tells me everything. Right from the beginning. What I hear helps, and although I know I shouldn't, after everything he did, I empathize with Eugene Belmer—the person who started it all—because he thought he was protecting his children.

When Lola found out her brother died, she broke and told the FBI what her mother did to her and her brother, and what happened after their stepfather found out. I don't try to understand Duane. I can't go there. Maybe one day I will, but I'm not even close to being ready.

Psychosis triggered by grief is how Evan explains it all, and I know better than anyone what a dark place grief can be, in all its shapes and forms.

But in life, we always have a choice. And just like Britney said, we can take a step back, we can remain stuck, or we can move forward. I'd take the latter every time, because everything else is too painful.

A cold breeze stirs around us as we stare down at their graves in the bright sunlight.

"Do you regret shooting him?" Evan asks, reaching over and holding my hand.

I stare at Duane's name. "A very wise man once told me that sometimes, to be the hero, you have to be the villain first. But I was never the villain, Evan. Duane was a monster ... the things he did ..." my voice breaks, and he squeezes my hand. "If it wasn't me, he would have found others, and my peace is knowing no one else has to go through that. You told me if I fired a gun, I needed to be certain. I was, and I still am certain that I did the right thing. So, no, I have no regrets knowing that another innocent life might have been saved because of what I did."

"What are you doing?" he asks, when I take my bracelet from my wrist and take off the wings charm.

I drop to the ground and bury it in the soil that's covering Duane. "I'd like to believe that one day he will fly, and somewhere up high, he will learn from his mistakes." I stand back up and brush the dirt from my knees. "I already have my wings, because I have you."

***

Josie – One year later

"Why aren't you ready?"

"I am," I snap back at Evan, sitting on my suitcase, trying to get it to close.

"Would you like me to help?" he smirks.

"No." I try to move the zip, but it doesn't budge. I admit defeat. "Please."

Ten minutes and a lot of effort later, we're ready.

"I still can't believe they accepted me," I say as we walk down the stairs.

The *they* I'm referring to is Le Cordon Bleu cooking school. I totally nailed it. Two birds with one stone, as far as my charm bracelet is concerned. I've spent the past couple of months like a pig in shit after I made it in my own way, even though Michael offered to wave his 'rep' around to help.

"It's because you didn't make chowder," says Evan under his breath. I pinch him, and he grins.

We make our way into the living area and almost all the gang are there, waiting to say goodbye, including Mara, Hewson, Swiss and Cheese. Oh, and one little, extra-small, incredibly blonde human who has us all wrapped around her little finger.

"Gah!" huffs Britney. "I need to pee, again!"

She darts out of the room, and my brother laughs, watching her go. Pregnancy problems ... again. They didn't take the whole 'you're incredibly fertile after having a baby' advice seriously and are now a prime example as to why you should.

An ear-splitting shriek has us darting after her.

We make it into the entryway at the exact same time Britney backs away from the downstairs bathroom with her hands covering her mouth.

"I'm so sorry," she says, horrified.

Michael's mouth drops open, taking in what has her spooked. My mom and Coach Langford wrapped around each other. Everybody else already knows. Like I said before ... he's oblivious.

"What the fuck?" Michael hisses, not caring that he has a small, impressionable infant in his arms.

"Language!" snaps my mom, pulling herself out of Coach Langford's embrace.

A horn blares outside, alerting us to the arrival of mine and Evan's car for the airport.

My mom and Coach Langford step outside the bathroom, cheeks flushed.

It really is a goodbye to remember.

Britney places a brief kiss on my cheek. "Sorry, I really do need to pee. Have fun in Paris. Don't do anything I wouldn't!" She slams the bathroom door behind her, and I doubt she'll return, wanting to avoid dealing with the aftermath of my mom and Coach's grand reveal with my brother.

Michael scowls at Coach. "My mom?"

Mom waggles a finger at him. "Now isn't the right time."

He throws his hands up in the air. "There's never a right time for something like this! It's gross and inappropriate. Aren't there rules against this kind of thing?"

Coach Langford shakes his head in despair and offers me and Evan a sheepish wave. "Have a great time in Paris."

Mom pulls me into a hug, refusing to let me go. Only when the Uber's horn blares again does she move back. Sobbing, I might add.

I chuckle. "Mom, I'm coming back."

"You say that now …"

"I promise," I reply. "I'm coming back."

"And it's my turn to say goodbye. Move aside, Coach stealer," interrupts Michael. "See you soon, José."

"Could you be any happier to see me leave?" I ask, rolling my eyes.

He taps his watch. "Tick tock, you're going to miss your flight."

I lean over and press a small kiss on Aisling's head. Her name symbolizes everything she's given us. Hope.

"Bye."

Evan and I wave as we wheel our cases over to the car. The driver jumps out and places them in the trunk. While he does, I listen to my mom and brother in the background.

"You're taking this surprisingly well," she comments.

"I'm getting rid of the downstairs bathroom," he replies.

Smiling to myself, I slide into the back of the car and tuck myself into Evan's side, giving them another small wave when it pulls away.

"Are you excited?" I ask Evan a few hours later as we roll along the runway, preparing to take off.

He places a long, slow kiss on my lips, one I feel in places that he hasn't touched in too long.

"I am," he replies.

When we get to Paris, he will be working closely as security for the US Ambassador to France. For now. Mara's been trying to convince him to go rogue with her, but I don't know if he has that kind of wild in him. We'll see.

"Let's do this," I grin, bracing myself right before the wheels of the plane lift from the tarmac.

A few minutes later, somewhere above Jacksonville, I stare out the window. The lights of the city glitter below the dusky sky, getting smaller.

When we get to Paris, with the past finally behind us, Evan makes love to me for the first time since that night, and it's even better than our first time in Santa Monica.

When we jump off the cliff together, I don't feel like I'm flying, I feel like I'm soaring into a future full of promises.

Epilogue
Evan Two years later

The melody of the bridal chorus fills the church. Nerves swirl in my stomach as I wait to see her walk down the aisle.

An eternity passes before she comes into my vision, and when she does, the breath catches in my throat. Josie always looks beautiful, but with her sandy blonde hair swaying around her shoulders and the soft lilac silk of her dress clinging to her every curve, she looks exquisite.

She gives me a wink before branching off to the other side of the bridal party, standing beside Britney who's wearing a matching-colored dress.

Mara, my new business partner, waves at us all frantically from the pews.

An organ joins the soft melody from the violins, and everyone stands, turning and waiting for the bride to start walking down the aisle. Coach Langford shifts at my right, bouncing the abundance of weight between his feet. Watching him and Becket both struggle their NFL grade bodies into their tuxes is something I'll never forget.

He shoots me a nervous glance.

"You've got this," I whisper, right before his face transforms when his eyes settle on Angela Becket.

She glides toward us with Michael by her side. His eyes shine when he leaves her, and he spends the majority of the service sniffling beside me. When the vows are exchanged, and cheers fill the church, we both watch his mother finally get her happy ending.

"Your turn next," he whispers before walking away.

I smile to myself and follow him. We both know I've had a ring burning a hole in my pocket since the day Josie and I left for Paris.

***

Josie

"I love it when you get the bat gear out," I smile, trailing my hand down Evan's chest.

"Josie, it's a groomsman suit," says Evan, laughing.

"Minor details," I reply, circling a finger in the air. "Turn. I want to appreciate it."

I squeak when Evan tugs me into him and places a kiss against my lips that sparks every part of me to life.

"I've been waiting for that all night," he says against my lips.

"You could have just asked," I reply. "I'm always up for a bit of wedding nooky."

"Wedding nooky?"

"Want me to describe the ins and outs?" I wiggle my eyebrows. "Literally."

"I need a shower," he laughs, but he doesn't say no. "Join me?"

I place another quick kiss on his lips, then saunter in the direction of the bathroom. "You don't need to ask twice."

Thirty minutes later, with my palms flattened against the bathroom tiles, he thrusts inside me. As he does, he kisses the wings tattooed on my back.

Beneath the ink are the names of Duane Belmer's victims; the ones he never wanted to be forgotten. They're etched in my skin, and I wear their names with pride. They remind me I can fly, even after everything I've been through. Each day, I pray they're soaring through the sky somewhere. I like to think they're watching over me like guardian angels.

"You don't want me on my knees?" I ask when he starts to tease me with his fingers.

Under the steady stream of water, he holds my chin in a firm grip. "I don't want you on your knees. I want you by my side, Josie, always."

***

Three months later

It's the opening night for the critics and my nerves get the better of me. After finishing cooking school, I spent time learning everything I could, ready to open my own restaurant one day. That day is now. I hide away, behind the pass, pouring my emotions into my cooking, allowing them to shape and enhance the flavors of every dish I prepare. My sous chef, Flo, busies herself beside me, and with every dish we send out, we move into a steady rhythm along with the rest of the team.

I'm dancing through the steam billowing from the boiling pans to the steady rhythm of chopping and meat being seared when Britney darts in, looking alarmed. She's working PR along with Abby West's firm, my brother's ex-girlfriend from New York. She was The Becket Foundation's first client.

I take in Britney's terrified expression. "Shit," I mutter, wiping my hands on the towel hanging from my chef pants. "What's wrong?"

She bites her lip. "One of the critics is complaining they've found something in their food."

I close my eyes and inhale. "Which table?"

"Follow me," says Britney, and I follow her through the restaurant.

She looks over her shoulder and smiles. I pause for a second, wondering what the hell is going on, before following her to the offending table. With each step I take, my pulse races faster, especially when my eyes settle on the back of a head I'd recognize anywhere.

"Evan?" He doesn't acknowledge me, so I walk forward and face him.

My stomach dips when warm brown eyes smile up at me before he drops to one knee.

"Please, tell me you're not proposing right now?!" He winks, the silver band with a diamond shaped like a pair of wings glinting for everyone to see. "I smell like raw meat."

He grabs hold of my hand, then slides the band onto my ring finger.

I arch a brow. "You're assuming I'm saying yes?"

His dimple pops when he laughs. "Like your answer would be anything else."

Standing up, he doesn't let go of my hand. The name of my restaurant, Espoir, glows behind him.

Hope.

When he leans down and kisses me, he does so like there's no one else in the room, leading us into our own version of a happily ever after.

There are still moments when things are hard, and unwanted memories of the past creep in. But when they do, I remind myself that I don't want to be a candle fighting to light the darkness. I want to be a star shining brightly in a universe full of possibilities.

Acknowledgements

When I started this series, I never imagined that this is where it would get to.

Evan and Josie's story is one I don't ever think I'll forget, and their journey has stayed with me long after writing 'The End'.

As always, a big thank you to all those in the background, supporting me every step of the way. My alpha's Babs and Kris, for always being there whenever I need help, and providing me with their expertise that has helped shape and take my stories to the next level. Thank you to Cheryl, Bex, Kirsty and Laura, for being passionate about these characters, even in their rough form and always being around for me to bounce ideas off.

To my editor Hayley. Thank you for going above and beyond your role, helping to make my story sparkle, but also encouraging me to have confidence in my words.

The biggest thank you goes to my family. This one was difficult. Lots of hours alone, late nights, lots of tears and wobbly moments. You always stand by me, even when it's hard.

Finally, a huge thank you to you, my readers. Every day I'm blown away by the love people have for this world and these characters. The enthusiasm and passion I saw on some of my hardest writing days helped me to get to the end, to finish the story not just for myself or the characters, but for you.

Now I need to figure out how I'm ever going to top Agent Price.

OTHER WORK BY LIZZIE MORTON

The Always Trilogy:

Always You
Always Us
Always

The Always Series:

Wanting You Always
Needing You Always

The Fool Me Duet:

Fool Me Twice
Fool Me Thrice

Summer Nights Series:

Just One Kiss
Just One Night
Just Once More – Coming Soon

Always You

You never forget your first love, and mine and Jake's, was the kind songs are written about.

I thought we were forever …
He promised me the world …
Then tore mine in two.
With my heart shattered into a million
unrecognizable pieces, I ran.
Out of the city. Out of the state. Out of my life.
Now I'm back for one summer, with one life changing
decision to make, and one goal: steer clear of Jake
Ross, the person who ran me out of Brooklyn.
Unfortunately, fate has other ideas and when
our careers become entangled,
avoidance proves impossible.
Together we were magical …
Apart we're a disaster.
Everyone deserves a second chance.

**But what happens if that chance leaves you
questioning everything, even when he
promises that it was always you …**

Always Us

**What hurt more than losing Jake Ross the
first time … was losing him the second.**

It's been two years since I turned my back on the one
that got away, doing what I thought was right
for both of us.
Instead, I'm more confused than I've ever been
before, fighting to forget what it felt like
being in his arms.
Now, it's another summer and another
life-changing opportunity.
This time I'm running around Europe,
surrounded by Rock Gods.
It's the life most would dream of, but things are never
that straightforward, and a chance meeting with a
stranger is a recipe for disaster.
The heart wants what it wants,
regardless of the consequences.
But just when I might finally be able to move forward
… the tables turn.
The choice is no longer between my head or my heart.

**It's a question of whether love, really is
enough.**

Always

**My life's about to change and I can't decide if
it's for better or worse.**

There was a time when I thought meeting Jake Ross,
was fate …
When I thought our love, was written in the stars …
When I hoped we'd find our way back to each other …
Now I'm left wondering if the path I'm about to take,
will be one I'll walk alone.
The one I want. The one I need.
Doesn't want me back.
Then the person I least expect gives me exactly
what I need.
A break from reality.
But there's only so long I can hide, and when the
truth comes out, it's explosive.
They say what will be, will be.

**But what if we were never meant to be
together?**

www.ingramcontent.com/pod-product-compliance
Lightning Source LLC
Chambersburg PA
CBHW061216190726

48288CB00001B/198